For Ashley

with best wishes
for every success

January 2002

M. D. Ano

amazon

THE COMPLETE **13** ADVENTURES OF

DETECTIVE-LIEUTENANT
CATHY CARRUTHERS

MEL D. AMES

Mosaic Press

TORONTO PARIS NEW YORK

Canadian Cataloguing in Publication Data

Ames, Mel D, 1921-

Amazon: the complete 13 adventures of detective-lieutenant Cathy Carruthers

ISBN 0-88962-666-9

1. Title.

PS8551.M477A82 1998

PR9199.3.A43A82 1998

Published by MOSAIC PRESS, P.O. Box 1032, Oakville, Ontario, L6J 5E9, Canada. Offices and warehouse at 1252 Speers Road, Units #1&2, Oakville, Ontario, L6L 5N9, Canada and Mosaic Press, 85 River Rock Drive, Suite 202, Buffalo, N.Y., 14207, USA.

Mosaic Press acknowledges the assistance of the Canada Council and the Dept. of Canadian Heritage, Government of Canada, for their support of our publishing programme.

Cover design and artwork: Mel D. Ames
Cover graphics: Dave Watland
Typesetting: Roger & Bonnie Ames

Copyright © 1999 Mel D. Ames
ISBN 0-88962-666-9

Printed and bound in Canada

THE CANADA COUNCIL | LE CONSEIL DES ARTS
FOR THE ARTS | DU CANADA
SINCE 1957 | DEPUIS 1957

MOSAIC PRESS, in Canada:
1252 Speers Road, Units #1&2, Oakville, Ontario, L6L 5N9
Phone / Fax: (905) 825-2130
E-mail: cp507@freenet.toronto.on.ca

MOSAIC PRESS, in the USA:
85 River Rock Drive, Suite 202, Buffalo, N.Y., 14207
Phone / Fax: 1-800-387-8992
E-mail: cp507@freenet.toronto.on.ca

CONTENTS

OTHER BOOKS BY MEL D. AMES

1993
THE OGOPOGO AFFAIR
MOSAIC PRESS

1996
TALES OF TITILLATION
AND TERROR
MOSAIC PRESS

ACKNOWLEDGEMENTS

By acknowledging the generous assistance of family, friends, colleagues, editors, *et al*, in the putting together of this anthology, I tread a virtual minefield. It is a sad reality, that in spite of every best intention, some hapless soul is destined to suffer the sting of inadvertent omission. Still, one cannot deny those who have given so freely of time and effort, in devoting untold hours to the ponderous word-on-word compilation of thirteen novelets, which is the embodiment of this work. To them, and to every *one*, who even marginally has lent their kind assistance to this, the long-awaited rebirth of the **AMAZON**, I tender my sincere and grateful thanks.

Special mention, however, must go to a notable few. To my son, **Roger**, together with wife **Bonnie** and family who so graciously shouldered the biggest burden and turned a wholly awesome task into a labor of love, I extend my deepest appreciation. Many thanks.

And I would be remiss, indeed, should I neglect two loyal friends, fellow wordsmiths, **Chuck Fritch** and **Peter Sellers**, whose separate contributions have seemingly fashioned a matching set of testimonial bookends. By way of an INTRODUCTION and an AFTERWORD, they have provided an ideal forum for the legendary **Cathy Carruthers** and her handsome hunk, **Mark Swanson**, in which to romp, roil and regale at friends and foe alike, with the utmost impunity, for all time. Thanks guys.

A very special word must go, yet *again*, to **Howard Aster**, one of my staunchest supporters in every respect, and on more than just this one important occasion. Thank you, Howard.

Finally, to my readers, I confer this fondest wish. As you now begin to mind-meander between these covers, (Chuck's and Peter's magical bookends), may you experience with each and every Amazonian adventure, the same outrageous fun and phantasy in your reading of it, as did I, in the writing.

The Author

INTRODUCTION
Charles E. Fritch
Editor, Mike Shayne Mystery Magazine

I first crossed quills with Mel D. Ames in the fall of 1979. It was just after I had taken over the editorship of MIKE SHAYNE MYSTERY MAGAZINE and Mel's story, *The Enigma of Andrew Marler*, had found its way to my desk. Yes, I liked the story, but I didn't much care for the title. And I told him so. That was a mistake; I should have simply changed the title then and there. I was soon to learn, working with Mel, that given slack, he'd likely have his way in the end. The story was published a few months later (MSMM July 1980), the title intact.

That first submission to MSMM proved to be the precursor to a flood of manuscripts from Mel's prolific pen, including a series of novelets featuring Detective-Lieutenant Cathy Carruthers (**the Amazon**) and her insouciant side-kick, Detective-Sergeant Mark Swanson. It was an indomitable duo that would quickly establish Mel D. Ames as one of MSMM's most gifted writers.

First and foremost, Mel is a storyteller. He gave Cathy and Mark their debut in a story called *A Matter Of Observation* (MSMM Nov 1980), and never looked back. The **Amazon** and her loyal 'hunk' would continue to grace the pages (and often as not, the covers) of MSMM until the magazine's untimely demise in the summer of 1985.

All thirteen of the **Amazon** novelets were written in a fast-moving easy-to-read style (typically Mel) with ever engaging undertones of pathos and humor. In addition to his lead protagonists, Cathy and Mark, Mel went on to invent a cast of supporting characters that were truly unique and enduring. There was *Cap'n Hank Heller, the Leprechaun, just-plain-Sam Morton, Too-Tall Bones, Fisk and Mayhew,* to name a few. But there were many more, as you may soon happily discover.

Still, it was Cathy Carruthers, the **Amazon**, who carried the ball, with consort, Mark Swanson, ever at her side. In the novelet, *Blood In The Rigging* (MSMM May 1984), Mel described his star performers thusly:

"... one, a woman, was a stunning six-foot Amazonian beauty, with long flowing hair the color of ripe wheat. She moved with the inborn power and poise of a jungle cat, a long loping stride that seemed to test the seams of her snug grey skirt with every step. At her side, an equally tall, heavily-muscled male kept pace with her, his rugged, unassuming self-assurance clearly evident even in the distracting presence of his remarkable companion ..."

What mere mortal, fiend or felon, could ever hope to triumph over such a magnificent pair? Even as they romped through issue after issue of MSMM, to the delight of its editor and its readers alike, their creator was already reaching out into other genres. But to me, as editor of MIKE SHAYNE MYSTERY MAGAZINE, Mel had already made his mark. His staunch commitment to the preservation of MSMM, as the only *true* pulp magazine of the day, was second only to my own. Other purveyors of crime and mystery fiction were fast forsaking their traditional roots and readership by becoming too 'slick,' too 'trendy' in story content, even though they still retained the old pulp format. And while we may have won the battle, for a time, we did eventually lose the war.

Still, I like to think that we, who were there at the end ... at the end of that magnificent and legendary pulp era, did manage to carve a kind of victory out of closure. Mel D. Ames' contribution to MIKE SHAYNE MYSTERY MAGAZINE, and to the declining pulp gestalt in general, was considerable. Proof of that is right here in these pages, in the stirring adventures of Cathy Carruthers, the **Amazon**, and her unforgettable cohorts.

Enjoy.

Charles E. (Chuck) Fritch

NOVEMBER 1980
$1.50

47744

MIKE SHAYNE
MYSTERY MAGAZINE

The New Mike Shayne
Short Novel
KILLER'S EVE
by Brett Halliday

ED NOON'S MINUTE
MYSTERIES
by Michael
Avallone

MIKE'S MAIL
Letters
from
Readers!

Stories and Features by

MEL D. AMES
JOHN BALL
JOHN C. BOLAND
JON L. BREEN
VICKI CARLETON
FRED FREDERICKS
JOHN LUTZ
ARTHUR MOORE
GENE MURRAY
PERCY PARKER
PATRICK SCARRETT

0 71896 47744

*The nude body of a woman hung by its
neck from the light fixture, and an overturned chair lay within kicking distance
of a daintily pedicured foot. Suicide?
Detective-Lieutenant Cathy Carruthers
thought not. Murder, more likely.*

a matter of observation

ROOM 804, AT THE HOTEL WESTMORE, HARBORED A grim pantomime of death. The nude body of a woman hung from a light fixture, by the neck, and an overturned chair lay within kicking distance of a dainty, pedicured foot. There was an eerie attitude to the body; to the limbs, mostly, as they stood out a little from the perpendicular. It was as though death had come suddenly in a throe of panic. The weight of the body on the thin leather belt from which it hung, had pulled the light fixture partly away from the ceiling, and a few pieces of plaster were strewn on the dark pile of carpet. Some of the plaster fragments, between the rungs of the overturned chair and beneath the body, were scrunched deeply into the rug fibers. The room was furnished with the usual, tiresome trappings, peculiar to all second-rate hotels: bed, dresser, night table, a mate to the fallen chair, and a television set. The rapid flip-flopping of the TV screen gave a weird, psychedelic aspect to the scene, and a tuneless rock-group, blaring from the FM band, seemed only to fuel the illusion.

Detective-Lieutenant Cathy Carruthers stood in the open doorway, surveying the room with a cold, calculating eye. No sign of emotion, no feminine impropriety, marred the composure of her finely-wrought features. She was six feet from head to heel, and blonde; and as she paced the hotel room in silent deliberation, she did things to a straight-cut, gray business suit that had never been intended. And even though the garment ended mid-thigh, it fell well short of its given purpose; to subdue, and otherwise divert attention from the superb body that moved within it. Her vital statistics had become classified information at Metro Central's Eleventh Precinct.

"Suicide?"

Detective-Sergeant Mark Swanson regarded his partner with manly deference. The questioning tone in his voice had not been unintentional, though the fact seemed self-evident. Bitter experience had taught him to accept the obvious with caution.

It had not been that way to begin with. But in recent months, he had found many compensations working with the 'Amazon,' an epithet that had been bestowed upon her (with affection) from her burly colleagues in Homicide. Mark had felt no sense of umbrage in their gender disparity, nor was he phased by the constant derision he endured at the hands of his macho cohorts. In addition to her obvious physical attributes, he had found his new partner to be a highly engaging individual and a detective of rare acumen.

"Shall I cut her down, lieutenant?"

"Do that, Mark." Her smile was butter on his daily bread. "Use the same chair."

Mark set the chair upright, beside the hanging woman. The pointed toes hung about an inch below the level of the seat. "With that kind of clearance," he said, "she'd have had to stand on tip-toe. A bit of a stretch, but certainly not impossible."

Lieutenant Carruthers winced with womanly qualm as her partner mounted the chair, sinking his feet deep into the well-upholstered cushion — with typical masculine indifference, she thought — but then returned her attention to the dead woman, as he parted the thin leather belt that held her, and lowered her gently to the floor.

SHE HAD BEEN PRETTY, ONCE, ABOUT MID-TWENTIES, with short dark hair and a good figure. Now, her face was a purple horror. The lieutenant knelt beside the body and drew a few strands of tightly curled hair from one clenched fist.

"Could be her own," Mark observed, over her shoulder. The lieutenant turned contemplative eyes upon him that temporarily took his mind off his work. This was one of the compensations.

"Take a sheet from the bed and cover her," she said demurely, slipping the hair samples into a small white envelope, then into her jacket pocket.

A little man with black hair and swarthy features came into the room. "My name's Forbes," he said curtly, "I'm the hotel manager." He leveled his words at Mark, who, busy with the sheet, directed him with a nod of the head to his imposing colleague.

"Thank you for coming," said the lieutenant, pleasantly, "I should like to ask you a few questions."

The little man turned his head from one to the other, unable to decide where his obeisance lay. Cathy Carruthers had long since resigned herself to this hesitancy on the part of some men in accepting her, a woman, in what they considered a man's domain. But precious few hesitated for long.

"What was the woman's name?" she asked with practiced authority.

"Valeri Smith," replied the hotel man.

"Miss?"

"Yes. At least that is how she registered."

"And when might that have been?"

"Yesterday evening, around seven." Forbes squirmed nervously.

"Have you seen her before, Mr. Forbes?"

"No... well, I mean... this wasn't her first time to stay at the hotel. Yes, I've seen her before."

"But you were not acquainted with her?"

"No."

"Do you know anybody who was?"

"No, I don't."

The lieutenant gave him a searching look "Is there any thing else you'd like to tell me?"

"No, except I don't see what you're making all the fuss about. The creature obviously took her own life."

"What makes you say that?"

"Well, for one thing, we had to break in this morning. Both doors to this room were bolted from the inside... and the transom. The window is almost a hundred feet off the ground — no ledges or balconies. I'm no detective, mam, but that adds up to suicide in any man's language."

"Yes, Mr. Forbes, I agree," Cathy Carruthers said sweetly, "you are not a detective. Because, you see, I am, and it is quite obvious to me that this woman was murdered."

Mark cast an enquiring glance at his superior He knew from past experience that this was no idle speculation.

"Now, perhaps you can tell me, Mr. Forbes, who was the first to find her?"

Forbes was visibly disconcerted. "One of the maids, I believe, a Mrs. Grebski."

"Is she in the hotel now?"

"Uh — yes." Forbes raised his eyes in an attitude of reflection. "Shall I send for her?"

"Please do. And, Mr. Forbes, before you go — " The lieutenant was standing by the door to the hall and she drew the man's attention to the light switch on the wall. It was the type with two flat surfaces that you push rather than flick, and on the lower OFF switch was a fingerprint so clearly visible that it seemed almost to have been put there intentionally.

"You will notice," the lieutenant told him, "that someone has left their calling card. That is, if you can remember with certainty whether or not anyone else has used this switch."

"Yes," Forbes said quickly, "I do — I mean, it was me. The light was on, so I turned it off. Force of habit, I guess."

"That was this morning when you found the girl?"

"Yes."

"Thank you, Mr. Forbes."

AS THE HOTEL MAN LEFT, THE LIEUTENANT ANSWERED her assistant's unspoken query with an audacious wink, then with one blood-red fingernail, she pushed the ON surface of the switch and looked up at the broken fixture. The bulb did not respond.

"What do you make of that?"

"Must be a short in the fixture."

"Must be," agreed the Amazon absently. Mark withdrew the bulb from its socket and tried it in the lamp on the night table. This time it lit up.

"Success," he said, but as he turned, he found himself to be alone in his conclusions, however illuminating. The lieutenant was already deeply engrossed in a new line of contemplation.

"Let us consider the dilemma of the doors," she mused aloud. There were two; one door opened out into the hall, the other to an adjoining room. The hall door, she noticed, had a night latch and the customary hotel night-chain, which now hung broken and useless from the doorjamb. The other door, which connected to room 806, had a common slide bolt with a projecting knob that fell, as it was moved forward, into a notched locking slot. There was also a locking slot at the other end of the bolt housing, which engaged the knob when the bolt was in the open position. The lieutenant tested the easy action of the bolt, then withdrew it and tried the door. It was apparently locked from the other side.

Mark, close at her elbow, had been running parallel with her observations until she stooped to retrieve a toothpick from the floor carpet, and here he lost contact in a flash of Amazonian leg.

"Interesting," mused the lieutenant, toothpick held twixt thumb and forefinger.

"Very," said Mark, with some ambiguity.

When she straightened, Forbes was standing in the hall doorway. He ushered in a middle-aged, nondescript sort of woman, in a blue thin-striped uniform.

"This is Mrs. Grebski, lieutenant. She was the one who found her."

"Thank you, Mr. Forbes." The lieutenant turned compelling eyes upon her assistant. "Mark, while I'm talking to Mrs. Grebski, would you endeavor to open this connecting door from the other side. Perhaps Mr. Forbes would assist you. I should like to have a look at that other room."

SAM MORTON, CORONER AND CHIEF MEDICAL EXAMINER,

M.C.P.D., took that precise moment to arrive, followed closely by photographers and lab-men. The lieutenant guided Mrs. Grebski to a spot by the window, out of the ensuing chaos.

"Mrs. Grebski, do you remember what time it was when you found her?"

Mrs. Grebski had the look of a frightened child.

"Yes, sir — ah — mam, 'bout quarter to eight, I'd say."

"What made you investigate so early?"

"804 had an early call, mam, I thought the room would be empty."

"I see. Now tell me what happened."

"I knocked first, mam, then used the pass key. The door wouldn't open but a few inches, because of the night-chain, but I could still see inside." She shuddered. "It was horrible."

"What did you do then?"

"I screamed," she said looking as though she intended to again, "then I went for Mr. Forbes."

"And Mr. Forbes broke the door in," the lieutenant filled in for her, "saw that she was long dead, and called us."

"That's right, mam."

"Mrs. Grebski, did you follow Mr. Forbes into the room?"

"No, mam, not likely."

"Did anyone?"

"Uh — no, mam."

"You're sure of that?"

"Yes, mam."

"Thank you, Mrs. Grebski, you may go."

As the maid stepped gingerly around the luckless Ms. Smith, on her way to the door, the Medical Examiner looked up to see the top half of Lieutenant Cathy Carruthers disappearing out the open window. She was prevented from disappearing entirely only by the tender balance of the remaining half (which he regarded with unprofessional interest) as it maneuvered her through an examination of the window's exterior, and an exquisite re-entry

"Intriguing," she mused, regaining her lofty stature with a toss of her blonde head.

"Very," Sam Morton agreed, averting his eyes.

"Sam." She favored him with a disarming smile. "You've

something to tell me?"

"Nothing you don't already know, lieutenant."

"Strangulation?"

"Yes."

"Can you pin the time down?"

"You want an educated guess?"

"In the absence of anything better, yes."

"I'd say — six to eight hours."

"Mmm — was the neck broken?"

"I think not."

"That was something I didn't know, Sam. Thank you."

Mark came through the connecting door just as Valeri Smith was being borne horizontally out the other. He found the lieutenant inspecting the contents of the dead woman's overnight bag. The bag looked as though it had been rifled.

"Has this been disturbed?" asked the lieutenant.

"Not prior to your arrival," Mr. Forbes volunteered from the doorway.

"And these?" She indicated some clothing that hung in a doorless alcove, serving as a clothes closet; a gaily patterned dress, a slip, and a three-quarter coat. The coat was beltless, but the leather trim on the collar matched the belt that had circled the pretty neck of Valeri Smith.

The hotel man shook his head. "Not to my knowledge," he said.

"Mr. Forbes," the lieutenant favored him with a long look, "I wonder if you would get me the name of the person, if any, who occupied room 806 last night."

"I already have that information, lieutenant," said Mark. "It was a Mr. Wilson Greaves, sales representative from out of town, in plastics, or so the register says; fiftyish, a hundred and fifty pounds, five-foot-six and bald as a billiard ball. Booked in at about 11 P.M. and left with the night owl."

"What time did the night owl leave?"

"The night clerk saw a man answering Greaves' description leave the hotel just after midnight, about 12:15. And, incidentally, both rooms were arranged-for a day ahead, simultaneously, by someone who identified herself as Greaves' secretary."

"Thank you, Mark." She projected a just reward. "Now let's

have a look at this other room."

IN THE OPEN DOORWAY, THE LIEUTENANT STOPPED TO trace a barely distinguishable line with her fingertips, across the varnished surface of the doorjamb. There was an identical mark on the now accessible edge of the open door. By closing the door, she was able to bring the lines together. Both marks were the same approximate height as the bolt in 804.

"Has this room been cleaned yet, Mr. Forbes?"

"Not yet."

The bed showed no sign of having been slept in and there was no luggage, or clothing, or any sign of occupancy. A door key, stamped 806, was on the bureau.

"And the door to the hall, Mr. Forbes. Was it locked when you came through, just now?"

"Yes, it was. I used my pass key."

"Good. Mark, see if you can't find traces of burning in that metal wastebasket. I'll check the bathroom."

Under the lip of the toilet bowl, the lieutenant found several irregular pieces of ash residue. She was slipping them into a white envelope when Mark came in holding up a blackened hand.

"Somebody's burned something in there," he said, "but how did you know?"

"I didn't," she smiled, "but I do now."

She continued to poke around the room until a seascape above the bed caught her eye. It was slightly askew, and she straightened it. A half inch strip immediately below the picture was noticeably lighter than the surrounding wall.

"Mark," said the lieutenant, without a smile, "I want you to put out an all-points on Mr. Wilson Greaves. I'm afraid we shall have to detain that gentleman for questioning." She stopped on her way out the door, and turned, and as though on second thought, she added; "And Mr. Forbes, we shall want you as well."

"Me? — want me?" Forbes was livid. "For what?"

The lieutenant spoke softly, with a forced calm.

"The part you have played in this affair, Mr. Forbes, poses no mystery for me. Your bungling, obvious attempts to hide one crime, has implicated you in another. I am in doubt at this point, only, as to why."

Mark's look of amazement was paralleled by the show of utter disbelief on the face of the hotel manager, and he wondered if he would ever have enough answers of his own to withstand the initial impact of these oracular bombshells. But when the dust had settled, there were only questions, still. Before he could put voice to them, the Amazon was fast disappearing down the hall.

LIEUTENANT CATHY CARRUTHERS SAT ATOP HER desk in the squad room, adorning her fingernails with a fresh coating of blood-red lacquer. Behind his own desk, Mark Swanson had propped his feet on an open drawer and was regarding his attractive colleague with mild chagrin.

"Okay," he said, "give — "

The lieutenant smiled, sphinx-like. "A simple matter of observation," she said lightly. She crossed one majestic leg over the other, contributing nothing to local jurisprudence.

"Out maneuvered again," muttered Mark.

"To begin with," began the lieutenant, "let's examine the unlikely premise that Valeri Smith committed suicide. Frankly, Mark, I thought it inconceivable that any woman (and a vain one, in particular — did you notice those pedicured toes?) would deliberately suffer the indignity of being found stark naked and, at the same time, so horribly visaged. Dead, yes; dead and naked, perhaps; repugnantly dead and/or naked, no. There was just no point in it. I thought it more likely she had worn a nightie, or a slip of some sort, that it was perhaps torn during a struggle, and subsequently removed from the scene, as not in keeping with the suicide idea."

"Mmm," said Mark.

"Then, again, it appeared to me most inconsistent, that a person, sufficiently disturbed as to contemplate the act of suicide, would switch on the television for a little viewing before hand. I'm more inclined to think that the television was used to cover the sounds of struggle, and whomever, after doing her in (so to speak), simply neglected to turn off the set."

"Logical," said Mark, "but hardly conclusive. Surely you had more to go on than that when you told Forbes we had a murderer on our hands."

"Not conclusive?" The lieutenant held up a red-tipped hand for inspection, her blonde head tilted appraisingly. "...to a man, perhaps. Honestly, Mark, sometimes the lack of insight in you men astounds me. But then, women are built so differently, aren't they?"

Mark conceded, silently and with approbation.

"Besides, it was physically impossible for Valeri Smith to have hanged herself from that chair."

"What? But I measured — "

"I know," said the lieutenant, beginning now to paint the nails on her other hand, "but only after the body had hung there for some time, and the leather belt that held her had been given time to stretch. Leather stretches frightfully, you know. And, if you remember, the light fixture was pulled down away from the ceiling, somewhat, which would tend to widen the gap still further — in as much as it was higher in its original position. Then, too, the weight of her body, if she had stood on the chair, would have depressed the upholstered seat by two or three inches. There just wasn't sufficient margin to accommodate any one of these factors, never mind all of them."

The lieutenant hung her nails up to dry, wrists limp, hands high.

"One more thing," she said, "there were pieces of well-trampled plaster that had broken away from the ceiling when the light fixture was pulled from its fastenings, littered over the floor below the body and the overturned chair, where the feet of Valeri Smith would not have stood (due to them being suspended in mid-air before the plaster had fallen), and where no other feet, save those of her hangman, could have stood, and then only prior to, or simultaneous with, the staging of that gruesome little charade, bolted doors and all, that subsequently greeted Mrs. Grebski, Mr. Forbes, and our unhappy selves, in that precise order. So you see, Mark, the suicide supposition would appear to have very little left to support it."

Mark lit a cigarette.

"If she didn't hang herself, then how do you suggest someone went about staging a private neck-tie party on the eighth floor of a busy hotel in the middle of the city? It seems to me — "

"I strongly suspect," the lieutenant put in serenely, "that she was hung there, by a person, or persons, yet unknown. Recall now, from

your anatomical studies at the Police Academy: the relative strength
of a woman's neck, in relation to her bodyweight is such, that even
a short drop of this kind would normally break it. I say *normally*,
because it is not inevitable; just probable. But Valeri Smith's neck
was not broken; she died of strangulation. Not conclusive, mind, not
in itself, but every substantiating clue serves to strengthen the
premise as a whole. Don't you agree?"

Before Mark could respond, agreeably or otherwise, the
telephone jangled with sudden alarm. The lieutenant tilted on her
ample axis and reached for it, stretching over the desk top with the
fluid grace of a panther.

This was no longer employment, Mark told himself; it was a form
of entertainment.

"Lieutenant Carruthers here." She listened a moment, then said,
"fine. Have them bring him up when they get in. And sergeant,
would you send an escort for Forbes. Yes, we're holding him now.
I'd like him here when we talk to Greaves."

The sound of the sergeant's voice crackled discordantly through
the receiver, and with a show of agitation she held the instrument
away from her ear. When she could get a word in, she said,
"Sergeant, I'll sign it — when I come by the desk. Right — and while
you're at it, see if you can chase up those reports from the coroner's
office. No — and I still haven't heard from lab, or records — as you
say, sergeant."

When she had replaced the instrument and regained her
equilibrium, she said, "Men!"

Mark said. "So they've got Greaves."

"Yes, and I've got hunger pangs." She looked at her watch.
"How about some lunch?"

"Thought you'd never ask."

"Let's try Lil Olys' — it's close, and it's quick."

"Match for the damage?"

"Uh-uh." The lieutenant shook her golden head.

"Dutch?"

"Dutch."

On the street, Cathy Carruthers walked tall and tempered at his
side, with a naked animal stealth that made Mark astutely aware of
the almost awesome intelligence and strength possessed by this

amazing woman.

SEATED ACROSS FROM CATHY CARRUTHERS AT LIL Olys' Cafeteria, Mark was aware that he was sheltering a callow sense of pride, a feeling of outright resentment, and a thin disguise of professional pedantry; pride, in his sometime-role of escort to the magnificent Amazon, resentment, in the endless turning of male heads, and, the inevitable ogling. To suppress any such activity, he knew, would require an exercise that would be tantamount to the total arrestment of crime itself.

He allowed his mind to wander these avenues for a time, until wild conjecture carried him into a nightmare of such outlandish fancy that he was happy, at length, to turn his thoughts back to the only somewhat less untenable complicacies surrounding the demise of Valeri Smith. With a hot corned beef sandwich under his belt and a cup of coffee warming his palate, Mark began to feel a little less like a student cadet at the police academy.

"Okay," he said with a sigh of resignation, "so Valeri Smith did not take her own life — then what explanation do you have for this business of the locked room?"

The lieutenant sipped thoughtfully on a glass of milk.

"Well, once we had ruled out the possibility of suicide, it followed categorically that *someone* had come and gone through one of the two locked doors, or an eighth-storey window. Of the three, the connecting door seemed to me the least formidable. That was where I found the toothpick, remember, directly beneath the bolt; which, incidentally, gave me my first clue as to how it was accomplished."

"Do tell," said Mark.

"If you recall, the bolt housing had a notched locking slot that engaged the projecting knob (by the simple expedient of gravity) in both the locked and the open position. It was to off-set this gravitational action that the toothpick, presumably, had been inserted between the bolt and the housing, thereby preventing the bolt from revolving and the projecting knob from dropping into the locking slot. This would permit the bolt, while still in the open position, to be drawn forward (by whatever means) without interception. Once released, the toothpick would simply fall to the floor."

"I'm with you, lieutenant. A common piece of string could have done it; one end tied to the knob on the bolt, the other passed around the end of the door. Then, with the door closed, the string could have been manipulated from 806."

"Exactly," said the lieutenant, adding impishly, "but then, how would you dispose of the string?"

"Yeah, how?"

"It puzzled me, too, until I spotted the seascape in 806. The painting had obviously been disturbed; taken down in fact, and the picture wire removed, then hurriedly replaced so that the frame rested higher on the wall than before. This, you remember, was not noticeable while the picture was askew, but only after I had straightened it, which was probably why it was overlooked. The wire, of course, made a perfect tool with which to draw the bolt; a wide, non-slip loop would easily have moved the bolt horizontally, then when slackened, would tend to spring away from the knob, allowing it to fall of its own accord into the locking slot. The wire could then be drawn back into the other room, and replaced. I suspect the end of the wire, twisted to effect the loop, was responsible for the light scratches on the edge of the door and the doorjamb."

"And I suspect you're right," said Mark. He followed her with unbidden eyes as she deserted her chair long enough to acquire a second glass of milk. He sighed. The Amazon in repose was disturbing enough; in motion, she was mesmeric.

"I will admit, though," she said, on resuming her seat, "I did not expect Greaves to be bald (as a *billiard ball*, you said, which was worst still). After all, Greaves had to be our prime suspect. It meant the hair we found in Valeri Smith's clenched fist could not have come from him; at least, not from his head. In view of this, I permitted myself the somewhat improbable supposition that Mr. Greaves was well haired below the neck, if not above it. Purely an assumption, you understand, but still, the hair sample did more closely resemble body hair than the scalp variety. And if it were so, (Greaves being our culprit) it would mean that he had not been fully clothed at the time of the murder. Then, when you consider that Miss Smith, too, had been scantily clad, if at all, there seemed little doubt they enjoyed a passing familiarity. As a matter of fact, it was possible — and to my thinking, even probable — that Valeri Smith and Wilson Greaves were involved in something of an affair, in the most lurid sense of the word. Their meeting last night, in those rooms, obviously had been no accident. We can safely assume, I'm sure, that the reservations had been made by the luckless Miss Smith, herself, and with the full knowledge and consent of our Mr. Greaves." The lieutenant knitted her brows. "But the relationship struck me as being most incongruous."

"How do you mean?"

"Well, for one thing, their ages weren't compatible. She just didn't seem the type, even dead, to become unselfishly involved with a man twice her years, and particularly one who appeared to have no physical attractiveness. Nor did the surreptitiousness of their meeting seem overly indicative of true love. To me, their intimacy suggested something more. Something — sinister."

"I smell a motive," said Mark.

"And well you might," said the lieutenant, "for it is my contention that Wilson Greaves was the victim of blackmail, that for whatever reason he met Miss Smith last night, he eventually recovered and subsequently destroyed, certain incriminating documents. From the disheveled state of her luggage and those traces of burning in 806, we can reasonably assume that he accomplished his purpose."

"Then why would he kill her?" asked Mark.

"Why, indeed."

AT THE FRONT DESK, THE SERGEANT HAD A SMILE, A pen, and a dotted line for Lieutenant Carruthers. She accepted all three, graciously.

"You absent-minded-professor types are the bane of my life," he said. The lieutenant smiled, indulgently.

"Any word from the coroner?"

"Not yet, but the lab reports are on your desk, and if you stop in at records, I think they've got a couple of surprises for you."

"At this point," said Mark, "nothing would surprise me."

As the lieutenant moved off down the hall, the sergeant's eyes went with her. (Quixotically, Mark gave the sergeant a brief kangaroo hearing and sentenced him to life in purgatory.)

The records department harbored the smallest policeman on the Metropolitan Force, hired some years ago for his status rather than his stature, and whatever his name had been then, he had been labeled the *Leprechaun* by all and sundry ever since.

The lieutenant took the proffered brown manila file. "Anything of interest?"

"That's putting it mildly," said the leprechaun, only too pleased to share the fruits of his labors. "It seems that your Mr. Wilson Greaves is not Wilson Greaves at all, but Wayne P. Grayson, vice-president of Halton Mills, the Eastport Plastics Complex."

Mark whistled softly.

"And," said the little man, delighted at the affect of his revelations, "until some time last night, Mr. Grayson's private secretary was a cute little brunette by the name of Valeri Smith."

"This ties things up a bit," said Mark, then, with a look at his partner, he added, "or does it — ?"

"Good work, Garfield," said the lieutenant to the little man behind the counter, apparently having done sufficient research of her own to ascertain his true appellation.

The leprechaun beamed. "No trouble at all, lieutenant."

Mark was less generous. "Is Garfield your first name," he asked with mock servility, "or your last?"

The leprechaun leveled a long malevolent look at Mark, and turned on his heel.

"Scheee — "

In the squad room, the lieutenant went over the records file in its entirety.

"Apparently Forbes was better acquainted with the late Miss Smith than he was prepared to say," she said. "According to this, he's been seen with her on a number of occasions." Then, with a sly smile, she added, "Garfield is his first name — it's on his report — G. Leprohn."

Mark laughed. "You mean you really didn't know?"

Cathy Carruthers shook her lovely head and burst into a fit of laughter. And, together, they guffawed loudly and long. Through tear-misted eyes, Mark shared a rare and precious liaison with his goddess. In an unguarded moment, it seemed, she had descended briefly, but with equivalence, to his own earthly level.

A SHARP RAP ON THE OFFICE DOOR HERALDED THE arrival on Wayne P. Grayson, alias Wilson Greaves. The uniformed policeman who announced him, shoved him into the room, then left immediately, closing the door behind him.

"Won't you sit down, Mr. Grayson?"

Grayson stood there looking like a fugitive from a Yul Brynner movie. He was an unpleasant little man, hairless from the neck up, except for a pair of bushy eyebrows that kept his already deep-set eyes in perpetual shadow.

Grayson addressed himself to Mark. "What's this all about? Nobody will tell me a thing."

Lieutenant Carruthers towered above him. "Mr. Grayson," she said, "please sit down."

Grayson looked about nervously, then lowered himself into a chair. He was visibly upset.

The lieutenant went to her desk and exchanged the records file she had been holding, for the folder containing the lab reports. Without a word, then, she began to circle the chair in which Grayson was seated, slowly, perusing the papers in the file. Her heels clicked with a hollow echo against the floor, each step seeming to heighten the little man's discomfiture. His eyes reached for her as she came from behind him, then followed her through the arc of his vision, until they lost her on the other side. Mark, watching him, saw no aesthetic favor in the dark, sunken eyes; only a brooding fear. He had seen the Amazon perform this little ritual before, unnerving her prey, and he never ceased to wonder at the effect of it.

"What is it you want of me?" Grayson was having some difficulty in keeping his voice steady.

The door opened, and the same policeman ushered in an anxious-looking Forbes. The hotel manager did not display the same self-assurance he had rendered earlier. To the lieutenant, he said: "I certainly hope you know what you're doing."

"Sadly enough, for you, Mr. Forbes," she said, pleasantly, "I do. Please be seated."

Mark ushered Forbes to a chair.

"I've just been reading about you, Mr. Forbes." said the

lieutenant, indicating the file in her hand. "It seems the fingerprint on the lightswitch in room 804 was, in fact, yours."

"I already told you it was mine," said Forbes, uncertainly.

"So you did."

Forbes pulled nervously at his tie. "You've got the wrong man, lieutenant. I did not kill that woman."

"No, Mr. Forbes, you did not," said the lieutenant, "but you did hang her."

Mark raised his eyes in a sign of hopeless bewilderment. At this moment, as co-inquisitor, he felt not a little superfluous. He watched as the lieutenant seated herself on the edge of the desk and wondered, as he feigned a casual disinterest at the crossing of one Amazonian leg over the other, whether these diversionary tactics were altogether unintentional.

THE LIEUTENANT TURNED HER ATTENTION TO THE little man. "Suppose you begin, Mr. Grayson, by telling us when you first became enamored of your secretary."

Grayson cast a furtive glance at Mark, then back to the lieutenant. But his hesitancy was short lived.

"I don't suppose there's much use in hiding anything, now."

"We already know what happened, Mr. Grayson. We only want your corroboration."

Grayson shut his eyes in weary resignation, and began to talk.

"Yes, I did get involved with Valeri Smith, lieutenant. It began about three weeks ago. They say there's no fool like an old fool, and I suppose I set out to prove it. She led me on until I actually believed she was genuinely interested in me. I know it must sound ridiculous, at my age, but last night was supposed to have been a — well, a sort of betrothal."

"It was Miss Smith, was it not," said the lieutenant, "who arranged for the rooms at the Westmore?"

"Yes."

"But it wasn't love you found there, was it, Mr. Grayson?" The lieutenant's voice had an omniscient ring. "It was avarice - and the threat of blackmail."

Grayson looked surprised, but he continued, undeterred.

"You must understand that I loved her, lieutenant, damn fool that I was — and I trusted her. She managed to lay her hands on documents that would reveal, with further investigation, a shortage in the books of almost $80,000. Administration is my responsibility, you see; my partner is in charge of production. It was my shortage alright, but I needed a little time — "

"The price of silence was too high?"

"It wasn't that, exactly," said Grayson. "I think I would almost have agreed to pay her off if it wasn't for the way she went about it. She made an utter fool of me. She told me she already had a lover, her partner in this blackmail routine. She called me repulsive, and loathsome — a little, ugly old man — "

The words, tumbling out so fast, appeared to choke him. "I didn't want to kill her — I didn't *mean* to — it was just that grinning, taunting mouth — God, what a fool I've been — "

Grayson began to sob, quietly — a sort of guttural hysteria.

"What was she wearing, Mr. Grayson, when you left her?"

"Wearing?"

"Yes, what did she have on?"

"A kind of negligee, I think.".

"You're not sure?"

"Yes, I'm sure. It was a negligee, of sorts."

"Pink?"

"Yes."

"And by bunching this garment up around her neck, you were able to strangle her with it?"

"Yes, yes — "

"Then what did you do?"

Grayson took some moments to compose himself.

"It wasn't until I had recovered the documents from her suitcase that I realized she was dead. I went to my own room where I burned the book entries in the waste basket, then flushed them down the toilet."

"Did you burn anything else?"

"No."

"What then?"

"I dressed, quickly, as quickly as I could, and I left the hotel."

"Do you remember what time it was?"

"I'm not certain," said Grayson, "shortly after twelve, I imagine."

"And Miss Smith?"

Grayson gave the lieutenant a look of perplexity.

"But I told you, lieutenant, she was dead — "

"How did you leave her?"

"She was on the bed — on her back."

Lieutenant Carruthers slipped off her perch on the desk and began to pace. "Don't you think it passing strange, Mr. Forbes, for a man to admit to murder, yet deny the inconsequential act of hanging the body to the ceiling?"

"Why ask me?" muttered Forbes. "You have all the answers."

"Even if his motive was to hide his crime, to escape detection — "

"I don't know what you're saying," cut in Grayson. "I've already told you what happened."

"You have, indeed, Mr. Grayson. But if *you* didn't hang the unfortunate Miss Smith by her neck — *who did?* And *why?*"

GRAYSON LOOKED FROM ONE TO THE OTHER, AS though genuinely mystified by the entire conversation.

"You were seen leaving the hotel by two people, Mr. Grayson; one by chance (the night clerk), the other by design." The lieutenant looked squarely at Forbes. The hotel man said nothing.

"Let us suppose, Mr. Forbes, that *you* are Valeri Smith's mysterious lover and cohort (purely for the sake of discussion, you understand), and, on seeing Mr. Grayson leave the hotel, you beat a hasty path to room 804 to ascertain the success of your infamous scheme, to claim your share of the proceeds. You knock furtively on the door, but due to Miss Smith's unhappy estate, she is unable to respond. If the door is not locked, you simply walk in; a locked door, though, would require a key — your pass key, perhaps — but either way, you enter."

The lieutenant paused before the open window, her back to the three men, a silhouette of uncommon contour against the afternoon sun. To the world at large, she said: "No plan or counterplan had foreseen this contingency. Your first instinct is to put as much distance between you and your dead partner as possible, and so you leave, your mind dancing with the grim and sudden imminence of disaster.

"Precisely how long it took you to conclude you were in no apparent danger — providing, of course, that Valeri Smith had not disclosed your identity — I do not know; but I do know that it was at least five or six hours later, before you returned, having in the interim concocted a most ingenious, but nonetheless preposterous, hoax, which you were then preparing to execute. Sadly, it was ill-conceived, and had little chance of success from its very inception."

"This is ridiculous," said Forbes, "you've got no proof — "

"But Mr. Forbes, we are merely posing a supposition — Now, let us again assume that you are Miss Smith's accomplice. Armed with a scheme to divert the course of justice to your own ends, you re-enter room 804 and make a hurried appraisal of the death-scene. To cover the sounds of your activity, you select an all-night, FM channel on the television, ensuring its volume is loud enough to adequately camouflage your movements, yet not too loud so as to disturb the other guests. The torn and twisted negligee does not lend itself to your project, so you remove it and burn it, as best you can, in the toilet bowl in 806. This you do on the premise that the adjoining room will not be as closely investigated."

The lieutenant turned to Mark. "Some of the burned pieces I retrieved from the bowl were paper," she said in explanation, "and some were charred remnants of a pink nylon fabric — it's in the lab reports."

"Mmm," said Mark. He had been trying to envisage what Cathy Carruthers, the woman, would look like in a pink negligee, of sorts. Her interruption had been unpropitiously inopportune.

THE LIEUTENANT BEGAN TO PACE AGAIN, MORE quickly. "With the belt from Valeri Smith's coat, the end passed through the buckle-guard to fashion a slip-loop, and then attached to the light fixture, you are able to elevate her body sufficiently to allow the loop to pass over her head and tighten around her neck. You take great care, Mr. Forbes, to measure the distance carefully, from chair to toe, so that it will look as though she had taken her own life, but (*tch, tch*) you overlooked so many details. Most glaring, was the fact that Valeri Smith had been dead for at least four hours and rigor mortise had already begun to set in. This was evident by the way her limbs hung out away from her body, instead of perpendicularly. From this fact, alone, I have known from the moment I first set foot in room 804, that the entire scene was a grim and shallow burlesque."

The lieutenant stopped mid-floor and assumed a thoughtful pose, one hip thrust elegantly awry, a finger pressed to pursed lips. Mark guessed she went 38-25-39 under the sackcloth.

"If that light fixture was to give way under the weight of the body, Mr. Forbes, it would have done so almost immediately. I would guess that as the belt took the strain, the light flickered ominously, and you quickly switched it off at the wall to prevent a short circuit. The finger that pressed the switch, moist from your heinous toil, left a vivid telltale print. You see, Mr. Forbes, you would not have turned the light off at the time the body was discovered, as you said you did, because the light, having been broken earlier, was already off. That was a stupid lie."

"I must confess, though, that you carried on from there rather well. The locked room, though by no means novel, was quite tricky. I find it incongruous in the extreme that now, rather than extricate you, it will serve only to ensure your ultimate conviction."

"I hope you're prepared to prove all this?" Forbes' manner was one of enquiry rather than of affirmation.

"Have no illusion there, Mr. Forbes." To Mark, she said: "Two pertinent factors pointed to Mr. Forbes in the second half of this double-barreled felony — motive, and accessibility."

"Right," Mark agreed, "his pass key gave him accessibility, both coming and going. But what possible motive... ?"

The lieutenant turned to Forbes, "It's inconceivable, isn't it, that any motive would induce a man to undertake so grim a labor. Motive? Extortion, what else? — a vice with which this gentleman is well acquainted. Forbes was the only person who knew, without any doubt, that Grayson had killed Valeri Smith. By hiding this fact from the police, Forbes would have saved Grayson's life, literally. He had visions of selling this same commodity back to Grayson, in installments — it was a blackmailer's dream."

Grayson spun on Forbes. "You swine," he said with

vehemence. Then, to no one in particular, he whimpered; "God, I would have given my life for that girl."

The Amazon looked at Grayson. "You might yet," she said flatly.

Who would kill Santa Claus in a store window in front of dozens of witnesses? And how? The beautiful and efficient Detective-Lieutenant Cathy Carruthers would have her lovely hands full on this case!

the santa claus killer

"LIEUTENANT, SOMEONE JUST KILLED SANTA CLAUS!"

Detective-Lieutenant Cathy Carruthers lifted her honey-blonde head and levelled quizzical blue eyes at the man who had come bursting into her office.

"What *are* you talking about?"

Detective-Sergeant Mark Swanson regarded his immediate superior with chagrin. He wondered if there was *anything* that could ripple that queenly calm.

"It's true," he persisted, "Santa Claus is dead."

The lieutenant smiled indulgently and proceeded to scatter piles of official-looking papers with her elbows, to make room in the center of her desk for a vial of blood-red nail polish. Mark watched in rapt frustration as she drew a red swath over the tip of an elegantly arched finger.

"That's like saying God is dead. Really, Mark — who would want to kill Santa Claus?"

Mark thought about it.

"Mrs. Claus?"

Cathy Carruthers favored her two i.c. with another disarming

27

smile and carried on calmly adorning her nails.

"Sit down, Mark. Tell me about it."

Mark pursed his lips, sighed obeisantly, and lowered his rugged frame into a chair. Working with the "Amazon", as she was known to her burly colleagues in Homicide, demanded certain compromises that might have daunted a lesser man than Mark. It had taken him several months on the job to see beyond the stunning, six-foot, honey-haired female he had been assigned to as partner, but when he did, he discovered a remarkable individual, a true friend and a detective of rare sagacity. Watching her now, as she hung her freshly painted nails up to dry, wrists limp, her classic features inscrutably unperturbed, he felt a mild alarm at his growing attachment to this larger-than-life Amazonian goddess.

"You were saying?"

Mark yanked his mind back to the moment.

"Dispatch," he began, "just took a call from a Lloyd Drexler, security man at Martindew's Department Store. He said there's been a killing in that big display window on Central Avenue, the one they doll up every year to look like Santa's Workshop. You know, a bunch of dwarfs making toys and things for Christmas, and some guy in a red suit and white whiskers dressed up like Santa Claus. Well, that's one sad Santa that won't be going down any chimneys this Christmas — some one just choked the life out of him."

"Did they apprehend the killer?"

"That's the strange thing about it, lieutenant. It apparently happened while he was sitting in the window going Ho-Ho-Ho to a crowd of starry-eyed Christmas shoppers."

"And?"

"No one saw it happen."

"Hmm."

Mark recognized that contemplative "Hmm." The Amazon, he knew, loved nothing better than a puzzling mystery. Mark remembered having once used the word "unsolvable" in connection with a particularly abstruse murder case. She had been quick to admonish him. "No such thing," she had asserted. "If murder can be done, it can be solved." And solve it she did.

Mark scrambled up on his size twelves as the lieutenant suddenly shouldered a red leather purse and headed for the door.

The purse matched her newly painted fingertips, he noticed (as a good officer should) — and her lipstick.

"Where to?" he asked.

"To find out who would want to kill Santa Claus on the very Eve of Christmas," she tossed back over her shoulder, "and why."

CHRISTMAS AT MARTINDEW'S WAS ADVERTISED AS A family affair. They had used the "family" motif from the beginning, back to thirty years ago when it was known as Martindew's General Store, and run mostly by family members. The business had flourished over the years, evolving rapidly into one of the largest departmentalized stores in the entire state. The seasonal window display, "Santa's Workshop", had grown with it, from a small nativity scene in an old storefront window, to an annual happening of almost legendary acclaim. Today, it was a major Christmas event in Metro, welcomed, and viewed with delight, by Santa fans of all ages.

Lieutenant Cathy Carruthers stood now in the center of Santa's Workshop and looked about her with coldly perceptive eyes. The window area, she observed, was about twenty feet wide, by maybe thirty, with a floor-to-ceiling plate glass window on one side that covered its entire length. The drapes were drawn now, but the whole exhibit was still operating at full tilt. It was a busy scene.

Toys were everywhere, toys of every make and mold, and a dozen look-alike elves, with big grinning heads and white gloved hands were still hammering, sawing, chiselling away at them, all in rhythm to a tinkling yuletide arrangement of *Whistle While You Work.* A huge pine Christmas tree stood in one corner, slowly turning, dazzling, with the glitter of a thousand ornaments and a magic mile of tinsel. And in the center of it all sat Santa, swaying gently in his automated rocker, with his glassy eyes staring vacantly ahead, and an uncharacteristic blush of purple in the once rosy hue of his cheeks.

"Has anything been touched?" The lieutenant directed her question to a uniformed police officer who, together with his partner, had been guarding the murder scene against well-meaning-bunglers and the just-plain-curious.

"No, sir — uh, mam — uh — "

The Amazon turned her back on the officer's confusion with an amused grin. "Wait outside, please."

When they were alone, she said, "Mark, it seems incomprehensible, does it not, that some one, or some thing, could have strangled the life out of our unhappy Santa — or whomever — and not been seen by someone, some *one*, in the crowd outside the window."

"Yeah, it's got me stumped."

"The most obvious suspects, of course, would be the elves — "

"Lieutenant," Mark's tone was disparaging, "how could a mechanical elf —?"

"Or someone dressed up like one?"

"Uh-hu," said Mark with skepticism, "and what about the thirty odd men, women and kids who were standing on the other side of that window, watching?"

"Yes," the lieutenant said quietly, as she moved to a spot behind the body. "As the late John Steinbeck might have said: *'Tis a puzzlement.*" She lifted the white hair at the nape of Santa's neck and exposed the sinister home-made garrote. It looked evil, Mark thought, even just lying idly there against the skin. It was fashioned of white nylon cord, with the replica of a small metal clothes-line tightener (also white) at one end, and a loop the size of a man's fist at the other. The cord, which was about four feet in length, dangled down behind the rocker and matched its tireless rhythm in a slow swinging arc.

"Recognize this, Mark?" The lieutenant rotated the small white "tightener" between an immaculately-lacquered thumb and forefinger. It was the cylindrical type, slightly narrowed at one end and with three tiny metal balls trapped inside. When a line was passed through it in one direction, from the narrow to the wide end, it moved freely; if the direction of travel was reversed, the cord was halted by the jamming of the metal balls in the narrow end of the cylinder.

"An effective clincher," Mark observed, "and available at almost any hardware store — but why so long a cord?" When he extended the length of nylon straight back from the rocker, it reached well into a small cluster of elves.

"Maybe that's your answer," said the lieutenant, and she drew his attention to the fact that only nine of the mechanical elves were animated. The three positioned directly behind Santa's chair wore happy grinning faces, but were otherwise non-productive in the Christmas effort of imaginary toy making.

"Lieutenant?" One of the uniformed officers had thrust his head through the partly open door. "There's a Lloyd Drexler here, wants to come in. Says he's in charge of store security."

"Let him in, officer."

A LARGE MAN, SIX FOOT PLUS AND BUILT LIKE A LINE backer, crammed his way through the door.

"Mark," The lieutenant spoke in quiet even tones to her colleague, but her eyes were on Drexler, "I'd like you to get the Medical Examiner down here, soon as possible. The Lab people, too, and the Photogs. We're going to need all the help we can get on this one. And Mark, have these two officers round up as many witnesses as they can find, anyone who was in front of that window during the past hour and a half." Then, as Mark turned to leave, "Mr. Drexler, I'm glad you're here, There are a few questions — "

"Yeah," the big man interrupted, "and I've got a few of my own. This here is my territory, and don't you forget it. And I don't want no guy in a monkey suit telling me where I can go and where I can't." He let his eyes travel up, then down, the lieutenant's imposing frame, "Now, I guess I got some dame giving me the I'm-in-charge routine."

The Amazon drew herself up to her full height. Her eyes had the glint of cold steel.

"Mr. Drexler. I am Detective-Lieutenant Cathy Carruthers, Metro Central, Eleventh Precinct. You can talk to me now, or not, as you wish. But kindly be advised that I am not intimidated by your supercilious, machoistic posturing. As a matter of fact, I'd be less them honest if I did not reveal to you that I find your behavior tiresome and churlish in the extreme, something more befitting a witless adolescent than a Martindew's store detective. Now — we can just as easily continue this conversation downtown, at headquarters, at my convenience, or we can resume where we left off a few moments ago. What is your choice?"

It was not possible for a man of Drexler's bulk to wilt, but he did slump a little.

"I — well — " he stammered, not knowing precisely how, or to what extent, he had been so imprudently squelched.

"Anyhow," he muttered, "there's not a whole lot I can tell you."

"Tell me this: are you acquainted with the victim?"

"Yeah. That's the *man*, himself. Nathan P. Martindew, President and owner of Martindew's Department Store."

The lieutenant registered her surprise. "What on earth would a man of that caliber be doing in a Santa Claus suit?"

"Nothing new. He takes an hour shift every day. Family tradition, or something. Says he's been doing it for thirty years."

"He took the same shift every day?"

"Yeah. Never failed. Nine to nine-fifty. Then the display closes down for ten minutes. Coffee break, a change of Santas. Goes on that way all day; every hour on the hour."

"Who takes over at ten, when Mr. Martindew leaves?"

"A couple of old guys take turns. They work out of the Display Department. Christmas extras. Nathan P. always hires them himself — you know, doing the interviews, training them to Ho-Ho, like that — "

"One thing, Mr. Drexler, strikes me as rather strange."

"What's that?"

"With Nathan P. Martindew, himself, sitting here, dead — why isn't there more of a commotion in this place?"

"No one knows about it, that's why. If it wasn't for those two cops — "

The lieutenant cut him short. "I seem to recall, Mr. Drexler, that Nathan P. Martindew was somewhat incapacitated, confined to a wheel-chair, if I remember correctly."

"That's right. It was polio, or something. Anyway, he was pretty well paralyzed from the neck down. A lot of good all his money was to him. We had to wheel him in, then lift him from the wheel-chair to the rocker. The same again, in reverse, when his hour was up."

"I see. And weren't you the one who phoned the police?"

"Yes."

"And you also discovered the body?"

"Well, yes, I did. But Penny Lamb was right there with me. We closed the drapes, opened the door, and there he was, just like he is now, deader than a Christmas turkey."

"Where will I find this Penny Lamb?"

"Miss Penelope Lamb, if you don't mind."

The lieutenant turned to see a large heavy woman, equally as tall as herself but obviously not poured from the same classic mold, sharing the doorway with a frustrated police officer.

"Officer, let her in."

"As if he could stop me." said Penelope Lamb. She came bursting through the door like a Marine hitting the beach at Okinawa. She wore faded blue jeans and a matching denim shirt, both of which seemed to be stretched to the limit of their capacity.

"Please stay over here near the window, Miss Lamb," the lieutenant cautioned, "our people from HQ will not want anything disturbed."

"For all the good it'll do them."

"Now what makes you say that?"

"You tell me, lieutenant." Penelope Lamb pointed a plump finger at the defunct Santa Claus. "Old Nathan P. was in here all alone for fifty minutes, until Drexler and I came in together and found him dead. Even if someone else did come in here during that time, which they did not, it still remains that no less than thirty pairs of eyes were on Nathan P. every second of that time. I just don't see how it could have happened."

"Perhaps not, Miss Lamb, but happen, it did. And I intend to find out precisely how, and by whom. Now suppose you start by telling me where you were this morning, when Nathan P. Martindew first assumed his seat in the window."

"I was right here with him, lieutenant. It was Drexler and me who lifted him onto the rocker."

"And then?"

"Then we turned on the display machinery, opened the drapes, and left."

"That how you see it, Mr. Drexler?"

"Yeah. I was the one who opened the drapes. Penny switched on the rocker. She was still fussing with his beard, straightening his hat, you know, last minute touches — "

"But he was still visibly alive when you both had finally withdrawn from the display area?"

"Oh, yeah," said Drexler emphatically. "Nathan P. was an old dragon at the best of times, and a real stickler about starting on time. He made no bones about telling us to get outta there and get the show started. He was still nattering away at us when we closed the door on him."

"Miss Lamb," The lieutenant pursed her lips against an extended finger. "What is your particular function, here at the store?"

"You're standing in the middle of it, lieutenant." She swung her pudgy arm to take in the entire exhibit. "I'm assistant manager in Display. This whole show is our brain child — mine and Reggie Martin's."

"And who might Reggie Martin be?"

"He might be me, damn it. And tell this clown to keep his hands to himself."

A LITTLE MAN, WITH A HEAD THAT LOOKED TOO large for his body, suddenly appeared at the door. He was about four-foot zilch in his hush puppies, and no bigger than one of the elves that were still banging away at the toys in the window. He was dressed in jeans, like Penny Lamb, and a denim shirt that was open almost to his navel. A bronze medallion swung from a leather thong around his neck and shone like a small sun from the black jungle of hair on his little chest. A pair of white cotton gloves dangled from his back pocket. He was prevented from entering further into the room by the restraining arm of the law, one hand of which had seized him firmly by the scruff of his neck.

"Another one for you, lieutenant." The officer struggled valiantly to hold onto the little man who was apparently much stronger than his size would suggest.

"It's all right, officer. Let him go. But, please, no more."

Reggie Martin waddled in and took up a position near Penelope Lamb. He was about eye-level with her belt buckle. He had a ruddy, just-scrubbed look, like a reluctant little boy on his way to church on Sunday morning.

"And who might you be?" he said, looking skyward at the

Amazon who towered above him like a giant gray sequoia.

"I'm Lieutenant Cathy Carruthers, Mr. Martin. And I am currently investigating the death of the unfortunate gentleman in the Santa Claus costume. Is there anything you would like to tell me about it?"

"What is there to tell? He's dead, isn't he?"

"Yes, he's that all right." The lieutenant smiled thinly. "And where were *you*...this morning, when Mr Martindew took his place in the window?"

"I was in Display, right behind Miss Lamb and Drexler when they opened the drapes at nine."

"And when he was found dead?"

"I was still in Display, just where I was supposed to be."

"Do you two concur?" The lieutenant looked at Drexler, then at Penelope Lamb. They nodded their heads in acquiescence.

"I remember him there at nine," Drexler added reflectively, "but I can't say for sure he was there when we found the body."

"He was there," Penelope Lamb said unequivocally.

The lieutenant turned her attention back to the little man.

"What is your capacity, Mr. Martin, in the Display Department?"

"I'm the manager."

"I see. And the Santa Workshop exhibit is the creation solely of you, and Miss Lamb?"

"Yes."

"Has anyone else from Display been permitted to work on it?"

"No."

"Why not?"

"Because Penel — Miss Lamb and I have been doing it for years. No one else has ever worked on it. It's our baby, that's all."

"Yes, well — "

"This exhibit is not as superficial as it may at first appear, lieutenant." The little man sounded somewhat put out by the lieutenant's seeming indifference. "Take Santa's chair, for instance," he pointed with pride to the object in question, "it will not only rock on its pedestal, back and forth, but it will also move in a fifteen degree arc either side of center. If the mechanism is activated promptly on the hour, the rocker will complete one full arc to the right, and return, in exactly ten minutes. It will then automatically repeat the maneuver to the left. After a fifty minute shift (or ten complete arcs) the chair will end up precisely where it began, facing the crowd at the window. It requires a great deal of skill, lieutenant, to achieve that kind of precision."

"I'm sure it does."

The lieutenant dropped to one knee and ran her fingers appraisingly over the ornate pedestal on which the chair was perched. The switch that activated the rocker was at the back of the base and the mechanism itself was skillfully hidden behind a gayly colored facade, an elaborate rendering of fairyland fantasia around a horde of little elfin gargoyles that winked and grinned with the spirit of Christmas. The tiny grotesque heads were carved from solid wood and bolted securely to the base on all sides of the pedestal.

"I'm duly impressed," said the lieutenant with apparent sincerity.

"Thank you, lieutenant."

Their eyes met briefly on the same level before the Amazon resumed the perpendicular. "The elves, Mr. Martin," she said reflectively, "the twelve mechanical elves. They seem to bear a remarkable resemblance — "

"To me?" The little display manager moved obligingly to the group of three elves behind the Santa's chair. He donned the white gloves from his back pocket, assumed an elfin pose, and grinned. With a little make-up, he would have been indistinguishable from any one of them. "I'm the original, lieutenant. All the elves were patterned after me."

"Remarkable," said the lieutenant, but her voice suddenly took on a warm confiding quality. "Mr. Martin. I sense that you are inordinately disturbed about something, that you are not totally at ease with me. Are you able to tell me why?"

Reggie Martin tugged nervously at the bronze medallion and shifted his weight from one little foot to the other. He glanced hesitantly up at Penelope Lamb.

"Look, lieutenant, maybe there is something. But I think we should be talking about it up on the seventh floor, in Nathan's office."

"I don't understand."

"Reggie — " Penelope Lamb put a lot of concern into that one word.

"It's got to come sooner or later, Pen. No point in hiding it any longer now." He turned to the lieutenant. "It's not generally known around the store, but I'm not really Reggie Martin. What I mean is, Reggie Martin is a simple diminutive of my real name: Reginald Martindew. That dead Santa Claus, lieutenant, is my brother."

Lloyd Drexler's jaw dropped in silent disbelief. Penelope Lamb's rotund face was expressionless.

"Very well, Mr. — uh, Martindew." If the Amazon was surprised, she did not show it. "I see no reason why we should not accede to your request. I still have a few loose ends to see to down here, but we will all four of us reassemble on the seventh floor in say, fifteen minutes. But before — "

The lieutenant stopped abruptly in mid-sentence and looked up. The star at the top of the Christmas tree had suddenly burst into a series of brilliant, eye-blinding flashes. The lieutenant blinked as all eyes darted to the tree.

"What is that about?"

"Star of Bethlehem," Penelope Lamb said proudly. "It's new this year. People love it."

"I'm sure. How often does it happen?"

"Every hour, on the half hour, for a ten second duration," Miss Lamb explained, "I've seen people wait the better part of an hour just to see it come on."

"Well, we were fortunate indeed," The Amazon ventured with a dubious smile, "we got zapped without having to wait at all."

LIEUTENANT CATHY CARRUTHERS AND SERGEANT Mark Swanson struggled through the main floor crush of Christmas shoppers toward the elevator lobby at the rear of the store. The frail familiar strains of Holy Night permeated the air, making something almost sacred out of the crass Christmas con game that had everybody clamoring over each other to give up their money. The elevators were taking off as fast as a bevy of young girls in abbreviated Santa costumes could cram them full. The lieutenant and Mark stood in line behind the others, waiting their turn.

"Well, lieutenant." Mark unbuttoned his coat and jammed his

hands into his pants pockets. "What do you make of it?"

"Not much." The lieutenant panned an exasperated eye over the milling heads of the shoppers.

"I mean this Santa Claus business."

"Oh." She nudged her nose thoughtfully with a genteelly flexed knuckle. "I find it somewhat intriguing, to say the least."

"Well, I don't mind admitting, I'm stumped. There just isn't anyway it could have happened. Someone must be lying."

"Mark, how can you say that? We've just finished checking it out." The lieutenant's tone was more speculative than assertive. "The two relief Santas have corroborated the statements of Penelope Lamb and Lloyd Drexler, as well as that of the little guy, Reggie — whatever. I can't believe that everyone is lying. By the way," she added, "did you get that self-styled garrote to the Lab?"

"Yes I did,"

"Good." She turned eyes on Mark that seemed to be looking right through him. "I find it difficult to justify that loop, or hand-grip, at the end of the cord. And why was the cord of just sufficient length to reach into that grouping of elves behind the rocker?"

"It doesn't look too good for the elves, does it?" Mark grinned.

"Nothing about this case looks particularly good for the elves," The lieutenant replied soberly, as though there had been nothing facetious in his comment.

"Yeah, I see what you mean," Mark reflected. "According to three independent witnesses, Nathan P. was alive and well at nine o'clock, and in full view of a crowd of Christmas shoppers until ten minutes of ten, when Drexler and Penny Lamb drew the drapes and found him dead. The only company he had during that fifty minutes, were the twelve grinning, four-foot elves. But even so, lieutenant, what could they have done (assuming a mechanical elf could do anything) with all those people watching?"

"Yes," the lieutenant mused softly, "what?"

"*THIS WAY, PLEASE.*"

One of the girls beckoned from the door of an elevator and they allowed themselves to be swept inside with a dozen other sardines. But Mark found no discomfort in being crammed into such close quarters with his enchanting partner. After the initial squirming, he found himself face to face with her, gazing breathlessly into those unbelievable blue eyes, just inches from his own,

"Hi," he said, with a crooked little grin.

"Hi, yourself."

She gave him a smile that promised to keep his fantasies flaming for a week.

The elevator clanked to a stop at the seventh floor with tummy-turning abruptness. An attractive black girl met them at the reception desk.

"Lieutenant Carruthers?" She addressed herself to Mark. The Amazon gave the girl a tolerant smile. She had long since resigned herself to this hesitancy on the part of some, to readily accept her, a woman, in what was generally regarded to be a male role. The girl conducted a brief woman-to-woman appraisal of the Amazon and said, "Follow me, please."

They trailed the black girl's engaging back through an immense, open room filled with desks, filing cabinets, rapidly clicking typewriters, and people. Everyone and every*thing* seemed to be in a hectic state of regulated confusion. They zigzagged through it all to a row of offices on the far side where they were ushered through a door that read: Nathan P. Martindew, President.

The office was impressively spacious. A thick pile rug lay underfoot, and luxurious furnishings in soft leather and deep red walnut enriched the decor. A huge desk dominated the room, behind which, the new-born Reginald Martindew sat looking like a midget mushroom on a two-dollar pizza.

"Come in, lieutenant." The little man was effusive. "You know everyone, of course. Miss Lamb, Drexler, Miss Gayle (who has just escorted you from the elevator) and old faithful, himself, Elmer Sawatsky. Elmer has been with the firm for almost thirty years. He is our chief accountant."

"How do you do, lieutenant?"

A bespectacled, nondescript sort of man in his middle fifties offered a limp hand to the lieutenant. She took it briefly, nodded to the others, and folded her elegant form into one of the leather chairs. Mark took the chair beside her.

"Mr. Martindew." The lieutenant spoke directly at the man's

head, which was all she could see of him above the polished surface of the desk. "Don't you feel that you might be jumping into your new role as president, somewhat precipitously, if not without a certain presumptuousness? After all, your own brother has just been killed — murdered, his body not yet cold."

"Presumptuous, lieutenant? Precipitous?" The new president had to raise his elbows to shoulder height to place his forearms on the desk. His little fingers toyed excitedly with the bronze medallion. "Hardly. I've waited years for this moment. The news of my brother's death this morning could not have come at a better time: Christmas Eve! How does that carol go now — *Oh ti-idings of co-omfort and joy.* You see, I make no illusions as to how I feel. Lieutenant, this promises to be the most momentous Christmas of my entire life."

"Reggie, not now." Penelope Lamb filled a leather chair to overflowing, a little to one side of the desk. "This is not the time," she pleaded.

"She's right, of course." Reginald Martindew tried several times to raise his head above the level of his hands. "My relationship with my brother, with my family, is undeniably a personal matter, and I would not normally discuss these things before the people who are presently in this room. But because of the way my brother died, and the circumstances that have preceded my rightful ascension to this chair today, the story, quite frankly, will be unrepressible. Every sordid detail will soon be splashed over newspapers, tabloids, and two-bit scandal sheets from here to Vladivostock. What would be the point in withholding anything at this juncture?"

"Then you won't mind," the lieutenant said as she settled back in the chair, "imparting some of those details you refer to, for our edification."

REGINALD MARTINDEW LOOKED AROUND THE ROOM, from one expressionless face to another, then shrugged his tiny shoulders.

"I was the oldest, the rightful heir. I had every appearance of a normal, healthy child, the first born, the pride of the Martindews, until it was noticed that I wasn't growing as rapidly as I should. By

MEL D. AMES

the time I was six, it was obvious that something was wrong. That was in the days before they knew too much about pituitary malfunctions which, of course, was my problem. Today, a series of natural-hormone injections would have remedied the situation, quite simply, and I would probably have grown eye-to-eye with your remarkable self, lieutenant."

All eyes turned momentarily to the lieutenant as though to see for themselves what Reggie might have grown eye-to-eye with, under more favorable circumstances.

"Nathan was born then, and I was shuttled off to one side, out of sight and mind. I never even knew my two younger sisters, whose twin births followed Nathan's by some eighteen months. As I grew older, the family law firm legally changed my name, and I was sent away with a modest, but livable, allowance. But, at the age of maturity, I returned, mortified at this rejection by the family, and by threatening to reveal my true identity, I was able to get a sizable increase in my allowance and a job for life, here at Martindews. What I did not know, at the time, was that only a few weeks prior to my re-appearance, the Martindew family had been touched by the hand of divine retribution (in my view, at least): Nathan, the favorite son, had been struck down by polio. The disease (acute anterior poliomyelitis, to be precise) left him totally devastated, and paralyzed from head to toe. Elmer, here, will attest to all that I have said, thus far."

Elmer nodded his nondescript head in agreement.

"Seven months ago," Reginald continued, "both my parents were killed in an automobile accident. The entire corporate estate, of course, went to Nathan, except for minor, non-voting stock allotments to my two sisters, who have since married and left Metro for sunnier climes. I tried to contest it — secretly — but I could not find a responsible law firm willing to risk the resultant pressures that would inevitably follow a suit taken against the highly influential Martindew administration. That is, until recently. Nathan, of course, was fully cognizant of what I was up to before he died, and did not actively oppose the action. Its ultimate success is ultra vires (as they say), inevitable. Simply a matter of time."

"How will Nathan's death affect your claim?"

"Not at all, really. Except that now I will inherit all — not half

41

— of the Martindew corporate holdings."

"That could be a sizable motive," said the lieutenant softly, "for permanently removing your brother from the scene."

"Oh, come now, lieutenant. I was already a potential millionaire before Nathan was killed. Why would I risk all that, for money I could never hope to spend?"

"It's my job to examine every motive," the lieutenant replied. "Motives, like life itself, are sometimes obscure and irrational."

"What about the rest of these people?" Penelope Lamb rushed to Reggie's defense. "Take Drexler, there. His job was on the line. Nathan P. was going to fire him right after Christmas. Tried to get himself into bed with a young, pretty shoplifter, by promising to drop the charges. She went to the boss with it —"

Lloyd Drexler's face had turned the color of cranberry sauce.

"I don't have to sit here and listen to this," he fumed, "I'm not the only one with egg on my face. It ain't no secret that Miss Gayle here has been fraternizing with the office manager, and vice versa, apparently. How do we know old Nathan P. wasn't getting ready to dump him and her both? And Penny Lamb's relationship with Reggie wasn't all nip and tuck in the Display Department — he's been sharing her apartment for the better part of two years, that I know of. What they could've been cooking up together is anybody's guess. A regular old *Peyton Place*, ain't it, lieutenant?"

"Oh, my," said Elmer Sawatsky.

"And you, too, you old fraud." Drexler was not yet finished. "How do we know you aren't cooking the books and embezzling yourself up to those ice-cube eyeglasses you wear? Like they say, lieutenant, nobody's perfect."

Mark looked from face to face for the reaction to Drexler's outburst. Miss Gayle had turned a slightly lighter shade of black while remaining painfully aloof. Penny Lamb's flaccid face was an overt mask of indignation and anger, and Elmer Sawatsky squirmed in his chair as though involved in a private little struggle with himself for the courage to raise his hand to ask to leave the room. Only the little president seemed immune to the store detective's vindictive tirade. The face that peeked up from behind the enormous desk was wreathed in a tolerant, beneficent smile, a product, it would seem, of his new-found authority.

"PLEASE. GENTLEMEN. LADIES." REGINALD MARTINDEW had now assumed a self-appointed role as mediator. "Let's not be carried away. The untimely death of my brother will touch on all of us, of course, one way or another. That is inevitable. But no one has yet been accused of anything. Have they? And I very much doubt that anyone will be. I would suggest that Lieutenant Carruthers is going to be hard put to tell us just how Nathan was murdered, much less by whom. Right, lieutenant?"

"Wrong." The lieutenant slowly uncoiled from the depths of the leather chair. She stood tall and silent for a moment, then paced out a small circle in the center of the room, as though modeling the latest thing from Frederick's, her exquisite body moving with the naked stealth and power of a jungle beast beneath the gray material of her suit. Mark knew a time of revelation was close at hand, and he wondered if he would ever become accustomed to the breath-robbing beauty and intelligence of this astounding woman.

The lieutenant stopped in front of Elmer Sawatsky. He seemed to pale a little behind his occular ice-cubes. Mr. Sawatsky," she said, not unkindly, "I cannot believe that you possess either the motive or the means — not to mention the fortitude — to cause the death of your late employer. If, in fact, you were "cooking the books" as Mr. Drexler had so groundlessly implied, it will soon come to light in the audit that will inevitably follow the death of Mr. Martindew. You may leave, Mr. Sawatsky, and I suggest you take Miss Gayle along with you."

The lieutenant turned to the young black with a condescending lift of her flawless brows.

"The allegations that your services to your immediate superior may not have ended with dictation, typing and filing, is of no concern to me in this investigation. You are an attractive young lady, Miss Gayle. It is my fervent hope that you will show better judgement in future when endeavoring to advance your career."

Miss Gayle hurried after the accountant and closed the door softly behind her. The lieutenant then turned to Mark.

"See that these other people are taken downtown, Mark, given their rights, and held."

Reginald Martindew's smile faded. Then the face behind the smile suddenly disappeared. A moment later, the little man came running out around the side of the desk, the bronze medallion flying in the breeze. He stopped about three feet from the lieutenant, his hands on his hips, looking up at her.

"Are you serious?" he choked. "You can't hold us. You don't have a damn thing to go on."

"I wouldn't be too sure of that."

"Are you accusing *me* of murder?"

"That," said the lieutenant, "could be a distinct possibility."

"You're making a big mistake, lady." He endeavored to convey with his tone of voice what a threatening posture had laughingly failed to achieve. "I'm not without influence now, you know."

"Nor, sir, am I."

Reginald Martindew's exasperation was suddenly more than he could rationally endure. He drew back a little foot and levelled it with irreverent spite against an hitherto sacrosanct Amazonian shin. "Damn you," he sputtered.

The Amazon winced, but made no sound as she calmly reached down and collared the little man with one well-groomed hand and lifted him, kicking and squirming, to shoulder height. "Cuff him," she said quietly to Mark, "and take him in."

Mark was no stranger to the occasional display of the Amazon's awesome strength and agility, but each new manifestation left him a little crushed, with yet another bruise to his hairy-chested ego. He took the weight of the midget president from her outstretched arm with a grunt of mild surprise, then answered her embarrassed grin with one of his own. "The Dragon Lady strikes again," he said with a whimsical little groan.

THE RECORDS DEPARTMENT EMBOSOMED THE SMALL-est policeman on the Metro Force, hired on the strength of his status rather than his stature. Few of his colleagues were actually aware of his legal name, Garfield Leprohn. Someone, somewhere, sometime, had labelled him the *Leprechaun,* and the name had stuck. Cathy Carruthers was leaning over the counter, talking to the Leprechaun when Mark caught up with her.

"It wouldn't take much to make this place into another Santa's Workshop," Mark observed wryly, "a saw here, a chisel there, someone wearing white gloves and whistling — "

"If you don't mind," the Leprechaun scowled, "we're discussing official business."

The lieutenant contained her amusement behind a mask of pretended interest in the file on the counter.

"This simply confirms Martindew's sad little story," the lieutenant said in a tight voice. "There was certainly no love lost between him and his brother."

"There is one point of interest," said the Leprechaun, eager to share the results of his seldom appreciated labors, "Penelope Lamb has apparently been with the Martindew family for almost as long as Reginald. She was the daughter of a servant, a housekeeper. They knew each other as children."

"Interesting," said the lieutenant, "anything on Drexler?"

"Not much, except that he's been cited half a dozen times for the same kind of thing that was getting him into hot water at Martindew's"

"That figures," the lieutenant said matter-of-factly.

"The two relief Santas are just what they seem to be, innocent by-standers. And I haven't been able to come up with much, yet, on either Sawatsky or Gayle."

"Let me know when you do."

As they left, the lieutenant smiled her appreciation, and Mark went out whistling: *Whistle While You Work —*

SEATED IN HER OFFICE, LIEUTENANT CATHY CARRU-thers went through the Records file again, in its entirety. As she closed the folder, Mark came in with another one just like it.

"The M.E.'s preliminary," he said, "The full report won't be available until after the autopsy."

"Is there anything in it?" the lieutenant asked as she accepted the unusually thin file.

"Precious little, lieutenant, and nothing we don't already know." Mark lowered his rugged frame into a chair. "Strangulation. Neck unbroken. No other marks. And a time of death that we've already come closer to ourselves."

The lieutenant flipped disparagingly through the half dozen or so pages. She looked up at Mark. "Did you establish the sequence I gave you to have the suspects brought in?"

"Yes. Officers Fisk and Mayhew have been alerted." He consulted his watch. "They should be here any minute."

"And what about the Lab report?"

"Whenever you're ready for it. I'll be right by the door."

"Good."

"But there won't be anything in it, lieutenant. After all, what can you say about four feet of nylon cord and a clothes-line tightener that had been rubbed smooth by the motion of the automated rocker?"

"Not much," the lieutenant admitted with a grim sigh, "especially if it should happen to be around your own neck." She planted her elbows on the desk and cradled her beautiful face in the palms of her hands. "We don't have much to go on, do we?"

"Even our own private little dwarf from Records wasn't able to give us anything," Mark grunted. "Say — maybe he's in on it. Yeah, I can see it now: the Leprechaun, moonlighting as one of the twelve mechanical elves, picking up a couple of extra bucks for Christmas. He killed Santa Claus because he didn't like what he was going to get for Christmas — a pocket periscope for watching parades, a reclining highchair, and the latest 8-track release of *Short People* —"

Cathy Carruthers tried unsuccessfully not to laugh at him. "Mark, don't you think you come down a little hard on the Leprechaun?"

"Temptation leaves me weak," Mark confided with mock innocence, "just can't help myself."

"I've noticed."

"And yet — " Mark's manner was suddenly, deadly serious. "That could be the answer."

"The Leprechaun did it?"

"One of the elves," Mark persisted, ignoring his senior partner's thinly veiled sarcasm, "maybe one of them was rigged."

The lieutenant settled back in her chair with a thoughtful sigh. She hooked a strand of spun gold from her forehead with a deftly curled third-finger and regarded her two i.c. with concern.

"I must confess, Mark, that your supposition is not without merit. However, I did have the elves checked out. There was nothing particularly sinister about any one of them."

"But the three that stood directly behind Santa's rocker were not mechanized," Mark asserted. "What if some four-foot phony had dressed up like one of the elves, and taken its place in the window before Nathan P. had even been wheeled in?"

"Little Reggie?"

"Why not? Nobody would have known the difference. After all he was the original elf, wasn't he? He was the model for all the others — he said so, himself." Mark thoughtfully rubbed the back of his neck. "The only problem, of course, is how he could have done anything, *anything*, with all those people watching."

"Well, that might not have been as difficult as you think, Mark. It would be my guess, that if someone *had* stood behind the rocker, as you suggest, waiting for the right moment to tighten the noose on Santa's chubby neck, he would have done so at precisely nine-thirty."

"Why nine-thirty?"

"For two reasons. First, whomsoever would have to distract the attention of the Christmas shoppers who were all standing at the window, watching, and what better diversion could they have than the Star of Bethlehem? Every hour, on the half hour, remember? And I can personally attest to how successfully it would turn every eye to the tree, then leave them all blinded for several seconds after it had stopped flashing."

"Of course," Mark said excitedly, "that would have given him lots of time to — " His enthusiasm seemed to droop with sudden doubt. "What's the second reason?"

"The rocker," replied the lieutenant. "We were briefed on its mechanical precision by little Reggie himself – remember — and on its side-to-side movement in particular. Each fifteen-degree arc (according to Reggie) took exactly five minutes to complete. Therefore, thirty minutes after the rocker started moving (at nine o'clock) and six five-minute-fifteen-degree arcs later, the time would be precisely nine-thirty, and Santa Claus would be facing directly toward the window."

"So?"

"Don't you see? If an overt act was to take place behind the rocker, there would be less chance of being seen if the back of the victim were facing away from those who were watching at the window. The slightest movement, to either one side or the other, would only serve to diminish the cover. That factor, coupled with the precise timing of the Star of Bethlehem — "

"Right on, lieutenant." That's the only way it could have happened."

"Not necessarily."

"But you just said — "

"I said the supposition was *possible*, and it is, but from the facts we have, I don't see how Reginald Martindew qualifies as a credible suspect."

"How many four-foot suspects do we have?"

"Unfortunately, only one. And he was in the Display Department, according to witnesses, *after* the exhibit had been put in motion, and the door closed. He had no way of getting in there without being seen."

Mark turned his palms up. "Which puts us right back where we started," he muttered.

"Not really. Sometimes, in order to determine what *is*, one must first peel away the obfuscating illusion of what is *not*." She gnawed pensively at an asymmetrical fingernail. "The anatomy of a mystery, after all, Mark, was best exemplified twenty centuries ago, by Salome, in her celebrated *Dance Of The Seven Veils*."

Mark sighed. " — and the punch line?"

"Only when all the veils have been removed," she smiled, sphinx-like, "does one perceive the naked truth."

Mark lifted his eyes to the ceiling in a gesture of hopelessness. "Let's face it, lieutenant, the only "naked truth" we've managed to unveil, so far, is that nobody could have done it."

"Precisely," said the Amazon.

A SHARP RAP ON THE DOOR SIGNALLED THE ARRIVAL of Penelope Lamb. She stood in the doorway, bristling with indignation. Policewoman Fisk shoved her gently into the room, then left, closing the door softly behind her.

"Miss Lamb, please sit down."

"I don't like this, lieutenant." Penelope Lamb was visibly nervous. She squeezed herself into a captain's chair and inflated her heavy chest with a deep, tremulous intake of air.

"Miss Lamb, your friend and colleague, Reginald Martindew, will be with us momentarily, together with Mr. Drexler. But before they arrive, there is a question I would like to put to you."

"Hmmph." Penelope Lamb squirmed uncomfortably on the hard wooden chair.

"I realize that one can feel a certain misguided loyalty, or protectiveness, perhaps, to those with whom they work from day to day. Understandably. But I feel I must caution you that what we are presently involved in is not a simple misdemeanor. We are dealing here with premeditated murder. And in this state, the penalty for murder-one, is *death*. I want you to think about that, Miss Lamb. I want you to think about it, to remember it, and to govern yourself accordingly."

Penelope Lamb appeared to pale a little, but she said nothing.

"Now then." The lieutenant caught the nervously darting eyes and held them with her own. "I ask you straight out: did you conspire this morning, with any other person, in any way, to bring about the death of Nathan P. Martindew?"

"No. No, I did not."

"Are you certain of that?"

"Yes."

"You're not shielding anyone?"

"No."

"And you are presently under no threat?"

" — no."

The door rattled in its frame as Penelope Lamb mumbled her last denial, and an amused Officer Mayhew ushered in a much unamused Reginald Martindew. A moment later, Lloyd Drexler followed them into the room and quietly took a chair.

"Officer Mayhew, wait outside, please."

"I'm not saying a word," the little man sputtered as he shook loose from the policeman, "not one word, until my attorney gets here."

"That is your privilege, Mr. Martindew. I assume that you have already been permitted to call him?"

"Yes."

"Very well, then. We will simply wait for his arrival. Please sit down."

Sit *up*, Mark thought, would have been a more accurate invitation, as he watched Martindew's new president climb up into the only vacant chair. The over-sized head seemed to wobble precariously atop the little body.

"Don't tell them anything," he said to Penelope Lamb, who sat biting disconcertedly at her lower lip. "They don't have a leg to stand on."

As though to disprove the little man's statement, Lieutenant Carruthers stood up on (not one, but) two perfectly good legs and strode thoughtfully to the window. Mark watched expectantly from his chair by the door as she turned slowly to face Penelope Lamb. Her voice, when she spoke, was quiet and deliberate.

"I sincerely hope, Miss Lamb, that you are fully cognizant of your situation. However Nathan Martindew might have died, the fact remains that you were the last person to have contact with him."

"Don't listen to her, Pen. She's just trying to trap you. You don't have to — "

Penelope Lamb turned on the little man with sudden vehemence. "Shut up, Reggie! Just *shut up!*" Her face was flushed and beaded with perspiration. "I'm not talking; I'm listening — okay?"

"Sure, Pen — I didn't mean to — "

Mark could not suppress a smile as the elfin body suddenly cowered — then jerked awkwardly forward again. The leather thong that suspended the medallion around the little neck had inadvertently caught on the wooden arm of the chair. But Mark's smile slowly faded in the graphic hush that followed as all eyes turned to watch the tiny fingers untangle the offending snare. It seemed a silent eternity before the lieutenant finally spoke.

"Miss Lamb," she said calmly, her eyes still on Reggie's busy fingers, "I now must formally charge you with the murder of Nathan P. Martindew — "

PENELOPE LAMB'S FACE WAS THE COLOR OF NEW SNOW.
" —you may remain silent if you wish— " As the lieutenant's monotone recitation continued, little Reggie squirmed in his chair like a recalcitrant child.

"Don't buy it, Pen. She's bluffing — "

"I told you to *shut up*, you little weasel." Penelope Lamb turned eyes on the lieutenant that were bright with fear. "How could I have killed him? He was still alive when I left the exhibit. Drexler, here, can prove it."

Lloyd Drexler vacantly nodded his head.

The door opened then, as though on signal, just wide enough to allow a uniformed arm to shove a brown file folder in at Mark. He accepted it with a nod, and closed the door as the arm withdrew.

"Lab report," he said, handing the folder over to the lieutenant. The self-styled garrote was coiled into a poly-bag and stapled to the front of the file.

"Recognize this?" The lieutenant detached the bag from the file, extracted the garrote, and tossed it across to Penelope Lamb. She intercepted it with nervous fingers, deflecting it back at the lieutenant as though it were white hot, or alive. "Damn you, lieutenant. I never saw that thing before."

Lieutenant Carruthers caught the snaking cord on one red-tipped finger and held it up for all to see. She read slowly from the open file in her other hand: "*Dactylography: two discernible whorl-type impressions have been reimpressed from the smooth surface of the clothes-line tightener, one right thumbprint, one right index finger. Identification, as follows — *" She looked searchingly at Penelope Lamb from behind an unruly fall of golden hair. "Miss Lamb, need I say more — ?"

"Oh dear God!" Penelope Lamb slumped back in a dispirited heap. She looked at her little colleague with eyes that were glazed with fear and despair. "I told you it wouldn't work."

"No, Pen. No — "

Mark looked on in astonishment as the Amazon moved in swiftly, looming over her quarry like a cat with a mouse. "We know *how* you did it, Miss Lamb, can you tell us *why?*"

Penelope Lamb's pudgy face turned apprehensively from the lieutenant to Reggie, then back again. "I didn't want any part of it, lieutenant. It wasn't my idea. Reggie set it up. All I did was — was — " A sudden sob choked off the words. Tears welled up in her eyes.

The lieutenant stooped beside the woman's chair. "Miss Lamb, what was your relationship with the Martindews?"

"My — my mother — " The big body began to jerk spasmodically with a repressed sobbing. She blew her tears noisily into a tissue, and began again. "Mr. Martindew (Reggie and Nathan's father) was — was my father, too. My mother was housekeeper at the time, so — so it was all hushed up, for obvious reasons. He promised my mother that he would always look after me, even after his death. When — when my mother died, there was no legal claim, but he kept his word. But then, he — he died, and I went to see Nathan. Nathan just laughed at me. Ca — called the whole story a shallow fraud — that I was just — just — "

"But you found a ready ally in Reggie?"

"Y — yes. Reggie promised that if I did what he wanted me to, he — he would "deal" me into the Martindew fortune — legally, when he became president. There was plenty for both of us, he — he said."

"That's preposterous." Reginald Martindew suddenly sprang to his own defense. "Why would I want Nathan dead, lieutenant? I was already assured more money, in *half* the estate, than I could ever hope to spend."

The lieutenant sat back on the edge of the desk and crossed one silken leg over the other. Mark noticed a small bruise on the left ankle where little Reggie had vented his ire.

"The way I see it, Reginald Martindew, hate was your motive, not greed. Hate, for the man who (in your mind, at any rate) had robbed you of your heritage — your birthright. It had become, over the years, a driving, waking obsession. There could be no rest for you, no peace of mind, until your brother was dead and in his grave."

The little face on the too-big head was flushed with frustration. "I hope you're prepared to prove all this."

"Miss Lamb?" The lieutenant's voice was suddenly as cold as a winter wind. "Is it your intention to be a patsy to this man's appalling hatred, to shoulder all the blame, while he goes on his lucrative way, free as a breeze? Or do you prefer to make a statement, to tell the truth, and let the justice of your peers temper your punishment, and his, in a more equitable manner?"

The withering look that Penelope Lamb levelled at Reginald Martindew seemed to preclude the need for an answer, and to reduce the little man's irate pomposity to the figment of a Christmas wish.

"I — I'll make a statement," she said.

WHEN OFFICERS FISK AND MAYHEW HAD ESCORTED Metro's most unlikely looking pair of felons from the room, the lieutenant regarded Drexler with an amused smile.

"What you said earlier, Mr Drexler, about Penelope Lamb and the late Reggie Martin "cooking something up together" has turned out to be strangely prophetic. But it wasn't quite what you had in mind, was it?"

The burly store detective rubbed his heavy jaw. "To tell you the truth, lieutenant, I don't really know what I had in mind. And I still don't know how Nathan P. was murdered."

"Well, it was actually quite simple," said the lieutenant as she resumed her seat behind the desk. "But it was only when we had established, unequivocally, that *no one* could have done it, that it became more obvious how someone *had*."

Mark grinned at Drexler. "Got another question?"

"Yeah, How was Nathan P. murdered?"

The lieutenant took their sarcasm in good humor. "Well, it seemed to me that if some *one* could not have done it, then, *ipso facto*, it had to have been some *thing*. And the people who were best qualified to rig that exhibit were, of course, Penelope Lamb and little Reggie. No one else was even permitted in there."

"But you said you had all the elves checked out," Mark reminded her, "and that they hadn't been tampered with."

"Nor had they. But to be perfectly candid with you, it wasn't until about ten minutes ago that I realized precisely how they had accomplished it. Remember, when little Reggie got his medallion caught on the arm of the captain's chair? It almost jerked his head off."

"That gave you the solution?"

"That *was* the solution. If the loop at the end of the four-foot nylon cord was not meant for the hand of an elf, then it must have been intended for something inanimate— some projection, perhaps, on the automated rocker."

"But — "

"Mr. Drexler, you attested to the fact that Penelope Lamb was the last one to leave the side of the victim. What appeared to you as "last minute fussing" was, in fact, the surreptitious fitting of the deadly garrote around poor Santa's neck. The whiskers and the hair effectively hid the device, which was also white, once it was in place. Then, when she stooped behind the pedestal to switch on the mechanism, she simply slipped the loop on the end of the nylon cord over one of the protruding gargoyles."

"But surely," Mark protested, "Nathan would have known that something was happening. He would have been noticeably upset— "

"And so he was. But, unfortunately, he could only move his head. Drexler, who was at the "drape switch" by the door, put it down to his usual feisty irascibility. The *Whistle While You Work* music would easily have drowned out his actual words. And the facial whiskers, which were created purposefully by the conspirators themselves, would have hidden any recognizable expression on the face of the victim, then, or later."

Drexler shook his head. "I still don't see — "

"The rocker, you will recall, moved from side to side, the pedestal did not. Once the loop was in place, the lateral movement of the rocker, combined with its jerking forward roll, would slowly tighten the garrote, cutting off the air supply to Santa's lungs. It is my guess, that he was dead by nine-o-five, after the first fifteen-degree arc of the rocker. Then, as the rocker slowly returned to its starting position, the cord would slacken off, and the loop would eventually fall away from the gargoyle, leaving it to dangle aimlessly behind the rocker. And that, of course, is precisely how we found it."

"Unbelieveable," said Drexler, "Penny Lamb and little Reggie." He rose uncertainly to his feet. "Well, anyway, it puts me in the clear. Am I free to go now, lieutenant?"

"Yes Mr. Drexler, you may go. But please keep yourself available. There'll be a preliminary hearing in a few days." When the store detective was half out the door, she added, "and Mr. Drexler, in the future, let us endeavor to keep our detective work separate from our sex life."

Drexler, with a red face, softly closed the door.

MARK LOOKED TO BE THOUGHTFULLY PREOCCUPIED as his senior partner tugged on a pair of fur-trimmed mukluks, checked the contents of her purse, and reached for her coat. "Before you go, lieutenant," he said, "what was that ballyhoo about the fingerprints?"

Cathy Carruthers grinned. "I never did get around to saying whose they were, did I?"

"They were yours?"

"Uh-hu." She laughed. "Just a little Christmas humbug." She was half way across the room before she saw it. "What's that above the door?"

Mark had risen to his feet, blocking her exit. "Mistletoe," he said, without looking up. "It's a good thing Drexler didn't see it."

The Amazon moved in with a bedeviling smile. "Merry Christmas," she said.

MARCH 1982
$1.75

47744

MIKE SHAYNE
MYSTERY MAGAZINE

The New Mike Shayne Adventure HAVOC IN HIGH PLACES by Brett Halliday

stories by:
**MEL D. AMES
JON L. BREEN
HAL CHARLES
JOSEPH COMMINGS
JAY FOX
JERRY JACOBSON
SUSANNE SHAPHREN**

A Momentous Encounter: HOLMES MEETS WATSON!

STIFF COMPETITION Book Reviews by JOHN BALL

The Amazon was back on the job, investigating the murder of a mermaid with an arrow through her head!

valentine
for a
dead lady

SHE LAY FACE DOWN IN THE POOL, HER BLONDE HAIR
splayed out over the water like drifting seaweed. She seemed to
dangle there like a puppet, her shoulders floating high in the water as
though buoyed by an invisible bubble, her shapely hips and limbs
undulating limply below the surface. It was not until she had been
taken from the water, and stretched out on her back at pool-side,
could it be seen the way she had died. Her once pretty face, now
blue-lipped and mottled, had been run through with an arrow, the
feathered end of the long shaft still protruding grotesquely from the
center of her forehead.

The pool stood back about a hundred and fifty feet from the open
end of the "U"-shaped ranch house, where the owners of Conklin
Ranch had resided in comfort and conflict for half a century. A
roofed-over patio filled in the "U" and a column of lofty poplars rose
out of the green carpet of the grass to encircle the expansive grounds
like silent sentinels. Beyond the trees, on three sides, the flat lands
stretched away into gently rolling hills, their distant crests dotted with
grazing cattle. And to the north, a scant five miles from the towering
timber gates to the Conklin properties, Metro's concrete jungle

sprawled over the unsuspecting horizon like a malignant cancer. The sun was already high in the heavens as a large, weathered-looking man in western attire stood waiting beside the dead woman, watching the approach across the lawn of two imposing figures.

One, a woman, was a striking six-foot Amazonian beauty with hair the color of ripe wheat. She moved with the effortlessness of a jungle cat, and even from a distance, the subtle power and grace of the body that moved beneath the camouflage of the brief gray suit was clearly manifest.

The other, a male, equally as tall, but thick-set and obviously well-muscled, walked in step beside her. He displayed a quiet self assurance that was evident even in the obfuscating shadow of his remarkable companion. As they drew near, Conklin addressed himself to the man.

"Lieutenant Carruthers?"

Detective-Sergeant Mark Swanson smiled indulgently and re-directed the query with a nod of his head to his attractive cohort.

"*I'm* Lieutenant Carruthers," the blonde beauty responded brightly. "Officially: Detective-Lieutenant Cathy Carruthers — Metro Central, Eleventh Precinct." She flashed her badge, then topped off the official dissertation with a dazzling smile. Mark knew that his senior partner was simply playing games. She no longer took offense at the hesitancy of some to accept her, a woman, in what had traditionally been a male role. He could not remember anyone, however, hesitating for long.

IT HAD BEEN THE BETTER PART OF A YEAR, MARK recalled, since Cathy Carruthers had first invaded Homicide, Metro Central's last bastion of male chauvinism. She had met the challenge of her initiation with the femininity of a fire-breathing dragon, and had emerged miraculously unscathed some weeks later with the respect and somewhat reluctant admiration of her burly colleagues. They now called her the "Amazon", with affection, but showed no quarter in their good-natured taunting of Mark Swanson, her self-appointed and trusted side-kick.

"You must be Mr. Conklin," Lieutenant Carruthers said now with practiced charm.

"Yes." Conklin looked to be discomfited more by her smile than the revelation of her authority.

"You are the owner and manager of the Conklin properties?"

"That's right."

"Are you acquainted with this unfortunate young lady, Mr. Conklin?"

"Yes, of course. That's Melody — Melody Slade. She's my sister."

"Then, perhaps, you can tell me what happened."

"I don't *know* what happened, lieutenant. The pool is visible from my suite in the west wing of the ranch house. "There," he pointed a leathery finger, "you can see it from here. I had just got back in from the south range when I noticed her from the window, floating face down in the water."

"When was this?"

Conklin looked at his watch. "About an hour ago. Say, 10:20? I phoned you people as soon as I saw the way she had died. She looked so strange, lieutenant, laying there like that, her head and limbs dangling under the water. My God, who would want to do this to Melody?"

"Did you see anyone else?"

"Yes, Crampton, the grounds man. He helped me get her out of the pool."

"Where is Crampton now?"

"I sent him after Slade. Stephen Slade, Melody's husband. I figured he'd probably be at the Country Club. That's his usual haunt."

AS THEY TALKED, THE LIEUTENANT'S DISCERNING blue eyes had been probing the mirrored surface of the pool. She turned to her colleague. "Mark, there's something floating in the water — there, just below the surface. See if you can fish it out. And there's something else over there, in the corner at the shallow end."

Mark reached for a gaff-pole from a pool-side rack and pulled a deflated rubber air-mattress from the water. Then from the far side of the pool, he retrieved an archer's bow. The lieutenant inspected the bow first, balancing it with professional familiarity by the taut string on the tip of a finger.

"Mr. Conklin," she said at length, "who at Conklin Ranch is able to manipulate this weapon with any degree of accuracy?"

"Me, for one, lieutenant. And Melody, there. We are both experienced archers. But we never thought of it as a weapon."

"Anyone else?"

"Not that I am aware of."

"Well, that seems to narrow things down a bit, doesn't it?" She regarded him intently from behind an unruly fall of golden hair.

"Now see here, lieutenant, if you think I had anything to do with this ghastly business, you're sadly mistaken. Why, in God's name, would I want to kill my own sister?"

Mark was not surprised when the lieutenant chose to quietly ignore the man's question and to center her attention on the bikini clad figure of the victim. She had been a lovely young woman, in her late twenties perhaps, with a good body that was evenly tanned from long leisurely hours under the sun.

"Mr. Conklin," the lieutenant said idly, "did you get along well with you sister?"

"Yes. She was devoted to me, and I to her."

"Did she also have a financial interest in the Conklin properties?"

"Yes. We are — were the only surviving family. We had equal interest in the estate."

" — until now."

"Now, look here, lieutenant — "

The rancher broke off as Cathy Carruthers suddenly dropped to one knee beside the body. In so doing, she inadvertently flashed a length of silken thigh that required no official dissertation to be recognized or appreciated.

"Look at this, Mark." The lieutenant had turned the impaled head to one side and drawn a red-tipped finger along a slight abrasion on the side of the neck.

"I'm looking," he muttered, with some ambiguity, but his eyes dutifully followed the path of her fingers as she cleared back some of the blonde hair that had matted behind the skull. The rounded tip of the arrow, now exposed, jutted out a full inch beyond the scalp. He noticed, too, with a slight flip of his stomach, that a certain amount of interior matter had come through with the arrow, although there appeared to have been little or no bleeding.

"It would require a well placed arrow to achieve that kind of penetration, wouldn't you say, Mr. Conklin?"

"Yes," Conklin agreed, "it would."

"And from relatively close range, with this weight of bow. Say — fifty feet. Seventy-five, maybe — at the outside."

"I'd say that."

"That distance would have put the bowman (or bow *person*) well out in the open, away from the cover of the house. Not the ideal site from which to launch an arrow with any semblance of stealth. The entire area between the pool and the patio is clearly visible from both wings of the ranch house. A rare and puzzling speculation, I must say." Mark looked on with interest as the lieutenant thrust out one supple hip and assumed an archer's pose before the rancher; one arm extended, the other drawn back as she sighted down an imaginary arrow. "It would almost suggest that Melody Slade had stood willingly beside the pool, face to face with her murderer, the very fiend who unleashed that deadly dart."

She let the arrow fly. "*Ziiip!*"

"Uh — yeah." Conklin had flinched at the release of the invisible arrow and tried now to cover his embarrassment. "I see what you mean."

"But still, if it was someone she knew, and trusted — "

The lieutenant's words drew some color to Conklin's weathered cheeks, but the man did not respond.

"Have you ever hunted with a bow and arrow, Mr. Conklin?"

"No, I damn well haven't."

"Well, I have, sir. I have no hesitancy in stating that I am an accomplished toxophilite of no mean ability. And you can take my word for this: the skull is an extremely resilient part of the human anatomy, especially at the point where this particular arrow made entry. The trajectory of the arrow in flight would have to be shallow indeed, in order to strike the surface of the skull at precisely the right angle. And I do mean *right* angle. Otherwise it would tend to deflect, to ricochet off the malleable bone structure and, at best, to achieve a minimal, angular penetration. As an experienced archer, Mr. Conklin, would you agree with those observations?"

"With all due respect, lieutenant, you're speculating in an area of which I know little or nothing. I — "

Mark Swanson looked on with some amusement as the Amazon again ignored the rancher in mid-sentence. It was a deliberate ploy, of course, to throw the man off balance, to get him to reveal something in anger that he would ordinarily have sufficient composure to withhold from her. But Conklin, though clearly annoyed, remained silent.

THE LIEUTENANT, ENGROSSED NOW IN AN INCH-BY-inch search through the folds of the deflated air-mattress, absently fingered a screw valve that appeared to have loosened, then suddenly straightened with an I-thought-so smile as she poked an immaculately-lacquered finger through a small hole in the pillow end of the mattress. Her finger probed the hole, then emerged through the material on the other side.

"In one side and out the other," she said matter-of-factly, "just like the hole in the head of our unhappy sunbather. By the way, Mark, do you know what day this is?"

"Yeah, Saturday. February 14th."

"That's a man for you." She curled a crimson lip and arched the eyebrow nearest to him. "It's also St. Valentine's day. A little ironic, don't you think?"

"I forgot to send you a Valentine?"

The Amazon smiled patiently. "Don't you find it something of an irony that Melody Slade should receive *the* original Valentine — imagine, an *arrow* — delivered by Cupid, himself, and right on St. Valentine's day?"

"Yeah, some Cupid — and *some* Valentine." Mark made an appropriate grimace. "But I guess it is kind of ironic, when you put it like that."

"Especially," the Amazon parleyed, delivering her *coupe de grace* with a bedeviling smile, "when you consider that the lady was dead when she received it."

"Huh?"

The two men gaped at her, then at each other. But before they could speak, she had given Mark an esoteric wink and was moving off across the lawn toward the ranch house, where a number of police vehicles had drawn up with lights flashing. Mark regarded the familiar contours of her receding silhouette with a blend of affection and chagrin. He wondered if he would ever become accustomed to these oracular broadsides — so casually expounded. And he knew from his relatively brief experience with this astonishing woman, that her startling comment would be anything but idle speculation.

MARK WATCHED CONKLIN TAKE OFF AFTER THE lieutenant as the various police teams began to converge on the pool area to perform their specialized functions. The Medical Examiner was the last to arrive.

"What've we got this time, Mark?"

"You're looking at it, Sam."

"*Sonofagun.*" It took something bizarre to get a reaction out of Sam Morton.

"The lieutenant figures she was dead before Cupid delivered the arrow," Mark proffered.

"That so?" The M.E. emitted a disparaging grunt as he bent over the body. "You still teamed up with the Amazon?"

"Yeah."

"Might have known. That lady's sure got an uncanny eye for detail. Anything else?"

"You tell us." Mark had turned and was heading for the ranch house "And before you move her out," he called back over his shoulder, "you better have the lab dust that arrow."

"Gotcha."

THE LIEUTENANT WAS IN THE MAIN CENTRAL ROOM of the ranch house when Mark caught up with her. Here, the Conklin money was clearly visible. The room was immense. From the high, vaulted, heavily-beamed ceiling to the mammoth fieldstone fireplace that claimed the entire north wall, it was the epitome of rustic luxury. The furnishings, like the room, were large and sumptuous, a pastoral fantasy of swirling wood-grains and soft, richly-scented leathers. Mark moved gingerly over the deep, sculptured carpet to where the lieutenant stood with Conklin, talking to a somewhat pallid, dapper-looking man with sleek black hair and a thin moustache.

"Mr. Slade," the lieutenant was saying, "do you think you can recall the precise time you left the ranch house this morning?"

"Around nine, I'd say." There was a thin thread of antagonism in the man's voice. "Melody was still in the pool. We left together, Conklin and I."

"Well, not quite together," Conklin put in quickly. "We left the patio at the same time, but your car was still in the driveway when I drove out."

Slade shrugged his thin shoulders.

"Then you *were* the last to leave, Mr. Slade, except, of course, for your wife."

"Looks that way."

"Were there no servants in the house?"

"No," Conklin volunteered. "Mrs. McInnes had set up a buffet breakfast on the patio, then left for the local Farmer's Market. I don't believe she has returned even yet." He lifted his eyes in a gesture of pained forbearance. "Her penchant for thrift is something we endure, rather than encourage."

"I take it that Mrs. McInnes is the housekeeper."

"Yes."

"Which means then, there were only three of you for breakfast. You two, and Melody."

"And Helen," said Slade.

"Helen?"

"Helen Mundy." Slade stroked his pencil-lined moustache. "She's my wife's physiotherapist. Melody was a health freak, lieutenant — you know, organic foods, yoga, massage, and now (believe it or not) pool therapy."

"I see. And when did Miss Mundy arrive?"

"She lives in. She has her own rooms in the east wing — just down the hall from ours."

"Yeah," said Conklin with a derisive curl of his lip, "real cozy like."

Slade's reaction was instantaneous. "Why don't you go milk a cow or something?" he spat out.

Conklin ignored this sudden hostility. "Helen and Melody were the first ones down," he said to the lieutenant. "They were in the middle of some kind of therapy session, splashing about in the pool, while Slade and I were having breakfast. Helen was also the first one to leave. Melody was on the air mattress in the pool, sunning herself, and we were still swilling coffee on the patio when she pulled out of the driveway."

"And where was Crampton during this time?"

"I sent him on an errand," Slade mumbled. He seemed to be in something of a sulk. "I didn't see him again until he came looking for me, after Melody was — killed."

"Was that before, or after breakfast?"

"Lieutenant?"

"The errand. When did Slade leave on the errand?"

"Oh — just before breakfast, before I came out on the patio."

"*Stephen!*"

AN ATTRACTIVE YOUNG WOMAN HAD SUDDENLY appeared in the doorway. She wore a chalk white tennis costume that set off her trim figure with stunning effect and gave sharp contrast to a head of beautiful black hair that tumbled loosely about her shoulders. Her voice was on the quiet side of panic. "What happened? Why are the police — ?"

Slade went to her quickly and took her hands in his own. "It's Melody, Helen. There's been an — an accident."

"Accident?"

"Melody's been shot. She's — dead."

"Oh dear God." Helen Mundy sunk deeply into one of the huge leather chairs. Her face had paled under a look of utter bewilderment. "Sh — shot?"

"With an arrow," Conklin added. "She must have died instantly."

Slade jerked his head up to stare open-mouthed at Conklin. Then at lieutenant Carruthers. His face was a veritable question mark. "Have they taken her away yet, lieutenant?"

The lieutenant glanced at Mark.

"Not yet," Mark said.

Slade headed for the door. "I've got to see her," he muttered, as though suddenly, inexplicably shaken by the full realization of her death. "I — I've got to see her." As he swept out of the room, Mark made a move to follow, but in response to an almost imperceptible tilt of the lieutenant's golden head, he held his ground.

"Mr. Conklin." Cathy Carruthers turned to the rancher with a condolent smile. "Miss Mundy appears to be somewhat shaken at the moment. Perhaps while she pulls herself together, you wouldn't mind showing the sergeant and me over the rest of the house. I'd like to start with Slade's east wing suite, then Miss Mundy's rooms."

"If you insist," the rancher grunted. Courtesy was apparently not a priority item on Conklin's list of things-to-do-today.

"And Mark." The lieutenant drew her colleague toward the door that opened out onto the patio. "Have a police woman see to Miss Mundy here, then assign an officer to go after Slade. I want him back here when we return. And, yes, we'd better have a team to give us a hand on our tour of inspection."

"Right, lieutenant."

As Mark left the room, the lieutenant motioned Conklin to one side, out of hearing. "You made an inference a while back, Mr. Conklin, about Mr. Slade and Miss Mundy. Would you kindly elaborate now, for *my* benefit?"

"Well," the rancher glanced uncertainly toward the girl, "it's no secret, damn it. Not anymore. Even Melody knew what was going on."

"And she still kept the girl in her employ?"

"Why not? If it wasn't Helen, it would be someone else. This way, Melody probably felt she could keep an eye on them."

"There was no bad feeling between them?"

"I didn't say that. Melody just seemed to keep things under control. In fact, they were quietly going at it this morning, when I came down to breakfast. Melody was threatening to tell Slade something she had found out about her — something from Helen's past."

"Did she?"

"No. The little creep wasn't down yet, and they had already left for the pool when he finally did show."

"What was it, that Melody had on Miss Mundy?"

"I have no idea."

"Do you think their affair had any substance, Mr. Conklin?"

"Substance?"

"Were they genuinely in love with each other?"

"On Helen's side, possibly — but Stephen Slade has no more fidelity in his pagan soul than a range bull in a herd of heifers."

THE ROOMS IN THE EAST WING WERE TWO MICRO-cosms of the main central lounge. But for the frilled canopy over the king-sized bed, and the flowered pattern in the drapes that hung on the floor-to-ceiling windows on the south wall, there was no feminine influence in evidence anywhere. Lieutenant Carruthers drew Conklin's attention to the obvious omission.

"My father," the rancher said in his explanation, "has been dead now about two years. The ranch house is a kind of moment to his memory. Melody and I agreed, soon after his death, to respect his wishes and maintain the house the way he originally designed it. The west wing, my side of the house, is virtually no different from this — except for a welcome lack of flowers and frills —"

At the window, Mark listened absently to Conklin history while looking out across the lawn toward the pool. He could see Melody Slade being borne away under a white sheet, the shaft of the arrow making a small tent at one end of the stretcher. And Slade, in the company of a uniformed policeman was walking slowly, head bent, back toward the house. Here and there, an officer poked about in the flower beds, or probed the loose soil at the base of the encircling trees. The entire grounds were under search for some small clue to the identity of the missing bowman.

The inspection of Slade's suite of rooms had turned up nothing of interest to the lieutenant, and so the entourage had moved in a body down an inside hall to Helen Mundy's quarters. Again, there was no feminine decor, but here there could be little doubt as to the identity of the attractive occupant. The odd piece of therapeutic equipment had been left haphazardly about on the floor, or stuffed carelessly into a closet, and tell-tale wisps of feminine attire created a kind of nylon jungle in the bathroom. And in the bedroom, a fashionable "cubic-foot" tote bag, made of clear polyethylene with a leather draw-string opening, had been tossed carelessly onto the counterpane. An assortment of massage oils, creams and emulsions lay strewn, half in and half out of the bag. The lieutenant ran her finger lightly along the leather thong.

"It's wet," she said. "Did she have this bag with her this morning?"

"Sure thing — it's part of her stock in trade," Conklin attested. "She's seldom without it."

IN THE WEST WING, CONKLIN'S SIDE OF THE HOUSE, they discovered a rifle, a 30.30 lever-action Savage. One of the officers held it out, cradled in a handkerchief, to the lieutenant. She was standing in front of the window, looking thoughtfully out toward the pool. It was the same view that Mark had from the east wing only minutes before, but from a slightly different angle. *It would make an unbelievably easy target,* she mused, *an unsuspecting sunbather, framed by the pool —*

"Lieutenant?"

"Huh — ?" Taken unawares, Mark noticed, her face could be as soft and ingenuous as that of a schoolgirl.

"It was in a gun case," the officer was saying, "closed, but not locked. It's been fired."

The lieutenant took the rifle with an impatient toss of her blonde head. She eased the lever half way ahead, sniffed. The empty cartridge, she saw, was still in the breach. "What can you tell me about this, Mr. Conklin?"

"I haven't used that gun in months." A flush of color had risen to Conklin's leathery cheeks.

"It's been recently fired."

"Not by me, damn it."

She handed the rifle back to the officer. "Have the Lab dust the entire case, as well as the gun. You'd better hurry before they leave. And officer, have the swimming pool drained immediately, and the entire pool area searched. We are now looking for an expended piece of lead."

"Yes, sir — uh, mam."

The lieutenant smoothed over the officer's confusion with an understanding smile before addressing the rancher. "Mr. Conklin, I'm afraid you'll have to come downtown with us. I'm sorry to inconvenience you this way, but we'll need a statement, you understand, as well as a paraffin test."

"Where? And a what?" Conklin's tone reflected his mounting irritation.

"Headquarters," the lieutenant replied patiently, "and a simple procedure to determine whether you have recently fired a gun."

"Save your candle wax for the power shortage, lieutenant." The big man was becoming increasingly more irate. "I shot a coyote this morning, no more than an hour'n'half ago, out on the south range. At least I shot *at* it."

"And the gun?"

"A Remmington 30.06. It's in my pick-up. I never go out there without it."

Mark nodded to the second officer, who immediately left to retrieve the Remmington from the truck. Seeing the officer go seemed to trigger Conklin. He suddenly exploded.

"Listen lady," He stood squarely in the center of the room, his hands on his hips and a look of ugly frustration on his face. He was plainly used to *giving* orders, not taking them. "I've had just about all of this I can handle," he seethed. "Are you sure you know what the hell you're doing? I thought lady cops were supposed to be out checking parking meters. So what're you doing here anyway? All this crap about guns, and paraffin, and draining swimming pools — It's obvious to anyone with half an eye that Melody died from an arrow through her brain, and I don't intend to stand around here while you mark time in a pair of men's shoes that are clearly three sizes too big for you." He spun to face Mark with the anger still boiling within him. "Now take this dumb broad outta here before I really lose my temper."

The lieutenant spoke softly to Mark. "Take him in," she said simply.

"Lady," Conklin fumed, "you're not taking me anywhere." The enraged rancher turned suddenly and headed for the open door. In two fluid strides the Amazon had moved up beside him. One flawlessly manicured hand grabbed the back of his collar, while the other fastened itself to the belt at his waist, and in one herculean swing, she had lifted the big man clear off his feet and slammed him face first into the panelled wall. With her superb body coiled like a steel spring, she held him there, three feet off the floor, while her wide-eyed two i.c. obligingly snapped on the cuffs.

"Male chauvinism is one thing," she said with an embarrassed little grin, "but, dumb broad — ?" When she let the man go, he dropped like a worn-out winter benny that had missed a coat hook. Mark picked up the dazed rancher and steered him through the door. He stopped on the threshold and turned to look back at his senior partner. Mark had seen the Amazon in action before, but each new manifestation of the awesome strength and agility of this astounding woman never failed to shake him. She returned his haunted gaze with a look of sublime innocence and a dimpled smile that would have melted the heart of a hangman.

STEPHEN SLADE AND HELEN MUNDY WERE SHARING an overstuffed leather couch in the main central lounge when Mark Swanson and Lieutenant Carruthers returned to the capacious room. A uniformed police officer was standing just inside the door.

"Mr. Slade," the lieutenant said affably. "I regret that I must ask you to accompany us to Headquarters. We'll need you, too, Miss Mundy."

If the alleged lovers were upset with the lieutenant's request, it did not show. They both looked more confused and frightened, than annoyed.

"Miss Mundy." The lieutenant seemed to tower above them like the jolly gray giant. "Where was Mr. Conklin and Stephen Slade, when you left the ranch this morning?"

"They were on the patio, lieutenant."

"Did you see anyone else?"

"No, I don't think so — except Crampton."

"Crampton?"

"Yes, I passed him on the road. He was heading back toward the ranch."

"Lieutenant." Slade was having an impatient chew at his lower lip. "Is this going to take very long?"

"No, Mr. Slade. When you're all through downtown, you'll be driven back here. And I must ask you then, to remain within the residence. There will be guards posted."

"Guards?"

"Just routine procedure, Mr. Slade."

"How long is this going to go on?"

"We'll need you at H.Q. again, probably sometime tomorrow afternoon. The department will send a car for you."

"And then?"

"That should wrap it up."

"But — " Slade seemed to be searching for the right words. "What about Melody — the way she died?"

"Mr. Slade," the lieutenant said patiently, "I already know the way she died."

"Yes, of course. But — "

"But who killed her?" The Lieutenant's piercing gaze drifted slowly from one upturned face to the other before she answered her own question. "Let's just say that it wasn't Cupid."

IT WAS A TYPICAL LATE SUNDAY MORNING AT THE Eleventh Precinct. The hectic weeklong hustle had slowed to a crawl, and a skeletal staff moved leisurely from one department to another, enjoying a welcome respite.

Lieutenant Cathy Carruthers sat with her back to her desk, a pair of tweezers in one hand, a mirror in the other, and a seeming disinterest in anything beyond maintaining an element of discipline in the eyebrow department. But reflected in the mirror, beyond the foreground image of one beautiful blue eye, she noticed Mark Swanson as he entered the main office. She watched him wave "Hi" at the duty sergeant, pick up the mail and a few call slips from the switchboard operator, then stroll nonchalantly toward her glass-partitioned office. The slight, involuntary brightening of that one blue eye betrayed the unspoken warmth of affection and the high esteem in which she held her chosen partner. She turned to face him as he entered.

"Anything interesting?"

Mark tossed half a dozen letters onto her desk. "I'll get the calls," he said with uncustomary curtness, "while you're checking out the mail." Then, to his partner's mild surprise, he turned on his heel and walked out to one of the empty desks in front of the office.

Mark was on his third call when the lieutenant finally got to the letter on the bottom. He watched slyly as she opened it and drew out a heart-shaped card. The sudden smile she projected at him through the glass partition made the whole gag worthwhile. The card, with his own scribbled verse, read:

> **Valentines are**
> **Decidedly *dumb*,**
> **But (*broadly* speaking)**
> **You're sure a Hon.**

The lieutenant made a gun out of her fingers, pointed it at Mark, and pulled the trigger. He was still savoring her wide happy grin, watching her slip the card into an inside pocket, when something in his peripheral vision made him look around. A little man, standing eye to eye with him, had stopped beside his desk.

Garfield Leprohn (the *Leprechaun*, as he was called by all and sundry) was Metro Central's shortest police officer. He was also head of the Records Department. His status on the force was commensurate with his ability, not his size, which was a happy circumstance for the Leprechaun, but he could never seem to escape the good-natured bantering of his life-size colleagues. Mark took a certain perverse pride in being one of his prime irritants.

"Well, Godzilla, what do *you* want?"

"It is not a question of what I want," the Leprechaun said, with all the dignity he could cram into his abbreviated stature. "I have the file on the Slade case, and I would like to discuss it with someone intelligent."

"Sure thing," said Mark, "it'll be a welcome change from talking to yourself." He got to his feet and ushered the little man into Lieutenant Carruthers' office.

"Garfield." The lieutenant's use of his given name was a courtesy the Leprechaun cherished. "I've been expecting you. Is that the Slade file?"

"Complete," he beamed. "I'd like to go over it with you."

"Please do."

"Very well then," Mark watched Garfield Leprohn make an irritating ceremony of selecting a chair, before he finally settled back with an open file and a closed mind. The Leprechaun was in his own, narrow, little data-gathering heaven, and he intended to make the most of it.

"Both Conklin and the dead woman," he began, "are (were, in the case of the victim) veritable pillars of society. There's not a blemish on either one of them, that is, if you can overlook Melody's recent, rather impetuous marriage. Slade, on the other hand, is a good-time Charlie from way back. He was implicated —but never charged —in a couple of bunko beefs in Seattle, about ten years ago. And that pretty well sets the stage for his whole penny-ante career. Always involved, but never convicted. His marriage to Melody was his third. One previous marriage ended in divorce (the first one) and the other in the wife's death. That was a drowning, where (once again) foul play was suspected, but never proven. Stephen Slade, lieutenant, is unquestionably one slippery customer."

THE LEPRECHAUN CAME UP FOR AIR, AND AN encouraging smile from the Amazon. "Now we get to the good part," he said almost gleefully, "Helen Mundy." He treated them both to a sly, off-the-record leer. "She is not, as she claims, a bona fide physiotherapist. She is, however, a masseuse —of a kind. She learned her trade well in a massage parlor on the seamy side of Vancouver, where she was picked up for soliciting on three separate occasions. She was sprung each time by the same four-bit lawyer who was known to be on the payroll of a local pimp. That was more than two years ago. She seems to have made a valid effort, though, to play it straight ever since her last bust."

"That must have been what Melody had threatened to tell Slade," the lieutenant speculated.

"I don't know about that," the Leprechaun added, "but I do know that Melody had a shamus on the payroll. That fit in?"

"It does indeed. That was how she knew about Helen Mundy's lurid past."

The Leprechaun was delighted with the response he was getting. "Well then. Now for Crampton. Ellias J. Crampton, to be precise. He started working for the Conklins when he was twenty years old. He hired on when he first arrived in the Metro area, nineteen years ago, with nothing but torn underwear and broken finger nails." He snuck a quick peek to appraise the effect of his colorful prose. "He's had a few run-ins with the law over the years, but nothing serious. He's a lush. And, for what it's worth, Conklin senior was apparently devoted to him."

"Hmm. By the way, Mark." The lieutenant jotted something on a note pad. "Have we been able to locate that particular gentleman yet?"

"Yeah. Picked him up early this morning. He was holed up in some sleazy hotel on Slater Street, drunk as a skunk. They've been trying to sober him up ever since."

"Good." She turned her attention back to the Leprechaun. "Did you get anything on the disposition of the estate?"

"Sure did, lieutenant." The Leprechaun looked like a toy poodle that had just earned a pat on the head. Mark was almost tempted to look down and see if his tail was wagging. "There was a will, of course, left by the senior Conklin. His wife pre-deceased him, and he died himself approximately two years ago. The beneficiaries (Mervin and Melody) were given equal shares of the estate. Melody also had a will, in which she left her entire share of the property to her new husband, Stephen Slade. The Conklin lawyers intimated that Melody fully intended to change her bequest, which was made in *temerarieta* (while under delusion) immediately after her marriage. She just hadn't gotten around to it."

"Interesting," mused the lieutenant.

"Ellias J. Crampton was also included in the old man's will," the Leprechaun rambled on. "He was given a life-time annuity, calculated each year-end at one percent of the current book value of the estate (which, you understand, is much less than the market value) with a proviso entitling him to commute the annuity (to age seventy-five) should both the principal beneficiaries pre-decease him. Stephen Slade, by the way would not be considered a principal beneficiary."

"And the book value of the estate?"

The Leprechaun consulted his file. "In the neighborhood of eight-hundred thousand dollars."

"Some neighborhood," Mark muttered.

"Not," the Leprechaun pointed out, "when you consider that the market value would probably be over two million."

Mark emitted a low whistle and the lieutenant did a quick calculation on the note pad. "So, to sum it up," she said thoughtfully, "Melody's murder leaves Crampton with his eight thousand dollar annual stipend (which he had anyway), while Slade and Conklin stood to gain roughly a million dollars each."

"That's about it." The Leprechaun handed the file to the lieutenant with a look of smug satisfaction.

"And, of course, there's Helen Mundy." The lieutenant made a steeple of her fingers against her lips and tilted her beautiful head. "With Slade free to re-marry, she stood to acquire (as his spouse) a fifty percent share of half of a two million dollar property. It looks like motives and suspects are a dime a dozen this morning."

"Four suspects, maybe," said the Leprechaun smugly, thinking he was stating the obvious, "but only one of them is guilty."

"Quite the contrary," the Amazon added quietly. "The way I see it, *only one of them is innocent.*"

THE SQUAD ROOM WAS CUSTOMARILY A QUIET place in the early hours of the afternoon. Sunday, February 15th, was no exception. It was this that had prompted lieutenant Carruthers to commandeer the room, her own office being too small to accommodate the four principal suspects in the still unresolved St. Valentine's Day murder.

There was a hush in the room. A policewoman and a male uniformed officer stood just inside the double doors. The lieutenant, at a desk on the narrow, room-wide podium, appeared to be totally engrossed in the files and reports that were spread before her. Sitting off to one side, Mark was thoughtfully searching the faces of the four unwilling guests. Just why, he was wondering, and by whose hand, had Melody Slade come to her grotesque and untimely end?

Sitting nearest to him, an unkempt and somewhat subdued Mervin Conklin showed the strain of spending the night as a guest of the city. He sat scowling at everything and nothing, tugging irritably at the tangles in his sun-bleached hair with thick stubby fingers.

Slade, though natty as ever, was cadaverously pale. His broody little eyes darted nervously about the room, looking like two lived-in maggot holes in a lump of gorgonzola.

If you could rely on appearance alone to establish guilt, Mark thought, Slade would be head of the list.

Between the two men, Helen Mundy sat stiffly on the edge of her chair, assiduously pressing out the wrinkles in a square of rumpled facial tissue. She seemed to have withdrawn into some dark inner refuge, her downcast eyes rivetted on the aimless activity in her lap.

The fourth guest, the illusive Ellias J. Crampton, had chosen a chair behind the other three. He was a gaunt and angular man, still in his work clothes, and bristling a two-day growth of beard on his thin square jaw. He appeared to be dozing, his skinny frame swaying mindlessly on its wooden perch, like a dry weed in the wind. And he looked to be more troubled by his unwilling withdrawal from the foggy world of the inebriate, than what was about to happen in the squad room.

"Lieutenant." It was Conklin who spoke. "I don't mean any disrespect," he said cautiously, "but I'd like to know just why I've been herded in here like a dogie at round-up. And why, may I ask, was I forced to spend last night in that crummy cell?"

Cathy Carruthers lifted her blonde head as the rancher spoke, her beautiful features inscrutably void of all expression. "Your brief detention, Mr. Conklin, was obviously self induced. Your impetuous behavior yesterday left us little choice. But I do otherwise agree with you. You have not been charged, and we no longer have any reason to detain you."

The lieutenant rose to her feet and picked up one of the files from the top of her desk. "You may go now, if you wish, Mr. Conklin. I had you brought here this afternoon because I thought you would be interested to know the final outcome of our investigation."

"You know who killed Melody?"

"Yes."

"Then why not just come out and say it? Why all the dramatics? Damn it, lieutenant, let the innocent people go."

The lieutenant gave him a condescending smile. "I have just done that, Mr. Conklin. The only innocent person in this room, is you."

"What the hell're you saying?" Crampton's bleary eyes jerked open. His head wobbled unsteadily atop a turkey-like neck. "I didn't kill nobody."

"No, Mr. Crampton, you did not. But you did attempt to divert the course of justice. And, strange as it may seem, even though all three of you are seriously implicated, there's not one of you who is totally aware of what happened."

"What's to be aware of?" Slade was visibly a frightened man.

"Melody was killed by an arrow, and the only people who had access to the archery equipment was Melody herself, and Conklin."

"And Crampton," the rancher added.

Crampton's stomach took that moment to gurgle. He shrunk back in his chair, grinning sheepishly under his bushy brows. Mark could not restrain a smile.

The lieutenant raised her hand for attention and got it. To Mark, watching from the sidelines, it was an electrifying moment. She could be so authoritative and so incredibly beautiful at the same time, without depleting one from the other. He saw her straighten to her full stature, and sensed a subtle change in her mood. It was as though she had elected, then, to terminate the myth, and put living flesh and blood to Homicide's most controversial legend. And, in that instant, it seemed to Mark, she was the Amazon, myth and maiden alike.

"I THINK WE HAD BETTER BEGIN," SHE SAID IN A LOW decisive voice, "by dispelling any notion that Melody Slade was killed by a bow and arrow. She was not." She opened the file she had in her hand. "The report I have here, is from Ballistics. It confirms by an indisputable match-up, that an expended round we picked up yesterday afternoon in the bottom of the drained pool, came from the 30.30 Savage we found in Mr. Conklin's west wing suite."

Slade stirred uncomfortably in his chair. "Then how come Conklin's off the hook? It was his gun."

"Yes, and on top of that, his paraffin test was positive (as was yours) — nevertheless, he did not fire that rifle."

"How can you be so sure?"

"Well, for one thing, Mr. Slade, I find it difficult to accept that any man would be so transparently stupid as to commit a murder with his own gun, in his own room, and then leave the murder weapon in full view where it was certain to be found later by the police. On such a premise, we could almost logically expect to find his fingerprints conveniently left on the rifle. We did not."

"So what does that prove?" Slade pressed his point in desperation. "He probably wiped them off."

"Now why would he do that? His fingerprints were supposed to be there — it was his gun. No, Mr. Slade, it was not Mr. Conklin who wiped off that rifle. It was you. And even though you were otherwise very thorough, you'll be distressed to learn, I'm sure, that you overlooked one tell-tale surface."

"Will I, now?" Slade's attempt at bravado was not convincing.

"I'm referring to the cartridge case, Mr. Slade, that you inserted into the breach with thumb and forefinger, and subsequently forgot to remove."

A light seemed to flick on in Slade's head, to flare briefly in the hollow eye sockets, then slowly dim. "Damn," he said.

"THEN IT *WAS* SLADE." CONKLIN ALMOST TIPPED HIS chair over in his excitement. "Of course — it had to be him. He was the last one to see Melody alive." He swung to face his brother-in-law. "You murdering louse — "

"Mr. Conklin," the Amazon cut in sharply. "I will caution you only once to keep yourself under restraint." Mark had tensed instinctively, only to relax a moment later as the rancher reluctantly settled back in his chair. "It has been relatively obvious from the beginning, Mr. Conklin, even without the paraffin test and fingerprints, that Slade was the one who shot Melody. But even so, he is not your sister's murderer."

Conklin squirmed. "You mean he missed?"

"No. The bullet hit her all right. It passed through her head on a path identical to that of the arrow. The only reason he did not kill her was because Melody was already dead."

"Lieutenant." Some of yesterday's belligerence was beginning to threaten the rancher's Sunday behavior. "I chose to remain here to get some answers, not more riddles. If Slade didn't kill her, then who the hell did?"

"Think, Mr. Conklin, to when we first viewed your sister's body." She spoke quietly, as though she were mentally re-living the moment. "The clues to this whole charade were there then. They had only to be interpreted. And frankly, I found the supposition that Melody had actually been impaled by an arrow (and — *tch! tch!* — through the skull) extremely hard to accept. Not an impossible feat, mind you, just difficult, and highly improbable."

"Then how — ?"

"You may recall, Mr. Conklin, that the pillow of the mattress had *two* holes in it. One, where your sister's head might well have rested, and the other in the material on the underside of the mattress. If the mattress was inflated at the time (and it must have been, to support the weight of our unhappy victim) then those two rupture points would have been several inches apart. When you weigh this observation against that of the arrow having projected a meager inch beyond the back of the skull, the discrepancy becomes untenable. A bullet, I was quick to assume, would more logically have made those holes."

"But the arrow *was there*," Conklin insisted.

"Yes, it was. But I would think it more likely that the arrow had been inserted into a hole that had first been reamed through by a bullet. And to support this premise, there was the interior matter that appeared to have been *pushed out* ahead of the arrow. Had the arrow gone through the skull with the speed and force necessary for that kind of penetration, it would have done so (in my opinion) cleanly. It would have tended to sear and cauterize the wound and, ultimately, to prevent such leakage by its very presence."

Conklin raised his eyes to the ceiling in a gesture of utter frustration. "What you're saying now, lieutenant, is that Melody was not killed by the arrow, that she *was* shot by Slade, but he did not kill her, and that she *was already* dead before he did it. Will you kindly get to the mother-lovin' point?"

"The point is, Mr. Conklin, that Melody was not killed by an arrow or a bullet. She was asphyxiated. The blue, mottled appearance of her face was the first attestation of that. And, I might add, the unusual absence of any meaningful bleeding would further suggest that her heart had stopped pumping, well before her skull had been punctured, by whatever means."

Conklin straightened excitedly. "But — but, lieutenant. If what you say is true: that Slade didn't kill her, and Crampton only "diverted the course of justice" (as you so aptly put it), and that I am the only innocent one here, then that just leaves — "

"Yes, Mr. Conklin. That leaves — Helen Mundy."

THE TROUBLED EYES OF HELEN MUNDY MET THOSE of the Amazon for the first time since she had entered the squad room. The paralyzing fear that had gripped her appeared now to have abated, and it seemed almost with a measure of relief that she now faced her accuser. Her voice, when she spoke, was a fragile whisper.

"You've known all along, haven't you?"

"Just about."

"And all along, I've known that you knew. I could sense it. I'm glad now that it's over." Her eyes blinked at the gathering moisture. "But how could you be so certain, lieutenant, just from the way she looked, the blotches — ?"

"There was also the unexplainable abrasion on the side of her neck," the Amazon put in quietly.

"Yes, but that could so easily have been self-inflicted — in so many ways. Surely, you had more to go on than that."

"In the main lounge," the Amazon recalled, "you were eminently more startled by the fact that Melody had been shot, than you were from the news of her death (as was Slade, when he first heard about the arrow). You had left her, dead, from asphyxiation; Slade had left her, dead (or so he supposed), from a gun shot wound. It must have been a disconcerting moment for both of you."

Miss Mundy breathed a low reflective sigh and looked over at Slade. His pasty face was expressionless, his eyes were empty hollows. The maggots seemed to have drawn quietly back into their holes.

"It was not until we searched your rooms, Miss Mundy, and I saw the polyurethane tote bag, that I realized how you had managed it. Until then, drowning had seemed to be the only means at your disposal, but that didn't coincide with the way the body had floated so high in the water, with the air so obviously still trapped in the lungs.

The M.E.'s report, by the way, has since confirmed asphyxiation as the mode of death, and conversely, ruled out drowning. But it was the wet leather drawstring that put the clincher on it."

"It was her own damn fault," Helen Mundy sobbed into the crumpled tissue. "She just wouldn't keep her mouth shut."

"It was then, of course, when she threatened to expose you, that you decided to silence her, once and for good. How long could it have taken to empty the tote bag of its contents — one, two seconds — and then to slip it over Melody's unsuspecting head?" The girl's dark hair covered her face and hands as she wept uncontrollably. "Then by expelling the excess air with the flat of your hands, and tightening the leather thong — "

"Oh God." Conklin had cradled his head in his heavy hands. "And we were right there, watching it happen."

"The clear plastic of the bag could hardly be noticed from that distance," the Amazon pointed out, "even had you been looking for it. The drawstring, of course, is what caused the abrasion on her neck, and the inevitable struggle that ensued was the 'splashing about' that you had attributed to the pool therapy."

"But how could she have gotten Melody onto that mattress without our seeing?"

The lieutenant directed the query to the distraught woman. "Miss Mundy?"

"I — I didn't," she replied after a tortured pause. Her hysteria had lapsed into a series of jerking sobs. "I — slid the mattress under her, using the side of the pool as a kind of - of third hand. It's a maneuver I learned in a life-saving class when I — I was a teen."

"And then (correct me if I'm wrong) you loosened the air valve in the mattress so that it would deflate slowly, giving you time to leave and to establish an alibi. Then, when everyone had left the scene, the weight of your victim (who appeared to those on the patio, to be happily sunbathing) would eventually sink into the pool along with the deflated air mattress. You had set the stage, Miss Mundy, for what you hoped would seem to be an accidental drowning. Unfortunately, as in most unpremeditated crimes, you overlooked so many things."

HELEN MUNDY'S PRETTY FACE WAS TWISTED IN

anguish and the eyes she lifted to the podium were red-rimmed and glazed with fear.

"Are you prepared now to make a statement, Miss Mundy?"

The girl nodded dispiritedly, and the policewoman, on some obscure signal, moved in quickly. Helen Mundy accepted her escort's hand on her arm without protest until they had reached the door to the hall. Here, she stopped abruptly, and turned.

"The arrow." Her voice was a thin, bewildered plea. "How could the arrow — ?"

The lieutenant condoned the delay with a slight lift of her chin. "That was Mr. Crampton's contribution, Miss Mundy. You said yourself you passed him on the road as you left the ranch. Mr. Conklin, having driven south, would logically not have seen him. In any case, he arrived back at the house just in time to witness Melody's 'second demise'. He simply hid, and waited, until he saw Stephen Slade drive away. And it was then that he went about the grisly and appalling task of inserting the arrow into the hole that had been made by Slade's bullet."

Crampton, oblivious to all, licked a dehydrated lip and belched dispassionately. His crapulent expression reflected only the relief that had come with the gastric eruption.

Conklin glared at the grounds man with intense loathing. "But why? For the love of God, *why* — ?"

"By the terms of your late father's will, Mr. Conklin (which I will never live long enough to fully comprehend), this bibulous reprobate had been bequeathed an annual annuity of approximately eight-thousand dollars, until the ripe old age of seventy-five. That is, unless both principal beneficiaries (yourself and Melody) should pre-decease him."

"Yes, I know, but — "

"But, Mr. Conklin, that was the *key*. If given that unlikely circumstance, the will granted a proviso of commutation which, in layman's terms, was the right to receive the annuity in one lump sum, rather than have it doled out to him in small amounts over the next thirty-six years. Crampton, of course, was delighted by the death of one beneficiary, and he reasoned (if we may be permitted to use the word that loosely) that should you also be eliminated, he would have effectively removed both legal obstacles to his right of commutation, in one fell swoop. The bow and arrow charade was perpetrated in the belief that you would be suspected *al principio,* as the only person on the ranch capable of killing Melody in that particular manner. He undoubtedly saw you, in his besotted mind's eye, being charged, held for trial and, eventually, executed, in place of the real murderer whom he believed to be Slade. Slade, he knew, could never pose a threat to him without putting his own neck in a noose."

Conklin was staring at Crampton with his mouth open. "Incredible," he breathed.

"What he actually stood to gain, Mr. Conklin, was thirty-six years of eight-thousand per, or, two-hundred and eighty thousand dollars, in one lump sum. Almost enough to buy a small brewery."

As Helen Mundy was led silently away, the other officer moved into the room and tapped Stephen Slade on the shoulder. "Follow me," he said flatly, and turning to Crampton, "you too."

Mark could not repress a smile as he watched them leave, with Crampton bringing up the rear, carroming off both sides of the door as he stumbled through it.

In the meantime, Conklin had risen to his feet. He approached the podium with his western hat gripped knuckle tight in his ham-like hands.

"Lieutenant," he faltered, "I — I'd like to apologize — I didn't realize — "

Lieutenant Carruthers offered her hand to the rancher with a forgiving smile. "It's a big man, Mr. Conklin, who can say he's sorry."

When finally they were alone, the Amazon turned to Mark almost shyly. "I haven't thanked you yet, for the Valentine," she said, warming him with a smile that was worth roughly two years of his pension. "I'm not too sure, though," she added, "whether I'm being hallowed — or hassled."

"Don't you?"

"The Amazon gave her two i.c. a long look. When their eyes met, she said softly, "And then again, I guess I do."

MIKE SHAYNE

MYSTERY MAGAZINE

JUNE 1982
$1.75

47744

A New
Mike Shayne
Mystery
THE
ASSASSINATION
OF
MICHAEL
SHAYNE
by Brett Halliday

Novelets by
MEL D.
AMES
PATRICK
SCAFFETTI

Short Stories by
PAUL BISHOP
HAL CHARLES
EDWARD D. HOCH
DICK STODGHILL

06
0
7 1896 47744

*Killing someone's mother was bad
enough. To do it on Mother's Day was
adding insult to injury!*

to mom
without love

SHE WAS MURDERED ON MOTHER'S DAY.

They were seated at the long table in the dining room, all eight of them, with mother Julia Endicott at the head. A festive occasion, with flowers, and candelabra, and champagne in long-stemmed glasses. The entire family was there; mother, of course, three sons and a daughter, and three more, kindred by marriage. Karl, the eldest, had risen to his feet, and was in the process of offering up a toast "on this propitious day," to all the mothers of the world, and his own in particular, when a muffled explosion echoed like distant thunder down the length of the table. Seven pairs of eyes turned as one to see mother Endicott's gentle face flare in sudden, exquisite agony. And as they sat rooted to their chairs, the tortured features turned grimly pale, then slowly, silently slumped, as in an old silent movie, to descend squarely into her plate of roast prime rib and Yorkshire pudding, with a dull unpalatable plop.

No one moved. Karl remained on his feet in stunned immobility. It was Elsa, Karl's wife, who finally pushed back her chair and went to the woman's side. "She's dead," she said after a close examination. "She's been shot. Someone had better call the police."

DETECTIVE-LIEUTENANT CATHY CARRUTHERS STOOD at her office window in Metro Central's Eleventh Precinct, a superb silhouette against the blood red sky of a dying day. Beyond the window, lights were winking on in the deepening crimson dusk and slow-moving streams of traffic had already begun the ritual daily blood-letting from the city's heart. She looked to be deep in thought.

"A penny for your dreams, lieutenant."

She started, then turned with a wry smile as Detective-Sergeant Mark Swanson's imposing frame filled the open doorway.

"Wouldn't thoughts be more precise?"

Mark shrugged his heavy shoulders. "Who wants precise?" he said. "I live and breathe precise." His ruggedly handsome features took on a distant look. "It's dreams, lieutenant, that can turn a man into a lion — a woman into a tigress." He growled softly.

The lieutenant chuckled as she took the chair behind her desk. "Enough already," she protested. "Lions and tigers make lousy detectives. So do dreamers." She tilted her beautiful blonde head. "What's on the agenda?"

Mark dumped his hefty carcass into a chair with a disparaging grunt, leveling a wistful eye at his senior partner. Six magnificent feet of honey-haired female could be a monumental distraction at the best of times, but working two i.c. to the "Amazon," as she was known to her burly colleagues in Homicide, had been a bucket of mixed blessings for Mark, and an exercise in manly frustrations. His good-natured verbal passes (and her mild rebukes) had lately become routine. A thinly veiled attempt, perhaps, to self-censor the deep bond of respect and mutual affection that had grown between them.

"There's been a killing," Mark began, "out in Thornston Heights. You know the area, *Mortgage Hill*, where Metro's "elite" live. A guy by the name of Karl DeVries phoned it in. He claims someone shot his mother."

The lieutenant arched a flawless eyebrow. " His *mother?* Mark, isn't this Mother's Day?"

"Right on lieutenant. Sunday, May 9th."

"Tch, tch — Well, so much for mother-love." She hooked an unruly lock of spun gold from her forehead with an elegantly curled middle-finger. "Suspects?"

"Seven. All family. They were having dinner at the time."

"Then we know who did it?"

Mark shook his head as he raked a wooden match across the sole of his shoe and touched the flame to a cigarette. "No one saw a thing."

"Nothing?"

"Nothing."

"Hmm." The lieutenant seemed to see something of interest on the ceiling. "That's a bit unusual. Still, matricides of this type are not normally too complicated. The silent seven will probably turn out to be one murderer and six reluctant witnesses. Everything being equal, Mark, I'd guess a quick wrap-up on this one."

Mark drew heavily on the cigarette. "You can forget the everything-being-equal, lieutenant. This guy DeVries is a psychiatrist, his wife is his nurse. He said they made a cursory check of the victim before he phoned. She'd been shot all right, but the only wound they could find was in the abdomen."

"So?"

"It was an *exit* wound."

"So? again."

"There was no *entry* wound."

"That's not possible, Mark. What came out must have gone in. Somewhere."

"Yeah, well — it's got DeVries flipping through his own inkblots."

The lieutenant placed the tips of her fingers and thumbs together, pressed them to her lips and closed her eyes. She almost looked to be praying. Mark knew better. *Preying*, he thought, might be more to the point. "Mark," she said at last, "unless bullets have started to make U turns, we might just have a puzzler on our hands."

Mark gave her a knowing grin. The Amazon, he knew, was in her element. There was nothing that intrigued her more than a "puzzler."

"I've already alerted the meat squad," Mark said, pushing himself out of the chair. "They'll be there ahead of us. And there was a black-n-white in the neighborhood, lieutenant. Fisk and Mayhew. I gave them instructions to get individual statements from the seven suspects, and to keep them on the premises, under escort. They're all related, one way or another, to the victim, Julia Endicott."

"Endicott? I thought you said the man's name was DeVries."

"I did, and it is. DeVries is apparently Julia Endicott's son from a former marriage. And apart from his wife, Elsa, each of the other six is either an Endicott, or married to one. Same mother, different father."

"I see." The lieutenant humored him with a doubtful smile. "We'll sort that out later." She rose from the chair, smoothed the creases from her snug gray skirt, slipped a matching jacket over a form-fitting white shirt-blouse (much to Mark's disappointment) and shouldered a well-worn red leather purse.

"Let's go," she said, as she made for the door. "Let's find out just what kind of person would actually kill their own mother — on Mother's Day."

THE ENDICOTT HOME TYPIFIED THE OLD-WORLD affluence of Thornston Heights. It was an ancient rambling colonial on half an acre of extravagant landscaping. Lawns were vast and green, flower beds rife with color, and a mingling of stately pines and poplars embraced the brooding old house with a somber, verdant dignity. A rank of white pillars stood guard at the entrance and dark-lidded dormers, like armed loopholes, seemed to defend a way of life that was already history. There were a dozen vehicles in the parking lot, six of them police cars, when Mark and Lieutenant Carruthers pulled up in an unmarked Chevy.

"We're not exactly the early birds, are we?"

Mark with a sly grin, was quick to point out that birds did not make any better detectives than lions and tigers. The lieutenant winced. "Touche," she said. And a moment later, she had slipped out of the car and was headed off across the gravel toward the house. Mark caught up quickly, coasting into step beside her.

They climbed wide stone steps to a kind of portico, where a black uniformed officer, the size of Too Tall Jones, stood stoically before the door. He directed them across a large entrance hall, through a lavishly furnished lounge, and into a dining room that still smelled pleasantly of food. The candelabra continued to burn brightly over the table but what was left of the champagne had all but given up its last bubble. The tragic figure of Julia Endicott was still firmly ensconced in her half-eaten dinner.

Sam Morton, Chief Medical Examiner for Metro Central, looked up from the body as they entered.

"Ah, lieutenant. Glad you're here. I've been waiting to get this lady onto a stretcher."

"Have the camera crew done their thing, Sam?"

"Just finished."

The lieutenant's vivid blue eyes turned grimly cold as she methodically surveyed the scene of the crime. Were it not for the missing dinner guests, the shooting could have taken place just a moment before. Chairs were pushed back from the table, as though in a kind of panic, and uneaten portions of roast beef and pudding had been left to cool on the plates. Someone, the lieutenant noted, had already chalked the outline of the body and its relative position to the table, the chair, and the floor.

"Okay," she said, "but do it carefully. I don't want anything disturbed. And Sam, I'd like a preliminary as soon as possible."

"No problem, lieutenant. I can give it to you now, but I don't think you're going to like it."

"Oh?"

"Well, for starters, she's been shot."

"That's very astute, Sam."

Sam Morgan grinned good-naturedly. "This lady's been shot, lieutenant, from the inside — out."

"Can you be more explicit?"

"The body has only one wound that I can see. It's in the abdomen. And it's an *exit* wound."

"Come on, Sam. If a bullet did an exit through her stomach, it must have entered somewhere."

"Tell me more, lieutenant."

The Amazon acknowledged his sarcasm with a lopsided smile. "What about the body's natural orifices?"

"Not likely."

"But you're not certain."

"That's right, lieutenant, I'm not. This is a prelim, remember? The "I'm certains" will have to wait until after the autopsy."

"Was there more than one bullet?"

"I doubt it."

"Has anyone found the one there was?"

"Not to my knowledge."

"Anything else you can tell me, Sam?"

"Not really — except, judging from the hole it made coming out, I wouldn't think there'd be much of a bullet left to find."

"That's encouraging."

With the aid of an assistant, Sam Morton moved the lifeless mother Endicott from her seat of honor at the table to a waiting stretcher. They were about to wheel it away when the lieutenant leaned over the body, peering closely at the grisly wound.

"Just a moment, Sam. What are these little black flecks in the wound?"

"You're guess is as good as mine, lieutenant. Maybe she put too much pepper on her roast beef. *Jeeeez*, let me do my job, will you? I'll write a whole book about it, later. Much later. Yeah — I'll call it the Autopsy Report, by Samuel Morgan, M.D., and I'll personally see to it that you get a free autographed copy *sometime tomorrow*. Now will you *please* let me get the hell outta here?"

THE LIEUTENANT WATCHED HIM GO WITH A WIDE GRIN. She turned to Mark who had stooped to inspect the wood behind the blood-splattered table cloth.

"Find anything?"

Mark opened a pen knife and dug gingerly at the polished wood. "Just a few lead fragments, lieutenant. Very soft lead. Scattered. Hardly penetrated the varnish." He dropped his gaze and his hands to the carpet beneath the table's edge, combing the thick pile with his fingers. "There's a few fragments down here, too."

"The lieutenant examined a piece of the soft metal. "I want this whole table area gone over thoroughly by the Lab team," she said to Mark, "with particular attention given to the underside of the table. Regardless of how it was done, we must assume that this woman *was shot*. And whoever shot her was apparently sitting at this table. Since no one saw it happen, we can only conclude that the gun was fired from below the table, out of sight of the others."

"Gotcha." Mark was quick to pick up her train of thought. "A paraffin scan under the table would not only tell us if a gun was fired, but where it was fired from. All we'd have to do then, would be to find *who* was sitting *where* at the table. And if the suspects were tested as well, a positive match-up on one of them would give us a pretty tight case. Maybe you were right, lieutenant, about a quick wrap-up, I mean."

"We should be so lucky."

Mark's enthusiasm quickly ebbed. "You don't think we'd have a case?"

"It's all too easy, Mark." The lieutenant was slowly circling the long table. "Too pat, somehow. Besides, we still don't know how that bullet (or whatever it was), managed to come bursting out of the lady's stomach when it had no obvious way of getting in."

"Any ideas?"

"Well — one possible solution might be a bullet that had been rigged to explode on impact. The explosion at the skin's surface could conceivably give the *illusion* of an exit wound, even if, in fact, it was not."

"Yeah." Mark brightened. "It might at that. But will Sam be able to pick that up in the autopsy?"

"I don't see why not."

"Then we'll just have to wait for the autopsy report." Mark grinned, remembering Sam's parting edict. " — sometime tomorrow."

"Not necessarily, Mark." The lieutenant was standing behind the chair at the foot of the table, looking down its cluttered length. "If an impact slug was used, and only one shot was fired, there would have to be (not one, but) *two* reports. One, when the bullet left the gun, the other, when it exploded on impact. And the other six witnesses — "

"Of course." Mark thumped his head with the heel of his hand. "Lieutenant, you never cease to amaze me. Mind you, DeVries never mentioned hearing two reports, but then he didn't mention hearing only one, either. Maybe it's time we started asking a few questions."

The lieutenant turned as the friendly black giant entered the room with a precautionary duck of his head. The Lab crew came trailing in behind him.

"Officer, where'd you stash the seven suspects?"

"In the library, lieutenant. The door at the end of the front hall."
He pointed behind him. "Officers Fisk and Mayhew are in there
now, taking statements."

"Thank you." The lieutenant returned the officer's easy smile
with one of her own, then watched him duck out of the room and head
back to his post at the front entrance.

"He's a tall one," she said to Mark. "What's his name?"

"Bones."

"As in Jones?"

"Uh-hu. George Washington Bones."

"What do they call him?"

"Too Tall."

The lieutenant looked heavenward as though in search of help.
"I'm sorry I asked."

One of the men from the Lab team detached himself from the
group. "Anything special on this one, lieutenant?"

"Mark, here, will clue you in, officer. And, Mark, you might have
them drop off a sample of that lead you found, to Ballistics. I've
never known a slug fragment to be so pliable. When you're through,
I'll be in the library."

"You got it, lieutenant."

As she turned to go, all eyes went with her, like a well-trained
drill team. They followed her engaging back through the dining room
door and across the vast carpeted floor of the lounge, metering her
long-legged loping stride with awe and approbation. When she
reached the door to the hall, those same eyes suddenly jerked wide
in shock.

"*Stop him!*"

The frantic shout had come from the direction of the library. Too
late. A man came hurtling through the doorway like a bull out of
loading chute. Taken by surprise, the lieutenant was dumped roughly
to one side, momentarily staggered. The intruder had run clear into
the center of the lounge before he spotted Mark and the Lab team.
He was cut off. He had obviously tried to detour around Too Tall
Bones, whose massive frame was literally obliterating the front
entrance. But now, with escape thwarted a second time, he swung

quickly around and headed back the way he had come. A flushed and shaken Cathy Carruthers apparently did not strike him as being much of a threat.

That was his mistake.

This time, the Amazon saw him coming. In one unbroken, fluid movement, she hiked up her snug gray skirt, well past the midway mark of her long thighs, and swung to face him (which in itself, Mark thought later, should have been enough to stop any man) and with the reptilian grace of a striking cobra, she drove a nylon-clad knee fiercely into the man's stomach. He collapsed in pain and nausea. But before he could hit the floor, the Amazon had spun around, her golden mane flying, and with one hand at his collar, the other at the seat of his pants, she blithely picked him up and started down the hall with him, toward the library. The man's feet were churning thin air a good foot above the floor.

"I don't believe it," said one of the Lab men.

"I don't believe *them*," said another.

"Hey, Swanson," a third man said to Mark, "where do you get the brownie points to play in the same sandbox with that carnivorous kitten?"

Mark eyed the man grimly. "First off," he said, in a soft menacing voice, "you gotta be able to shift a motor-mouth outta high gear, and into neutral."

The Lab men went quietly to work on the table.

WHEN MARK CAUGHT UP WITH THE LIEUTENANT, SHE was standing in front of a red tile fireplace in the library, with policewoman Fisk at one elbow, and officer Mayhew at the other. They spoke in low voices, comparing notes, while the other seven people in the room sat quietly waiting. Book shelves lined all four walls with only a high narrow window here and there, and the door, to break the continuum of hoarded knowledge. An occasional moan drifted up from a deep leather chair where the would-be escapee was slouched low, nursing his stomach.

"You, then, are James Endicott," the lieutenant said to the moan. When it failed to answer, officer Fisk said, "That's him, lieutenant. He answers to Jimmy — at times."

"What made him bolt out of here?"

The officer shrugged her shoulders. "He just didn't like being detained, I guess. He said he had a heavy date. He's the youngest of three sons, lieutenant. Twenty-six. Not married. And not terribly broken up, it seems, at the death of his mother."

"Occupation?"

"He's a gentleman of, uh — leisure." Officer Fisk's soft brown eyes looked almost apologetic. "He told me he 'subsists' on an allowance from his father's estate. He would not divulge the amount."

The lieutenant looked at the young man in question with mild disfavor. "Gentleman, you say."

"Lieutenant?"

An untidy looking man who appeared to be in his early forties, stood up as he spoke. He was dressed in a tweed jacket, with leather elbows, and a badly trimmed full beard. A curved pipe drooped congenitally from a protruding lower lip. There was a patronizing manner about him that he was given to flaunt like a badge of merit. This man, Mark guessed, bearing all the usual sad pretensions of the academic milieu, would no doubt be the psychiatrist.

"I'm Karl DeVries," the man unwittingly confirmed. "This is my wife, Elsa."

The woman who had now risen to his side, was forbiddingly austere in a shapeless black dress. Her hair was straight, without fullness or color, and her thin sharp face gave her the look of a gaunt wingless bird.

"Do we not have your statement?" the lieutenant asked the psychiatrist.

"Yes, you do. Officer Mayhew took it, but — "

"But, what?"

"Well, Elsa and I examined the wound, lieutenant, before I made the phone call, and there just isn't any way it could have happened — "

"But it did happen," the lieutenant said curtly.

"Yes, well — perhaps you could tell me if you've found out how or who — I mean, there was only one — "

The lieutenant bristled. "I do not intend to discuss the complicacies of this case with you, sir, nor the progress of our investigation. You are a suspect, Mr. DeVries, nothing more. Now please sit down."

"Doctor," DeVries said, obviously miffed at being so abruptly dismissed.

"Eh?"

"*Doctor* DeVries," the man insisted.

The lieutenant regarded him coolly, then left him with an irreverent "Hmph" as she turned her attention back to officer Fisk's notebook. "Now, which of you is Julia Endicott's daughter?" she asked the room at large.

A woman about thirty, with long flowing auburn hair and a pleasant round face, raised her hand. "I am, lieutenant. I'm Susan Endicott — I mean, Cross." She giggled nervously at her own confusion. "I've been an Endicott for thirty years, and a Cross for one. I guess I'm just not used to it yet." She looked sheepishly at the man beside her. "This is my husband, Brian."

Brian Cross had an affable, easy way about him. He was younger than his wife, deeply tanned, with boyish good looks and a shock of blonde hair that had been bleached almost white by the sun. He returned her embarrassed look with an understanding smile and reached for her hand.

"What's your occupation, Mr. Cross?"

"I'm, uh — between jobs, lieutenant."

"What did you do previously?"

"He's a competitor," Mrs. Cross put in quickly, defensively. "He's a top ranking surfer. We've just come back from Hawaii where he placed — "

"Top ranking beach bum, you mean."

The unfriendly interruption had come from a man who could only be Herman J. Endicott (being the only unidentified man left) and, according to officer Mayhew's notes, a bank manager by profession. The woman at his side, the lieutenant assumed, would be his wife, Cybil.

"What bank are you with, Mr. Endicott?"

"Metro Civic Savings," the man replied.

Herman J. Endicott not only was a banker, he looked like one. He had a huge pudgy body that was (at the moment, at least) humanely hidden from view beneath the folds of an expensive gray business suit, but three obscenely bloated chins still remained, unadorned, in the public domain. Sitting there, with his lard and his chins, and a pair of thick-rimmed spectacles perched on a dab-of-putty nose, he looked for all the world like a giant pink frog in mufti. His wife, Cybil, who obviously shared his table as well as his lily pad, was only sightly less obese than he.

"*Ribbit, ribbit* — "

The humiliating sound had come from somewhere in the vicinity of an angelic looking Brian Cross. Herman J. glowered at his handsome young brother-in-law who, in turn, politely acknowledged the glower with a nod and a smile. Susan Cross dug an elbow into her husband's ribs, then seemed to find something amusing in her lap.

"PLEASE?"

Lieutenant Cathy Carruthers waited patiently until the room was silent. All eyes were on her. There were times, Mark mused, when his stunning partner truly put live meat on the bare bones of a mythical jungle legend. *The Amazon*. A goddess from another planet, he thought, could not have been more incredibly unique, more outrageously beautiful. She stood now with her feet braced firmly apart, hands on hips, chest high, her luminous blue eyes sweeping the room like an airport beacon.

"There are some questions," she told the gathering, "that I'd like to ask you all in unison. Please think carefully before you attempt to answer." She looked to each waiting upturned face before she went on. "Now, was there anyone else, *anyone*, other than you seven, in or around the house at the time of Mrs. Endicott's death?"

The seven suspects shook their heads as if wired by a single string.

"Not a maid? A handyman? A housekeeper?"

"Not today, lieutenant," Susan Cross volunteered. "There is a full-time housekeeper, a Mrs. Griffith, but she was given the time off while the family was visiting. I helped my mother prepare and serve the dinner." She lowered her eyes, visibly saddened. "She wanted this to be a close family re-union."

"Then you all planned to spend the night?"

"Everyone," Herman J. put in, "but my wife and me. We live

only a few blocks away, lieutenant. Besides, we felt it would be crowding things a bit."

"Plenty of room," Jimmy muttered, having suddenly found his voice. "Couple of stuffed shirts, that's all."

The lieutenant ignored the interruption. "Did anyone of you see any kind of weapon — a gun, perhaps?"

The heads moved negatively for a second time.

"Does anyone own a gun?"

"Karl does," Jimmy piped in. "He's a real gun freak. He even makes his own bullets."

The lieutenant turned to face the psychiatrist. "Is that true?"

"I certainly don't consider myself to be a freak, lieutenant, but, yes, I do have an interest in guns."

"You make your own ammunition?"

"Yes. But what I choose to make myself, anyone over eighteen can purchase at will. I fail to see anything sinister, lieutenant, in what has lately become a rather popular hobby."

"Murder," the lieutenant noted quietly, "has also become rather popular of late." She swung her attention back to the group. "The shot," she asked them, "was it loud? Or faint? Muted? What did it sound like?"

"Faint," said Jimmy.

"Muted," said Herman J.

"Muffled," said Susan Cross. She looked at her husband for corroboration.

"Muffled," he agreed with an affable nod.

"Now think, before you answer this last question." The lieutenant paused significantly. "Can any of you remember, *precisely*, how many shots were fired?"

"One," they answered in a chorus.

The lieutenant's eyes flicked from one face to another. "You're sure of that?"

Jimmy Endicott put voice to their collective response. "One shot," he said unequivocally. The rest of them nodded.

"There goes our solid case," Mark muttered close against Lieutenant Carruthers' ear.

"So it would seem," she sighed. To the seven witnesses, she said, "That's all the questions for now, but I must ask that no one leave this house unless authorized." She disregarded Herman J.'s angry snort. "Guards will be posted to ensure that you comply. I must also ask that you cooperate with officers Fisk and Mayhew while they conduct an immediate search; first, of your persons, then this room, the dining room, the lounge and the kitchen, and the traveled areas between."

The lieutenant spoke to Susan Cross. "Will you be able to accommodate your brother and his wife, Mrs. Cross?"

"Why, of course," she said. "This place has more bedrooms than the Metro Hilton."

"The rates aren't bad either," her husband quipped.

The lieutenant smiled. You could not help but like this pair. To Mark, she said, "I guess it's back to square one for us."

"Yeah." Mark tagged along as she made for the door. "Got any more bright ideas?"

"Just one." She treated him to a win-some-lose-some look. "Let's grab a salami on rye. Maybe we'll 'detect' better on a full stomach."

WHEN THE LIEUTENANT AND MARK RETURNED TO the house on Thornston Hill, an hour and some twenty minutes later, they were met at the door by Too Tall Bones.

"Evening, lieutenant. Sergeant."

Nodding, the lieutenant hesitated. "Have you been relieved for a lunch break, officer?"

"No sweat, lieutenant," the big man replied. He pointed to a brown paper sack just inside the door, big enough to hold a week's groceries. "My wife fixed me a lunch."

"Well, you'd better get at it," the lieutenant said, with a wondering look at the bag. "You're only on shift for another four hours."

Once inside, they found the overnight guests wandering freely about the house. Officers Fisk and Mayhew were seated before the fireplace in the lounge, with their lunch pails open. As the lieutenant and Mark approached, Mayhew was trying to talk the brown-eyed Fisk into swapping a turkey sandwich for one with jelly and peanut butter.

"Forget it, Mayhew," Fisk was saying, "you must think I'm stupid, or something. I didn't burn my brains with my bra, you know — " Her words trailed off into an embarrassed silence as she realized they were no longer alone.

The lieutenant grinned. "Sorry to interrupt such an enlightened discussion, officers, but can I safely assume that you have completed the search I ordered?"

"All done, lieutenant." Mayhew spoke with difficulty around a mouthful of jelly and peanut butter.

Did you turn up a weapon of any kind?"

"No gun, no weapon of any kind — no nothing."

"Hmm — the further we get into this case, the more perplexing it seems to get. Just one dead-end after another." The lieutenant chewed thoughtfully at her lower lip. "Well, let's try extending the search to their homes. We might just turn up a new lead."

"Tonight?" Officer Fisk looked dismayed. "There's three of them out there, lieutenant, not counting Jimmy's quarters, upstairs."

"Two," Mayhew put in. "DeVries lives across the state line in Huntsville. Out of our jurisdiction."

"So now what do we do?" Fisk gulped the last of her turkey sandwich and washed it down with a tug at her thermos.

"You start by checking out young Endicott's rooms, upstairs, then pick up the other two. Herman J. and his wife live only a few blocks from here. The Cross's, if I remember correctly, are out in Beachville, close to the surfing.

"Whatta we do for search warrants?" Mayhew asked.

"You don't." The lieutenant was looking a little exasperated. "You solicit their cooperation. And don't forget their keys."

"What if they refuse?"

"Just remind them that we can always do it the hard way — tomorrow morning. Why delay the inevitable?"

"And DeVries, lieutenant. What about him?"

"Mark will handle it." She turned to her two i.c. "Get on the blower to Huntsville, Mark, and arrange a proxy search of the DeVries home. They'll need time to pick up a warrant, so you better get with it. And don't forget to fill them in on the case so they'll know what to look for."

"What *are* we looking for?" Fisk asked ingenuously.

The lieutenant regarded the young brunette with measured patience. "We're looking for three of those five illusive *W*s, officer Fisk. We already have the *When* and the *Where*. It's the *What*, *Why* and *Who* we're after now. Are there any more stupid questions?"

No one seemed inclined to risk her further displeasure by responding. It wasn't until the lieutenant and Mark were half way across the room that officer Fisk found the courage to call after them. "Lieutenant?"

The big blonde detective halted abruptly and slowly turned, then stood, silent, watching the young policewomen apprehensively narrow the gap between them.

"I don't know if this is important," the officer said meekly, "but I found it in the kitchen during our search." She held out a blue plastic folder about the size of a large wallet, loosely wrapped in a paper napkin. It had a white label affixed to the front of it. "It's a prescription, lieutenant. The label is made out to Julia Endicott."

The lieutenant took the folder and read the label aloud. "Three capsules a day, before meals." She opened it. Both interior sides were lined with a series of small celluloid pockets, each about a half inch in diameter, and most of which still contained a deep red gelatin capsule.

"Very good, officer Fisk." The lieutenant rewarded the young rookie with a smile. "This could prove helpful."

Officer Fisk beamed.

FOLLOWING HIS CALL TO HUNTSVILLE, MARK WENT in search of his senior partner. He found her in the library, seated at a small reading table. She had the plastic prescription folder before her, studying it closely. She looked up as he entered.

"Mark, have a look at this."

He drew a chair up beside her as she edged the folder and herself closer to him. He was not unhappy with the resulting shoulder-rubbing propinquity.

"You can see, Mark, how the prescribed capsules are arranged chronologically on each side of the folder. Three in each row (breakfast, lunch and dinner), seven rows on each side; in all, a two-week supply. And see how each row of three is dated." She pointed with a brightly lacquered, blood-red fingertip. "She apparently began taking them at breakfast on May 4th, here, which is the first date shown. Now, notice that all the celluloid pockets on this left side, are empty (May 4th through May 9th), except for the last row, dated May 10th. That means she took her medication, whatever it was, up to, and including, the one before her fateful last dinner."

Mark's face reflected the puzzling turn of his thoughts. "This is all very interesting, lieutenant, but aren't we dealing with a shooting?"

"Indeed we are, Mark. But what if one of these capsules had contained an explosive of some kind?"

"Come again, lieutenant. There just isn't any way that an explosive charge in a casing *that small*, could carry a detonating timer — or even some far-out kind of remote electrical impulse mechanism. It just is not physically possible."

"It isn't physically possible for a bee to fly, Mark, but it damn well does."

"Meaning?"

"Impossible, is not one of my favorite words."

"I'll remember that," Mark confided meaningfully, "next time I get a couple of tickets to the ball park."

The slow unfolding of her wide grin at such close quarters, Mark decided, was tantamount to watching the parting of the Red Sea.

"Am I interrupting anything, lieutenant?"

The two detectives drew apart like a couple of errant kids. Susan Cross stood in the doorway and there was a teasing, knowing twinkle in her eyes.

"No — of course not." This was the first time Mark had ever seen Cathy Carruthers in less than total control of her composure. "What can I do for you?"

"I'd like your permission to clean up the dining room, lieutenant. Brian and Jimmy have offered to help."

"Yes, well — " The lieutenant straightened authoritatively with a defiant toss of her honey-colored tresses. "I see no reason why you can't. As a matter of fact, I plan to use that room, hopefully sometime tomorrow, for a revelatory reenactment of the crime."

"We'll have it ready for you, lieutenant." She turned and quickly left.

"Where were we?" Mark asked innocently.

"Where we've been since we took on this case," the lieutenant replied in a brisk, back-to-business voice, "back at square one — where else?"

IT WAS THE FOLLOWING DAY, MONDAY, MAY 10TH. Cathy Carruthers sat nursing a cup of coffee at a table in Lil Oly's Cafeteria, one short block from the Eleventh Precinct. Her attention seemed to vacillate between the papers she had spread out over the table, and the entrance to the cafeteria, The noon lunch crowd had thinned to a few stragglers and she was beginning to show signs of mild exacerbation when Mark's husky frame suddenly filled the doorway. Her eyes brightened as she returned his friendly glance of recognition.

She watched with amusement as he headed directly for the coffee bar, while dogging tenaciously in his footsteps, a little man, taking three steps to Mark's one, followed close behind. She recognized at once the abbreviated Garfield Leprohn, Metro Central's shortest police officer, and the controversial head of the Records Department. Mark seemed to be totally unmindful of the little guy who struggled along in his wake, trying desperately to keep up, while balancing a cup of coffee in one hand and a briefcase in the other. When finally they were seated at the lieutenant's table, the *Leprechaun*, as he was known to his life-sized colleagues at the precinct, sank back in his chair and breathed an audible sigh of relief.

"Whew!" he gasped. "I'm a little short on breath." He glanced at Mark, regretting at once his unhappy choice of words.

"What else is new?" Mark muttered dryly. He seemed incapable of resisting any opportunity to rub the little cop the wrong way.

The lieutenant fought back a smile as she gathered up the scattered papers and fed them into two separate file folders. She then leveled her startling blue eyes at the Leprechaun.

"Thank you for coming, Garfield. What have you got for me?"

The lieutenant's courtesy in calling him by his given name, instead of that ugly Irish epithet, was not lost on the Records man. "I've got a run-down on all the suspects, including DeVries," he said brightly, basking in the warmth of the lieutenant's smile. "Would you like a summary?"

"Please."

Mark bristled while the little man made a Hollywood production out of opening his briefcase and extracting, one by irritating one, a number of manilla folders from its hidden recesses. Finally, Mark raised one curled fist in front of his eyes and rotated the other as though he was turning an old-fashioned movie camera. "Mummy's Little Helper Tells All," he announced in the servile tones of a Hollywood set director, "take one."

The Leprechaun flushed angrily. "All these people," he began between clenched teeth, "are without a police record of any kind. The Herman J. Endicotts are an integral part of Metro's exclusive upper crust. Socialites, of the first order. On the other hand, young Jimmy Endicott, and the Cross's, are only tolerated. The DeVries, as you know, reside in Huntsville, where they keep pretty much to themselves."

The Leprechaun paused to take a sip of coffee. "Jimmy Endicott, in spite of his immaturity, is warmly embraced by his peers, and grudgingly respected by his elders. He was the favorite son, in every sense of the word."

"That doesn't seem to jibe with the uncaring way he reacted to his mother's death," Mark observed.

"That business back at the house, Mark, was most likely just a gut reaction," the lieutenant replied. "Each one of us has to deal with grief in our own way."

"Yes, well — if Jimmy was the favorite son, then Susan was the favorite (if, only) daughter." The Leprechaun plowed relentlessly on. "And Brian Cross, her husband — well, he's just an out-and-out enigma. He graduated with honors in corporate law, but subsequently rejected numerous, lucrative offers to stand before the bar. He did a voluntary stint in Nam, then gravitated to a wastrel's life with the sun-sand-and-sea set of southern California. About thirteen months ago, he met and married Susan Endicott. In short, this obviously talented young man, aided and abetted now by a coddled wife, has simply turned his back on success to become a beach bum."

"Hmm," the lieutenant mused. "Perhaps one should stop to

ponder the true definition of success, Garfield."

The Leprechaun chose not to respond. "DeVries is currently registered at Huntsville U.," he continued. "He's been there most of his adult life; first as a student, then as tenured faculty. He now enjoys his own practice while still affiliated with the university on an honorary basis. Quite a lucrative arrangement. And prior to their marriage, (some six years ago), his wife worked with a pharmaceutical firm. She is now his nurse and receptionist. The DeVries, by the way, are not much liked, apparently — by anyone."

Mark took out a cigarette and lit it. "All this seems to bear out the results (or lack of them) of the searches made by Fisk and Mayhew last night," he said. "They didn't turn up a damn thing, either. Mind you, we still don't have anything yet on the Huntsville call." He squinted thoughtfully at the Leprechaun. "What about the money angle?"

"The banker," replied the Leprechaun, referring to his endless heap of data, "is wealthy in his own right. The rest of them depend, with varying degrees, on Endicott money, voluntarily meted out by mother Endicott. I say 'Endicott money' but it is (or *was*) DeVries money. Julia Endicott was a wealthy widow with one small son, Karl, when she met and married Walter J. Endicott. Endicott died of prostatic cancer about a year and a half ago, but Julia had never relinquished control of her first husband's money — until, of course, yesterday. There is a will, which was only recently drawn up, leaving the entire estate to all her children equally — "

"There goes the money motive," Mark put in.

" — but it was never signed."

"Oh? Why not?"

"Well, that's what this Mother's Day dinner was all about. She was going to sign it in front of everyone."

"Interesting," the lieutenant reflected, "but not very helpful. The more info we get, the less we seem to know."

"No hidden debts?" Mark probed hopefully.

"None that I could dig up."

Mark turned to his senior partner. "What about Lab, lieutenant, and Ballistics?"

"Another blank. The capsules contained a common medication for chronic osteoarthritis. There were no powder burns (or residues) under, over, or anywhere near the table, except, of course, directly in front of where Mrs. Endicott was sitting. All paraffin tests were negative. Can you believe it? *No one at the table fired a gun.*" Mark blew a billowing cloud of smoke (with malice aforethought) directly toward the Leprechaun. "Maybe Sam Morton was right," Mark recalled. "Remember what he said, *This lady's been shot, lieutenant, from the inside — out.*"

The lieutenant gathered up her folders. "Yes, and anybody who makes a statement like that had better come up with some answers to back it up." She got to her feet, "Let's go find out what they are."

Before vacating his chair, Mark unleashed another billow of smoke at the Leprechaun. The little man coughed and reached for a cigarette of his own.

"Do you think that's wise?" Mark asked.

"Wise?"

"Cigarettes," Mark grinned, as he turned to leave, "have been known to stunt your growth."

IT WAS AFTER THREE O'CLOCK WHEN MARK SWUNG the unmarked Chevy out of the Metro Morgue parking lot. The lieutenant sat beside him, clutching her collection of folders in one hand while bracing herself against the dashboard with the other. "Now I know why they call this the suicide seat," she complained, as Mark made a taxi stop at the curb, then hung a ferris-wheel right out onto the main drag.

"Keep your shirt on, lieutenant. We're not in orbit yet."

"Mark," the lieutenant's voice was menacingly quiet. "I have no more intention of going into orbit with you than I have of removing my shirt. Now, slow this vehicle down to legal speed."

Mark decided it would be expedient to change the subject with the gears. "So what's the M.E. got to say?"

With a parting glance at the speedometer, the lieutenant opened one of the files. "Hmm, what's this?"

"Looks like a will," Mark proffered with a quick sidelong glance.

"It *is* a will," the lieutenant said as she leafed through the legal document, "and it is still unsigned. Now how in blazes did the Leprechaun know that, when it must have gone with the dead woman to the morgue?"

"You just can't sell that little guy short," Mark acknowledged with a wide grin.

The lieutenant muttered something under her breath as she consulted the autopsy report. "Here's what was found in her stomach," she said after a short perusal, "or what was left of it: *one empty shell casing, .22 caliber, short — inch-long length of twisted wire* (from the roast beef, do you suppose?) — *globules of partially dissolved gelatin — minute lead fragments — widespread cauterizing of tissue — powder residues —* "

Mark emitted a low whistle. "That lady sure had a belly full."

Just what you might expect, Mark, if you can buy a bullet being fired from *inside* someone's stomach. Oh, here's something else: *detonation in mid to lower sector of stomach — rupture of anterior and posterior wall — shell casing reversing through pancreas — lodged solidly against first lumbar vertebrae —* "
The lieutenant looked quizzically at her two i.c. "What do you make of it, Mark?"

"Not a damn thing. You?"

"Well, for one thing, it proves, unequivocally, a bullet *was fired* from inside Julia Endicott's stomach."

"Uh-hu." Mark voiced his disbelief. "You said so yourself, lieutenant — that just isn't possible."

"Precisely." The Amazon settled back with a smug, satisfied smile. "You see, Mark, when the 'impossible' becomes a *fait accompli,* the *if* is no longer in question — only the *how.*"

Mark gave his beautiful partner a searching stare. "Know something, lieutenant? You're *weird.*"

ONCE AGAIN, EIGHT INVITED GUESTS SAT AROUND the long table in the Endicott dining room. On this somber occasion, however, the candelabra had not been lit and there was no champagne in long-stemmed glasses. Detective-Lieutenant Cathy Carruthers now occupied the seat at the head of the table where mother Endicott had so abruptly, and so mysteriously met her death less than twenty-four hours before.

In the background, Mark was making himself as inconspicuous

as possible. Officer Fisk stood at the entrance to the kitchen, while Too Tall Bones hovered like a dark cloud just outside the open door to the lounge. Officer Mayhew had assumed the post at the front entrance. The time was precisely 5:35 P.M.

The lieutenant surveyed the seven anxious faces that ringed the table with a cool candor. "You are all seated just as you were, last evening?"

There were seven assenting nods.

Elsa DeVries sat to the lieutenant's left, with Susan Cross next, and then her husband, Brian. On the lieutenant's right was Karl DeVries, Herman J., and his wife, Cybil, in that order. Jimmy Endicott sat alone at the foot of the table. The mood of the group was one of suspense.

"The purpose of this get-together," the lieutenant began, "is to ascertain precisely what happened last evening when Mrs. Julia Endicott — "

"Lieutenant?"

The lieutenant looked up with some annoyance.

"Sorry to interrupt, lieutenant." Too Tall Bones had thrust his great head through the doorway. "Phone call, from Huntsville. They say it's important."

"Thank you, officer." Rising, she said, "Excuse me," to those at the table, then left to take the call.

It was fully five minutes before she returned. All eyes were on her as she resumed her seat.

"A slight change in plans," she announced soberly. "A search of the DeVries' Huntsville home has now given us sufficient substantive evidence to make an arrest. Pardon me, a *joint* arrest." She turned to the bearded professor on her right. "Suppose you save us all a lot of time and speculation, Mr. DeVries, by telling us just how you armed that deadly capsule that took the life of your mother."

A look of horror clouded the face of everyone at the table. They turned fearful, questioning eyes on the psychiatrist, grimly aware that a murderer sat among them. DeVries swallowed noisily. "What? Are you mad, lieutenant? You don't know what you're saying — "

"Oh, but I do, Mr. DeVries. The Huntsville police have brought to light your frantic attempts to burn and otherwise destroy the materials that were used in the trial-and-error manufacture of that lethal capsule."

"I didn't agree to a search. Lieutenant, you had no right — "

"A duly processed warrant gave us the right, Mr. DeVries. Besides, you were careless in more ways than one." She drew the blue plastic prescription folder from an inside pocket of her jacket and held it out to him. "If you look carefully at the *inside* of the third empty celluloid pocket in the row of three, dated May 9th, you will see that the Lab has dusted for a credible thumb print. There just isn't any way a print could get there after the pocket had been sealed, or resealed, as the case may be. What possible reason, Mr. DeVries, can you give for having tampered with a sealed capsule in your mother's prescription folder, other than to rig it for detonation?"

"Oh, Karl — " Elsa DeVries' gaunt face was the color of chalk, her voice a thin filament of fear.

"Shut up, Elsa." DeVries, too, had paled under his scraggly beard. "What you say, lieutenant, is absurd. Why, in heaven's name, would I kill my own mother?"

"I can only answer that question by conjecture, Mr. DeVries." The other members of the family watched and listened in stunned silence. I suggest that you were alienated from your mother the day she married Walter J. Endicott, years ago, when you were still a child. Only the existence of your father's fortune could have persuaded you, over the years to remain close to a mother you felt had sullied the memory of your father. You felt betrayed; her love for you diluted, and divided; first by the man she married, then successively by each child she bore him."

"Rubbish," DeVries was livid. "Utter nonsense."

"It was the proposed reading of your mother's will," the lieutenant went on, "that finally fanned the long-smoldering hatred into a murderous flame. This was *your* money (or so you envisaged), left to *you*, in your mother's care. Now it was to be divided among the progeny of your mother's shame. The signing of the will, last night, was to have been a demonstration by Mrs. Endicott, of her impartial love and respect for each of you. But you, Mr. DeVries, did not see it quite that way."

"But how would Karl stand to gain by the death of my mother, lieutenant?" Herman J. was visibly shaken.

"Not at all, monetarily. The ultimate disposition of the estate, which will now go to probate, will not (in my opinion) differ substantially from the provisions already proposed by your mother. But while the money was undoubtedly the catalyst, it was not the motive. Hatred, Mr. Endicott, *long-nurturing hatred*, can be eminently more obsessive and violent a motive than simple greed."

Elsa DeVries' hawk-like features suddenly slackened into a convoluted mask of fear and remorse. "Karl," she cried, "it's no use —"

THE BEARDED ACADEMIC GLARED HEATEDLY AT his distracted wife. "Damn you," he seethed. "Damn you all!" His eyes darted wildly about the table from one startled face to another. "Bastards. That's what you are. An illegitimate pack of thieving bastards. You have no more right to the DeVries fortune than you have to the name — " After a time, his anger subsided, slowly, into a subdued, breathless sobbing.

"Mrs. DeVries." The lieutenant placed her hand gently on the woman's arm. "It was you, was it not, who procured the capsule blanks for your husband? Did he, perhaps, threaten you?"

"Yes." She hesitantly covered the lieutenant's hand with one of her own, as though seeking a new ally in the face of her husband's anger. "He knew I had access to any number of them, all sizes, from the pharmaceutical firm where I used to work."

The lieutenant's voice, when she spoke, was soothingly quiet. "Do you want to tell us about it?"

The distraught woman glanced apprehensively at her irate husband, wondering whether to proceed. In quick response, the lieutenant caught the eye of Too Tall Bones, "Take this man into another room, officer. Cuff him and detain him, out of earshot."

The scraggly professor sprang to his feet. "You're not getting rid of me that easily," he fumed. "*You!*" He glared at his wife. "You're no better than the rest of them." He lunged across the table at her, but she cowered away from him like a frightened ostrich.

At that instant, the Amazon's left hand flashed out with the speed of lightning. She caught the one extended wrist closest to her in a grip of steel. She squeezed. And as her knuckles whitened, the pallid face beneath the beard contorted with pain, and the struggling body slumped against the table, limp and helpless.

Moments later, Too Tall Bones was snapping on the cuffs while assessing his amazing colleague with wide, white eyes. "My, my—" he said, with undisguised awe and admiration. And with a puzzled, wondering, final glance at the Amazon, he yanked the disheveled academic to his feet and led him whimpering from the room.

"You were saying, Mrs. DeVries."

AS HER HUSBAND WITHDREW, THE VEIL OF TERROR that had so quickly cloaked the beady, bird-like eyes, appeared now to lift. "What is it you want to know, lieutenant?"

The lieutenant opened the prescription folder on the table and extracted a capsule. She held it up so that all could see it. "It was a capsule, then, identical to this, that a .22 caliber short round — "

"*Two* capsules, lieutenant. One, slightly smaller than this, was telescoped into the other, to provide a more solid sheath."

"Then the bullet?"

"Not exactly. A conventional round would have been too long, and too heavy. Karl removed the heavy lead slug and filled the cavity with a weightless cotton fluff, then capped it with a thin disk of a soft lead alloy. But before that, he had weakened the detonating cap by plying it with a kind of acid solution, softening the metal to a point where the slightest impact would set it off."

"Kind of like a hair trigger," the lieutenant suggested. "The spoiled casings of those he had been experimenting with, were found in his workshop. But, tell me, Mrs. DeVries, how was it detonated?"

The other five people at the table leaned forward, straining to catch each tremulously spoken word.

"A small, tightly coiled spring, that had been shaped at one end to facilitate a 'firing pin', was imbedded in the end of the capsule, in line with the detonating cap. It was held there in a specially molded 'saddle' of coated gelatin. This 'coating' effect, lieutenant, is achieved by treating common gelatin with a methanal solution, which causes it to 'harden' and become less soluble when subjected to the gastric juices of the stomach. Variations of this process are widely used today in the manufacture of 'time-release' medications."

"Yes, we're all familiar with them, but — "

"Yes, lieutenant, I'm getting to it. The spring was secured in the coiled position by a 'keeper' of *untreated* gelatin, leaving it vulnerable to the first eroding effects of the stomach fluids."

"Ah — now I see." The lieutenant held the capsule curiously between thumb and forefinger. "The keeper was designed to dissolve first, while the balance of the capsule was essentially still intact. Then the spring, when released, would propel the firing pin forward, against the detonating cap, and *zaaap!*"

She tossed the capsule lightly in her hand. "Ingenious, to say the least. The deep red color of the capsule would, of course, hide its contents. It would be a simple matter, then, to substitute the deadly capsule for any other in the prescription folder, and thereby predict the very time of death."

She hesitated a moment, her eyes narrowed in retrospection. The *manner* of Mrs. Endicott's death, however, the so-called 'exit wound', was simply a matter of chance. Had the device been facing any other way but forward when it exploded, there probably would have been no exterior wound at all. Death, however, would have been just as swift, and just as permanent."

Elsa DeVries reacted with an agonizing moan. "He made me do it, lieutenant. I didn't want to. I — I *loved* her — "

"Whatever."

THE LIEUTENANT NODDED TO OFFICER FISK WHO came forward to escort the sobbing woman from the room. She turned to the others at the table. "That wraps it up," she said curtly. "You are all free to go."

Stunned and shaken by the bizarre turn of events, the five remaining Endicotts filed silently from the room. When only Mark remained, the lieutenant said, "I hope God won't get me for that one little white lie."

"You mean the one about the fingerprint?"

"That's the one. But how did you know?"

"Lieutenant." It was Mark's turn to look pained. "Those capsule pockets are only half an inch in diameter. It would have had to be the thumb of a leprechaun to make contact with one of those concave inner surfaces." He held up his own stubby thumb in evidence.

"Hmm." The lieutenant grinned. "It's plain to see a leprechaun is something you ain't."

"Well," Mark was looking pleased with himself, "you've got to admit I was on the ball — and I didn't give your little game away."

"Ball, you say? Game?" Cathy Carruthers, the earthling, widened her beautiful eyes in mock naivety. "How about that? I thought you were never going to ask."

MEL D. AMES

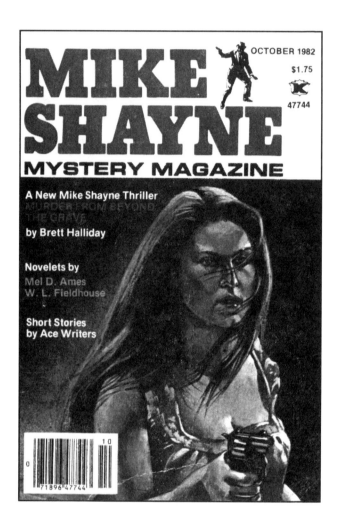

MIKE SHAYNE

OCTOBER 1982
$1.75
47744

MYSTERY MAGAZINE

A New Mike Shayne Thriller
MURDER FROM BEYOND THE GRAVE
by Brett Halliday

Novelets by
Mel D. Ames
W. L. Fieldhouse

Short Stories
by Ace Writers

71896 47744

Beautiful Amazon Detective-Lieutenant Cathy Carruthers looked up inquisitively as Sergeant Mark Swanson entered her office. "We've got ourselves a beaut, Lieutenant," he said. "There's a real weirdo out there tonight! One of the kids found a human finger in her trick or treat bag!"

hallowe'en madness

IT WAS HALLOWE'EN. JACK-O'-LANTERNS GRINNED like orange sharks from darkened windows and elfin monsters roamed freely through the streets. Covens of witches, ghouls and goblins converged on porch-lit doorways with gaping sacks and happy cries of "trick or treat!" It was a time of innocent masquerade. The long dark hours of revelry, mischief and mayhem had not yet begun in Metro. Or so it might have seemed.

Six year-old Tammy O'Toole, alias Wolf Man, her tight blonde curls betraying her presence behind the fright mask, arrived home a few minutes past seven with a sack full of treats. She removed the mask and her heavy outer clothing, then dumped the contents of the sack out over the kitchen table, and began to sort her garnered treasure into piles. When Maureen O'Toole entered the kitchen a few minutes later, she saw her daughter peering intently at a small object about the size and shape of her own lipstick tube.

"Mummy, what's this?"

Maureen took the thing in question between thumb and forefinger and held it up curiously. Her eyes suddenly widened in horror as recognition dawned, and with a violent shudder she let it fall back to the table.

"Oh my *God*! It's a human finger."

IN THE HOMICIDE DIVISION OF METRO CENTRAL'S Eleventh Precinct, at precisely 7:29 P.M., Detective-Sergeant Mark Swanson returned the telephone to its cradle and shoved himself away from his desk. He covered the distance to the glass-partitioned office of his immediate superior in three quick strides, rapped twice and entered.

Detective-Lieutenant Cathy Carruthers looked up as Mark's heavily-muscled six-foot frame filled the doorway. She watched him dump himself unceremoniously into a chair and assume a comfortable slouch before she said "Come in," with obvious sarcasm, adding, "is there a law, Mark, that prevents you from closing doors?"

Mark gave the door a jab with one of his size twelves and grimaced as he waited for the slam. When it come, he grinned sheepishly at the lieutenant, then quickly tried to divert her mood, "We've got ourselves a beaut, lieutenant. There's a real weirdo out there tonight."

The lieutenant leveled her vivid blue eyes at him. "Something of a weirdo has just invaded my office," she said with a feisty mix of annoyance and amusement, "Would you care to convince me otherwise?"

Mark produced a cigarette and a wooden match. He ignited the match with a flick of his thumbnail and considered his beautiful partner through a haze of smoke. It had been a good year since he had teamed up with Cathy Carruthers. This remarkable six-foot blonde beauty possessed all the physical attributes of a Playboy Bunny plus a hidden wellspring of such uncanny strength and intelligence that her burly colleagues in Homicide had dubbed her *The Amazon*, a manifestation of their incredulity, respect and affection. But only to Mark, her trusted and self-appointed side-kick, had she ever permitted a glimpse of the warm and vital woman behind the epithet. And even to him, rarely.

"I just took a call," Mark began, with a heavy pull on his cigarette, "from a Mrs. Maureen O'Toole, out in the old section of East Metro.

Says her daughter came home with a sack full of Hallowe'en goodies about twenty minutes ago, and when she dumped it all out on the kitchen table, there was a lady's finger in amongst the candy bars and popcorn balls."

"So? I'm rather fond of lady fingers myself."

"This, lieutenant, was a lady's *finger*, as in fore, index, ring, or little."

"That's a little gross, isn't it? Are you sure it's not just a hoax, Mark, a plastic or rubber counterfeit?"

"No hoax, lieutenant. No counterfeit."

"Oh, wow! So now we've got a finger freak to go along with the crazies who bury razor blades, broken glass and fishhooks in Hallowe'en handouts. The lieutenant's usually inscrutable features betrayed her extreme abhorrence to these senseless attacks on innocent children. "But, Mark, what are we doing with this call? We're supposed to be handling homicides, remember?"

"Yeah, well, there have been two similar calls within the last half hour, from distraught parents who found 'fingers' in their kids' Hallowe'en haul. Black-and-whites have already checked out both calls, and radioed back in a verification that the fingers were, in fact, genuine — uh, human. So Chief Heller instructed the Desk to route any further calls through to Homicide. He says there's got to be at least one body out there to go with the pinkies, and he wants us to find it."

"Mmmm." The lieutenant got to her feet and began to pace. "That's a little like handing Robbery a couple of hubcaps and asking them to come up with a stolen car."

"At least they'd know the year and make," Mark put in.

"That's true, Mark, but hubcaps don't have fingerprints, at least not their own. Where are those first two fingers now?"

"One was on ice in the Lab when I got the call. The other was on its way in."

"Good. Get down there right away and have a set of prints sent over to Records for a possible match-up. And, Mark, are Fisk and Mayhew on tonight?"

"Yeah — " Mark tugged his eyes up three pulchritudinous levels to a face that was becomingly furrowed in deep thought. "I spotted them in the squad room as I came on tonight."

"Okay. So we'll commandeer them for this one. I want the Metro Central and County Morgues checked out for any fingerless corpses, the hospitals for amputations, the Coroner's office for recent exhumation permits, and the Med staff at Metro U for an accounting of all cadavers in their possession, along with all their spare parts, during the past seventy-two hours."

Mark levered his rugged carcass out of the chair. "Are we going to take that O'Toole call, lieutenant?"

"Indeed, we are. I'll meet you down in the garage in, say, five minutes. That will give you time to reach Fisk and Mayhew, and me to get through to the M.E. Sam Morton's been bragging for years how he came up with the sex, the approximate age, the build and weight, and even the probable occupation of one leg bone—a femur, that had been salvaged from the Metro Dump. I wouldn't like to miss this opportunity to see what he can do with three severed fingers."

"Aren't we jumping the gun, lieutenant, in assuming that all three fingers came from the same hand?"

"You've got a point, Mark. But to think otherwise, would suggest that we're dealing with three fingerless corpses, instead of one. Also, all three have been described as *lady's* fingers, which, at the moment anyway, seems to point to only one victim." The lieutenant gave Mark a grim look. "And there is still one other possible false assumption that we've been making: That the hand and body belonging to those fingers is, in fact, a corpse. Whoever once owned those fingers, Mark, could well be alive and kicking at this very moment."

The telephone sounded before Mark could respond.

"Carruthers."

He watched her beautiful face darken as she held the instrument against her ear. "Right, sergeant. Yes. We'll pick up both calls on the way out." She broke the connection with her other hand and turned to Mark. "Better get with it. That was a report on another finger. Looks like our crazy's having himself a ball tonight."

IT WAS ALMOST 8:30 WHEN THE UNMARKED CHEVY pulled up in front of Maureen O'Toole's split-level bungalow. The trick-or-treat crowd had thinned to a few stragglers.

"Don't forget to lock the car," the lieutenant cautioned as she stepped out onto the sidewalk. "I don't want any Hallowe'en pranksters doing a number on us."

"Don't you think it's a little early for that?" Mark countered as he followed her up the walk.

"It wasn't too early an hour ago for some psycho to start handing out human fingers for Hallowe'en treats."

Mark thumbed the doorbell. "You've got a point there," he said grimly. "By the way, I checked the map in the garage while I was waiting for you, and all four of those calls originated in this same general area."

"That's interesting."

The curtain on the door was drawn aside and a pretty face looked out at them. Mark said "Police," and flashed his badge. The face disappeared and a moment later the door swung open.

"Mrs. O'Toole?"

"Yes. Please come in."

Maureen O'Toole was a typically attractive blue-eyed colleen. She was all of five-feet-two, with abundant auburn hair and a slender engaging figure. She led the two detectives into the kitchen, where six year-old Tammy was still busy with her now slightly depleted hoard of goodies.

"This," Maureen O'Toole said proudly, "is my daughter, Tammy."

The lieutenant took a chair beside the child, which brought her down to eye level and made her seem a little less imposing. "Hello, Tammy. I'm Lieutenant Carruthers, and this is my partner, Sergeant Swanson."

"Hi," she said, ignoring Mark altogether. "Are you a lady detective?"

"Yes, I am."

"*He's* not."

There was a thread of belligerence in the girl's voice as she shot a quick glance in Mark's direction. Mark looked mildly surprised. He usually got along well with kids.

The lieutenant reached for the child's hand. "We girls have to stick together, don't we, Tammy?"

"Uh-hu."

"'Specially when we're doing detective work, right?"

"Right."

"Well then, do you think you could tell the sergeant, for me, exactly where you went tonight? The names of the streets? The blocks you covered? Like that?"

"I guess so."

Mark took out his notebook and sat down on the other side of the youngster. "Sergeant Swanson at your service, Tammy," he said with a quick salute and a smile. "Ready when you are."

The lieutenant got to her feet then, and Maureen O'Toole headed for the refrigerator. "I scooped it up into a plastic container and put it in the fridge like the sergeant said." She reached in and took out a plastic medicine vial about three inches high by an inch and a half in diameter. "Who could do such an awful thing, lieutenant?"

"We don't have an answer to that yet, Mrs. O'Toole, but we will, in due course."

"It's enough to give a person the creeps," the young woman said nervously.

The lieutenant eyed her closely. "Is your husband not at home tonight, Mrs. O'Toole?"

"My husband and I are separated, lieutenant. The Family Court served him with a restraining order about six weeks ago, to keep him away from Tammy. He had been, uh —" she lowered her eyes — " — abusing her. You know what I mean? Intimately — "

"I understand." But Cathy Carruthers, the woman, did not, in truth, understand at all. She looked wonderingly at the natural warmth and beauty of this young wife and mother, and the sweet innocence of her child, and she questioned how any man could deviate so far from the norm as to willfully forfeit such a treasure. In an effort then, to reify her somber thoughts, she pried the top off the small container and peered in at the severed finger. It was pitifully shrunken, a dirty ashen-gray thing, and it looked grotesquely alone and purposeless lying there in its plastic sheath. It was, nevertheless, unmistakenly a human finger.

Later, as they were leaving, the lieutenant said, "Mrs. O'Toole, where is your husband living now?"

"He has an apartment downtown, close to the Metro General Hospital. That's where he works."

"What are his duties at the hospital?"

"He's an orderly, in O.R."

"O.R.?"

"That's what they call the wing where the operating rooms are located. He actually works in Recovery, which is on the same floor."

"Thank you, Mrs. O'Toole."

When Mark and the lieutenant were back in the car, Mark said, "That little tyke sure covered a wide area. We've got somewhere between three and five square blocks to check out, door-to-door."

"If the kid can do it, Mark, so can Metro P.D. Besides, we should have it narrowed right down by tomorrow morning."

"How so?"

"We received four phone calls, Mark, reporting on four dismembered fingers, that were allegedly picked up by four separate kids, right?"

"Right."

"Well then, if we can assume that each kid covered roughly the same area that Tammy did —"

" — we'll have four times the area to check out," Mark cut in, "about twelve to fifteen blocks in all. It's getting worse all the time."

"Not really, Mark. Those kids might have all started out tonight to trick-or-treat from totally different locations, but you said yourself that all four fingers were given out in the same general area. This would suggest to me, that some of the houses in the overall area would have been visited by more than one of the kids, some houses by more than two, and some, presumably, by more than three. And if we can give any statistical credence to Bernoulli's famous *Law of Averages*, there would be relatively few in the latter group that were called on by *all four kids*. And they, Mark, are the only houses that should interest us."

"Lieutenant," Mark groaned, "you're snowing me again. I've got to agree with your reasoning, but how do we go about putting a handle on only those houses that all four kids went to by pure chance?"

"That's the easy part, Mark. And one simple, graphic method of doing it, would be to draw out the route that was taken by each of the kids, to scale, on separate sheets of paper, then superimpose them, one on top of the other, over a street map of the total area. The houses we'd be looking for would be located only at those points where all four of the routes intersected and/or overlapped."

Mark studied his beautiful partner silently for several moments through a one-eyed squint. "Lieutenant, you must have been sired by a mother-lovin' computer." He let out a long sighing breath. "Now tell me, if that was easy, what's the hard part?"

"Getting the information from the kids to make up the four route maps."

"Yeah, I'll buy that one. I just hope they're all as articulate as little Tammy. And, lieutenant, speaking of Tammy, that kid sure seems to have a thing going against anyone who isn't female. I've never had any trouble relating to kids before tonight."

"Nothing to do with you, Mark. She's a victim of that ever-growing malady: *child abuse.* Her father, in fact, is currently on a restraining order."

"Do tell? And he works at the Metro General in O.R.? Maybe we've got ourselves a fish, lieutenant."

"Maybe. But it's a little early yet to start counting our chickens. Or should I say, fingers?"

Mark grunted dispassionately. "Where do we go from here, lieutenant?"

"I think we'd better pick up that fourth finger before checking out the other calls for route maps."

Mark sighed as he turned the ignition key and slipped the gearshift into Drive. "Something tells me this is going to be a lo-o-ong night."

IT WAS THE FOLLOWING DAY, 11:33 IN THE A.M., AND Mark stood at the entrance to the Metro Central City Morgue watching his favorite police person approach him from the direction of the parking lot. The sinewy grace of Cathy Carruthers as she narrowed the distance between them, her long loping stride, and the superb blend of movement between hip and shoulder was, he mused, a symphony of anatomical perfection. His trance-like abstractions ended abruptly, however, as she bore down on him with a wide smile and a congenial "Hi."

"Hi, yourself."

Mark swung into step beside her as they entered the building and started down a long marble-lined hall. Their voices and footsteps echoed off the high cold walls.

"I asked you to meet me here, Mark, because I thought you'd enjoy being a witness to the big cop-out."

"Cop-out? I don't get it, lieutenant."

"Mark, Sam's been bragging for years about the time he solved the case of the *phantom femur*, single-handed, by coming up with a make on the murder victim from his examination of a single thigh bone. The way he tells it, he saved the day for the prosecution by making it possible to comply in *supersedeas* with the court's imposition of a writ of *habeas corpus*."

"It all sounds Greek to me," Mark said, stifling a yawn.

"Well, it's not. It's Latin. Anyway, first thing this morning, I had the Lab send our four phantom fingers over to Sam's office with a requisition for an 'identity prognosis'. I thought I'd give him an opportunity, once and for all, to put up or shut up."

"You don't think he can do it?"

"Let's just say that I think his tales are taller than his track record."

At the door labeled: SAMUEL MORTON, M.D., CORONER AND CHIEF MEDICAL EXAMINER, M.C.P.D., they knocked and entered. Sam Morton, short, balding and grumpy, looked up over thick-rimmed spectacles from behind his desk.

"Ah, Metro's finest. I've been expecting you."

The lieutenant caught Mark's eye with a confiding wink. "What have you got for us, Sam?"

The M.E. shoved his glasses up higher up on the bridge of his nose and reached across his desk for a brown manilla file folder. "Now understand," he said preemptively, "we can't expect too much from the examination of a mere finger — "

"Uh — just a moment, Sam." The lieutenant, Mark knew, was going to milk this little scenario for all it was worth. "I think Mark had better get all this down. We know your reputation in the field, and I wouldn't care to trust to memory — "

"Forget it!" Sam scowled. "You can take the bloody file with you when you go. Now—you want to hear this, or not?"

"Whenever you're ready, Sam."

" — but," the M.E. glanced up, ready to thwart a further interruption, and when it didn't come, he continued, "in view of the fact that, on this occasion, I had (not one, but) *four* fingers to work with, and I was able to establish almost at once that all four were from the same hand, my prognostications were accordingly somewhat routine and (I add in all modesty), substantive."

The lieutenant gave Mark a look that seemed to begin somewhere in Texas and end up in Missouri.

"I'm going to skip the gobbledygook on techniques and methods (you probably wouldn't understand them anyway) and get right down to a biological reconstruction of the *disjecta membra* in question."

"The *what?*" Mark muttered.

"More Latin," the lieutenant told him with a grin.

Sam Morton ignored the interruption. "My tests have shown this alleged victim to be a fair-haired, light-complexioned, female Caucasian, approximately eight years of age, rather slight in build and of average height for her years. She either resided, or attended school, in the greater Metro area, and was, at the time of her dismemberment, connected in some meaningful way with the modeling of clay."

He looked up from his notes to see the lieutenant's open mouth snap shut, then wreathe into a smile of genuine approval and esteem.

"That's incredible, Sam. I owe you an apology. I do. I really didn't think — "

Sam Morton closed the file with an ill-humored growl. "What did you expect, for Chrissake — chopped liver?"

"I don't know what I expected," the lieutenant laughed uncertainly, "but it wasn't this. I'd take my hat off to you, Sam, if I had one on. I don't suppose you'd care to enlighten us on how you arrived at those conclusions?"

The crusty M.E. sighed indulgently. "It's all here in the file," he grumbled, "but, okay. In layman's terms: the hair color, complexion and the Caucasian factor is determined by skin pigmentation; the sex, age, height and general build, by bone analysis and growth projection; her domicile and probable hobby, from under-nail residues; and the approximate time of dismemberment, by cellular decomposition."

"Time of dismemberment?"

"Oh — I didn't mention that, did I? Those fingers were severed from the hand to which they were once attached, lieutenant, about a year ago."

"*A year ago?*" The lieutenant could not contain her surprise.

"Then how have they been so well preserved?"

"They've been frozen." The M.E. smiled patiently. And *that* was deduced from cellular fragmentation in both the epidermis and the muscle fiber itself — "

"Enough already — " The lieutenant was suddenly all business. She reached across the desk for the file folder. "You say it's all in here?"

"It's all there, and it's all yours."

At he door, the lieutenant paused and turned. "Sam." She appeared to be a little discomfited. "I'd just like you to know that it's good to have you on the team."

When the door had closed behind them, SAMUEL MORTON, M.D., Coroner and Chief Medical Examiner, M.C.P.D., shrugged off a fleeting smile and went on with his work.

12:57 P.M. THE TOP OF MARK'S DESK WAS HIDDEN under an enlarged street map of East Metro. On one portion of the map, three squares of transparent drafting paper had been thumb-tacked into position, one above the other. At an adjacent desk, the department artist was drawing out to scale, the fourth and final route on a similar square of tissue. Mark stood over the man, watching the red line that was Tammy O'Toole's route last night, lengthen in an irregular loop that zig-zagged over the paper, then doubled back on itself to the point where it started.

"There. That does it, Mark. Let's get this last one pegged out on the big map."

The route of each Hallowe'en trick-or-treater had been drawn in with a different color. Blue, green, yellow, and now red. The lines spidered through the streets of East Metro, intersecting and overlapping at numerous points, but only on three short block-long streets, in an "H"-shaped configuration, did all four colors come together.

"That nails it down to just three short blocks," Mark grunted appreciably. "See what you can do, O'Malley, when you've got a God-given brain instead of a shillelagh between your ears?"

O'Malley lifted one disparaging eyebrow in Mark's direction, gathered up his paraphernalia, and walked away without comment. Lieutenant Carruthers paused and turned as she came into the room, just in time to watch the artist stomp angrily out the door.

"What's with O'Malley?" she said to Mark.

"Search me, lieutenant. Maybe somebody crumpled his crayons."

The lieutenant grinned. "Guess who," she said. She tossed Mark one of two paper sacks she carried. "I bought you some lunch. A couple of salamis and a danish. I thought we'd eat in and save time."

"You're all heart," Mark muttered.

"Any success on the search pattern?"

"Yeah — we've got it narrowed down to three single blocks."

"Good. We'll get Fisk and Mayhew on it." She glanced at her watch. "They were due in here at one."

As though on cue, officer Mayhew and policewoman Fisk appeared at the door. The lieutenant beckoned them with a tilt of her chin. "You better get in on this," she said to Mark.

"First off," the lieutenant began when they were all seated, "I'd like to hear what you came up with last night."

"One big zero," Mayhew said.

"With the ring removed," Fisk added for emphasis.

"You covered all the ground?"

"We started with the city morgue," Mayhew explicated, "then those in the County as far as Ridgewood. We had to take on two extra men —"

"Persons," Fisk put in.

" — to cover the hospitals (the Chief okayed it, lieutenant), and the Coroner's office informed us that there had been no disinterments in the last three months. Finally, Fisk and I finished it off this morning with a trip out to Metro U. It was zilch all the way, lieutenant."

"Well, that's not surprising, I guess," Mark said with perverse good humor, "when you consider that the mutilations we're looking for, happened a year ago."

"*What?*" Mayhew did a double-take on Mark, then addressed the lieutenant. "Then what were we doing — ?"

"Relax," Mark grinned, "we just got the news, late this morning."

Fisk looked disheartened, "So now we've got to do it all over again, in a wider time frame — " She made a sour face and shuddered. " — *ugh*, I guess it's back to those horrible cadavers."

"That might not be necessary." The lieutenant chuckled at the young brunette in spite of herself. "We've got a door-to-door for you today — "

Mayhew groaned.

" — and where you go from there will depend on what you come up with."

Fisk brightened. "Anything," she said emphatically, "would be an improvement on going shopping for fingers in that human-parts department at Metro U."

The lieutenant drew back a fall of golden hair that had strayed over her forehead. "Line them up on that map, Mark, so they can get on it right away." To Fisk and Mayhew, she said, "Take your hand-radios with you and keep in close contact. Report anything, *anything*, that appears in any way irregular."

"You got it, lieutenant."

WHEN MARK RETURNED A FEW MINUTES LATER, the lieutenant had her elbows spread before her on the desk with her fingers interlocked and her chin resting on the backs of her hands. "I've got a hunch," she said.

"Uh-hu." A hunch with Cathy Carruthers, Mark knew, was not a hunch at all, but a well-considered expectation. When he had settled back comfortably in his customary slouch, he said, "Are you going to tell me about it?"

The lieutenant looked at him, moving only her eyes. "I think it's a Hallowe'en thing," she said.

"How about that?" Mark thumped his forehead with the heel of his hand. "I wonder where I got side-tracked into thinking that this was the Fourth of July?"

The lieutenant appeared (or chose) not to hear him. "I believe this is more than just the twisted humor of a Hallowe'en sickie, Mark. I think this is the second chapter in a two-part drama, one that began, perhaps, a year ago, or longer—but *when*ever it was, and *what*ever it was, it's got Hallowe'en written all over it."

Mark began to munch on a salami sandwich. "What makes you think there's more here than meets the eye, lieutenant?"

"I should have brought something to drink with this," the lieutenant said absently as she unwrapped one of her sandwiches.

"How about some battery-acid from the local urn?" Mark offered.

"I guess we don't have much choice."

Mark had returned with the coffee and settled down once again into his awkward slouch, before the lieutenant responded to his initial question.

"To begin with, Mark, there isn't anything very casual or spontaneous about freezing four severed fingers for an entire year before handing them out on Hallowe'en as trick-or-treats."

"Maybe they were already frozen," Mark suggested, "and whoever it was, just thought about the trick-or-treat bit at the last minute."

"Yes. but why freeze them in the first place?"

"I see what you mean."

"And then, there's the ghoulish fact that these fingers are not even from an adult hand, but from the hand of an eight year-old girl. A mere child."

"Yeah. You'd think if a kid that age had lost all her fingers, alive or dead, we'd have heard about it."

"That's just it, Mark. Maybe we *have* heard about it. Maybe we just haven't made the connection."

"Lieutenant." Mark spoke around a mouthful of salami. "Don't you think you're reaching just a little? You're saying that something might have happened, but you don't know *what*, last year at Hallowe'en, *maybe*, connected in some way with the severed fingers, *perhaps* — Jeeeeez! We don't even know who the victim is, much less the killer. That is, *if* there is a killer."

"The trouble with you, Mark, is you don't have a woman's intuition."

"I wonder why?" Mark muttered as he started in on his danish. The lieutenant reached for the telephone and dialed an inside line. "Garfield? This is — oh, you recognize my voice — "

Mark polished off the rest of his danish and his coffee as he listened to his senior partner clue in Garfield Leprohn (the *Leprechaun*, as he was known to his department cohorts) on the known details of the case. The Leprechaun had the dubious distinction of being the shortest policeman on the Metro Force, "or any other force," Mark had once suggested, "with the possible exception of Gravity." He went four-foot zilch in his sweat sox and, happily for the Leprechaun, he had been hired to head the Records Department on the strength of his data-gathering status, rather than his stature. Mark took a perverse pleasure in needling the little man at every opportunity.

"I suggested to him," the lieutenant said when she had hung up the phone, "that he start down in the 'morgue' at the *Metro Examiner*. If he draws a blank there, he's always got his own Data-Bank in Records to fall back on."

"Still playing your hunch?"

"What else have I got to play with?"

Mark looked wonderingly at his beautiful colleague and opened his mouth to respond, but didn't. There were times, he decided with some reluctance, that discretion really was the better part of valor, not to mention its amorous equivalent.

IT WAS NINETEEN MINUTES PAST FIVE O'CLOCK WHEN the Leprechaun put out a call for Lieutenant Carruthers. She and Mark were in the unmarked Chevy, heading back to H.Q. after a field check on Fisk and Mayhew. The voice of the girl in Dispatch crackled through the car radio.

"Message for Lieutenant Carruthers. Respond, please." The staccato buzz of the radio took over briefly.

"Carruthers here. Proceed."

"Lieutenant. The Lepre — uh, Corporal Leprohn has important information for you and requests your location."

"No need. We're on our way in. Instruct the Corporal to wait."

"Yes, Mam. Can you give me an E.T.A.?"

"Five minutes."

"Yes, Mam. Over and out."

When the lieutenant hung up the mike, Mark said, "It sounds like our Irish elf might have come up with something."

The lieutenant nodded speculatively. "I'm counting on it," she said.

The Leprechaun was at his desk in the Records Department when the lieutenant and Mark burst in on him. The little cop grinned up at them, delighted to once again be the center of attention. "Have a seat," he said, "I've got a story to tell."

"Just keep it pertinent and concise," the lieutenant said a little impatiently.

"He only tells short stories," Mark reassured her. "As a matter of fact — "

"Mark." The one word, quietly spoken, was enough to still her partner's wily wit as he hunkered down into his usual happy slouch with a wide-eyed look of innocence. The lieutenant then turned her own startling blue eyes on the Leprechaun. "Let's have it," she said.

"Well, you were right, lieutenant, about it being a Hallowe'en caper." The Leprechaun handed the lieutenant a number of photo-copy sheets from an open file on his desk. "These are copies of a story that broke in the morning edition of the *Huntsville Herald*, exactly one year ago today. I started with the Examiner, as you suggested, but drew a blank. I tried the Huntsville paper on a hunch, even though it *is* over the state line. There were follow-ups on the story, both in the Herald and on television, but I don't think we picked up much of it in Metro. But I am certain, lieutenant, that this story has some connection with the severed fingers that were handed out last night here in Metro as Hallowe'en treats."

"There's a lot of reading here, Garfield." The lieutenant flipped through the photo-copies. "Suppose you give us a brief summary."

The Leprechaun settled back with a see-who's-got-the-floor-now look at Mark, and after an annoying preemtive cough and a meaningfully bated pause, he began his story.

"On Hallowe'en," he said, "last year, eight year-old Cindy Crawford started out in Huntsville on her trick-or-treat rounds. It was about 6:30 P.M. and already dark. Cindy was dressed as "Mary" of Mary-Had-A-Little-Lamb fame, and her pint-sized poodle, Piddles, was dolled up as the lamb. Piddles was a *Heinz-57* variety purebred and Cindy had him on a leash. In the course of her rounds, Cindy was apparently lured, on some pretext that was never made totally clear, into a seldom-used lane by a couple of eager pubescent boys dressed as Pirates. One of the boys had a real sword as part of his costume, a souvenir his father had brought back from Nam, and when young Cindy resisted their less-than-honorable intentions (can you believe it, lieutenant, at that age?), the boys threatened to decapitate her 'little lamb' unless she became more cooperative."

The Leprechaun paused for a breath and for oratorical effect, which managed to evoke a stifled yawn from Mark and a weary sigh from the lieutenant.

"It was all a tasteless prank, of course, but it turned suddenly sour. The boys had no intention of actually harming the dog, but as the sword descended, and Cindy reached out unexpectedly to save her precious Piddles — well, the rest is history. The dog was released at the last moment and the sword struck the girl's outstretched hand, lopping it off at the wrist. Cindy passed out and the boys fled in disbelief and horror. The bottom line was: by the time Cindy was found, about two hours later, by a neighbor and his wife out walking their mutt, she had bled to death. The boys were ferreted out the next day and confessed readily. Because of their ages, however, they were given suspended sentences, which apparently sent Crawford, Cindy's father, into a public tirade. Cindy's mother had been killed in a traffic accident about eighteen months prior to the Hallowe'en tragedy and the little girl was all he had left in the world. It was a rough scene for the poor guy."

The lieutenant looked sadly into space and spoke slowly, softly, as though from memory,

"But when to mischief mortals bend their will,
How soon they find fit instruments of ill.

Alexander Pope said that at the turn of the eighteenth century, Mark," she said. "Things haven't really changed all that much, have they?"

The Leprechaun was fidgeting impatiently. "There's more to it, lieutenant. While we weren't able to establish an I.D. from the fingerprints sent to us by the Lab, we *did* learn that both Cindy and her father were engaged in a pottery making project just prior to her death."

"That could be all the identification we need, at this point, anyway."

"Maybe so, but here's the clincher. The neighbor who found the girl, sent his wife home to phone the police, then remained at the scene to wait for them. He was there when the police arrived."

"So?"

"So to this day, lieutenant, *they have never found that severed hand.*"

"Hmmm. And you're suggesting that maybe the neighbor took it?"

"I'm not suggesting anything, lieutenant. I'm merely pointing out that the only person who was alone with that girl, after the hand had been severed, was, in fact, the neighbor."

"Who in hell would want to steal a hand?" Mark said in disgust. "And why?"

"Why, indeed," the lieutenant said thoughtfully. "do you have an address on Crawford, Garfield?"

"Yes. And the neighbor, too." The Leprechaun scrawled both addresses on a sheet of canary-yellow and handed it across the desk. "And here's where it all starts to come together. Crawford, you'll notice, moved to Metro about six months ago and now lives on the south-west leg of that search pattern you've got mapped out on Mark's desk. The Crawford house is at the end of the street —"

The lieutenant got quickly to her feet. "I wish you had mentioned this earlier," she said with obvious concern, "Fisk and Mayhew should be half way down that street about now, and they could be heading into trouble. Get a back-up out there for them right away, Mark, and let them know we're on our way."

"You got it, lieutenant, but what makes you think there's any urgency about this? I mean, we still don't even know what happened to that hand —"

"Oh, come now, Mark. I think it's fairly obvious what must have happened to the hand. I'm surprised they didn't pick it up a year ago. Now get that back-up team out to the Crawford address, S.A.P., and tell them to keep out of sight and wait until we get there."

The Leprechaun looked both puzzled and frustrated. "You

mean you think Crawford took the hand?"

"No, Crawford didn't take it. There was no way he could have. Nevertheless, I'm fully convinced that it *did* come into his possession. And it's my guess, gentlemen, that he's still got it." The lieutenant sighed grimly. "Or what's left of it."

A FULL MOON HAD TURNED THE NIGHT INTO AN EERIE blend of silvered images and black velvet shadows. Mark flicked off the headlights before the unmarked Chevy made a slow turn at the corner, then ghosted to a stop at the curb where a vacant lot made a toothless gap in the row of houses. A black-and-white was parked a few yards ahead of them and Mark watched a towering shadow detach itself from the gloom and approach the Chevy.

"That can only be Too-Tall Bones," Mark observed, "either that or Fisk has managed to talk Mayhew into carrying her on his shoulders."

The lieutenant chuckled. As the black giant neared the car, she said, "It's Bones, all right. Run your window down, Mark."

Too-Tall Bones lowered his great head to the level of the open window. When he smiled, his teeth and eyes glowed florescently in the dark.

"Where's Fisk and Mayhew?" the lieutenant asked.

"They're in the next house, lieutenant. The one between the vacant lot and the one on the end. They haven't come out yet."

"How long have they been in there?"

"Better part of twenty minutes," Bones replied, "they were just going in when we got here. Want us to bring 'em out?"

"No." Mark could see the lieutenant shake her golden head by the light of the dash. "We'll wait."

"No need," Mark interjected, "there they are now. I think they've spotted us."

As the two officers approached the car, the lieutenant said to the tall black, "Who are you on with tonight, Bones?"

"Dave Madson, lieutenant. He's right here." Bones moved sufficiently to allow Madson's normal-sized head to appear behind his own. "And Mark," Bones added in a tired voice, "we've already been through the David-and-Goliath routine, so forget it."

The dashboard light did not do justice to Mark's thespian attempt at injured innocence. "Why do I suddenly feel like part of an unsung minority?" he muttered.

When Fisk and Mayhew had joined the group at the car, the lieutenant filled them in on the tragic story of Cindy Crawford.

"Wouldn't you know it," Fisk moaned. "That's the second time in as many days that we've been preempted by a break in the case, after putting in all the leg work."

"Would you rather have spent the day holding hands with the cadavers at Metro U?" Mayhew asked lightly.

"Scheee!" Fisk responded. "What kind of choice is that? Mayhew or the cadavers — ?"

The lieutenant climbed out of the car. "Can it, you two." To all five of them, as they gathered around her, she said, "This man Crawford is a psychopath and he may be dangerous, as much to himself as to any of us. I want him apprehended, unharmed. Remember, he's not so much a criminal as a victim."

"Don't worry, lieutenant," Too-Tall Bones rumbled, "we'll be gentle." Everyone, including the lieutenant, chuckled softly at the St. Bernard-like pathos of the big black.

"Lieutenant," Madson suddenly piped up, "how come there's six of us just to take one lousy looney?"

"That *looney*, as you call him, Madson, will be pretty well stretched out after hacking off his daughter's fingers to commemorate her untimely death at the hands of a couple of juvenile pirates. He's been licking his emotional wounds for twelve long months, and it's my guess he's just about ready to snap. I don't want anybody taking this guy too lightly. That clear?"

There was a low murmur of assent.

"Okay. Bones, you and Madson take the back of the house. Fisk and Mayhew, one of you on either side. I don't want him slipping out a window on us —"

"What if we're spotted?" Bones wondered.

"Don't be," the lieutenant cautioned tersely.

"No one's going to make you at night, Bones," Mark added, "just so long as you remember not to smile."

The big black's laugh was like a peel of quiet thunder. "There just ain't nothin' sicker'n hunky humor," he muttered as he faded into the surrounding shadows.

THE LIEUTENANT AND MARK WALKED SLOWLY DOWN to the front gate of the Crawford house, then stood waiting in the shadows until the others had taken up their positions.

"Wait here, Mark," the lieutenant whispered finally, "and stay out of sight. He'll be less likely to panic if he thinks I'm alone. Just keep me covered."

"You can count on it," Mark assured her.

The moon caught the lieutenant's fleeting smile. "I know I can," she said with feeling. A moment later, she was moving quickly toward the darkened front door of the house.

Mark watched the Lieutenant's dark shape climb the two short steps to the porch and rap heavily on the door. A porch light flicked on after a few tense seconds and a small dog began to yap-yap from somewhere within the house. When the door swung open, Mark could see a heavy, balding man in his middle years, standing behind the now sharply-defined silhouette of the Amazon. He heard her voice faintly, indistinctly, as she spoke to him. He saw her flash her badge.

Then all hell broke loose.

The man in the doorway appeared to turn, slowly, as though to move back into the house, but then, in the next instant, his body exploded into unexpected, violent motion. Mark saw the lieutenant's tall shadow suddenly double forward as the man's knotted fist plowed into her stomach. She let out a grunt of disbelief and pain. Then, before she could straighten, the same fist jerked back and pistoned forward again, this time smashing squarely into her unprotected face.

Mark was already on the move as the Amazon sagged back toward the edge of the porch, but as she fell, she reached out and caught the wrist behind that knotted fist in a vice-like grip. Mark was still thirty feet away when the Amazon hit the lawn. She landed heavily on her shoulders, the man hurtling toward her as he was drawn along by the impetus of her falling weight and her tenacious hold on his wrist. In the space of a split second, Mark saw the Amazon's long silken legs fold in under the plummeting body of the man, then snap violently upward with the force and fluidity of twin hydraulic rams.

Mark jerked to a stop as Crawford went rocketing into space, and he regretted later, that he had been too preoccupied at the time, to fully appreciate that superb launching pad. He was left with only the briefest recollection of those long, sinewy, shimmering thighs and the don't-blink-or-you'll-miss-it flash of white panties, in the talismanic light of a friendly moon.

The blurred and violent impact of Crawford hurtling squarely into his arms, cut off any further voyeuristic delights for Mark. When he had recovered sufficiently from the impact, the lieutenant was snapping the cuffs on a dazed and unresisting Crawford.

OFFICER FISK STOOD IN THE DOORWAY OF LIEUTENANT Carruthers' office, her soft brown eyes moist with concern. Mayhew's handsome face looked in over her shoulder.

"I'm really sorry about that belt in the eye you took, lieutenant," the young brunette rookie said feelingly.

"Thanks for the sympathy," the lieutenant replied, then added candidly, "but it was the eye in my belt buckle, along with that first punch that did the most damage."

The lieutenant looked for all the world like a movie star holding a press conference, Mark thought as he watched her closely from his usual slouching roost, her beautiful face even more inscrutable behind a pair of dark glasses.

"I've got a St. John's Ambulance ticket, lieutenant," Mayhew said glibly, "if I could be of any —"

A dark threatening glance from Mark and a sharp dig in the ribs from Fisk, cut short Mayhew's less-than-honorable mission of mercy. He flushed uneasily and drifted back out of sight.

"If you're feeling up to it, lieutenant," Fisk interjected quickly, "there's one thing about that Crawford case that still puzzles me."

"And that is?"

"Well, we all know that the guy confessed to having the girl's missing hand, and to *ugh* cutting off the fingers to hand out as Hallowe'en treats, but I still don't know how he came into possession of the hand in the first place."

"I'm surprised you haven't figured that one out," the lieutenant told her. "It was delivered to him the next morning by Cindy's constant and faithful companion, Piddles."

"The dog?"

"Or, Mary's Little Lamb, if you prefer."

"But why would a dog — ?"

"The dog, I'm sure, did not fully appreciate the horror of the situation, although I have little doubt that it knew something was terribly wrong. Cindy, after all, had obviously been hurt. I strongly suspect that Piddles picked up the hand and took it home in an instinctive attempt to summon help. Where the dog hid it then, until Crawford took it from him the following morning, is anybody's guess."

"But then why, in Heaven's name, would he keep the horrible thing for a whole year, then hack it up and hand it out to the trick-or-treaters on Hallowe'en?"

The lieutenant winced as she settled back in her chair. She pressed an immaculately manicured hand gingerly to her stomach. "The hand, remember, was all he had left of his little girl. It was not a 'horrible thing' to him. Still, he wasn't quite sure what to do with it, so he froze it in his home freezer to keep it from spoiling until he was able to make a decision. And that, of course, is where we found what was left of it, last night. I imagine he had thoughts, at first, of digging a private little grave, a memorial, of sorts, to the memory of one who had so suddenly, so tragically been taken from him. This, you'll recall, was his second great loss in the space of eighteen months. Little wonder he finally flipped."

"Then why the mutilations, lieutenant? That just does not seem consistent with the picture you've been painting of unbearable grief."

The lieutenant sighed. "It was the hand, you see, that kept the memory of that night alive and vivid in his mind. His grief had not been given the chance to subside in the natural healing processes of time. When Hallowe'en came around for the second time, it was just too much for him. He had been nurturing and wallowing in this horror for a year, and he wanted some kind of revenge. He wanted to jar the minds and souls of those 'juvenile killers' (his words) with the magnitude of the thing they had done. That he was now living in a different area was of no consequence. The trick-or-treaters everywhere were, in his eyes, all of a kind."

"Fisk." It was Mayhew's voice, calling from the outer room. "You coming, or not?"

"I think Helpful-Harry is getting impatient," the lieutenant said with some amusement.

Officer Fisk flushed prettily. "He's not really like that, lieutenant," she said defensively. "He's — well, he's a helluva partner."

"I'm very much aware of his abilities, Fisk, and yours as well. That's possibly why you find yourselves so frequently on our team."

Fisk beamed. "Well," she stammered, looking pleasantly embarrassed, "duty calls." She left quickly.

NOW THAT THEY WERE ALONE, THE LIEUTENANT EASED the dark glasses off to reveal a deep purple mouse where her beautiful right eye should have been. "I'm surprised you haven't made some smart-ass remark about this shiner, Mark, or the belt-buckle bruise on my — my abdomen."

"Well, I've seen the shiner, lieutenant, and frankly, it just don't look very funny —"

The lieutenant's one good eye reflected her mute gratitude at his concern.

" — but I haven't yet seen the belt-buckle bruise."

"And you're not likely to. But I can assure you, it isn't very funny either."

"You weren't so wrapped up in false modesty last night," Mark reminded her with a secret smile.

The lieutenant chuckled. "For a moment there, I wasn't wrapped up in much of anything, was I?" She added thoughtfully, "Maybe I should start wearing pant suits."

"Oh, come now," Mark said quickly. "Let's not over-react. I'm sure I can adjust to an occasional lapse of modesty — if I put my mind to it."

Cathy Carruthers had replaced her dark glasses and he could not see her eyes when she replied.

"I'm sure you can."

MEL D. AMES

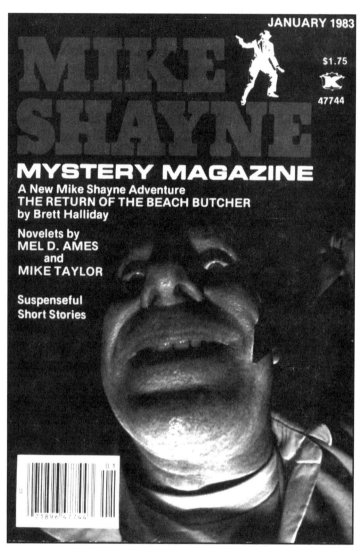

JANUARY 1983

$1.75

47744

MIKE SHAYNE

MYSTERY MAGAZINE

A New Mike Shayne Adventure
THE RETURN OF THE BEACH BUTCHER
by Brett Halliday

Novelets by
MEL D. AMES
and
MIKE TAYLOR

**Suspenseful
Short Stories**

On the floor between the bed and the window were two people. Their eyes were closed, their features were composed and peaceful. They seemed to be sleeping, but their bodies were as cold as carrion!

the happy-new-year murders

AN UNEASY QUIET HAD SETTLED LIKE A PALL OVER the first dark hours of the New Year. The maudlin strains of *Auld Lang Syne* had long since faded into the night and the old house had grown as cold and as silent as a tomb.

Upstairs, in the master bedroom, Brenda Weise woke with a premonition of death. Something was terribly wrong. She was alone in her bed, but that, in itself, did not alarm her. Hans had recently taken to sleeping on a mattress on the floor beside her bed, to be close at hand if she needed him, yet not to disturb her fitful slumbers.

They had already resigned themselves to her dying, she thought bitterly, and she had begun to sense a growing impatience in them as she clung tenaciously from day to day, to the thin remaining thread of her life. She turned with a twinge of pain to peer apprehensively over the side of the bed. She could see his face, impassive and pale in the half light. He was stretched out on his back, and in the crook of his arm, with her auburn curls spread out over his pajama-top, their five year-old daughter, Linda, was cuddled close against him.

She frowned, gazing down at them. And with some grim maternal insight, perhaps, and a slow dawning of horror, she became acutely certain that she was then no longer among the living. *Either she, herself, or (God forbid) the man and the child on the floor beside her, was dead.* And then, as though to preclude all ambiguity, a mortal moan escaped her own trembling lips.

THE STREETS OF METRO WERE UNCOMMONLY QUIET as Detective-Lieutenant Cathy Carruthers and her inseparable side-kick, Detective-Sergeant Mark Swanson, headed toward the Weise home in the early morning hours of January 1st.

"A brand new year," the lieutenant said brightly, "and almost no one out to greet it."

"Most people did their Happy-New-Year-ing last night," Mark replied, with a bleary-eyed glance at his beautiful, wide-awake companion. "They're all toes-up now, sleeping it off."

"More's the pity," the lieutenant said reprovingly. "So, what did *you* do last night?"

"Well —" Mark braked the unmarked Chevy to an idling stop at an intersection. "To tell you the truth, lieutenant, after I left you at the Precinct, I drove down to Slater Street on the East Side, picked up one of those sexy car-hoppers, a big, beautiful, bra-less blonde with a short skirt and willing ways, and we spent the night at my place with a bottle of Southern Comfort, making passionate love —"

Cathy Carruthers laughed. "Sounds like fantasy time to me." The light changed and the car began to move ahead. "Tell me, Mark, what did you really do?"

Mark sighed ruefully. "I had a quiet evening in front of the tube with two old friends, Johnny Walker and Guy Lombardo. I fell asleep before everybody started kissing everyone else's wife in Times Square."

"Now that, I can believe," the lieutenant said with mock accord, "but I do think you should do something, Mark, about that subconscious predilection you apparently have for blondes, booze, and depravity in general."

"I'm working on it," Mark grinned, "but I'm having trouble getting past the blondes."

THE CHEVY SWERVED INTO A SIDE STREET LINED

with wide boulevards and ten-foot hedges, typical of the area, then pulled over and stopped in front of a pair of towering iron gates. Mark touched the horn.

A man emerged from the gatehouse that sat back and a little to one side of the entrance. He was unordinarily large, a hulking brute of a man, and the face he pressed against the vertical iron bars of the gate would have curdled the milk in the breast of a pregnant witch.

"Watcha want?"

Mark flipped his badge at the man without getting out of the car. "Police," he said, "open up."

The face drew back and the gates opened moments later with squeals of protest from rust-encrusted hinges. "There are more police vehicles on the way," Mark said to the man as he drew abreast of him, "might as well leave it open."

"You do your job," the surly gatekeeper grunted, "and I'll do mine."

"Suit yourself, Igor." Mark flashed the man an irritating smile and headed the car up the long, gravel driveway.

"You certainly have a way with people," the lieutenant chuckled. She inspected her beautiful face in the mirror of a small compact. "What have we got on this case, Mark, other than it being a double homicide?"

"Not much," Mark said as he rounded a curve in the driveway and the huge, rambling, tudor-styled house suddenly loomed before them. "Father and daughter. The daughter's apparently only five years-old."

"Sad. Any suspects?"

"Sure. Plenty. But that's not the problem."

"Oh?"

"There's not a mark on either one of them, lieutenant, to indicate how they might have died."

"So? That's a job for the coroner," the lieutenant replied indifferently. "Besides, if they *are dead, something* must have killed them."

"Yeah, well — the guy who phoned it in, a Stanley Dunlop, said there were three people sleeping in the same room. Mother, father, and daughter. The mother was the only one who woke up this morning. And, oddly, she was the one who wasn't supposed to."

"May I ask why?"

"She's terminally ill with cancer, lieutenant. She's been on borrowed time for the past month."

The car ground to a gravelly halt and the lieutenant alighted quickly. "Mark, get on the radio and request a couple of special uniforms." She had turned, and her golden head was suddenly, beautifully framed in the open window. "Bones and Madson, if they're available. I want a man on the gate and that refugee from a horror movie brought up to the house. We may want to question him."

"Ah, yeth," Mark responded, mimicking the sinister Karloff lisp. "Who knowth what evil lurkth in the heartth of ugly gatekeeperth —"

"That's a good Shirley Temple, Mark," the lieutenant called back as she took off toward the house. "Can you do Boris Karloff?"

MARK WATCHED HIS SENIOR PARTNER CLIMB THE few short steps to the front entrance with mixed feelings. She was still the same Cathy Carruthers he had teamed up with more than a year ago, and their light-hearted gibes were nothing more than a verbal facade to cover the deep respect and affection that had grown between them. But, to those with whom she worked, she was also *The Amazon*. Not just in light of her magnificent, six-foot, honey-haired physique, but for her frequent manifestations of such uncanny strength and prowess, that she seemed literally to transcend all restraints of mortal blood and muscle.

Mark had long since given up trying to penetrate the legendary mystique of the Amazon; he had learned, instead, to be content just to accept and enjoy Cathy Carruthers, the beautiful earthling.

The lieutenant was standing in the lower hall at the foot of the wide, central staircase when Mark caught up with her. She was in conversation with a thin, gray-haired woman, a private nurse, Mark guessed, from the way she was dressed.

"Ah, there you are, Mark. We've been waiting for you."

Mark was conscious of a claustrophobic closeness in the rich decor of the old house. He was almost totally surrounded by dark, polished paneling and heavy floor-to-ceiling tapestries, and, conversely, the staircase that wound up to the second floor looked

MEL D. AMES

wide enough to be an off-ramp on the Metro Central freeway.

"Bones and Madson are on their way," he told the lieutenant.

"Good. Mark, this is Elly McBain, Brenda Weise's private nurse." The woman was visibly distraught. "She's going to take us up to the room where the deaths occurred."

"I put Mrs. Weise into another room, poor dear," Elly McBain told them as they climbed the stairs, "what an awful shock it was and all."

"You were the one who found the bodies then?"

"Well, not exactly. I heard Mrs. Weise crying, and choking, and carryin' on somethin' terrible, from where I slept in the room next to hers. Just at daybreak it was. And she was knowin' they was dead, poor dear. She knew before I even got to them. Cold and stiff as a line of winter wash they was, frozen rigid, just the way they was layin' there."

The gray old nurse hesitated at the door that opened off the upper hall. "They're in there," she said, standing back. She was obviously reluctant to enter the room.

"We'll take it from here, Miss McBain." The lieutenant opened the door and stepped into a room that was cloaked in semi-darkness. "Let's get some light in here, Mark."

Mark moved quickly to the window and a moment later, as the heavy drapes flew apart, the blinding light of day flooded into the room.

THE LARGE DOUBLE BED THAT DOMINATED THE ROOM was empty now, but on the floor, between the bed and the window, the bodies of Hans Weise and his daughter, Linda, lay silently entwined. They looked to be sleeping. Their eyes were closed, their features peaceful and composed. There was no sign of violence. No blood.

The lieutenant stooped over the bodies and touched their ashen temples with a red-tipped finger. "Hmmm," she mused. "Cold as carrion. They must have died shortly after midnight."

"Any idea what killed them?" Mark asked.

"Not really, but there is a skin discoloration that could suggest asphyxiation."

"Like a pillow held over the head?"

"Something like that, but yet, it's inconsistent with the total lack of any sign of struggle. People don't just lay there and allow themselves to be smothered, now do they?"

"Maybe it was something they ate, or drank," Mark suggested. "Poison of some kind."

"But again, Mark, one would think there would be some sign of pain or discomfort on their faces. These two look as though they quietly passed away in their sleep. It looks to me more like carbon monoxide poisoning — a gentle, painless death."

"Like from the exhaust of a car?"

"Yes. But if the girl and her father did die from CO fumes, how come the mother is still alive?"

"Well, the victims are close to the floor," Mark said thoughtfully, "would that have any bearing?"

"I think not, Mark. Carbon monoxide, if released in here, would quickly permeate the entire room."

"Maybe the M.E. will be able to shed some light on it," Mark said hopefully.

"I certainly hope so."

The lieutenant's vivid blue eyes surveyed the room with cold deliberation. A small, white, almost imperceptible stain caught her notice, just below the lip of the window sill. "Mark, see if you can get a sample of that white stuff down there. Have you got an envelope?"

"Yeah." Mark knelt over the stain and began to scrape at the surface of the carpet with his penknife. "Seems almost moist," he said.

The lieutenant had now lifted her attentive gaze to the window. It was closed but not locked; her fingers freely rotated the open crescent catch. Then, on the exterior surface of the lower pane, she could clearly see a small grouping of finger smudges.

"Miss McBain," the lieutenant called over her shoulder, "who would be responsible for the cleaning of these windows?"

The nurse stood nervously in the open doorway, unwilling, it seemed, to move in beyond the threshold. "Well, I'm not exactly responsible for them, lieutenant, but I do the windows in here."

"Can you recall when you last cleaned them?"

"Why — why, yesterday. Late yesterday afternoon. I do them several times a week. It's the poor dear's only look at the world, lieutenant — "

"I understand, Miss McBain." The lieutenant joined her at the door. "Did you clean both sides of the windows? Outside, as well as in?"

"Yes. Yes, I did."

"You're certain of that?"

"Yes."

"All right, Miss McBain. You may go. There will be more policemen arriving shortly. Perhaps you would be kind enough to direct them up here, to this room."

"Yes, mam."

AS THE NURSE'S FRAGILE PRESENCE LEFT THE OPEN frame of the doorway, another taller, more voluptuous figure took its place. An attractive, full-bodied girl in her mid-twenties studied the lieutenant with open hostility. "Just *who* in *hell*," she said, "are *you*?" Her blonde hair fell to her shoulders and she stood with arms akimbo, looking fit and trim in snug-fitting jeans and a white tailored shirt-blouse.

"My name is Cathy Carruthers," the lieutenant said with an officious smile. "Detective-Lieutenant, to be precise, Metro Central, Eleventh Precinct, Homicide." She flashed her badge. "Now, may I ask, who in the hell are *you*?"

The young woman was somewhat taken aback. "I — I'm Marilyn," she stammered. "Marilyn Dunlop. Brenda Weise is my mother. I — I didn't realize that you were a policeman — I mean — "

"I know what you mean." The lieutenant softened her tone in an attempt to take the edge off their conversation. "Dunlop is your married name?"

"No. I'm not married. Heaven bloody forbid. I'm Brenda Weise's daughter from her first marriage. She only married Hans about six years ago, eight bloody months after my father died. Would you believe it? Linda, thank God, is their only child."

"When did you learn about the death of your step-father, and

147

Linda?" the lieutenant asked.

"Elly woke everyone up when she found them. I helped her move mother to another room while Stanley phoned the police."

"Stanley?"

"That's my brother. Stanley Dunlop. He went back to his room to get dressed. That's if Denise lets him out of bed long enough to get his bloody pants on."

"Uh-hu." The lieutenant drew a patient breath. "And who might Denise be?"

"Stanley's ever-lovin', lieutenant. She steered him to the marriage waterbed about nine months ago, then threw out the anchor. They've hardly touched dry land since, except for an occasional midnight sally to stock up on booze and bloody band-aides."

"Hmm, yes, well — " The lieutenant cast a wondering look in Mark's direction. Mark seemed to have found something amusing in the stain on the carpet. "Is there anyone else in the house, Miss Dunlop, other than your brother and his wife, (yourself, of course), and your mother's nurse?"

"That's the whole Dunlop-Weise menage, lieutenant — or should I call you Cathy?"

"And the gatekeeper," the lieutenant added, ignoring the girl's flippancy.

"Oh, yeah." Marilyn Dunlop smiled indulgently. "Gunga Din."

"Gunga Din? That's his name?"

"His name is Gunther Dinsley. Everyone calls him Gunga Din. He's not too bright, you know." She made a wry face. "A bit of a — duh."

"Then why do you keep him around?"

"He's loyal," she said simply.

Officer Madson's face suddenly appeared over the girl's shoulder. "Lieutenant?"

"Yes, officer."

"That guy you're talking about — that freak at the gate?"

"Well?"

"He's refusing to come up to the house."

"That so? And you've come for reinforcements?"

"No, mam — Too Tall Bones is with him now. He just wanted

your permission to use, uh — necessary force."

The lieutenant chuckled. She had little doubt that Too Tall Bones could handle the hulking gatekeeper, but she shared the big black's obvious concern that it could prove to be a little messy.

"Tell officer Bones to wait until I get there," the lieutenant told Madson. "I shouldn't be too much longer here."

AS MADSON LEFT, THE OTHER POLICE CREWS BEGAN to arrive in force. Marilyn Dunlop was obliged to retreat into the hall.

"Perhaps you could get your brother and his wife to meet me downstairs in the living room," the lieutenant told the blonde girl. "I would like to ask them both a few questions."

"Whatever you say, Cathy." Marilyn Dunlop smiled disarmingly. "I'll see if I can catch them between tussles."

The lieutenant smiled in spite of herself as the girl moved off down the hall, then turned in time to see Elly McBain coming out of a door directly across from the death room. "Is that where you've put Brenda Weise?" the lieutenant asked.

"Yes, Mam." The nurse closed the door softly on the darkened room. "We've kept the poor dear heavily sedated for weeks now," she said in a hushed whisper, "but all this has upset her so."

"Is she asleep now?"

"Yes."

"Well," the lieutenant pursed her lovely lips. "We'll let her be for the time being."

Mark appeared at her elbow. "The lab crew kicked me out," he laughed. "They said I should stick to my own job, like being a snoop."

"Did you give them the sample?"

"No. They took it."

The lieutenant began to descend the stairs and Mark followed. "What now?" he asked.

"I think I'd better check on Gunga Din."

"That hulk at the gate? Too Tall can handle him," Mark told her.

"I don't doubt it, Mark, but that big ape is apparently lurching around on square wheels, and I don't want him hurt."

"I'll go with you," Marilyn Dunlop said from behind them. "He'll do what I tell him. Anyway, Sodom and Gomorrah won't be down for a little while yet. They're in the shower. Together."

The lieutenant laughed. "Be my guest," she said, then, turning to Mark, "Check in on Brenda Weise while I'm gone, Mark. If she should wake up, I'd like to know if she saw or heard anything unusual during the night."

"You got it, lieutenant."

As Mark left them, Marilyn Dunlop said, "Do all your stooges acquiesce with such lap-dog humility?"

"Don't confuse cooperation with weakness, Miss Dunlop," the lieutenant told her quietly. "The biggest mistake of your life would be to mis-judge that man you just called a stooge."

THEY WERE IN SIGHT OF THE GATEHOUSE, WALKING side by side across the expansive grounds, when Marilyn Dunlop suddenly staggered and fell, her left foot firmly wedged in a gopher hole. The lieutenant bent over her and attempted to free the trapped foot, but the blonde girl cringed away from her with a cry of pain. Then, from the vicinity of the gatehouse, there was a sudden, guttural roar of anger. The lieutenant looked up to see Gunga Din bearing down on her in an obvious rage.

"Run, Cathy!" the girl cried out. "*Run!* He thinks you're hurting me."

In the background, behind the advancing giant, the lieutenant could see Too Tall Bones scrambling out of the patrol car. "Come back here, you hunky horror," he thundered. But he was too far back to enforce the command.

The lieutenant came out of her crouch in an effort to side-step the ugly gatekeeper's first onslaught, but the blonde girl, in trying to take the painful pressure off her ankle, shifted the position of her trapped leg. The unexpected movement was enough to trip the lieutenant and send her sprawling into the flying ham-like fists of Gunga Din.

The Amazon was momentarily helpless. She felt a row of hairy knuckles slam into the side of her mouth, snapping her head to one side, hair flying; and a split second later, a club-like fist plowed brutally into her lower abdomen. Pain and nausea exploded through her body, and she seemed to just hang there, like a broken Barbie

Doll, half way to the ground, as though not yet willing to give in to the dizzying, inescapable tug of gravity. Then a giant fist grabbed a handful of her honey-colored hair and drew her into a suffocating, rib-crushing bear-hug.

"Gunther! Let her go!" Marilyn Dunlop's frantic cries fell on ears that were deaf to anything but that all-consuming rage, and Too Tall Bones was still fifty feet away from being able to lend assistance.

But the slow tightening of Gunga Din's vice-like embrace seemed to suddenly clear the Amazon's pain-fogged brain. She shook her golden head, and found herself looking squarely into the crazed and rheumy eyes of her assailant, her face just inches from his foul, rasping mouth. Her arms were pinned to her sides, her body crushed against him, her long legs dangling clear of the ground.

"Let her go! *Gun-ther!* Don't you bloody hear me? *Let her go!*"

The Amazon heard the girl's futile pleading as she now reached within herself, to draw upon that awesome power that lurked like a sleeping giant beneath the pulchritudinous surface of her body. She let out a cry that resembled the squall of a wounded beast, and Too Tall Bones stopped dead in his tracks. He watched in amazement as the Amazon's imprisoned body suddenly coiled and flexed, and two nylon-clad knees shot up with pile-driving force into the unsuspecting gatekeeper's groin. A terrible roar of pain and anger blared out of the big brute's mouth and his grip loosened abruptly.

Then, as she regained her feet, and her balance, the Amazon swung into action. With extended knuckles, Karate fashion, she leveled a stunning blow to the man's throat, and then another, in rapid combination, to the temple. The big man's knees buckled, but before he could fall, she had one hand at his collar, the other at his waist, and had jerked him clear off the ground. Her superb body seemed to contort like a steel spring as she sent him hurtling into the arms of a speechless Too Tall Bones.

"Chain him up to something," the Amazon said as she wiped a trickle of blood from the corner of her mouth, "before he really hurts someone."

Too Tall Bones cuffed the dazed gatekeeper and led him limping toward the house. "I just wouldn't never believe it," the big black mumbled as he passed the two women, "if I hadn't seen it with my own two eyes. And what's more," he turned to look back at the Amazon, "I still don't."

Marilyn Dunlop laughed nervously. "I know how he bloody feels," she said. "Wow! You don't mess around, do you, Cathy?"

Cathy Carruthers blushed with the ingenuousness of a school girl. "I think we'd better get you back to the house," she said. "If the M.E.'s still there, he can take a look at that ankle."

"Yes, mam," the girl said with a note of new respect. And she leaned heavily on the lieutenant as they turned and began to hobble painfully after the two men.

STANLEY DUNLOP AND HIS WIFE, DENISE, WERE standing at the door to the living room when the two women re-entered the house. Mark had just descended the wide staircase.

"What happened?" he said with quick concern, seeing the lieutenant's disheveled appearance and the smudge of blood at the corner of her mouth.

"Gunga Din got a little too friendly," Marilyn Dunlop told him. "Like I said, he's a little — you know." She rotated a finger around one ear.

Mark ignored the girl. "You all right?" he said to the lieutenant.

"I'll live." She gave him a crooked smile. Her upper lip was already beginning to swell. "Is the M.E. still here?"

When Mark nodded that he was, she said, "Don't let him leave without seeing me." Then as the group moved out of the hall, Mark went back up the stairs to the second floor. Too Tall Bones, Gunga Din, and Elly McBain were already in the living room, waiting.

"Well, lieutenant, got it all figured out?"

The man who spoke could not have been anyone other than Stanley Dunlop. He was a clean-cut, darkly handsome man of about thirty. The woman who stood close at his side, holding his hand, was so much like him she could have passed for his younger sister. She had raven hair and smoldering blue eyes, a striking combination, and she seemed very much aware of her slender, elfin body. The way she was dressed, it looked as though she had just painted on a short, powder-blue skirt and a matching blouse, without feeling the need for either a primer or a second coat.

"You, then, are Stanley Dunlop," the lieutenant said.

"Yes. And this is my wife, Denise."

The lieutenant drew herself up to her full, impressive height and looked searchingly from one to the other of the small gathering. "I must confess," she said with slow deliberation, "I'm not a little surprised at the apparent lack of grief, or even concern, in a family that has just been dealt a double tragedy."

"Well —" Stanley Dunlop shrugged his shoulders. "The girl's death is a tragedy, of course, but Hans Weise is no great loss, lieutenant."

"Amen," added Marilyn Dunlop.

"I find that rather callous," the lieutenant admonished the blonde girl. "However, our investigation will proceed. Sergeant Swanson and officer Bones will be taking statements from each of you. You will then be finger-printed and asked to remain on the premises until I specifically, and personally, give the release order."

"And when will that be?" Stanley Dunlop wanted to know.

"When we find out how two people out of three, in one room, mysteriously died during the night from no apparent cause, and who (if anyone) was responsible."

"What about my job?" Marilyn Dunlop limped over to a vacant chair and sat down with a low moan. "I'm not like these other free-loaders, you know. I've got to bloody work for a living."

"Where do you work?"

"M.R. & P.," the girl replied. "Metro Reefers and Packers. They'll be expecting me to show up tomorrow."

"I think you'd better call in sick," the lieutenant suggested. "You've got good reason with that ankle. And how about you, Mr. Dunlop? What do you do?"

"Nothing," Marilyn answered for him, "outside of the bloody bedroom, that is."

Denise Dunlop responded with a demure smile. "My, doesn't jealousy go well with your nasty nature, Marilyn dear?" she said sweetly.

Stanley Dunlop quickly interceded. "I manage my mother's estate, lieutenant. Our father, Marilyn's and mine — Oliver J. Dunlop — left a rather elaborate portfolio of financial holdings.

Mother seems to feel that it was more in keeping with father's wishes that I, a Dunlop, handle the purse strings, rather than her — her paramour."

"You refer, of course, to Hans Weise."

"Of course."

"Was there any resentment on the part of Mr. Weise?"

"Uh-hu," he reflected, with the hint of a smirk, "you could say that."

"Did you ever argue about it?"

"Constantly. But never in front of mother — "

"You wanted to see me, lieutenant?" A relatively short man with a balding pate stood in the doorway. He was carrying a black medical bag.

"Oh, Sam," the lieutenant called to him. "May I have a word with you?" She steered the usually grumpy M.E. to the far side of the room, out of earshot of the others. "Have you got anything yet that I should know about?"

"Sure. Two dead, one dying."

"Sam, be serious."

"Two dead, one dying isn't serious?"

The lieutenant attempted a thin smile.

"What happened to your lip?" the M.E. asked with a concern that surprised her.

"Somebody didn't like my face, I guess."

"They must have been blind or crazy. Want me to treat it?"

"I'd rather be treated to a couple of straight answers."

"Shoot."

"What killed them?"

"I don't know."

"Guess."

"Well, if all three had died, my first guess would have been CO poisoning, carbon monoxide. As it is, I just don't know. You'll have to wait until I get them on the table."

"Time of death?"

"Shortly after midnight, give or take a little."

"You're being unusually cooperative, Sam."

"Yeah. It's that thick lip. It looks like you're leering at me." He turned to leave. "I just got carried away for a minute."

THE LIEUTENANT DIRECTED HIM OVER TO WHERE Marilyn Dunlop was sitting nursing her ankle. "This is Dr. Morton, Miss Dunlop, would you like him to take a look at that leg?"

"Sure. As long as he confines his looking to below the knee."

"Relax, young lady." The chunky coroner was suddenly his usual, ill-humored self. "To interest me, the first thing you'd have to be, is dead."

The blonde girl grinned and held her leg out to him, but she yelped with pain a moment later as he began to examine the already swelling ankle. A low, menacing growl rumbled out of the throat of Gunga Din.

"I hope you've got a leash on that brute," the M.E. said, looking warily at Too Tall Bones.

The big black laughed. "Don't worry, Doc. His bark's worse'n his bite."

"That's easy for you to say," the lieutenant complained with a bit of a lisp.

Mark came into the room then, and drew his partner to one side. "I managed to have a few words with Brenda Weise. That's sure one sick lady."

"Did you ask her — ?"

"Yeah. She doesn't remember a thing, lieutenant, Just woke up and found them dead."

"She's kept pretty heavily sedated, Mark. I wonder what made her wake up when she did?"

"I asked her that. She said she felt cold."

The lieutenant turned to Sam Morton who had just finished taping the girl's ankle. Don't you think Mrs. Weise would be better off in a hospital somewhere?"

"Absolutely."

"She won't go," Marilyn Dunlop interjected. "Says she wants to die in her own bed."

"How long do you think she has?" the lieutenant asked the coroner.

"Twenty-four hours, at the outside."

Marilyn Dunlop stood up and tested her weight on the bandaged ankle. "That's what they said four weeks ago."

Sam Morton shrugged indifferently. "Want me to treat that lip now?" he asked the lieutenant.

"How, for Pete's sake?"

"He'll probably try to talk you into mouth-to-mouth resusci-bloody-tation," Marilyn Dunlop suggested dryly. "You can't trust a guy who'd rather cavort with a cadaver than a real live doll."

The M.E. picked up his bag and headed for the door. "This just isn't my day," he muttered.

The lieutenant laughed. "Call me when you come up with something, Sam." To Mark, she said, "Let's get things narrowed down. We don't seem to be any closer to an answer now than when we started."

"What'll I do with our heavy breathing friend, lieutenant?" Too Tall Bones wanted to know.

Cathy Carruthers ran the tip of her tongue over her fat lip as she looked at the hulking gatekeeper. "You can take the cuffs off, Bones, but keep your eye on him." She regarded Marilyn Dunlop thoughtfully. "I don't imagine he'll wander very far."

The blonde girl lowered her gaze, then hobbled over to where Gunga Din stood rubbing his wrists. "I'll be responsible for him," she said. "He just needs someone who cares."

"He could also use a collar, a distemper shot," Too Tall Bones rumbled, "and a very short chain."

IT WAS LATE THE FOLLOWING MORNING BEFORE Lieutenant Cathy Carruthers received the promised call from the coroner. She was in her office at Metro Central's Eleventh Precinct when the call came through. Mark Swanson was slouched comfortably in a captain's chair, facing the lieutenant's desk.

"Carruthers."

Mark watched his senior partner's beautiful face register, in quick succession: relief, hope, doubt and disappointment, in that order. "That's all you can tell me, Sam? On both of them?" The lieutenant gave Mark a look of helpless despair. The tip of her pink tongue toyed with her swollen upper lip as she listened. "Okay, Sam," she said finally. "I know you did your best. Yes, the lip is just fine. You, too."

"What, what?" Mark enquired anxiously as she returned the phone to its cradle.

"He says they died of suffocation. That's it, Mark. Suffocation, No marks, no bruises, no blood, no nothing. Their deaths, he says, are a direct result of a sustained lack of oxygen."

"But how — ?" Mark's puzzled features seemed to make the words superfluous.

"He has no more idea than we do."

"Sonofagun," Mark muttered. "Talk about your dead ends."

"Mark." The lieutenant leaned back in her chair in a thoughtful pose. "Get Leprohn up here right away."

"I talked to him half an hour ago," Mark replied. "He said he didn't have a full report yet."

"I want him here now," she said quietly but firmly. "And pick up the Lab report on your way, whether it's ready or not."

Mark knew better than to question the merits of her request. He'd seen her go into this thoughtful stance before, when faced with what she intriguingly refers to as a "puzzler." The solution to the double, New-Year's-Eve murders, Mark decided as he left the office, was on its way to being history.

CORPORAL GARFIELD LEPROHN, METRO CENTRAL'S shortest police officer, stood four-foot zip in his b.v.d.'s, and a dizzying four-foot four in his Elevators. His prowess in data gathering was fast becoming legendary at the Eleventh Precinct, but, for all his success, he could not escape that infamous epithet, *The Leprechaun*, as he was ungraciously referred to by his colleagues. Mark Swanson took a special, perverse delight in irritating the little cop at every opportunity.

When Mark re-entered Lieutenant Carruthers' office with the Leprechaun in tow, he stuck his head in first and did a credible imitation of Tatoo's opening line in the TV series, Fantasy Island.

"The plane, the plane!" he intoned with spiteful glee.

The Leprechaun was not amused. He stormed in under Mark's outstretched arm and stood red-faced in front of the lieutenant's desk. "To complain about your partner's childish behavior, lieutenant, would be to give it a dignity it does not deserve. Instead," he postured, with a withering look at Mark, "I simply choose to ignore it."

The lieutenant was doing her best to hide her own amusement by feigning discomfort with her swollen lip. "Were you able to complete the file, Garfield?"

"Yes, lieutenant. Except for a few loose ends that aren't really all that important."

"Good. And Mark, how about the Lab file?"

Mark handed the brown manilla folder across the desk. "In a nutshell, lieutenant, the fingerprints on the outside of the window belong to Gunga Din. And that white stain on the carpet is some kind of alcohol residue. They're still doing tests on it."

"Alcohol? A spilled drink, perhaps?"

"Search me," Mark shrugged, "but what's more important is the fact that Gunga Din was definitely at that window some time during the night. And by the way, lieutenant, there's a small balcony outside the window, with no fire escape and a second-story drop (I checked it out), and there's also an old elm with an overhanging limb that comes within half a dozen feet of the balcony."

"Hmm. It's beginning to look bad for Gunga Din. But what was he doing out there, I wonder? And if he did kill Weise and the child, how? And why?"

"Maybe I can shed some light on it, lieutenant," the Leprechaun chimed in. "Gunther Dinsley has only worked for the Weises (Dunlops?) for a few months. About two years ago, he was caretaker and off-season watchman at a Summer Camp that was owned and operated jointly by three private schools for girls. He was something of a conversation piece, needless to say, with both students and faculty, but they considered him harmless enough, until he was caught peeking in the girls' dormitory windows one night, just before lights out. He was severely admonished, of course, but when he was caught doing the same thing a week later, he was charged and institutionalized."

"You mean they sent him to the Funny Farm?" Mark interjected.

"That is precisely what I mean," the Leprechaun replied coolly. He consulted his files. "They kept him there for about a year, then released him. And he showed up a few months later at M.R. & P. (Metro Reefers and Packers), where Marilyn Dunlop works. He was soon in trouble again when someone spotted him peeking in the window of the ladies' washroom. They were going to call the police, but the Dunlop girl pleaded his case and offered to take him off their hands. For some reason, she seemed to be the only one who could control him, then, and now."

"Interesting," the lieutenant mused. "Do you have any more background on Miss Dunlop?"

"Not a lot. One thing, though, she's a real loner. She doesn't appear to have any close friends, either at work or at home. She has been employed by M.R. & P. for just over six years, first as their bookkeeper, then, about two years ago, she was moved up to Branch Comptroller. She is quite an accomplished person."

"Am I right, Garfield, in assuming that M.R. & P. is some kind of cold storage warehouse and shipping terminal?"

"That about covers it."

"Now what about Stanley Dunlop, and Denise?"

"Just what they appear to be, lieutenant." The Leprechaun flipped over a couple of pages. "He manages his mother's estate, and is expected to continue to do so (on a lesser basis, of course) after her demise. And that, as you know, is imminent. The remuneration he receives for his accounting efforts appears to be more than adequate to sustain his, and Denise's, somewhat reclusive life style, especially when you consider that everything is "found" for them. It's plain to see that Stanley was, and is, his mother's darling."

"Denise?"

"A local girl who married well. She hails from a middle-class, middle-income family, and is obviously much enamored of her new husband, not to mention the rather elite neighborhood she now calls home. They've been married nine months now, and she is looked upon by all (even Marilyn) as an expensive but harmless toy for Stanley.

"On the other hand," the Leprechaun went on, "Hans Weise, who also feathered his nest by marrying into Dunlop money, was regarded from the outset as a bit of a cad, a fortune hunter. He was thoroughly disliked by everyone, except, of course, Brenda. And even she seemed to have serious reservations about trusting him too far."

"What about Elly McBain?"

"Elly McBain?" The Leprechaun ruffled through his hoard of data, much to Mark's annoyance. "She seems to be genuinely fond of her patient. She has her R.N. ticket, which permits her to administer certain medications, and the light housework she does is purely voluntary, and gratuitous, on her part. She will, of course, be out of a job when Mrs. Weise finally succumbs."

"And that's it?"

"That's it, lieutenant." The Leprechaun closed his file with an exaggerated flourish. Mark groaned. "Oh, one thing more. There's a will (by Mrs. Weise, I mean, not Hans. He doesn't have a penny), and we can reasonably assume that it will name Stanley and Marilyn as principal beneficiaries (in view of it being Dunlop money), with a probable, generous settlement to Hans and their daughter, Linda, plus a small sum, perhaps, to Elly McBain. But I must emphasize that this is mere conjecture on my part. Only the death of Brenda Weise, and the legal disclosure of the will can tell us for certain —"

THERE WAS A SUDDEN RAP ON THE DOOR AND TOO Tall Bones leaned his great head into the office. "I hope I'm not interrupting anything, lieutenant, but I would like a word with you."

"Come in, Bones. Corporal Leprohn is just leaving." The lieutenant smiled her appreciation as the little cop handed her the file. "And as usual, Garfield, you've done a superb and thorough job. Thank you."

The Leprechaun beamed and did his Jesus walk out of the office, two inches above the floor level.

"I got a six year-old bigger'n him," Too Tall said with a deep chuckle when the door had closed behind the Leprechaun. "And the kid don't wear nothin' but sneakers, neither."

The big black took a chair, then settled comfortably into a slouch that seemed to compete with Mark's convoluted sprawl. The lieutenant smiled as she waited with measured patience. "Now that both you male brutes are firmly ensconced on your own shoulder blades," she said testily, "maybe we can get on with it."

Bones shifted his great weight uneasily. "I'm not sure whether this is important, lieutenant, but I figured you ought to know about it."

"Know about what, Bones?"

"Well, I'd been trying to keep an eye on that weirdo, Gunga Din, yesterday, like you told me to, but once in a while he managed to slip away from me. Last night, about ten o'clock, I missed him again, and I went looking for him. I finally found him up in the room where the bodies had been. It's empty now, and — Jeeez, lieutenant, you're not going to believe this."

"Try me."

"Yeah, well — he wasn't alone, lieutenant. Marilyn Dunlop was with him, and I do mean *with* him. They hadn't heard me come in and it was a few seconds before they spotted me."

"What were they doing?"

"She was just standing there, lieutenant, with her arms hanging limp at her side, letting him touch her with his bloody great paws, and nuzzle his ugly face against her cheek and her hair, and all the while he was simpering and fawning over her like some kind of dumb animal."

"There is no way that you could be mistaken about this, Bones?"

"No way, lieutenant."

"What did they do when they saw you?"

"The big creep was upset, as you might expect, but he didn't try any rough stuff. He looked to be too mesmerized by the girl to do much of anything. The girl, she gave me a look that could have iced over Hell itself, then she kind of straightened her blouse and limped out of the room. No one said a word."

"What do you think of it, lieutenant?" It was Mark who spoke.

"I think officer Bones has just unwittingly given us the solution to the New-Year's-Eve Murders." Cathy Carruthers' beautiful face was flushed with introspection. "And make no mistake, gentlemen, murder, it was."

"Which only goes to prove once again," Too Tall said, grinning at Mark, "that black is not only beautiful, but brilliant."

"Yeah," Mark was quick to respond, "and ignorance is bloody bliss." To the lieutenant, he said, "You mean you know who killed Weise and the girl?"

"I do. And not only *who*, Mark, but *how*."

"I don't suppose you plan on filling us in, lieutenant?"

"No time now, Bones. I want you to pick up your partner, Madson, and get out to the Weise/Dunlop place S.A.P. That means Sirens And Power. I want everyone assembled in that living room in twenty minutes. And, Bones, with the exception of Brenda Weise, I mean *everybody*."

THE SUN WAS HIGH OVERHEAD WHEN LIEUTENANT Cathy Carruthers stood once again in the center of the living room of the old tudor mansion. She looked around at the gathered family members and their retainers with a questioning mix of pathos and amusement.

Stanley Dunlop and his look-alike wife, Denise, sat together on an antiquated window seat, holding hands like a couple of children, and Marilyn Dunlop lolled lazily in the same chair she had occupied the day before when Sam Morton had taped her ankle. Gunga Din stood sullenly at the back of the room with Too Tall Bones close at his elbow. And hovering near the door to the hall, Elly McBain was shifting her weight restlessly from one foot to the other, as though listening for a summons from her dying patient on the second floor.

"All present and accounted for, lieutenant," Mark reported from where he had positioned himself at the room's only egress. "Officer Madson is on the gate."

"Thank you, Mark." To the room at large, the lieutenant said, "There is no easy way to inform a family group that one of its own is a murderer. You must all be aware by now, that the death of Hans Weise, and that of his daughter, Linda, was no accident. It was murder. Their untimely deaths were deliberately planned and executed by someone in this room. But before I reveal that person's identity — " Here she looked to the back of the room and leveled a meticulously manicured finger at the gatekeeper. "Bones, will you please cuff and restrain Gunther Dinsley."

The words had scarcely passed her lips when the *crrr-lick* of the big black's cuffs echoed metallically through the room. Gunga Din loosed a low growl of displeasure.

"This unfortunate, dumb brute of a man was coerced into becoming an accessory to murder," the lieutenant said with compassion, "but, in truth, he's more victim than villain." She flipped her own set of handcuffs from the belt at her waist, and turned to face Marilyn Dunlop.

"They won't be necessary," the blonde girl said with a deep sigh of resignation. "I know when I'm bloody licked."

"Then you're prepared to make a statement? To confess your part in all this?"

"I didn't say that. I told you the cuffs weren't necessary, that's all. I don't intend to say or do a bloody thing."

"That's your privilege, Miss Dunlop, but it's my duty to inform you at this juncture, and you, Mr. Dinsley, that you have the right to remain silent — "

"*Can that crap!* I already know my bloody rights." The girl was flushed with anger and humiliation. "You don't have anything more to go on than a bloody theory, lieutenant, you can't prove a thing."

"But why, lieutenant?" It was Stanley Dunlop who spoke. "Why on earth would Marilyn want to kill Hans and Linda? None of us liked the man, but — "

"Money, Mr. Dunlop. Marilyn resented the intrusion of Hans and Linda into the Dunlop inheritance."

"But, lieutenant, I have it on good authority that Hans and Linda would have received only a relatively small portion of the total bequest. Enough for them to continue living in modest comfort, plus a provisional amount held in trust for Linda's education — "

"Yes, Mr. Dunlop. We, too, assumed that such would be the case, as did Miss Dunlop. But what she realized, and you may not have, is that a will can be contested. With his status as legal spouse, and the only surviving parent of their natural daughter (with all the emotional implications a pretty five year-old girl could wring from a sympathetic court), Weise could have, and, I'm sure, would have, built himself a very credible case."

Stanley Dunlop exchanged a wide-eyed look with his nubile little wife. The lieutenant wondered, with some amusement, if the long-beleaguered groom could see TILT flashing in those innocent azure eyes.

"Hogwash!" Marilyn Dunlop slumped a little deeper in her chair. "Besides, I can't recall anyone ever going to jail just for — thinking about it."

"Which is fortunate for you, Miss Dunlop," the lieutenant

replied, "or we'd be trying you on four counts of murder, instead of two."

Denise Dunlop permitted her pretty jaw to drop and the flashing TILT suddenly gave way to GAME OVER. "Oh my *God*, Stanley, she was going to kill *us*!"

"How can you know that, lieutenant?" Stanley Dunlop choked, "how can you possibly *know* that?"

"Murder, like love, Mr. Dunlop, is always easier the second time around. And your sister felt she had the perfect means of disposing of the remaining heavy spenders. She wanted it all, you see, and she meant to get it. By simple attrition."

"How was she going to — to — ?" Denise Dunlop was a question mark beautifully, fearfully personified.

"It was really quite simple." Lieutenant Cathy Carruthers stood tall and statuesque in the center of the room, her long yellow hair glistening like freshly spun flax. Mark, from where he stood at the doorway, marveled at the poise and the beauty of this outrageously stunning woman. The time of revelation was at hand and the Amazon, he knew, was going to make the most of it.

"Now, if you will permit me," she said as she addressed the motley gathering, "I will endeavor to elucidate." She touched the tip of her tongue to her swollen lip. "Hans Weise, and little Linda, died on New Year's Eve of suffocation, *or*, to put it another way, they died from a sustained lack of oxygen — which you understand, is the same thing in one sense, but something vastly different in another."

"However, in view of the serenely composed state of the bodies, plus the total absence of any signs of violence, I immediately discounted suffocation, per se, which would have necessitated a strong hand or a gag over the mouth, or a pillow over the head — whatever. Instead, I thought it more likely that the air supply itself had been tampered with. But how? How to account for the fact that two of three people in the same room died, while the other remained alive?"

"Our first thoughts, of course, were of CO (carbon monoxide), a frequent killer in these modern times. But had there been sufficient carbon monoxide in that bedroom to have killed Hans Weise and Linda, Mrs. Weise would also have died. No. It had to be some form of gas, I reasoned, that had its own barrier — built-in so to speak."

THE AMAZON PERCHED HER ENGAGING RUMP ON THE edge of a table and crossed her long silken legs. The move was monitored by every eye in the room, including those belonging to Stanley Dunlop. A petulant dig in the ribs from his ever-lovin' abruptly ended whatever reveries he might have momentarily enjoyed.

"In his report to me this morning," the Amazon continued, "Officer Bones unwittingly made reference to something that (in his words) 'could have iced over Hell itself.' And that was the precise moment, ladies and gentlemen, when all the scattered pieces of the puzzle came tumbling into place."

"Do bloody tell," Marilyn Dunlop muttered sourly.

"The gas you used, Miss Dunlop, was CO_2," the Amazon went on undeterred, "carbon dioxide, which, when cooled sufficiently, becomes an easy-to-handle solid. *Dry Ice*, in other words. We're all familiar with it. And while the gas itself is not poisonous, a sustained dose of it can cut off the body's supply of oxygen. Mrs. Weise was not affected (other than being awakened by the resulting chill in the room) because CO_2 being heavier than air, sinks to the lowest level. The barrier between the two on the floor and the dying woman in the bed, was simple gravity."

"But there must have been some trace — "

"Carbon dioxide is colorless and odorless as it evaporates from its Dry Ice form," the lieutenant told an astounded Stanley Dunlop. "The only trace was a small alcohol stain by the window. Alcohol, you see, is frequently used in the manufacture of Dry Ice, as a control agent. The alcohol would be, and was, its only residue."

"Miss Dunlop, we know, had access to any amount of the coolant at M.R. & P., where she worked." The lieutenant regained her feet as she continued. "And while she could easily have put a block of the stuff in the sick room herself, there was a genuine risk of her being seen by some other member of the household. And so, to be on the safe side, she enlisted the services of Mr. Dinsley. She persuaded the poor dupe to scale the old elm to the balcony, with a block of Dry Ice clutched in his great paws. Once there, he simply opened the window (inadvertently leaving his fingerprints on the outside pane) and obediently placed the block of ice on the floor, just inside the window. He then closed the window and descended the way he had come."

Stanley Dunlop looked around at an abject Gunga Din, standing with his head on his chest, under the watchful eye of Too Tall Bones. "But *what*, lieutenant, could persuade even a dumb brute like Gunga Din to be a party to cold-blooded murder?"

Marilyn Dunlop struggled to her one good foot and turned to face the Amazon with her wrists extended. "Cathy," she said meekly, "is the rest of it really necessary?"

"No," the Amazon replied. "Not if you're prepared now to make a statement."

The blonde girl raised her eyes and met the Amazon's searching gaze. Then, as the cuffs closed snugly over her wrists, she said in a low voice that only her captor could hear, "will — will he be all right?"

"Gunga Din? I expect so."

"He was just like a — a kind of pet," the girl mused aloud, "a big dog, like a Great Dane or a St. Bernard. He'd do anything for me, you know."

"Yes, I know," the Amazon said dryly. "Even to committing murder."

MEL D. AMES

APRIL 1983

$1.75

47744

MIKE SHAYNE

MYSTERY MAGAZINE

A New Mike Shayne Adventure
SHADOW OF DEATH
by Brett Halliday

Novelets by
MEL D. AMES
JERRY JACOBSON

Short Stories
and Features by
the World's Greatest
Mystery Writers!

*The murder method was particularly ap-
propriate and blasphemous. It was Easter
Sunday, and the victim's body was attached to a cross with spikes driven
through his hands and feet!*

the crucifixion

THE REVEREND RUSSELL I.P. PHINNEY, BETTER known as *Rest-In-Peace* Phinney to his parishioners (and *I.P. Funny* to the unreverent young folk), had never before failed to enjoy the short, early morning walk to his beloved church.

The rectory was situated well back on the expansive church property, and it was from there that he would happily wend his way each day, down through the trees to the stone-and-cedar grandeur of St.Cuthbert's, where it fronted on one of Metro's busiest thoroughfares. Few moments had given the Reverend greater pleasure than when, as he rounded the last turn in the driveway, the giant wooden cross that rose so solemnly before the entrance to the church, suddenly would spring into view.

On this particular morning, being Easter Sunday, the Reverend Phinney was feeling doubly blessed. So great, in fact, was his euphoria as he maneuvered that last rewarding turn, that it took a full minute of stunned ogling before he could fully comprehend the tableau of horror that the Devil (who else?) had so cruelly wrought upon his church. For there (*God save us!*) on the hitherto empty face of the towering cross, *the body of a mortal man, clad in nothing but his own body hair, hung from three spikes that had been brutally driven through his hands and feet.*

It was, the Reverend Phinney later adjudged, the most blatant, blasphemous mockery of the Holy Crucifixion he had ever had the misfortune to witness.

THE SUN HAD NOT YET RISEN ABOVE THE TREES when Detective-Lieutenant Cathy Carruthers, chauffeured by her inseparable cohort, Detective-Sergeant Mark Swanson, drew up before the ecclesiastical elegance of St. Cuthbert's Church. The massive cross with its human adornment, looked, from where they had parked at the curb, like nothing more spectacular than an intended, life-like, life-size, replication of the Holy Crucifixion. No crowd had gathered to gawk, and the Sunday morning traffic continued to bustle back and forth, innocently oblivious to the outrageous sacrilege.

I'll be damned." Mark's ruggedly handsome face monitored his awe as he emerged from the unmarked Chevy. "Talk about your pinups."

The lieutenant stood eyeing the bizarre scene for some moments in undisguised amazement. "I thought I'd seen everything, Mark, but this is utterly maniacal. What do you suppose is the point of it?"

Mark rolled his eyes heavenward in what was meant to be pious contemplation. "Well, I doubt very much that he's up there counting Volkswagens, lieutenant, and, frankly, I can think of better ways to get a suntan — "

"Your sense of humor, Mark, can be positively obscene at times." She gave him a dark look of reproach. "It wouldn't surprise me to see you goofing off at your own funeral."

Mark grinned. "How about a bumper sticker on the coffin that reads: *Pardon me for not rising.*"

The lieutenant laughed in spite of herself. "Mark, you're incurable." She glanced back at the man on the cross and quickly sobered. "Get on the radio, Mark and have Dispatch requisition a firetruck, P.D.Q. That's Pretty Damn Quick, in case you're in doubt. Make sure they send a truck with a ladder. That guy must be over twenty feet up there. And you'd better alert the meat squad.

I want the Lab and Camera crews on that cross before any attempt is made to get the body down."

"You got it, lieutenant." Mark reached for the radio-mike but his eyes never left his senior partner as she turned and headed out across the church lawn toward the cross. His gaze lingered on her receding silhouette with fond reflection.

OVER THE PAST YEAR AND A HALF, MARK HAD WATCHED Cathy Carruthers evolve into something of a living legend at Metro Central's Eleventh Precinct; a remarkably beautifully, six-foot, honey-haired blonde, possessing all the sexual attributes of a *Penthouse* pinup, with a hidden reservoir of such awesome strength and intelligence that she had been nicknamed *The Amazon* by her incredulous colleagues in Homicide. They had become an effective team, she and Mark, and a deep bond of mutual respect and affection had developed between them.

Following a couple of terse moments with the dispatcher, Mark took off after the lieutenant. A lone, black-robed figure had joined her at the foot of the cross, and as he drew within earshot, Mark heard his partner identify herself, then flash her badge. "And this," she said, as Mark drew abreast of them, "is my partner, Sergeant Swanson."

"I am Reverend Russell I.P. Phinney," the man in the black cassock responded. "I am the person who phoned."

"Do you know the identity of the man on the cross, Mr. Phinney?"

"Reverend."

"Pardon me?"

"*Reverend* Phinney," the man insisted. "I am a Reverend; I am not a Mister."

"And *I* am not a hypocrite," the lieutenant replied coolly. "While I respect your right to practice your own religion as you see fit, Mr. Phinney, I feel under no obligation to cower before another mere mortal in mock reverence. Now, will you kindly answer the question: Do you know the man on the cross?"

"Uh, yes — lieutenant, I do." The Reverend Phinney was visibly discomfited by Cathy Carruthers' rather blunt assessment of his secular status. "That is Kevin LeMay up there. He is (or was) a member of my parish. I assume he *is* dead."

"You assume correctly. Now, have you any idea who might have put him up there?"

"None whatever."

"Or why anyone would want to?"

"None wha — uh, well, lieutenant, to be perfectly candid, he was reputed to be something of a — lady's man?"

"That, *leve*l*end*, would be putting it mild*ry*."

THE VOICE HAD COME FROM THE DIRECTION OF THE church. All heads turned to see a slight little man of Japanese extraction emerging from the cathedral-like entrance. And following subserviently three feet behind him, was an even tinier, doll-like woman of similar cast. The eyes of the woman were focused unwaveringly on the ground.

The man, with his one-woman entourage in tow, approached the group at the foot of the cross. He squinted up at them through thick-rimmed glasses that looked like the bottoms of empty Coke bottles. "A *l*otten basta'd," he said emphatically, "would be a mo'e fitting desc*l*iption."

"Perhaps you'd like to identify yourself," the lieutenant said with some amusement.

"My name is Ouchi. Yosh Ouchi." He pointed a tiny thumb over one shoulder. "My wife, Tomi."

"Yosh is our caretaker," the Reverend Phinney said in explanation. "And Tomi plays the organ for us. They are both a credit to St. Cuthbert's, lieutenant."

"I'm sure. How long have you been back there listening to us, Mr. Ouchi?" the lieutenant asked the upturned Coke bottles.

"We a*ll*ived just after the *l*eve'end, *r*ieutenant. We were with him when he phoned the po*r*ice."

"That is correct," the reverend attested.

"Well, then, what can you tell me about the man on the cross?" The lieutenant directed her question to the little man's wife, who seemed to be on an invisible leash. "Mrs. Ouchi?"

The tiny woman shot a fearful glance up at the lieutenant, at her husband, then back down at the ground. She was actually quite pretty, the lieutenant noted, and at least twenty years younger than her domineering spouse.

"Tomi would not know of these things," Yosh Ouchi put in quickly. "But *I* can tell you that Kevin ReMay was intimate with many *r*adies in the chu'ch. And thei' husbands we'e ve*l*y ang*l*y."

"You saw them?"

"Yes, *r*ieutenant, I saw them."

"And where did these trysts occur?"

"In ReMay's *l*ooms."

"You were there, in his loo — rooms, when this happened?"

"No, *r*ieutenant, but I did see them go in, and I heard — evelything."

"Perhaps I can elaborate, lieutenant," the reverend offered. "Yosh had already told me, in some detail, of these — indiscretions. LeMay, you see, was Resident Church-Activities Director, and had been for more than a year. He occupied a small apartment that is attached to the equipment garage where Yosh has a workshop. I gather, from what Yosh has told me, that the walls are rather thin — "

"And just what *did* he tell you?"

"He told me, lieutenant, that he had seen ladies from the congregation enter LeMay's apartment, alone with him, on several occasions. When I asked for specifics, he recited two instances, and named two married ladies, that he claims had definitely been in — in dalliance with the man."

"In *dalliance?*"

"They made *r*ove!" the little oriental stated unequivocally.

"Yes — well," the reverend continued, "to make matters worse, if that were possible, both of these ladies were then seen leaving the apartment by their respective husbands, who had apparently come looking for them. As Yosh tells it, it resulted in a couple of rather ugly scenes — and even uglier threats."

"I see." The lieutenant regarded the little man speculatively for several moments. "Mr. Ouchi," she said at last. "I want you to convey that same information to Sergeant Swanson, in every detail, and, of course, anything else you might have seen or heard that may be pertinent to the case. I want names, dates, and addresses, relevant to all parties involved. Is that clear?"

"Yes, si', rieutenant."

A HALF DOZEN POLICE CARS SUDDENLY APPEARED on the scene with lights flashing. Moments later, a lone firetruck mounted the curb and came rumbling across the lawn toward to cross. Ouchi watched in dismay as the heavy wheels pressed ruts into the otherwise unmarked carpet of the grass. Mark hauled out his notebook and steered the little oriental to one side, while his petite mate perpetuated her peripheral presence as though she'd been linked umbilically.

The lieutenant, meanwhile, had cornered the head man in the fire crew. "I want my Forensic team up there before you attempt to salvage the cadaver," the lieutenant told him. "And they're going to need your help."

"Not to worry, lieutenant. We'll float 'em up and down that cross like they'd just sprouted wings. But first hadn't we better check to see if the guy's dead?"

The lieutenant smiled condescendingly as she pointed up at the sagging corpse. "You've probably already noticed the marked absence of bleeding, right? Only traces of blood on his hands, and his feet, where the spikes were driven in. It seems rather obvious, don't you think, that his heart had stopped pumping before he was nailed up there. That man, I'm afraid, is as dead as he's ever going to get."

"Yeah, I guess he is at that." The fireman committed Cathy Carruthers' engaging rear-end to memory as she walked away to rejoin the Reverend Phinney near the entrance to the church. "I hate smart broads," he mumbled to himself, "especially good looking ones."

At her own request, while the police teams busied themselves at the scene of the crucifixion, the lieutenant accompanied the Reverend Phinney on a hasty tour of the church. They went to LeMay's apartment, where the lieutenant retrieved an apple core from the garbage pail, and a small black notebook from a dresser drawer. In the garage where Yosh Ouchi had his workshop, she stopped to run an immaculately manicured finger over grass stains on the base clamps of an aluminum extension ladder, noting that the ladder, when fully extended, would measure more than thirty feet. And the top rung of the ladder appeared to be shinier than the others, as though someone had deliberately burnished it. Then, in the wall that separated the garage from the apartment, the lieutenant uncovered a cleverly concealed peephole that looked directly into what had been LeMay's bedroom.

It seemed that Yosh Ouchi had been into more than just listening, while his fellow parishioners had been 'making rove.'

WHEN THE LIEUTENANT AND THE REVEREND RETURNED to the activity at the front of the church, the body of Kevin LeMay was sprawled grotesquely over the grass at the base of the cross, arms splayed and body cruelly bent, frozen in the relentless grip of rigor mortis. Sam Morton, Metro Central's Chief Coroner, was crouched over the body.

"Any idea what killed him, Sam?"

The M.E. looked up with a humorless smile. "I take it you don't buy the crucifixion bit."

"You can say that again, Sam."

"I take it you don't buy the crucifixion bit." The lieutenant narrowed her vivid blue eyes, with her inscrutably beautiful face just inches from his grumpy smirk. "Mark's pathetic one-liners aren't enough?" she told him with a tempered touch of malice, "now I've got you on my back?"

"As long as I haven't got you on the table, lieutenant, you've got nothing to worry about. And to answer your question, no, I don't know what killed him."

"Guess."

"Asphyxiation? Poison? Bubonic Plague?"

"You're not being very helpful, Sam."

"Lieutenant, this guy's as stiff as the cross he was nailed to. I can't tell you much of anything until I get him in where I can do a number on him. My guess is, he drew his last breath sometime around midnight. There are no outward signs of violence, apart from being hung up to dry, of course. But as you've already surmised, that came later."

"How much later?"

The M.E. drew a sheet over the convoluted corpse and got stiffly to his feet. "Don't ask me."

"Who do you suggest I ask, Sam, the Easter Bunny?"

"Why not?" The coroner's customary furrowed frown seemed to contort itself almost painfully into a grouchy-looking grin. "Try him with, *What's up, Doc?* I get it all the time."

Before the lieutenant could respond, one of the men from the Lab team suddenly stepped in front of her. He held up a small poly-bag. "This was stuck to the cross, lieutenant, just above the guy's head. It wasn't visible from the ground."

Inside the poly-bag, the lieutenant could see a strip of white paper. There was something printed on it in an awkward scrawl, with what seemed to be a red grease pencil. She held it up and read aloud: "THE WORKS OF THE FLESH ARE MANIFEST."

Over her shoulder, the Reverend Phinney said, "That's a quote or partial quote, from Galatians, I think." He fumbled in his black cassock and produced a small black Bible. As he flipped through the pages, the lieutenant handed the message back to the Lab man, together with the apple core and notebook she had taken from LeMay's apartment. They, too, were each protected by individual poly-bags.

"I'd like you people to check the dead man's apartment," she told him, "which is where this stuff came from. And you might have a look at the aluminum ladder that's hanging in the adjacent workshop. Mr. Phinney, here, will show you where to go."

The man looked around him. "You mean the Reverend Phinney?' he asked innocently enough. The lieutenant treated him to a long, reflective look. "Let's not get into *that* again," she said menacingly. The man shrugged, then moved off to one side to wait.

"Ah, yes, here it is." the reverend exclaimed triumphantly. "Galatians 5:19, 20 and 21 — *Now the works of the flesh are manifest,*" he read, "*which are these: adultery, fornication, uncleanliness, lasciviousness, idolatry, witchcraft, hatred, variance, emulations, wrath, strife, sedition, heresies —* "

"Let me know," the lieutenant sighed wearily, "when you get to *dalliance.*"

" *— envyings, murders, drunkenness, revellings, and such like: of the which I tell you before, as I have also told you in time* *past, that they which do such things shall not inherit the kingdom of God.*"

"Amen," said Yosh Ouchi, his Coke-bottle specs glinting with piety in the morning sun.

Mark shifted uncomfortably at the lieutenant's side. "That doesn't leave much room for a guy to maneuver, does it?"

Cathy Carruthers grinned. "It'd sure as hell cramp your style," she chuckled. "Have you finished with our little oriental snitch?"

"Yep." Mark held up his notebook. "It's all here."

"Let's go then. I think we'll have better luck with the *Book of Revelations* (according to Ouchi) than with the diatribe we've just been listening to."

TWO MINUTES LATER, MARK WAS BEHIND THE WHEEL of the Chevy, one hand on the gearshift, motor running, ready to roll. His favorite sleuth-person had just climbed in beside him. "Where to, lieutenant?"

"Well, Mark, I don't think there's much doubt, at this point anyway, that our prime suspects have got to be the husbands of the two ladies that were caught coming out of LeMay's apartment. Clark Goodman and, uh — Nigel Stirling. They were both fiercely irate, and with justification, perhaps, but they *did* make threats. I think we owe them both a visit, don't you?"

"Who do we start with?"

Mark watched Cathy Carruthers ponder the question silently for a few moments. He had become rather fond of watching her ponder. It wasn't what you'd call an arduous activity, but it had its thrusts.

"I think we'll begin with Nigel and Monica Stirling," she said at last. "You've got them down as owning and operating a peach orchard on the outskirts of Metro, off Interstate 5. It shouldn't be more than a half hour drive."

Mark did a U-turn off the curb and headed out toward North Metro. He shot a quick glance at his partner. "Lieutenant, there's some information I picked up from Ouchi that I didn't put in the book. I think you should know about it."

"I'm listening."

"Reverend Phinney failed to mention it, but he's got an eighteen year-old daughter, Elizabeth. She lives at the rectory. Ouchi claims that the girl was one of LeMay's conquests. It's kind of sad because the kid was deluded into believing the guy really loved her. You know the scene. Anyway, Ouchi didn't want to say anything in front of Phinney for fear of upsetting him. The girl is the only family the reverend has left; his wife died of cancer a couple of years ago."

"Now that *is* interesting." The lieutenant leaned back with an esoteric chuckle. "*Because*, according to I.P. Phinney, Ouchi's wife Tomi, was also one of LeMay's bed partners."

"My God! When did that guy sleep?"

"And here's something else to titivate the tale: Ouchi was not only a witness to the comings and goings of LeMay's playmates, he was actually watching their amorous activities through a peephole in the bedroom/garage wall. He was undoubtedly having himself a fine old time (the little creep) with a real, live, porno soap-opera going for him, until (chuckle) his own child-bride made her humble debut as the leading lady. He was then, as they say, *Hoist by his own petard.*"

Mark laughed. "That must have been some finale." He braked the car to a running stop at a turn-off, then hung a right onto an up-ramp to Interstate 5. "What a case," he said. "Everyone we've talked to has become a viable suspect."

"That may be true, Mark, but remember there are three contingencies to murder: Motive, Means, and Opportunity. And by the simple process of elimination, just on that criteria alone, we should be able to rule out most of them. But that's not what's bothering me now."

"Oh? Then what is ?"

"I just can't imagine how one person, even a trained and rugged, six-footer like yourself, Mark — "

"Don't forget handsome, and witty — "

" — and even with the aid of a good ladder, could drag a body up the face of that cross, and then go about pinning him up like a tail on a donkey."

"Yeah, I see what you mean. But maybe it wasn't just one man, lieutenant. Maybe it was some kind of a conspiracy. You know, two or more people in cahoots, or even a lynch mob. God knows — by the time LeMay had met his somewhat appropriate end last night, there must have been as many cuckolds as sinners parked in their pews at St. Cuthbert's."

"You do have a way of putting things, Mark."

Mark kept the car hurtling down 5-North until they reached the Dry Valley turn-off. He slowed to maneuver the cloverleaf, then swung east at a more leisurely pace, winding down through a magnificent valley that virtually teemed with lush, budding orchards. The noise of the freeway had fallen away behind them, and they seemed to float along in a new, gentle quiet, stirred only by the hum of a distant tractor and the whispering *chu chu chu* of sprinklers.

"Dry Valley Road," Mark said wonderingly, "what a ludicrous name for such a fertile valley."

"I agree, Mark, but this valley was named when there was nothing here but sagebrush and rattlesnakes. Irrigation water had to be flumed down from high-level reservoirs."

"Yeah? So how did they get the water up there in the first place?"

"To put it simply; the reservoirs are fed by a chain of small mountain tarns, which, in turn, are augmented by natural rainfall and the seasonal melting of a fairly reliable snowshed."

"I'm impressed, lieutenant. How come you know so much about irrigation?"

"I grew up on an orchard, Mark. I was driving a John Deere when most kids my age were still into kiddie cars."

At that point, a rural mailbox with the name STIRLING painted on its side, loomed up on their left, and Mark nosed the car into a long, gravel driveway.

"The trees are almost ready to blossom," the lieutenant noted absently, "the buds are just on the verge of erupting."

Mark chuckled grimly. "That's not all that's ready to erupt, lieutenant. Look ahead."

A HUGE, YELLOW AND GREEN DIESEL TRACTOR WAS angled across the driveway, blocking their path. A red-headed man in coveralls occupied the bucket seat, vibrating slightly from the idling diesel, his face a clouded, sun-weathered mask of inhospitality.

"This here's private property," the man shouted, "back up and get out!"

The lieutenant slipped out of the car and approached the tractor. Mark watched from behind the wheel as the lieutenant flashed her badge, identifying herself.

"Will you please shut that off!" she shouted over the noise of the diesel.

"I told you to back up and get out," the man shouted back. "Now move, b'fore you get hurt."

The lieutenant reached quickly in behind the dash and yanked at the shut-off knob. The tractor coughed and stalled, but because she had to hold the knob in the 'out' position for two or three seconds, she could not avoid the vicious blow the man had aimed at her wrist.

Momentarily stunned, the lieutenant fell back a pace, but was on the verge of retaliating when Mark suddenly appeared on the other side of the tractor. The man's hand was already on the key to re-start the motor, but a fist the size of a leg of mutton slammed into his biceps, just below the shoulder. The fingers on the end of the arm spread and stiffened in paralytic pain.

It was the lieutenant's turn then, to stand and watch as the orchardist was whipped out of his seat and unceremoniously dumped on his rump in the center of the driveway.

"You don't hear too well," Mark admonished the man quietly. "You gotta pay attention, sonny, when the lieutenant talks to you."

Cathy Carruthers turned her golden head to hide the wide grin she was unable to suppress. When she regained her composure, she said, "You *are* Nigel Stirling?"

The man nodded his head, then grunted in the affirmative as Mark nudged him with his toe.

The lieutenant grinned openly. "I'll back this mechanical brute up to the house and out of the way, Mark. You follow in the car. And, uh — bring Sonny with you."

MARK WATCHED HIS BEAUTIFUL PARTNER MOUNT THE tractor like she'd done it more than once before. She had to hike her skirt to straddle the transmission hump, but once in the saddle, she got it rolling like a pro. With one hand on the steering wheel, the other on a fender to support her back-ward looking posture, she sent the green and yellow monster barreling back in a cloud of dust, to an open area beside the old clapboard house.

Nigel Stirling led them, reluctantly, through the back 'mud-room' entrance, into a large country-style kitchen. A woman standing before the sink, turned as they entered. She had a plump, rosy face that was framed in a clump of tousled brown hair, and a figure that looked to have been nurtured on pork pie and peaches. If this was Monica Stirling, she was not what Mark had imagined an even quite-by-accident fornicatrix would have looked like. LeMay had obviously been willing to oblige most anything, as long as it was female and friendly.

"Are you Monica Stirling?" the lieutenant asked the woman.

"Yes, I am."

Mark found a kitchen stool to sit on as his partner went through the routine of identifying herself, and him, for the second time. "We're here about the death of Kevin LeMay," she said finally.

Monica cast a frightened look toward her husband, though to Mark, the man looked more comical than threatening. He was a thick-boned, stumbling lout of a man, with a wide mouth and a crop of wiry red hair that gave him the appearance of a clown without make-up. But there was an unmistakable fear, not amusement, reflected in the eyes of his disquieted wife.

"We were told about his death," Stirling mumbled, "jest a half hour ago."

"By phone?"

"Yeah."

"Who made the call?"

"Reveren' Phinney did."

"I see." The lieutenant did not appear particularly pleased. "You were, of course, both known to the deceased?"

"Yeah. He knew us." Stirling turned his eyes darkly in his wife's direction. "Both of us. And we knew him."

"On at least one occasion, Mr. Stirling, you were overheard to threaten — "

"You been talkin' to that little turd Ouchi, have'n'cha? Anyhow, even if I did, that don't mean I killed 'im."

"No, it doesn't. But it does give you a motive. Are you able to account for your whereabouts at the time of the murder?"

"Now when'n hell might that have been?"

"Around midnight, give or take an hour."

"Midnight?" There was no humor in the man's sudden, ugly chortling. "I was right where you'd expect a farmer oughta be, *loo*tenant, mam."

"You didn't answer my question."

"In bed, damn it. In bloody bed. Where else?"

The lieutenant turned to the dumpy 'Delilah.' "And you, Mrs. Stirling?"

"I was with Nigel, of course."

"Of course." The lieutenant echoed the words with some ambivalence, and Monica Stirling's pudgy face suddenly took on the color of an over-ripe peach.

"Can you corroborate that?" the lieutenant asked.

"If that means can we prove it," Stirling grumbled, "the answer is, no. We're not in the habit of having strangers in bed with — "

He stopped in mid-sentence, clearly flustered by his own clumsy ineptness. And his wife's already flushed face deepened to a feverish, cherry red.

"Look, mam." Nigel Stirling seemed almost as unhappy as his hangdog spouse. "We told you where we was, and we told you where we wasn't. Now if you don't mind, I got a' orchard to run — "

"Mr. Stirling." The lieutenant was patiently condescending. "I have only one more question for you, at this time: Do you own a cherry-picker?"

"A giraffe? Yeah, I got two of 'em. Don't pick no cherries with 'em though."

"Where are they now?"

"One's in my equipment shed. Other one I had to take inta town, for repairs."

"When was that?"

Stirling shifted his weight from one foot to the other. " - - uh, yestiday."

"Yesterday morning? Afternoon?"

The man hesitated. "Had to take it in last night," he said finally, "don't have no time durin' the day. Ain't nothin' wrong with that, is ther'?"

"You tell me," the lieutenant said from the door. "All I know is, it sure would have been one easy way to haul LeMay up that cross, *without the need of a ladder.*"

THEY HAD ALREADY MADE THE TURN AT THE END OF the driveway, heading back the way they had come, along Dry Valley Road, before the lieutenant spoke. She sounded pensive. What do you make of that Stirling character, Mark?"

"I think the man is not only an unmitigated bully, lieutenant, but a stupid one. And that's the worst kind."

"But did he kill LeMay?"

"Who knows? He certainly had the motive, the means, and the opportunity. He qualifies."

"He does, indeed. But then, so does Ouchi and that perfidious parson."

"The Reverend?"

"The same. I just wonder if he's tipped off the Goodmans, like he did the Stirlings?"

"Is that where we're heading?"

"Only if you can get this Detroit dinosaur out of low gear and into get-along. It's already after ten, and I'd like to squeeze in a workout at the Fitness Center before lunch. Feel up to it?"

"Are you kidding? Hang onto your seat!"

THE GOODMANS LIVED WITHIN A QUARTER MILE OF St. Cuthbert's Church. The top floor of a two-storey stucco building, housing Goodman's Arts & Signs, had quite obviously been converted into living quarters. Curtains, drapes and flower boxes adorned the upper windows. A door on one side of the storefront, gave access to an enclosed stairwell that led to the floor above.

Being Sunday, the business was closed, but Mark found a buzzer on the side door and thumbed it. A moment later an intercom squawked.

"Yeah?" A man's voice.

"Police," Mark intoned flatly. "We'd like to talk to you."

"How do I know you're cops?"

"You don't. And you won't, unless you come down here and let us identify ourselves."

"Just a minute."

A buzzer sounded, and the door-lock clicked. Mark tugged the door open. "Couldn't have been all that leery," Mark muttered as he followed the lieutenant up the stairs, "letting us in like that, without checking."

"He was probably expecting us," the lieutenant said tightly. "Phinney-the-Fink strikes again."

A door opened at the top of the stairs and a man dressed in undershirt and jeans admitted them into a spacious living room. He was a thick-set man, about five-ten, with a sagging chest and stomach that was fast losing its fight with gravity. He looked to be about forty.

"I'm Lieutenant Carruthers, and this is my partner, Sergeant Swanson." The lieutenant flipped her badge as Mark looked around for a comfortable place to sit. "Are you Clark Goodman?"

"That's my name."

"We're here about the death of Kevin LeMay, Mr. Goodman."

"Yes, I know."

"Phinney phoned you?"

" — uh, yes, he did. How'd you know?"

"Just a lucky guess." The lieutenant treated him to a secret smile. "Is your wife at home?"

"She'll be out in a minute. She's getting dressed." He ran his hand over his unshaven chin. "This is usually our day to sleep in."

"I was under the impression you attended St. Cuthbert's on Sunday mornings."

"We do, normally, but the service doesn't start until eleven. And today, after the phone call — "

"Mr. Goodman," the lieutenant cut in, "I have information that you had a rather unfriendly exchange of words with LeMay, after you discovered — "

"Damn!" Goodman's face had darkened. "You've been talking to that little Kamikaze creep, haven't you? Someone ought to crucify *him!*"

"You want to tell me about it?"

"What's to tell?" You obviously know what went on. I just warned LeMay to keep of my turf — or else."

"Or else, what?"

"I don't know." Goodman sank down in the second most comfortable chair in the room; Mark was already occupying the first. "It hadn't come to that."

"You could have fooled me there, early this morning," the lieutenant responded gravely.

A woman entered the room from a connecting passage. She had bleached-blonde hair with black roots, and a figure not too different from her husband's, except that it was female. *Right up LeMay's libidinous alley*, Mark mused with an inward grimace.

"This is my wife, Goldie," Goodman grunted. To her, he said, "They're here about LeMay's death."

Goldie Goodman had a bruised left eye and a grazed cheek that a heavy application of make-up had not been able to hide.

"What happened to your face, Mrs. Goodman?"

The woman lifted a nervous hand to her cheek. "Why, I — I fell. The stairs — "

"I hit her," Goodman stated matter-of-factly, with no suggestion of remorse. "LeMay was an unqualified bastard, lieutenant, but it takes two to tango."

"Yes, well, unless Mrs. Goodman wishes to file a complaint," the lieutenant asserted, "it's of no concern to me. What I do want to know, however, is where you were last night, around midnight."

Goodman shrugged his meaty shoulders. "I had a late job last night that took me until 10:30, 11 o'clock. When I got home, Goldie and I killed a bottle of wine and went to bed."

"And what was the nature of this 'job?'"

"I had to erect a small sign, that's all. At Prime Pizza Palace, over on South Main."

"I presume you had with you, the necessary sign-erecting equipment?"

"Of course. It's truck mounted. We couldn't operate without it."

"Did you have a helper?"

"You kidding? With overtime wages the way they are today? Who can afford it? Anyway, it wasn't that tough a job."

The lieutenant drew a stray fall of golden hair from her forehead. "How high will that equipment of yours lift, Mr. Goodman?"

"Thirty-five, forty feet. High enough."

"Yes," the lieutenant agreed, "high enough to lift the body of a man up a thirty-foot cross, wouldn't you say?"

"You're reaching, lieutenant," Goodman snarled. "I'm not sorry to see that raunchy bastard dead, and that's a fact, but *I* didn't kill him."

"I'd hardly expect you to admit it if you did," the lieutenant told him quietly, "but as the sergeant would likely say, *you do qualify.*"

AT 11:45, PRECISELY, MARK SWANSON STOOD WAITING in the inner hall of the Fitness Center, a facility provided for the exclusive use of Metro Central's law enforcement personnel. He was dressed in sneakers, shorts, and a sleeveless tank-top, revealing a powerful, sun-bronzed physique that drew double-takes from both sexes as they traversed the narrow hall between the gym and the locker rooms. Mark's eyes strayed repeatedly to a door with a block-letter sign that read: MUCHACHAS. On another door across the hall, behind which he had just changed out of his street clothes, a similar sign read: MUCHACHOS. He had often speculated on what delightful havoc might ensue *if* (one day) he was to surreptitiously switch the A on one sign, for the O on the other; or, of course, vice versa.

However, his wait (and therefor his speculation) on this particular day, was of short duration. Cathy Carruthers emerged from the MUCHACHAS side of the hall in a burst of energy; her abundant, honey-blonde hair drawn back in a ponytail that billowed and flew like a Cavalier's plume. She wore coal-black leotards and matching wool leg-warmers that came to just above her knees. A loose-fitting, white pullover completed her attire, and left her looking like a long-legged ballet dancer who'd outgrown her tutu.

"Well," she said brightly, "how do I look?"

Mark, who firmly believed (from the moment he had first set eyes on Cathy Carruthers) that there were eight, not seven, Wonders in the World, was momentarily speechless. He did finally manage something like, "Uh — great!"

"You don't sound too convincing," she laughed. She punched him playfully on a bulging biceps. "God, you're a big brute."

Before he could respond, playfully or otherwise, she had taken off toward the indoor track. Mark followed strategically three feet behind. He might have felt a little like Ouchi's tagtailing spouse, except that *his* eyes were not focused on the ground.

"Come up beside me, Mark," she called back over her shoulder, "I want to talk to you."

Mark, who was not adverse to getting a little behind in his workout, acquiesced with some reluctance.

"What do you think about Phinney, Mark, phoning ahead of us like that?"

"Well, maybe there's something in this conspiracy theory after all. Phinney, Ouchi, Stirling, Goodman; all in it together. Except—"

"Except, what?"

"Except that both Stirling and Goodman have about as much use for Ouchi as a born-again Geisha."

"That may be true, Mark, but there's still three of them left with a credible, collective motive. And we still don't know how they (or he, for that matter; or even she) managed to get LeMay up on that cross — "

" — or, how he was killed to begin with."

"We're just going to have to wait, Mark, to see what the Lab and Sam Morton come up with. And that probably won't be until sometime tomorrow. The way it looks now, we just don't have a leg to stand on."

Mark, who had been having trouble keeping his mind and his eyes above his partner's chin, could see no visible justification for her last remark.

"I'll race you the last lap," Mark challenged, "loser buys the lunch." And he surged ahead of her in a powerful, leg-pounding sprint. He was still in the lead and more than half way round the track, when a bionic blur went whistling by him like a black-and-white answering a Code 3. The only thing missing was the flashing lights and (happily) a rear bumper.

MONDAY MORNING CAME AND WENT WITHOUT incident at Metro Central's Eleventh Precinct. Lieutenant Carruthers kept close to the phone as she tackled the never-ending backlog of paperwork that strewed her desk. Mark was similarly engaged, just outside her glassed-in office; a necessary, but brutally boring task that kept him fidgeting like a hungry sinner at a soup-kitchen prayer meeting.

It was well past the noon hour when the long-awaited call came through from the Lab. Mark rang it through to his senior partner without breaking his own connection.

"Carruthers."

"Brewster, here, lieutenant, from Lab."

"Yes, corporal. You've got the report?"

"No, we'll need more time. But there is a couple of things developing that you may find interesting. Want to come down and talk about it?"

"Be there in five." The lieutenant caught Mark's eye through the glass-partition as she hung up the phone. "Let's go," she mouthed.

LENNY BREWSTER WAS BUILT LIKE A TEST TUBE. HIS coal-black short hair could have been mistaken for the business end of a Bunsen burner and his chalky, tight-lipped face looked more like a blank Lab report than a human identity. For all that, Lenny Brewster was undeniably a prodigy of Forensic Chemistry. It was rumored in the department, that when he and Sam Morton got together, they could concoct a pepperoni pizza, if they felt so inclined, out of a week-old cow patty.

Lenny was at his laboratory bench when the lieutenant and Mark entered the Lab, but he blended so well with his immediate surroundings that he was next to invisible — until he moved.

"Over here, lieutenant. Hi, Mark." He turned on his high, three-legged stool to face them, "They've sure dumped a weird one on you this time."

"What else is new?" the lieutenant said lamely. "We're hoping you might make it a little less weird, corporal. What have you got?"

Lenny consulted a raft of scribbled notes. "Let's start with the apple core," he said. "You did the right thing, bringing it in. It was laced with enough poison to kill a water buffalo."

"What kind of poison?"

"It's a poison that has been withdrawn from commercial use in many states, lieutenant, including this one, mainly because it's just too dangerous. There is no known antidote, you see. You'd probably recognize it as 10-80, used by ranchers for killing off marauding coyotes, and by farmers to control infestations of mice, pocket-gophers and whistlers, as well as sundry other rodents. The environmentalists raised merry hell about it though, and it was eventually taken off the market."

"*Whistlers?*"

"A whistler, Mark, is a large marmot, closely related to the common woodchuck. It makes a trilling sound, like a street-corner 'wolf' whistle."

"That is most interesting, corporal, to say the least." The lieutenant was jotting something in her own notebook. "Anything else?"

"Could be, lieutenant. We found traces of three separate foreign substances on the face of the cross, two of which we haven't yet analyzed, but the third is definitely a type of chemical fungicide: one of the *dithiocarbamates.* We haven't been able to isolate the precise one exactly (there must be dozens), but maybe that, in itself, will be helpful to you."

"I'm sure it will, corporal. At the moment, however, it doesn't appear to do much to narrow our list of suspects. Ouchi and Phinney, for instance, could both have legitimate access to fungicides and rodent poisons, in their joint care and responsibility for the acreage on which the church and the rectory is situated. And, Stirling, with his peach orchard, would even probably have a supply on hand."

"But 10-80 isn't available anymore, lieutenant, and hasn't been for years."

"There could still be plenty of it hanging around, corporal, in garages, storage sheds — "

"Yeah, I guess."

"But how does Goodman fit in?" Mark asked.

"If he wanted the stuff bad enough, he could always steal it," the lieutenant said impatiently, then, "But, *wa-a-ait* a minute! Hmmmm — " She tilted her beautiful head in an attitude of deep cogitation. "Something has come to mind."

"Everybody duck," Mark muttered. "Here comes the punch

line."

"Not yet, Mark, but I have a nagging hunch that might just wrap up this entire fiasco." The lieutenant turned to Lenny Brewster. "Have you alerted the M.E. about the 10-80?"

"Yes, about an hour ago. He'll be looking for it when he does the autopsy."

"Good. Now, Mark. I want you to round up all our suspects: Ouchi, Phinney, Stirling, and Goodman, and their respective wives, and, of course, Elizabeth. I want them all at the church within the hour. But before you leave the precinct, put in a call to Sam Morton and see if he'll give you confirmation that LeMay was, in fact, poisoned with 10-80."

"Sure, lieutenant, but where're you going?"

"To St. Cuthbert's, just as you are, but I'm going to have to meet you there. There's a stop I've got to make on the way." She gave him one of those vague looks that, he knew from past experience, signaled the beginning of the end. "Hypotheses, Mark, like alibis and arson, have to be substantiated before they become fact. And facts are what we need to nail the man who crucified LeMay." She turned and headed for the door. "See you in church."

Mark watched her go with a shrug and a long-suffering sigh. "Yeah," he said, almost wistfully, "see you in church."

THEY WERE IN THE CHURCH WAITING, ALL EIGHT OF them, when the lieutenant entered unexpectedly from the rear vestibule. Everyone but the reverend and his comely young daughter was seated in the front, right-hand pew. The Goodmans near the center aisle; and the sun-scorched Stirlings hugged the end of the pew, on the outer aisle against the wall. Elizabeth sat behind them, in the second pew, midway between the Ouchis and the Stirlings. The Reverend Phinney, draped in his customary black cassock, had assumed a somewhat theatrical, unmoving, prayerful pose, just inside the communion rail. And Mark, who had stationed himself at the main entrance, moved up now behind the group as the lieutenant swept down the aisle to mount the dias. She had a coil of heavy rope looped over one shoulder.

"I'm sorry to have kept you waiting," the lieutenant said to the motley gathering, "but having now arrived, I can assure you I will not detain you long. The exception to that, of course, will be the one culprit among you who so ignominiously dispatched your fellow parishioner, Kevin LeMay."

"Are you suggesting that the killer is someone in this room, lieutenant?" the punctilious parson exclaimed with a show of exaggerated horror.

"Indeed, I am," the lieutenant was quick to respond, "and I might also suggest that you follow the example of the other seven suspects in this case, and avail yourself of a pew. For the duration of this inquiry, sir, I will hold the floor."

"Uh, yes — yes, of course, lieutenant." The reverend was visibly nonplussed, but he managed to maneuver the lieutenant into a private huddle facing away from the other participants. "Lieutenant," he whispered against his palm, "that notebook you found in LeMay's apartment, do you think it could be, well — placed in my custody — ?"

"That notebook, sir, is evidence."

"Yes, of course, but — "

"But, nothing." The lieutenant shrugged the man's hand from her shoulder. "If you are curious to know if it contains the name of your daughter, it does. And will it be made public? No. Now, if you'll kindly park yourself in a pew, as I have already suggested, I'll endeavor to shed some light on the macabre death of Kevin LeMay."

When the reverend had reluctantly ensconced himself in the second pew, behind the Goodmans, the lieutenant stood stolidly, front and center on the dias. She surveyed her borrowed congregation with a look of saddened deprecation that bordered on outright pity. *What a pathetic bunch of bumblers,* her eyes seemed to say, *there's not a mother's blush of you who isn't guilty of some dark deed.*

"I was at a loss, at first," the lieutenant said aloud, "as to how anyone could lift LeMay's body (he *was* dead before he was crucified) up on that cross, and then proceed to nail him there. One answer could have been Stirling's 'giraffe,' as he calls it, or even Goodman's truck-mounted sign erector. But both of these contrivances would have left vehicle tracks on the lawn, and there were no such tracks visible the morning he was found, as we all noted at the time; except, of course, those of the firetruck, which arrived later, after the deed was done. That left only the unlikely use of a ladder with which to accomplish the task, and who among you (she chuckled disparagingly) would have the physical prowess to so prevail?"

The lieutenant swept the sorry-looking group with her eyes. They, in turn, looked wonderingly at one another.

"Tonight, however," the lieutenant continued, "I unearthed this coil of rope." She held it up for all to see. "It was adroitly hidden under the workbench in Mr. Ouchi's equipment garage, where it had been overlooked, or thought to be irrelevant, perhaps, by those who had searched the premises — "

"Not hidden," Ouchi countered angrily, "the *l*ope is a*r*ways kept the'e."

"That may be so, Mr. Ouchi, but it *was* used to hoist Mr. LeMay up on that cross. And it is my assertion, that whoever crucified him, also killed him. The rope was looped around the dead man's chest, under his arms, then over the top rung of the ladder, and in this manner, lifted to the desired height. Then, by simply climbing the ladder, unencumbered, the murderer was able to perform his grisly task at will. The shiny top rung of the ladder, burnished by the action of the rope, I am certain, under laboratory examination, will further attest to this — not to mention a microscopic scrutiny of the rope itself."

"You mean that by Lab testing the rope and the ladder, you'll be able to identify the murderer?" The reverend's voice carried a note of genuine awe.

"I already know the identity of the murderer," the lieutenant replied, "the Lab will merely give us the forensic proof we need to prosecute — "

The lieutenant suddenly straightened. "Damn!" she exclaimed. Her eyes spun around the inside of the church. "Where are the Stirlings? Did anyone see them leave?" The pew near the outer aisle was now empty.

"They went out that side door, lieutenant." A wide-eyed Elizabeth pointed to a curtained portal, close to where the Stirlings had been sitting. "I — I thought you saw them — "

"Where does that door lead, Phinney?"

The reverend was about to reply when the sound of a bell echoed hollowly through the cavernous interior of the church.

"The bell tower," the reverend gasped. "They're up in the bell tower!"

THE LIEUTENANT WAS ALREADY AT THE DOOR, tugging the drapes aside. Mark was close at her heels. A steep circular staircase rose up in front of them and, together, they took the stairs two at a time.

The bell sounded again. It came from directly above them, where daylight from the open spire illuminated their ascent. And as the lieutenant cleared the last three steps in one frantic leap, she caught sight of Stirling, standing on the outer ledge, looking apprehensively toward the ground a hundred feet below. He was clutching his cringing wife against himself in a grip fed by fear and frenzy.

The lieutenant's shoulder brushed the huge bell, and it tolled softly as both Stirlings turned their stricken eyes toward her.

"Get back!" Stirling growled, "or I'll jump and take her with me." He held the terrified woman firmly in his grasp, his eyes wide and wild.

The lieutenant had stopped dead at the top of the stairs, but now began to drift, almost imperceptibly, around the near side of the bell. Mark was already moving, unseen, around the other side. "Jumping won't solve anything," the lieutenant said gently. "It's not the end of the world, you know. And your wife is innocent — "

"She's 'bout as innocent as a two-bit whore," Stirling said with an ugly laugh. He shook the woman fiercely, his eyes irate and filled with loathing.

"Let's talk about it," the lieutenant coaxed in a soft voice, "you can still jump, if that's what you want, after we've — "

A loud bellow came from the top of the stairs as a distraught reverend Phinney emerged in a violent rush. "Don't jump!" he screamed. "My God, don't let him jump — !"

Panic suddenly flared in Stirling's face, and with one fist clamped firmly on his wife's wrist, he shoved himself away from the ledge. The lieutenant streaked forward, but Mark, who was closer, caught the woman's other wrist and braced himself against the wooden parapet. The sudden jerk of their two falling bodies against Mark's vice-like hold, loosened Stirling's fingers and with a gurgling cry, he plummeted toward the earth.

Monica Stirling had fainted dead-away before they gently hauled her back into the bell tower.

THE SUN WAS LOW IN THE AFTERNOON SKY WHEN the lieutenant stood watching the Coroner's black van cart away the body of Nigel Stirling. The vehicle's tires left deep indentations in the close-clipped lawn.

"So it was Stirling," Mark said as he came up beside her, "who gave LeMay the apple laced with 10-80."

"No, Mark, it was actually Monica Stirling. She confessed to her part in it while you were scraping her late husband off the lawn. But she did it under a threat of violence to herself. I don't imagine her involvement will go much beyond a Court of Inquiry."

"But how did you know it was Stirling, lieutenant?" It was the voice of the reverend who had just joined them in front of the huge wooden cross.

"It was really quite simple," the lieutenant replied. "The Lab crew found traces of *dithiocarbamate* on the cross, a chemical used in the manufacture of certain fungicides. With information gleaned from my own orcharding background (which I re-enforced with a visit to the office of the local Department of Horticulture, on my way out here), I was able to associate the chemical with fungicides produced primarily for the eradication of *Leaf Curl*, in the growing of peaches: *Ferbam, Zeram, Maneb*, to name only a few. And peaches, of course, were Stirling's major crop."

"Hmmph!" the reverend Phinney grunted. "I would have thought the Biblical reference that was stuck to the cross would have had greater significance."

The lieutenant turned to him patiently. "Goodman took the agony of his wife's infidelity out on *her*, personally. Ouchi dealt with *his* little deceiver by tightening her psychological leash. And you, too, reverend, seem to have found a way to deal with your daughter's indiscretions with compassion — "

"We are all sinners in the eyes of the — "

" — but Stirling," the lieutenant politely interjected, "just couldn't handle it. He was the only one who turned his initial anger almost totally toward LeMay, as the scrawled Bible message clearly intimated." The lieutenant sighed reflectively. "The answer to who killed LeMay, had to be hidden in the identity of the mental cripple who perpetrated the mock crucifixion. Find one; and you find the other. And there lay the tragedy — "

"The tragedy," the reverend moaned, "was that it had to happen here." He moved off disconsolately toward the church. "Oh, what a travesty," he lamented, "St. Cuthbert's will never be the same."

THE LIEUTENANT LAUGHED AS SHE WATCHED THE churchman walk away, then, turning to Mark, she said, "Know something? We haven't even had lunch yet."

"Don't I know it," Mark groaned. "My stomach's been growling like a junk-yard dog."

"Come on, then." She took his hand and led him toward the unmarked Chevy where Mark had parked it at the curb. "I know a terrific, little Italian restaurant over on the East Side. And this time, I'll even buy."

"Lieutenant," Mark said with a sheepish grin as he tagged along, "what do you think the guys in Homicide would say, if they saw us holding hands?"

Cathy Carruthers chuckled and tightened her fingers on his. "Something male and macho, I guess, like, *What's up, Jock?*"

JUNE 1983
$1.75
47744

MIKE SHAYNE
MYSTERY MAGAZINE

0 71896 47744
06

The voluptuous and incredibly efficient Detective-Lieutenant Cathy Carruthers had been up against rapists and killers before, but this one's M.O. boggled even her mind!

the rape
of the
mannequins

TUESDAY, MAY 3RD

Detective-Lieutenant Cathy Carruthers was alone in her Homicide-Division office at Metro Central's Eleventh Precinct. She was seated at her desk, hunched forward in the chair with her hands up under her rumpled blouse. She was in the midst of an unscheduled, but critical adjustment to a snarled bra strap. And at that inopportune moment, the door to the office was suddenly thrown open.

"'Allo, 'allo! Wot's going on 'ere, then?"

Detective-Sergeant Mark Swanson stood in the doorway rendering his sadly inept impression of a London bobby. He kicked the door shut as he entered the office, then stood back to deliberate on his beautiful partner's curious plight, with *un*seemly interest.

"The old 'ammock's finally come a cropper then, 'as it, Mum?"

Cathy Carruthers glared up at him from behind a curtain of disheveled golden hair, and abruptly swiveled her chair and herself out of his view and further embarrassment. To her silently struggling back, in his own voice now, Mark added, "Which reminds me, lieutenant, the chief wants to see us. Something about a rape."

When she turned again to face him, Cathy Carruthers, though flushed, was now "decent" and seethingly calm. "I don't know what bothers me most, Mark," she asserted evenly between clenched white teeth, "your sudden intrusion on my privacy; your snide reference to an intimate article of my attire as a *hammock*; or simply that seeing me so rudely indisposed, should evoke in your one-track plebeian brain nothing more uplifting than (of all things!) an act of rape!"

Mark's eyes were wide with innocent wonder. "*Uplifting?*" He seemed almost to weigh the word.

The lieutenant favored her chosen partner with dark disaffection for several tense moments, then, with a sudden expulsion of breath, she broke into a squeal of uninhibited laughter.

"That *was* a poor choice of words, wasn't it?" she admitted finally, grinning up at him through a mist of tears. "Still, you weren't being very gallant, you know. You could at least have turned your back."

Mark made a valiant effort to look the injured party. "Lieutenant," he said solemnly, "with all due deference to the British Constabulary, I feel duty-bound to insist that I *did* act in a true gentlemanly manner, which, I hasten to suggest, is why you now find yourself still delightfully unsullied and free from ravishment, and in spite of the almost irrepressible compulsions of my deepest and darkest urges — "

The lieutenant raised a hand in protest. "Enough already." She dabbed at her eyes with a Kleenex tissue. "Now, what's this business about the chief?"

"He wants you in his office, PDQ."

"About a rape?"

"So he says. But don't worry, lieutenant, I'll be there to protect you."

Cathy Carruthers leveled her glistening blue eyes on him as she got to her feet. "That's like asking a lion to mind a lamb," she chuckled. "Come on, killer, let's find out what's bugging the chief."

As Mark followed the lieutenant out the door, he treated her to his best, impromptu rendition of the MGM lion.

CHIEF HENRY (HANK) HELLER WAS A CRAGGY LOOKING man with short gray hair and deeply chiseled features. He rose with a genial grunt from his chair as Cathy Carruthers and Mark Swanson entered his office.

"Lieutenant, Sergeant." The chief extended a gnarled hand to each of them in turn, motioned them to a chair, then settled himself back comfortably behind his desk. "Got a P.R. problem," he said simply.

"So what else is new, chief?" The lieutenant arched a perfect eyebrow. "What's it this time, police brutality?"

In answer, Chief Heller made a steeple with his fingers, pursed his lips against it, and squinted thoughtfully at his top investigative team. They were, he decided, a truly remarkable pair.

Mark was ruggedly, almost boyishly handsome. A powerfully built six-footer, with tousled brown hair and laughing blue-grey eyes that seemed to be permanently crinkled with imminent mischief. Cathy Carruthers, better known as *The Amazon* to her loyal colleagues, though equally tall (with the help of 3-inch heels) was a paradox of such outrageous beauty and sheer physical strength and intelligence, that she seemed at times to go beyond the pale of mortal blood and bone. They had built between them, she and Mark, an unspoken, mutual bond of respect and deep affection.

"There's been a rash of burglaries," the chief told them, "in the large department stores across the state line. Huntsville, to be precise. Speers, The Bay Co., The Broadwalk and P.C. Peter's— they've all been hit, with Speers and P.C. Peter's coming down as two-time losers. Same M.O. in every one of them. No signs of forced entry, or exit. Weird. Then, last night, the Speers store out at Pinetree Park was hit, right here in Metro. And that, boys and girls, dumps the ball squarely in our court."

"They're blowing the safes?"

"It's not a 'they,' Mark, it's a 'him.' And if he was into safes, he'd probably have tripped an alarm by now, and they'd have nailed him." The chief gave a weary shrug. "This guy seems to have a real talent for spotting small, high-priced items that are easy to tote. And he comes and goes as if by magic. My guess is, he probably cases each location the day before he pulls the job. Easy enough to do when the store is full of shoppers. Anyway, he's managed to get away with a couple of thou in merchandise on every haul. But," he eyed them both, closely, "there's more to it than that."

"I sure hope so." Cathy Carruthers couldn't hide a certain impatience. "So far, all this adds up to is a penny-ante heist. Store security ought to be able to handle that kind of situation on their own. So, what else does he take?"

"It's not so much what he takes," the chief replied with a mirthless chuckle, "it's what he leaves behind."

"You've lost me, chief."

"Every time this guy commits a burglary, lieutenant, he rapes a mannequin."

Cathy Carruthers glanced uncertainly at Mark. She didn't appear to know whether to laugh, cough, or just blush a little. "You're putting us on," she said finally.

"I'm giving in to you straight, lieutenant. This guy's got the hots for mannequins."

"The hots?" Mark's ingenuous face reflected his total incredulity. "For *mannequins*?"

"Yeah. You know, those life-like dummies they stick in the stores and dress up like real people."

"I know what a mannequin is, chief, but how the hell — ?"

"And he has a preference for blondes."

"Oh?" This time Mark did laugh. "That should be a comfort to the brunettes and the redheads. So why don't they just stow away all the blonde mannequins until the guy's been caught? If nothing else, it would sure cut down on the laundry bill."

"Mark!" Cathy Carruthers gave her partner a grim look of reproach.

"Not a chance, Mark. Do you have any idea how many blonde mannequins there are, scattered around the country?"

"No, sir, I don't imagine he does." The lieutenant eased herself up out of her chair. She was looking somewhat miffed. "This is all very, uh — enlightening, chief, but Mark and I are assigned to Homicide, remember? This case (thank God!) doesn't quite fit into our pigeonhole — "

"Sit down, lieutenant." The chief waved her back down into the chair. "I haven't finished yet. Not by a long shot."

"You mean this gentleman has other talents?"

"That's exactly what I mean, lieutenant, and he's no gentleman. Last night, a watchman caught him in the act."

"The act of what?" the lieutenant asked cautiously. "Burglary, or rape?"

"Both, I guess."

"So then you've got an I.D.?" It was more a statement than a question.

"No. Lieutenant, we haven't. But we have got a killer on the loose. The watchman was found early this morning, *with his throat slit from ear to ear.*"

"WELL, NOW." LIEUTENANT CARRUTHERS NUDGED HER beautiful nose with an elegantly flexed knuckle. "That puts a different light on it. Why didn't you say it was a homicide to begin with?"

"Are you kidding?" The chief gave a lecherous snort. "And miss out on seeing your reaction to the part about the mannequins?"

The lieutenant acknowledged Chief Heller's quaint sense of humor with a derisive curl of her upper lip. "You're a regular four-alarm fire, chief," she said tediously. But a moment later she was leaning forward in her chair, her vivid blue eyes bright with interest.

"It's a bit like getting someone else's unsolved case-file, I must admit," she mused, "but it occurs to me that a guy as kinky as this one shouldn't be all that hard to pin down." She looked to Mark as though to confirm that here, indeed, was a "puzzler" worthy of her efforts. She turned to the chief. "We're going to need a catch-up file on this, chief, everything relevant to the case that has happened up to date, and back to the time of the first burglary — "

"You got it, lieutenant. As a matter of fact, Corporal Leprohn has already been alerted and he's working on it right this minute. But before you get carried away, lieutenant, there's something else we should discuss."

"Your P.R. problem," she prompted intuitively.

"Hmmm. Right on the ball, eh?" Chief Heller leaned back with a doubtful smile, his hands locked behind his head. He was a striking man. His age could have been anywhere between forty and sixty, in spite of the gray hair. "Let me see if I can put this together for you," he said reflectively.

"All through this epidemic of burglaries," he began, "store management has been belly-aching for a quiet investigation, for obvious reasons. Frankly, I can't say that I blame them. But the Media picked up on that fiasco with the mannequins right off the bat, and they're the culprits who began to label each one of the burglar's little escapades as a 'rape.' In blazing bloody headlines yet: MIDNIGHT MARAUDER RAPES HIS THIRD MANNE-QUIN! I mean (Christ!), *you tell me,* lieutenant, how the hell's a guy going to rape a dummy — ?"

"I'd rather not, thank you."

" — and even if he does, *so what?*"

"Yeah, so what?" Mark echoed the words with a lascivious chuckle.

"Anyway, the stores apparently all got together and threatened to hire on some private investigation outfit. They said the police were giving the whole thing too much publicity. Bad for business, they said. Bull! It was the snoops from the Media who were doing all the damage. And to make matters worse, by the time the guy had made his third haul, and diddled his third dummy, the burglaries were strung out over three separate shopping centers. There just wasn't any way to keep a lid on it."

"This was all prior to the murder, of course."

"Right. He hit the stores a total of six times before leaving the Huntsville area. And now, with the death of the watchman last night, here in Metro, and another deflowered blonde within arms-length of the body — well, that's it."

"That's it?"

"What I mean, is, we might have been persuaded to pull back to an advisory role (given the collective civic pressure from the management of four major store chains), as long as it was only burglary, and, involving their own crummy merchandise. We might have even considered turning a blind eye to their fetishistic rapist, as long as he didn't deviate (if you'll pardon the pun) from those paint-and-plaster dummies — *but murder?* No way, Jose!"

"Did it occur to you, chief, that this Metro caper might be the work of a copy-catter, and that your ithyphallic thief might still be in Hunstville?"

"Yes, as a matter of fact, it did. But at this stage of the game, who can say — *ithyphallic?*"

"Why, *you* can, chief. And very well, too." The lieutenant rewarded him with an irritating smile. "Which, as we all know," she said demurely, "simply means that he is not a very nice man."

The chief grunted noncommittally. "Just one thing more, lieutenant, before you leave — "

"Keep it low key," she interjected, widening her smile as she second-guessed him for the second time.

The chief let out a low moan as he rolled his eyes up in the general direction of Cop Heaven. "Maybe," he said to the peeling paint on the ceiling, "just *maybe*, that's what this cockamamie case needs."

"Chief?"

"A woman's intuition, lieutenant. A rare commodity with which you seem to be uncommonly well endowed. And need I remind you, that until last night's murder, all the victims in the case have been women — at least of a kind."

"Yeah," Mark agreed, "and blondes, to boot." He exchanged conspiratorial winks with the chief.

IT WAS WELL PAST THE LUNCH HOUR WHEN Lieutenant Carruthers and Mark Swanson sauntered into Speers' body fashions department in the Pinetree Park Shopping Center. The actual site where the murder had taken place was now indistinguishable from any other area in the store. The victim and the violated mannequin, the spilled blood, and even the chalked outline of the body, had all been removed or cleaned away. The lieutenant's questions to the salesgirls about the recent murder were met with detailed recollections of horror, but about the put-upon dummy, they evoked only embarrassed titterings.

"We might as well grab ourselves some lunch," the lieutenant said to Mark with a beleaguered sigh. "There's nothing left to see here but a bunch of empty hammocks, as you so brutally call them." She tugged at his sleeve, drawing him reluctantly away from an erotic, promotional display of lingerie that had been aptly entitled: GO PAGAN IN PINK.

"I'm just partial to pink," Mark objected lamely as she steered him toward the store's bustling cafeteria.

The lieutenant, however, was visibly perturbed as they maneuvered through the crowd of midday shoppers. "I hope the leprechaun has been able to put something meaningful together for us," she fretted. "You don't know how I hate to take over someone else's botched-up investigation."

"Cheer up," Mark said brightly, "maybe tomorrow we'll get lucky and have a lovely new throat slashing all to our very own."

The lieutenant ignored her partner's obvious sarcasm. "Did you let the little guy know where we'd be this afternoon?"

"The leprechaun? Unfortunately, yes. He'll probably turn up in the salad with the midget mushrooms, and with a file a mile long."

The lieutenant chuckled. "Speak of the Devil," she said.

Waiting for them, by a stack of empty trays, with a bulky bundle of files clutched under one little arm, was Corporal Garfield Leprohn, better known as "The Leprechaun" by his colleagues at the Eleventh Precinct. He was Metro's shortest cop, ever, as well as the legendary head of the Records Department. It was obvious that he had donned his "elevators" for the occasion, which enabled him now to stand at eye-to-eye level with a spiteful little pre-teen girl who had just jostled him out of his place in line. He was still glaring at her retreating back when the two detectives closed in on him.

Mark beamed at the little cop. "You're in luck," he said with a syrupy smile.

"In luck?" The leprechaun was justifiably wary of Mark, especially when friendly. The big detective had taken an almost obscene delight in needling his pint-sized cohort, at every God-given opportunity.

"You better believe it," Mark said, pointing to a sign over the cafeteria counter. "They've got your special on today." The sign read:

HALF-PORTION SPECIAL FOR TODDLERS
(Must Be Accompanied By An Adult)

"Don't worry about the last bit," Mark told him with mock concern, "we'll vouch for you."

The leprechaun turned to his only friend. "I'll have a coffee, lieutenant. If you'll be good enough to get it for me, I'll find us a table." Mark thought he spotted a thin curl of smoke rising off the little guy as he stalked away.

"KEEP IT BRIEF, GARFIELD."

The leprechaun took the lieutenant's admonition in stride. His notes and files, much to Mark's annoyance, were everywhere, between coffee cups, soup bowls and plates of salad, and a small pile had been pressed into service (literally) to elevate his tiny tush, so that a level of visibility could be attained above the edge of the table.

"I picked up the Autopsy Report on the way out here," the little man said importantly, "it'll save you a trip to Cadaver City."

"Can't argue with that," the lieutenant acknowledged. "Are there any great pathological revelations in it?"

"Not so's you'd notice, lieutenant. I'll just give you the highlights: Victim, Jake Pedley. Male. Caucasian. Sixty-three. Throat slashed, jugular to carotid (left to right). Murder weapon, sharp knife or razor (not recovered). Time of death, about midnight, Monday May 2. And the rest, lieutenant, is just so much bureaucratic I-hope-this-justifies-my-job gobbledegook."

"Did Sam Morton do that autopsy?"

"Uh — yes. Here it is: Samuel Morton, M.D., Coroner & Chief Medical Examiner, M.C.P.D."

"Mmmm. It's not like Sam to be so sketchy. Not too enlightening, is it?"

"No, it isn't. But then neither is the catch-up material I was able to pry loose from my counterpart in Huntsville." The leprechaun gave an exaggerated sigh of frustration as he opened another file. "But for what it's worth, lieutenant, here it is —

"There were six reported burglaries in the Huntsville area, occurring on seemingly random days (or nights) of the week, except Wednesdays, Saturdays or Sundays. Chronologically, they took place as follows: March 14th, a Monday, Speers; Thursday, March 24th, The Bay Co.; Tuesday, March 29th, P.C. Peter's; then another

Speers store on April 4th, a Monday; Friday, April 15th, The Broadwalk; and finally a second P.C. Peter's on Tuesday, April 19th. There doesn't appear to be any pattern to them, except, perhaps, that no store was burglarized more than once other than the Speers' and P.C. Peter's chains which were singled out for two burglaries each."

"The chief said something about there not being any signs of forced entry."

"Right." The leprechaun flipped a couple of pages. "The B&E Squad in Huntsville, however, were not overly mystified with the forced entry factor (or the lack of it), they figure he could have easily hidden himself somewhere in the store, prior to closing. It was the lack of forced *exit* that had them buffaloed. They just couldn't figure out where he went to — *after* making his haul. And they still don't know."

"The stores would have been locked up by then, I presume, and adequately guarded."

"Tight as a drum, lieutenant. There just wasn't any way he could have gotten out without 'breaking a seal,' so to speak."

"But he did."

"Apparently so."

"A regular Houdini," Mark grunted. "What about those so-called rapes?"

"Now there's a dollop of *Ugh!* That defies description." An involuntary shudder shook the leprechaun's little shoulders. "You're already aware, I believe, that the 'rapist' invariably chooses a blonde mannequin on which to vent his venereal aberration (isn't that gross?), but other than that one idiosyncrasy, there doesn't seem to be any pattern to it. All known sex offenders were, of course, rounded up and questioned, but, so far, nothing has come of it."

"And the stolen merchandise, corporal, has any of it been recovered?"

"No. Not yet. Not a single item."

"After six burglaries?"

"Seven," Mark updated, "if you count the one last night, here in Metro."

"True enough, Mark. Scheee! He must be sitting on a veritable hoard by now." The lieutenant chewed incredulously at her lower lip. "Sooner or later," she mused, "*sometime, somewhere,* he's going to have to start unloading the stuff."

"The Huntsville P.D. have had a special team working on it non-stop, lieutenant, ever since the first heist. Pawnshops, known fences, you name it. But, to date, they've drawn a blank."

The lieutenant shifted some of the files that were heaped in front of her. "There's a cup of coffee hiding in here somewhere," she lamented, "that *I'm* drawing a blank on. Is all this paper really necessary, Garfield?"

"You cannot create and maintain a record without paper, lieutenant." The leprechaun postured and pouted with appropriate aplomb. "Paper is a vital tool of my trade."

"So why don't you try putting it all on rolls of four-inch tissue?" Mark suggested. "Besides taking up less room, it'd be a helluva lot easier to dispose of."

The leprechaun fought to stem the rise of color to his little cheeks. He gathered up his files in stony silence, tossed four-bits on the table to pay for his coffee, and headed for the door without a backward glance.

"The little guy looks a bit 'flushed'," Mark allowed with impish innocence as he watched the leprechaun trundle away.

THURSDAY, MAY 12TH.

At precisely 9 o'clock in the a.m., Lou Drydon approached the all-glass entrance to The Bay Co. store in Central Metro. He was a tall, rangy man with a florid face and a small, firm, abdominal pot, that came from years of sitting behind the wheel of a car. He carried a large sample case in one hand and a brown leather order book in the other.

Drydon, now in his early fifties, had been a commercial traveler most of his working life. He was presently representing two well-received lines of ladies' wear, both of which had originated in the garment district of New York. They both were specialty lines of *Intimate Apparel.* One, COMFY CONTROL (bras, girdles, corselets, and such) had been designed on the premise that the female form required some measure of assistance from stretch-nylon and whale-bone to look its sexy best. Conversely, the other line, EVE'S RIVAL, assumed all women to be perfect, *au naturel,* and fielded garments that sought simply to adorn and titillate.

It was from this latter line that Lou Drydon chose from his most erotic samples each morning, a pair of panties to wear himself.

Drydon noted with some relief that there was only a smattering of early shoppers in the store. This would give him a clear field to take stock, draw up a fill-in order, and show a few new COMFY CONTROL styles without major interruptions. And that would leave the EVE'S RIVAL line for a similar showing tomorrow morning. Perfect. He went directly to the Lingerie Department where he was known and welcomed with courteous reserve.

"Keep the order to a minimum, Lou," a chunky, barrel-waisted woman called to him from behind a display of what looked like lace-trimmed armor. She was Pamela Jeffers, the manageress, a *corsettiere* of the old school who was obviously well wrapped up in her own advice. He had often speculated, that if the heavily boned garment she always wore under her nylon smock was ever to let go, she'd ooze out over the floor like a hundred and fifty pounds of Gillette Foamy.

"No 34As, and no large sizes, Lou. No smalls or XLs. Only 36s and 38s, B to D cup. Summer's a slow mover, Lou."

"Whatever you say, Miss Jeffers."

Drydon went about taking stock with a seemingly detached indifference, but his eyes strayed repeatedly over to the ladies' outerwear department, where he could just make out, between the racks of colorful summer dresses, the glistening, golden topknot of a blonde mannequin. She was new here, he could tell, even from that distance. He had long ago committed his favorite "girls" in all the stores to memory. The hint of a smile played across his lips. He would have to name her, he thought, as he had the others. Then later, when he had old Miss-five-by-five off his back, he'd meander over there and have a good look at her. In the meantime, while he worked, he would think of a pretty name — .

"LIEUTENANT — " MARK STRETCHED THE WORD out into a weary sigh. They were in the Broadwalk store, on the outskirts of Huntsville, and he was sitting with his beautiful partner at a worktable in the stockroom, behind the lingerie department. "How much longer," he said, "do we have to hang around this cruddy town, waiting for something to happen?"

"We've only been here since Monday," the lieutenant replied absently, as she watched a frumpy salesgirl search through a myriad of stacked boxes for a garment of a given size and color. "We've managed to do a thorough check of all the burglary sites in Huntsville, Mark, except one, and we should finish that one off some time tomorrow."

"If you've seen one, you've seen 'em all," Mark protested. "Here it is Thursday, lieutenant, and, I ask you, what do we know now that we didn't know last week, before leaving Metro?"

"Not much, I confess. But remember, Mark, the simple process of elimination is, in itself, a proven method of investigation. Besides, we're on a very cold trail."

"This trail is not just cold, lieutenant, it's *frigid* to the point of needing therapy."

Cathy Carruthers admonished him with her eyes as she reached into her handbag for her notebook. "Why must you put everything into a sexual context, Mark? If I didn't know you, I'd have you at the top of my list of suspects." She opened the book and turned a few pages. "Anyhow, let's see what we've got, so far."

"Zilch," Mark told her, "that's what we've got. You're just grabbing at straws, lieutenant."

"Maybe so." she ran a blood-red fingernail down a scribbled page. "But we've got to start somewhere. Look at this, for instance: where I've listed the six burglaries by the days of the week. See? It becomes apparent at once that two occurred on Mondays, and two on Tuesdays, but only one each on a Thursday and a Friday." She looked up at him as though she had just discovered America. "Now, where I've listed them by the 'chain,' rather than by the store, we can see that Speers pops up twice, P.C. Peter's twice, and the other two, only once. Mmmmm — " She squinted thoughtfully at her unreceptive partner as she appeared to consider a third possibility. "But then, by listing them *this* way, Mark, chronologically, by the day and the date — ?"

The lieutenant seemed suddenly to lose herself in her own speculations.

"Well?" Mark grunted impatiently.

"Well," the lieutenant said slowly, "where I've listed them like *that*, it shows that there is precisely three weeks between each of the Monday heists at Speers, and the two Tuesday heists at P.C. Peter's."

"So?"

"So, it suggests to me, Mark, that there are certain 'invariables' here. A kind of regularity. For example: (a), our lascivious felon, for some unknown reason, never rips off more than one store in any given week, (b), he never hits the same store location twice, and, (c), as I've already pointed out, he spaced the Speers jobs and those at P.C. Peter's by exactly three weeks, to the very day — "

Mark made a gun out of his fingers and put it to his right ear. "If I wasn't confused before," he said, "I sure as hell am now." He pulled the trigger. "Goodbye, cruel world," he sobbed.

"You're out of sequence," the lieutenant told him with a patient smile. "You should have said good-bye *before* you pulled the trigger – hey, *that's it!*" she exclaimed suddenly. "Don't you see, Mark? Those first six burglaries have a definite *sequence* to them."

"How about that?"

"Now," she mused as she buried her nose even deeper in the book, "if we can only establish what that sequence is, or the relevance of it, before he has a chance to strike again."

"But he hasn't made a move since the Monday before last," Mark reminded her, "out at the Speers store in Metro. That's almost two weeks ago. Maybe the sight of blood has scared him off."

"Somehow, I doubt that. It didn't seem to dampen his fetishistic ardor on that occasion, did it? But, come to think of it, we just can't be too sure of that either, can we?"

"How so?"

"We're still in the dark on his priorities, Mark. Like who strikes first, the lecher or the yegg?"

Mark held his nose in mock disdain. "Just the same," he admitted grudgingly, "we really don't know how he operates."

"Right. So let's look at another angle. The mannequins."

"Well, for one thing, they've all been blondes," Mark volunteered.

"Yes," the lieutenant added, "and they've all been fully dressed.

Sedately dressed, at that."

Mark grimaced. "You mean, to begin with."

"But doesn't that strike you as being somewhat incongruous?"

"And just what," Mark queried, "do you suggest would be congruous to a sex fiend?"

"Still, it could be relevant that he hasn't yet attacked a mannequin that was scantily clad, or nude, or even one that was left overnight by the display people, in a partial state of dishabille. The rapee, Mark, in every case, has been a *fully dressed figure*. That should tell us something."

"It should?"

The lieutenant screwed up her beautiful face in thought. "Of course," she said at last.

"Of course," Mark echoed with a facial shrug of mock accord.

"It is only then, Mark, that those things look for real. Or human, if you like. Don't you see? The least clothing a mannequin has on, the more it looks like just what it damn well is — a cold and sexless plaster dummy."

"What you're saying is that the clothes help to fuel the imagination," Mark acknowledged. "Agreed, but what does it prove?"

"It proves that we've got a genuine psycho on our hands, Mark, with a very real fetish. This bozo probably couldn't relate to a bona fide woman if his life depended on it."

"But what can we do about it? All known sex offenders have already been checked out. Both in Metro, *and* here in Huntsville. And all we've come up with so far is a goose egg." He gave it a moment's thought. "Unless, of course, the guy is a first-timer."

"A distinct possibility, Mark. Also, there's this business about there being no signs of break-in, or break-out. And when you start putting it all together, it begins to smell like a inside job."

Mark looked doubtful. "Lieutenant, what kind of an 'inside job' is going to give a man access to seven different stores, that are owned and operated by four totally different 'chains?'"

"Hard to say," the lieutenant conceded, "but it's the best angle we've come up with so far."

Mark glanced at his watch. "Hold your fire, lieutenant, it's almost 5:30. Don't you think it's time we called it a day?"

"Indeed, I do, Mark." The lieutenant folded her notebook and stowed it back in her red leather shoulder bag. "We've just got time to get cleaned up."

"We have? For what?"

"Well, Mark, seeing we're being held over for another night, I took the liberty of picking up a couple of tickets to the Huntsville Opera House. Pavarotti is appearing in Puccini's *La Boheme* tonight. It should be pleasurably edifying for you."

Mark groaned. "Being edified is not exactly my idea of pleasure," he muttered. "I don't suppose it would be possible — "

The lieutenant stifled his protest with a bewitching smile. "*La Boheme* is a love story," she told him in a propitious stage whisper, "when the house lights dim, *anything is possible.*"

FRIDAY, MAY 13TH.

When Chief Hank Heller's call came through at 4:15 a.m., Cathy Carruthers was fast asleep in her hotel room. They had chosen a small hotel in the central part of town, more out of convenience than preference. She groped in the dark for the phone, then grunted in the general direction of the mouthpiece.

"Lieutenant? This is Chief Heller."

"Huh? Chief? Good grief, man, d'you know what time it is?"

"I know precisely what time it is, lieutenant. And it affords me the greatest pleasure to jangle your comatose brains at this unholy hour. Unfortunately, the serious nature of my call tends to dilute my equally unholy joy, but only somewhat."

"Give," the lieutenant muttered.

"Romeo has struck again."

"My God," she said. "What this time?"

"You name it, we got it." The chief's voice was quietly, deadly serious. "Rape, burglary, and bloody murder. Not necessarily in that order."

"Where, and who?"

"The Bay Co. In the Pinetree Park shopping Center. The victim was a woman this time, a Miss Jeffers. Pamela Jeffers. She is (or was) the manageress of the ladies' underwear department, or whatever they call it."

"I doubt they call it that, chief, but what was a woman doing in the store in the middle of the night?"

"She wasn't. I mean, she was, but — "

"But, what?"

"But, well — let me give it to you from the beginning. I got the call about a half hour ago. Our guys were already on the scene. A watchman phoned it in. The M.E., Sam's assistant, pegged the time of death, tentatively, at five to six hours. That would mean she died around 10 or 11 o'clock, last night."

"The store was still open at that hour?" the lieutenant asked incredulously.

"Hell, no. She was apparently working late, taking stock, or something. She must have heard him and gone over to investigate. When they found her, she was over in the dress department with her throat cut from ear to ear."

"Seems I've heard that song before," the lieutenant said softly. "You said something about rape."

"Yeah. Not the woman, though. It was another mannequin, a new one they'd just moved into the evening wear section of the dress department. He sure messed up an expensive set of threads."

"Was the mannequin a blonde?"

"What else?"

"Chief." The lieutenant's voice took on a reflective note. "Don't you find that middling strange? Passing up a real woman, I mean, to rape a lousy dummy?"

"Not really, lieutenant. And you won't either, when you see the woman."

"Hmmm." The lieutenant was silent for several moments. "Did he get away with a haul?"

"He had a field day."

"Any weapon?"

"No. He must have taken it with him. We're still searching, of course."

"Anything else you can tell me, chief?"

"Only this. There were no signs of forced entry, or exit. We've checked out every door, window and vent. It's almost like we're dealing with a, a — "

" — a ghost?"

"You said it, I didn't."

The lieutenant laughed. "Okay, we're on our way." She checked the luminous dial of her watch. "We should be there before the store opens at nine. See if you can get the area roped and curtained off where they found her, and *it*. And, chief ?"

"Yeah?"

"Get the Lab Crew in at the scene before anyone touches that corpse or the dummy. This is the first warm bit of evidence we've had a chance to work with."

"Well, you'd better hurry."

"Chief?"

"That 'warm' evidence, lieutenant. It's getting colder by the minute."

MARK OPENED HIS EYES WITH A START, THEN GRINNED as he recognized who had awakened him.

"Well, lookie here now," he purred, "its's Aunt Cathy with her hair down." He slid over the far side of the bed and turned down the covers. "Be gentle with me," he pleaded in a feigned, frightened little voice.

The lieutenant laughed at him, in spite of a supreme effort not to. "Doesn't that lecherous libido of yours ever call it quits?" she scolded.

"Sure, if that's what turns you on," Mark replied agreeably. "So, okay — let's make 'quits'."

"The only thing you're going to make," the lieutenant told him in a voice that did not in any way reflect her sleepy, sultry appearance, "is tracks. It's time," she said, "to hit the road."

"What's up?"

The lieutenant quickly filled him in on the call from the chief. "We've just got time for a quick shower," she added. "Breakfast will have to wait."

Mark sat up in bed, wide awake. "I don't suppose I could interest you in the merits of conserving both time and water, could I?" He was suddenly at his persuasive best. "The Pure-Water Society of Bald Knob, Arkansas, has proven, posi*ti*vely, that two can shower as quickly and as pleasurably as one — "

The lieutenant picked up the pillow closest to her and threw it. "Five minutes," she asserted. "Dressed and packed."

Mark's garbled rejoinder was (fortunately) muffled by the pillow.

THE AREA IN THE BAY CO.'S DRESS DEPARTMENT where Pamela Jeffers had met her untimely end, was roped and curtained off from public view. A few early morning shoppers milled about the floor, unconcerned with what appeared to be the sequestered, innocent beginning of a new display. The news of the manageress's death had apparently not yet been leaked to the Media. And for that, the lieutenant was thankful.

"Yuck!" Policewoman Fisk, who had been assigned to guard the area, gave voice to the sentiments of all three of them, as they stood over the chalked outline that now replaced the body. Blood was everywhere, and a disheveled blonde mannequin lay about ten feet away, parallel to the outline. The pristine, gossamer folds of the sequined evening dress it wore, was rumpled and torn — and grossly soiled.

"I see they've dusted the mannequin for prints," the lieutenant said to Fisk, who stood at her elbow. "Do you know if they came up with anything?"

"Nothing but a bunch of smudges." The young brunette rookie was dressed in civvies, so as not to attract undue attention. "There wasn't even a decent print from the display staff who dressed her — uh, it."

"Well, at least we know now that we're not dealing with a copy-catter," Mark noted grimly. "There can't be any doubt that this is the work of the same guy."

"Yes, indeed," the lieutenant agreed, "and he seems to be right on cue."

Mark lifted his bushy brows as he fired up a cigarette. "Come again?"

"I'll get to that later, Mark. Right now, I'd like to have a few words with the store management." She turned to the young brunette who, in her summery blouse and skirt, looked like anything but the trained and capable policewoman she was. "Office Fisk, can you tell me where the Administrative Offices are?"

"Right on this floor, lieutenant." Fist pointed a dainty finger. "There, behind the Notions Department."

"Thank you. Fisk, you stay here. Mark, while I'm gone, see what you can come up with in the lingerie department. And I don't mean, pink pagans. I'll meet you over there in a few minutes."

"You got it, lieutenant." Officer Fisk acknowledged the order with a weary sigh.

She lifted the rope for them to exit under, then watched Mark thread his way, like a bull in a cornfield, through the racks of summer dresses toward the lingerie department. A well-endowed salesgirl was there to greet him with a questioning smile in front of an elaborate display of "Uplift" bras. Her opulent, cantilevered bosom seemed to be a living testimonial to the advertised claims of the product she was selling, *and* undoubtedly wearing.

"Is this where Miss Jeffers works?" Mark asked, trying to keep his eyes above the level of the girl's chin.

"Yes, sir. But she's not in this morning."

"Are you aware if she was working last night?" he asked.

"Yes sir." She gave him a curious look. "She was doing an inventory, I believe. That's probably why she's late getting in this morning. It's really not all that unusual."

From where he stood, Mark could clearly see the curtained-off area he had just vacated, and then, as he glanced to his left, he noticed a tall, gangly-looking man, with a balding pate and a small paunch, busily sorting through the bins of bras and panties that flanked the department on three sides. The man's eyes met his, fleetingly, then quickly flicked away.

"Sir?"

The girl had moved up close to Mark's elbow and as he turned, his cigarette dangling on his lower lip, he found himself suddenly squeezed into her somewhat generous, head-to-toe proximity.

"We have a 'thank-you-for-not-smoking' policy in the store," she said with a patronizing smile. But then, before Mark could respond, the ash fell off the end of his dangling cigarette and disappeared into the girl's protruding cleavage. She looked calmly down at her offended anatomy, then just as calmly back up to a discomfited Mark.

"I suspect," she said with irritating sweetness, "*that* is one of the reasons why."

Mark beat a hasty retreat to where the lieutenant now stood waiting, and watching, in the aisle. Her beautiful face was contorted with suppressed amusement.

"That's not exactly what I'd call making a clean breast of things," she choked through muffled laughter, as they headed back together toward the scene of the murder. "I'm just relieved that you didn't try to retrieve the ash."

"Nuts!" Mark grunted. "It wouldn't have happened if she hadn't been so — "

" — so forward?" the lieutenant suggested with pretended innocence.

IT WAS LATER THAT SAME DAY. CHIEF HANK HELLER'S graven face hovered over his desk like an incipient storm cloud. Cathy Carruthers and Mark Swanson stood in the doorway to his office, as though reluctant to advance any further into so hostile an environment.

"It will be exactly two weeks tomorrow since I put you two on this case," the chief was saying in a tone of voice that augured no good for anyone, least of all the two detectives who now stood before him, "and what do you have to report? You've got a theory. *A theory!* I don't want a theory, lieutenant, I want an arrest."

"Chief, if you'll just hear us out — "

"Lieutenant, the only thing I want to hear is the click of handcuffs on the man who murdered Pedley and Jeffers. Now, understand me, I'm giving you just three more days to come up with something substantial, something I can take to the commissioner. Three more days, lieutenant. Otherwise, you're off the case."

"But, chief — "

"No, 'buts,' lieutenant. Just results. Now, *if* you can find the bloody thing, close the door as you leave."

When the door had closed behind them, the chief smiled knowingly; while outside in the corridor, the lieutenant looked wide-eyed at a thoroughly discombobulated Mark Swanson.

"I just wanted to tell him," she seethed, "that we'd have the damn killer for him, Tuesday night."

Mark froze on the last swing of a double-take. "We'll *what?* You've got to be kidding, lieutenant. We're not even close to knowing who that creep is. All I can say is, it's a good thing he didn't give you the chance to stick your pretty neck out any further than it already is."

The lieutenant spun angrily on her heel and headed for the elevators. "If you think that's sticking my neck out, wait'll you hear what I've got in mind."

Mark caught up with her just in time to board the same elevator. There was only one other occupant in the car; a prune-like, precipitously ageing cleaning lady, standing alone and aloof at the rear of the elevator. The woman looked almost triumphant, Mark thought in passing, as though she had devoted her entire forty-odd years to the joyless pursuit of menopause, and had, at that very moment, finally achieved her goal.

"Well?" Mark nudged his beautiful partner. "How long are you going to keep me in suspense?" he asked in a husky whisper.

The lieutenant regarded him with one of those opaque stares that usually denoted some deep, inner cogitation. "We've been going at this all wrong," she whispered back.

The prune raised a spinisterish eyebrow.

"We have?" Mark queried, wondering vaguely why he was whispering.

"Yes. We've been dwelling too much on the murders."

"Yeah, well — "

"And all those rapes."

"But — "

"What we *should* be thinking about, Mark, is — "

The prune-like ear closest to them twitched.

" — Sex!" The lieutenant's one whispered word echoed off the walls of the elevator with alarming clarity. "*Perverted, maniacal sex,*" she appended, with somewhat unseemly zeal.

The doors gaped open and Mark turned to allow the matronly person he remembered to be behind him, to exit first. Oddly, she had already left.

MONDAY, MAY 16th

Mark was perched on a P.C. Peter's check-out counter, watching while Cathy Carruthers was doing her level best to look like a mannequin, and a prissy little man from the display department, was doing *his* best to make a mannequin look like Cathy Carruthers. The three of them were alone in the store, except possibly for a member of the security staff who would be somewhere out of sight, checking doors and punching clocks. The time was 11:05 p.m.

Since the store's opening at 9 a.m., the two detectives had spent most of their time with the General Manager, setting up what the lieutenant referred to as her "proposed ambuscade." They had been promised total cooperation, both in the acquisition of props, as well as the direct assistance of certain store personnel that would be necessary to the success of the lieutenant's risky ploy. Other than the G.M., however, and one trusted assistant, there were only two other employees who had knowledge of the scheme; the manageress of the ladies' wear department, and the little display man. Later, one guard would also be alerted.

The smile Mark now leveled at his comely partner, did not totally hide the concern he felt deep in his gut. It was a dangerous thing she was doing; but to watch her, you would think she was being fitted for a dress to go to the school prom. Her beautiful honey-colored hair was hidden under a tinsel-blonde wig that was styled in identical fashion to the wig on the mannequin. And the lavender dress she had been given to wear, was an elegant twin to the one on her hank-o'-hair counterpart.

"When you said you were going to stick your neck out, you weren't just kidding," Mark said with feeling. "Frankly, I don't like any part of this."

"It's the only way we're ever going to nail him," the lieutenant replied. "Anyway, it's too late now for second thoughts."

"Maybe he won't show," Mark said hopefully.

"Either way, Mark, we're between a rock and a hard place. And if I could have my druthers, I'd still prefer to deal with *El Sexo* than an irate Chief Heller."

"What makes you think this weirdo is going to take the bait, lieutenant?"

The lieutenant sighed soulfully. "I've already told you, Mark, I just don't believe we're after a murderer, *per se*, or even a burglar, or a rapist. The guy we're after is a gold-plated psycho. I believe we're dealing with a man who, until very recently, had been living a relatively normal life. I also believe he is known, and perhaps even respected by a lot of people in the stores that he has plundered and desecrated. The actual murders, and the burglaries, in my opinion, are merely 'extensions' of his compelling mania with the mannequins."

"I get the drift," Mark said impatiently, "what you're saying is that we're not about to catch a psycho by looking for a thief or a murderer"

"Right, Mark. And especially a thief who has made no visible attempt to profit from his crimes, or a murderer whose victims seem to be merely chance encounters, and whose deaths are totally bereft of method or motive. No wonder we've drawn a blank. We've been looking in the wrong places for the wrong guy."

"And you're sure this is the right place?"

The lieutenant turned her head and smiled. The combination of the tinsel-blonde wig and her own luminous blue eyes was not only stunning, it was positively magnetic. She was seated at a table in a make-believe nightclub. A third mannequin, a male, in black-tie and tails, sat opposite. The table was grandly accoutered and graced with a bottle of rare wine, crystal glassware, and a flickering candle centerpiece that almost looked like the real article.

"Only time will tell, Mark," she said around the fussing of the little display man. "But now we're into assumptions, rather than hard nosed facts. We have to assume that, *one*, these "rapes" (I deplore that reference) are intentionally, or *un*intentionally, a sequence, and *two*, that he's repeating the same sequence here in Metro that he began in Huntsville."

"But there's another P.C. Peter's store in Metro, lieutenant, out in Almond Gardens."

"Yes, I know. And that's a chance we'll have to take. My guess is, though, that he'll stay in this area. It would be more consistent with his previous pattern."

"*Fudge!*" The somewhat mild expletive was delivered with the flip of a delicate hand on the end of a limp wrist. Dickie Wilde, of the display department, was obviously annoyed. "Oh, I did ask you girls to stay still. Dearie me. I'll just *never* get you dressed at this rate."

Dickie Wilde took the lieutenant's head gently between his little hands and turned it back to where it had been. He fussed over her dress, molding the low-cut bodice to her breasts, arranging a casual fall to the material over her generously exposed thighs. A disapproving frown had clouded Mark's stolid features. Few men would risk doing what the innocuous Dickie Wilde was innocently getting away with.

To break the tension in his own demeanor, Mark said lightly, "What are you going to do about matching up their eyes, Dickie?"

"Oh, *yes*," he lisped, just inches from the lieutenant's vivid blue orbs, "aren't they just *darling?*"

He took a small bottle from the make-up kit with which he had been attempting to transform the mannequin into a Cathy Carruther's look-alike. "It's a luminous blue dye, of sorts," he said with a dither of excitement. "It's my own innovation."

The little man applied the dye to the mannequin's somewhat vapid blue irises. The result was startling.

"*There*," he beamed. He assumed a typical Jack Benny pose, with hands on hip and cheek, waiting for his kudos. Mark obligingly applauded, as much to cover his own amusement as in honest praise. The lieutenant rose and turned to have a look. "Oh, wow," she breathed. "Do I look like that?"

"I'll finish this off myself now, if you *don't* mind," Dickie Wilde told them with a note of petulant authority. "I'll have the *real* mannequin in the display during the day, of course, then at *closing* time, I'll be here to make the switch. She'll need some last minute *preening* you see," he said, as he fussed and plucked at the material in the lieutenant's dress. "I'll spruce this up for you tomorrow, sweet, so if you'll *just* slip it off — Oh!" he tittered, with a smirking glance at Mark, "we have a gentleman present, don't we? You'd better use the change room, dear."

Mark's eyes were saucers of incredulity as his beautiful partner in a fit of restrained laughter, trooped off to the change room.

"They're such *dears*," Dickie Wilde confided to Mark, as he turned his attention back to the mannequin, "but they do so *try* a person, don't they?"

TUESDAY, MAY 17TH

Lou Drydon crossed the parking lot of P.C. Peter's Pinetree Park store in a state of inner excitement. He glanced at his watch as he neared the entrance. Nine-thirty. He was in good time. The girls, of course, would already be there, waiting for him, standing serenely in their places, posing in their pretty clothes. He smiled wanly. Before the day was much older, he would be choosing among them for one to be his lover.

He hurried through the entrance foyer, feeling the first cool puff of the air-conditioning, then plodded down the wide center aisle toward the lingerie department. His sample case hung heavily from his right hand and, midway along the aisle, he decided arbitrarily on a detour through the dress department to shorten his trek. And it was there and then, as he circled a heavily laden rack of multi-colored summer dresses, that he saw her for the first time.

She sat at a table with a man in black-tie and tails, *but her liquid shimmering blue eyes were looking directly at him.* There was a half-consumed bottle of wine on the table, an array of sparkling crystal, and a dancing yellow candle that imbued the whole tableau with an aura of sheer elegance. But it was the girl in the lavender dress that swelled his heart, the girl with the golden hair and the most exquisite, heavenly-blue eyes he had ever seen.

He continued on to the lingerie department, reluctant to leave his new love, but ecstatic in the knowledge that he had found her so quickly. He'd have the whole day now to think about her, to fantasize, to dream up a pretty and appropriate name. He'd have to schedule his day just right so that he'd still be working in the department at closing time, ready to slip away, to lose himself in the stockroom; *just as he had done in so many stores, so many times before.*

He went happily about his task, counting bras and panties, negligees and nighties, with the image of his new-found love dancing sensuously in his thoughts.

WHEN THE LAST CUSTOMER HAD FINALLY STRAGGLED

from the store, it was precisely 5:37, and Cathy Carruthers slipped silently out of the fitting room, dressed in her blonde and lavender ensemble. Dickie Wilde, she saw, had already denuded her mannequin look-alike and was deftly tugging a chalk-white tennis outfit over its bald head. She watched him fuss with the dummy like a mother hen, then cart it off to a spot opposite Sporting Goods, where he stuck a racquet in its hand and endowed it with a page-boy hair-do and an instant back-hand.

When Dickie returned to the display, the lieutenant was already settled in the seat the mannequin had vacated. "Now," he whispered, "let's get you presentable — *Oh my*! What is this lumpy *thing* you've got under that pretty dress?"

The lieutenant gently open-handed him back a pace. "Wait," she whispered hoarsely. She took the earplug from the top of the battery unit that was strapped between her breasts and lodged it firmly in her left ear. From her purse, that she had slipped in under the floor-length table cover, she withdrew her own original Smith & Wesson .38 special, and tucked it snugly between her crossed thighs. "*Now* fix me up," she told him curtly, "and remember that we're here to catch a murderer, not to win the Miss America title."

Dickie Wilde swallowed noisily, with a nervous forward thrust of his chin. He suddenly seemed to see his assigned task in an entirely new light. With his busy little fingers, he hid the wire from the earplug beneath the cascading blonde tresses of the wig. The offending bulge between her breasts, he skillfully obscured by re-arranging the loose, lavender folds of her dress. And the gun that protruded so evilly from between her thighs, he cleverly concealed under a seemingly innocent bunching of her raised skirt.

As the little man fussed over her, the lieutenant pressed a button on the battery unit. "Mark? Do you read me? Come in, Mark." Her voice, to Dickie Wilde, was almost inaudible. The voice that answered, he didn't hear at all.

"I read you, lieutenant. Everything okay?"

"So far, so good. Dickie's preening me."

"Yeah, I'll bet. Tell the little fag to hurry up and get out of there."

To Dickie Wilde, the lieutenant said, "I think you'd better leave now."

The little guy needed no more prompting. He picked up the wig and the dress he had stripped from the mannequin, took one last critical look at his "display" and beat a hasty retreat.

The lieutenant was suddenly very much alone. It was just a few minutes shy of six o'clock, and still light outside (and would be, until well after nine) but without the overhead lights, the interior of the store was dingy with shadow and as silent as a tomb. Even her companion at the table, so quiet and unmoving, took on the unreal, spectral quality of an unwanted presence.

Cathy Carruthers tried to think of other things while the minutes began to tick by with painful slowness.

BACK IN THE POLICE VAN THAT WAS PARKED JUST beyond and to one side of the north entrance, Mark was monitoring the radio that was tuned in to the set on the lieutenant's chest. The reception was excellent. He could hear it when she breathed deeply, or sharply, and her occasional nervous swallow was clearly audible. Officer Too-Tall Bones sat beside him, his black face creased with concern.

Mark glanced at his watch. The second hand was just moving up to 7:35. He had been making contact with her every five minutes for the past two hours. He switched on the mike.

"Lieutenant?"

"Yes, Mark."

"You okay?"

"I guess. I never thought sitting still could be so painful."

"Have you heard anything?"

"Not since the watchman made his rounds. All I've heard since, is silence."

"You can't *hear* silence."

"Want to bet?"

"Okay, pardner, just want you to know we're with you, every second."

"That's good to know."

"Over and out."

The speaker in the van picked up the lieutenant's weary sigh of resignation.

"I'd feel better," Too-Tall said, "if we were hidden inside the building somewhere. The way it is, it's going to take us at least two minutes to get to her."

"You think I don't know that?" Mark said grimly. "But how can we hide from someone who's already hidden, and we don't know where? All we'd do is scare him off."

"If he's in there to begin with."

"So how else d'you figure he gets in there without cracking a door or a window?"

"Beats me." Too-Tall was silent for several moments. "Are you sure the guard has left the door open for us?"

"No, I'm not sure, Bones," Mark said impatiently, "but the guy did get his instructions. He was also told to clear the area, and keep clear, until we sound the all-clear." He chuckled dryly. "He was only too happy to oblige."

"I still wish there was some way we could check out that door," Too-Tall worried.

"Well, there isn't. Damn it, Bones, you're acting like an old woman."

"Yeah, I guess," the big black said lamely. "It's just that she's so alone in there, and so bloody vulnerable."

"Tell me something I don't know."

Bones put a gigantic black hand on the big detective's shoulder.

"Sorry, sarge. Let's just be ready to roll if anything happens."

"I'm ready," Mark muttered softly.

LOU DRYDON LIFTED HIS WRIST AND STUDIED THE dial on his digital watch. It was 9:41. There hadn't been a sound since the guard had passed through more than three hours before. He was stretched out on his back on the uppermost shelf in the stockroom, his jacket rolled up under his head like a pillow, and his sample case resting just beyond his feet. He was not uncomfortable. On the contrary; later, when it was all over, he'd simply come back up here and wait until the store re-opened in the morning. Then he would pick his moment to blend unobtrusively back in among the lingerie displays. He would be expected (welcomed, even) with his second line, "EVE'S RIVAL." In the meantime, he'd idle away the hours, as he'd always done, thinking about his past encounters.

It was then, his heart took an unexpected, anxious leap, as, suddenly, he recalled that one time, about two weeks ago, when he had looked up to see the watchman standing over him, *just standing there, watching him with the girl*— And then, again, last Thursday, that damn woman. *She had just stood there, with her fat ugly mouth open, looking down at them.* That was the night he had been with Marlene, he remembered. He'd just have to be extra cautious, that's all. Especially tonight. His girl, tonight, was really someone quite special.

He rolled over on his side, reaching down with one foot to get a toe-hold on a lower shelf. His descent was rapid and soundless; he had done it many times before. With his sample case tucked under one arm (to prevent it rattling at the handle), he headed for the door.

The interior of the store was now a haven of ever-lengthening shadows. He paused beside a circular rack of negligees and nighties and waited, listening, before crossing the open aisle into the Dress Department. And then (determined not to be caught unaware again), he drew the switch-blade from his pocket and with a dull click, he released the razor-like shiv from its scabbard.

THE FIRST INKLING THE LIEUTENANT HAD THAT SHE was no longer alone in the store, was a faint, almost imperceptible *click* that seemed to originate from behind a circular rack across the aisle. Then, a vague blur of movement silently came and went in her peripheral vision. The muscles in her arms and legs, already cramped from their prolonged immobility, tightened with painful apprehension, and the hair at the nape of her neck lifted in a cold sweat. The urge to turn her head in that direction was almost overpowering.

"Lieutenant? You all right? What's up?" Her quickening breath had betrayed her sudden alarm to the men in the van.

"Something," she breathed, "someone — "

"Can you see him?"

"No, but — "

"How close is he?"

"Thirty feet?" Her lips were frozen into a fixed position, slightly parted, so that the "f" in feet came out slurred and indistinct.

"Let me know the second you see — "

"*It's him.*" The whispered words were pressed out of shape against the roof of her mouth. She wondered if they could understand her. "*He's coming — knife — *" There was suddenly no response from the radio, only a flat silence. "*Mark,*" she hissed, "*it's him — *" The man was clearly visible to her now, tall and disheveled looking, no more than twenty feet away, moving closer. She fought to quiet her breathing, to keep it at an indiscernible level, but her quickening senses had sent the adrenaline pulsing through her body in a burgeoning, irrepressible wave. And then, when he stood, at last, directly in front of her, gazing wildly into her own wide blue eyes, she blinked.

His first reaction, she saw, was fear. Then, disbelief. Finally, there was a slow dawning of comprehension. He was no more than an arm's length away when she saw the knife again. He held it authoritatively, in an underhand grip, waist high, moving it menacingly side to side.

She was suddenly, coldly calm. All pretense gone now, she waited, watching his eyes for a sign that would telegraph his first move. When it finally came, she threw herself away from the table with all the strength she could summon, groping under her skirt for the gun, meaning to swing around as she landed, to face him again in a half crouch. But her legs, stiff and numb from long inaction, folded under her shifting weight, and she felt the point of the knife trace a searing arc across the inside of her right thigh. Her gun tumbled from nerve-deadened fingers that could not hold onto it.

The lieutenant felt, rather than heard, a rhythmic pounding she thought at first to be the drumming of her own heart. But a moment later, Mark's galloping size twelves left the floor and his rugged frame went soaring over her head like a Kamikaze WWII Zero. Her attacker saw the human missile coming and made an effort to dodge it, but the big detective's heavy shoulder caught him a glancing blow and he staggered back. Mark went hurtling on into a rack of ankle-length evening dresses, knocking the whole conglomeration to the floor.

The would-be rapist struggled to remain on his feet. The knife was still clutched in his right fist, the tip of it stained red with the lieutenant's blood. He turned on Mark who was on his back, frantically yanking at the tangle of dresses that had fallen around him. He saw Drydon coming, and he doubled up his long legs to take the impact.

The lieutenant had not moved. Her leg was bleeding profusely from the slash of the knife and she groped for the artery on the inside of her thigh. She saw the rapist stagger, then turn and launch a diving charge at Mark, and she yelled a belated warning. But in the next instant, she saw Drydon's gangly body shoot straight up toward the ceiling, a good ten feet into the air, as Mark's powerful legs pistoned him upwards like a giant rag doll. The knife swooping down in a vicious arc, seemed to miss Mark's throat by inches. And as the man dutifully answered the call of gravity, Mark slid to one side and slammed a fist the size of a leg of mutton into the rapidly descending face. Drydon landed hard, twitched once, and lay still.

"Amen," said a giant black shadow that had suddenly appeared behind the lieutenant. "I've triggered the alarm," Bones told them in a voice that sounded like a welcome roll of distant thunder. "This place will be swarming in about two minutes."

"WHAT DO YOU THINK WILL HAPPEN TO OUR SHIFTY phallic thief, lieutenant?"

"That's *ithy*phallic, Mark," the lieutenant censured him demurely, "which isn't quite the same thing." She was seated behind her desk with her right leg propped up on a half-open drawer. The leg was splinted and mummy-wrapped in white bandages.

"But as for Drydon," she said, "whatever he does draw in the way of a sentence, he'll be out in half that time to rape and murder again, thanks to our current crop of 'enlightened' do-gooders. Meanwhile, it'll cost the taxpayer about sixty-thousand a year to keep his sick brain alive."

"And if he pleads insanity," Mark speculated, "he'll end up in clover, out at one of those funny farms."

"Whatever." The lieutenant winced as she tried to shift the position of her bandaged leg. "But he's not about to be going anywhere for awhile, until he gets out of the hospital. You broke his face, you big lug."

"I should have broken his ithyphallic while I was at it," Mark muttered.

Cathy Carruthers returned her partner's Machiavellian grin with a wan little smile. "Mark, I honestly think you should be belled, and X-rated, for the public good." She shook her golden head in a gesture of utter hopelessness.

"Does that mean now that I don't get to help you change the bandages?"

"Dreamer," she chuckled.

MIKE SHAYNE

MYSTERY MAGAZINE

OCTOBER 1983

$1.75

47744

A New Mike Shayne Novella

DEATH STALKS THE CAMPUS
by Brett Halliday

A Cathy Carruthers Novelet

THE $1.49-DAY KILLER
by Mel D. Ames

Short Stories by
Top Suspense Writers

*Detective-Lieutenant Cathy Carruthers
was tall, beautiful, and efficient, but even
she occasionally made a mistake — like
this time, turning her back on a killer.
Without warning, the man struck!*

the $1.49-day killer

IT WAS AN EARLY, TUESDAY, MID-SUMMER MORNING. The main drag that ran through Metro's ethnic East End was deserted and ominously quiet. The only sound was the rhythmic scuffling of Hymie's slip-shod feet as he kitty-cornered across the empty thoroughfare toward his place of business.

HYMIE LIPSHITZ
KOSHER MEATS

He was relieved to see from a distance that the expensive, gold block-lettering was still apparently intact on the plate-glass window. Then, as he drew closer, he caught a first glimpse of the spray-can graffiti that had been added overnight, exhorting him to assault himself in all manner of obscene and impossible ways. But it was not until he stood directly in front of the window, peering between the "R" in KOSHER and the "M" in MEATS, into the dim interior of the store, that he saw the girl.

"*Oy! Vos iz dos?*" Hymie's gentle Jewish face took on the color of uncooked *matzah*. "*A naket mendle?*"

The previous night, before locking up, Hymie had dutifully cleared away all the meat he had on display, leaving clean, empty trays in both the counter and casement coolers. The three shiny meat-hooks that hung inside the window area, had been left dangling idly from the rack. Now, inexplicably, those same meat-hooks were crudely laden with two whole carcasses of dressed beef. And wedged grotesquely between them (God preserve us!), brutally impaled on the third hook, was the dead and denuded body of a young woman.

And *Oy!* (to add insult to infamy) one of his own plastic price-tags had been skewered into the shapely flank, *offering the comely cadaver for sale to the public, in whole or in part, for $1.49 lb.*

THE EARLY ORANGE SUN HAD ONLY JUST BEGUN TO rise above the rooftops when Hymie stood in the open doorway of his shop, waiting for the arrival of the police. He was doing his best to shoo away the rubbernecking ghouls who had begun to gather, drawn by the scent of death like flies to carrion. They seemed to materialize out of nowhere, to *Ooo!* and *Aah!* and add their flattened, runny nose-prints to the scuff of graffiti that already befouled his window. But for all his threats and wheedling, they refused to budge. That is, until Metro's finest came careening onto the scene in the guise of an unmarked gray Chevy, like a giant can of RAID (Hymie thought) disinfecting everything around it in a cloud of bureaucratic dust. He coughed, and blinked, and waited stoically for the dust to settle, then stood rooted in disbelief as the police car began to disgorge its human cargo.

This, Hymie marveled, was the *goyim politsey?*

A six-foot blonde beauty (*Lynda Carter, who else?*) had alighted from the near side of the car, with a flagrant flash of silken thigh that would have brought the law down on a Las Vegas peeler. And who should be coming around the car to stand shoulder-to-shoulder with her on Hymie's own little piece of sidewalk? *John Wayne (rest his soul), that's who.* He'd know him anywhere; with the swagger and the big grin, the laughing blue-gray eyes, straight up from Hollywood and Vine, no doubt, with barely time enough to switch duds and pick out a new leading lady.

"Good morning," Lynda Carter says to him, "are you Mr. Lipshitz?"

Hymie acknowledged that he was, indeed, that person, then waited a little apprehensively for her next move. He was half expecting her to go into a spin on the spot, then do a *ta-da*, moments later, and emerge from a puff of smoke in tiara and leotards.

Instead, she said, "I am Detective-Lieutenant Cathy Carruthers," with a melting smile, "Metro Central, Eleventh Precinct, Homicide." She flipped a badge before his eyes and nodded toward her companion. "This is my partner, Detective-Sergeant Mark Swanson."

The big detective shuffled his size twelves. "Ya got a dead body hereabouts?" he drawled in typical Duke-like fashion.

Hymie pointed nervously to the bovine and human remains that still hung cheek to jowl in the window of his shop. "There," he said with an involuntary shudder. "*Oy. Such a shmuts!*"

"I'm not sure what that means," the lieutenant said as she entered the shop, "but I think I can guess." When she caught sight of the youthful corpse, so rudely indisposed, she told Hymie, "Get a sheet or a tarp and curtain off that window." She glowered back in disgust at the ogling crowd. "And, Mark, get rid of that horde of weirdos out there, before one of them comes creeping in with $1.49, looking for a pound of flesh."

Hymie obediently shuffled away in search of a sheet for the window, wondering why he hadn't thought of so obvious a deterrent himself, while Mark let loose with a street-clearing bellow that sent gawkers and ghouls (and a few innocent bystanders) scrambling for cover. And every pigeon in a quarter-mile radius was suddenly wheeling skyward in frenzied flight.

The lieutenant seemed to vibrate like a tuning fork as she stood with her eyes closed, waiting stiffly for the din to die down. When it did, she said, "Mark," with measured calm, "in the unlikely event that H.Q. has not already heard you, will you please get on the horn and let them know we've got a female 'defunctee' out here?"

Mark hesitated, with a glance of feigned indecision toward the towering heart of the city, then he shrugged his heavy shoulders, winked, grinned, and headed for the Chevy.

The lieutenant called after him, "Tell them to stir their stumps,

Mark, I want prints and pictures of this mess before anything is touched. And you'd better let the chief know we've got ourselves another dead doxy — victim number four, looks like, in the $1.49-Day killings.

MARK SWANSON STOOD AT THE OPEN DOOR OF THE Chevy with the radio-mike clamped in his big fist. He was confirming to the young female dispatcher at H.Q. that a new murder had, indeed, taken place in Metro's infamous East End. He was telling her, with measured patience, that he would consider jurisprudence to be well served, if (between the snaps, crackles and pops of her No-Trouble-Double-Bubble), she could find the time to acquaint the Special Team in Homicide with that bothersome bit of trivia.

But even as he talked, his thoughts had drifted elsewhere. He was just trying to recall (with one reflective eye on his beautiful partner), just what he had ever done to occupy his time and his mind, before Cathy Carruthers had entered his life and chosen him as a team-mate.

The Amazon they called her. And with reason.

For the better part of two years now, in her relentless pursuit of law and order, Cathy Carruthers had been stalking Metro's concrete jungle with the mien of a marauding tigress, and (to Mark's libidinous delight), the unbridled pulchritude of a Penthouse Pinup. Her outrageous beauty and recurrent feats of sheer animal strength and cunning had long since become legendary. And while Mark was no more immune than his awestruck colleagues to the ego-bruising mystique of the Amazon, *he*, as her constant companion, had developed a special, more personal relationship with Cathy Carruthers, the woman. It was an intimacy that, though still mutually unacknowledged, had, from the very beginning, been secretly and shyly reciprocated.

When Mark re-entered the shop, the lieutenant had climbed into the window display area to more closely examine the bizarre, triple heft of slaughter that hung there. The little proprietor had joined her and was busy draping a canvas sheet across the window, muttering under his breath about what the world had finally come to, being now, in his view, no longer kind nor kosher.

Certainly, it had not been kind to the young lady who had been left to dangle forlornly on the hook. Her head was toppled forward, obscuring her face, and her long raven hair cascaded down her naked front like a billow of black water. A congealing of blood and hair had formed an ugly brown scab between her breasts, and a network of bloody little rivers had criss-crossed the velvet expanse of her torso. Like a maze of southbound routes on a roadmap of Wyoming, they zigzaged over and around the hills of her breasts, down and across the rolling plain of her abdomen, puddling here, and there, in the hollows and valleys — and converging, finally, in one copious, violent splash along the insides of her thighs.

The lieutenant reached out to part the veil of black hair that hid her face. She might have been pretty once. Now, two unblinking green eyes stared out at her, frozen wide in death and terror, the bloodless lips curled back in a silent scream. A startled fly crept from the open cavern of her mouth. It buzzed irately, as though to protest the intrusion, then darted away. A second mouth, the one that had given up her lifeblood, grinned up at the lieutenant from under the sagging chin, where it stretched from ear to ear.

"$1.49 doesn't seem much for a human body," Mark said grimly over the lieutenant's shoulder. "Even if it is only that of a dead hooker."

"Too true," the lieutenant mused, "especially when you consider (monetarily, of course) that it would cost at least twenty dollars for just the *loan* of a *live* one."

Mark laughed. "Are you kidding? That might have been true B.I., lieutenant. Not any more."

"B.I.?"

"*Before Inflation.*"

The lieutenant gave him a critical look. "How did *you* acquire all this sordid expertise?"

"I worked Vice, lieutenant, before I was transferred to Homicide." He smiled wistfully. "I've seen it all."

"Hmm. I can imagine. That would have been B.C., of course."

"B.C.?" Mark's ruggedly handsome face betrayed his bewilderment.

"*Before Cathy*," the lieutenant replied with a grin.

MARK WAS ABOUT TO RESPOND WHEN HE WAS JOSTLED to one side by the mass arrival of the Special Homicide Investigative Team. Photogs, Lab-men, Finger-printers, Morgue-meds, whatever; they all came crowding in through the door of the little shop, lugging the specialty equipment that would facilitate their separate and varied functions. The noise level was suddenly overwhelming. Every mother's son of them seemed to be speaking at once, obviously intent on the individual task at hand. Some barely gave a second glance to the broken body that hung so brutally from the hook.

In the midst of this orderly confusion, one man was struggling like a bedbug in a beehive to retain a modicum of dignity. He was short, dumpy and balding, but there was an unmistakable air of authority about him. Officially, he was Samuel Morton, M.D., Coroner and Chief Medical Examiner, M.C.P.D. *Unofficially* (he was fond of reiterating), he was "just plain Sam."

"So what do you make of it, just-plain Sam?"

The little M.E. looked up at the lieutenant without amusement. There was a condescending curl to his pursed lips. "*Pate de foie gras,*" he stated flatly.

Mark, at the lieutenant's elbow, raised his eyes and his eyebrows. "Whadhesay?"

"Chopped liver," she translated with a grimace, "or something just as nasty. And, as unenlightening."

"So what do you *want* from me, lieutenant?"

Cathy Carruthers ruffled the few remaining hairs on the M.E.'s peekaboo pate. "Sam," she said sweetly, "how about treating a lady to a crooked smile and a straight answer?"

The M.E. managed a reluctant, ill-humored grunt. A smile, even a crooked one, was out of the question.

"How long would you say she's been dead, Sam?"

"You want a wild surmise or a bold conjecture?"

"How about an educated guess?"

"Well," he mused grudgingly, "she's colder'n a dog's dinner. Rigor's pretty well established." He touched the inside of his wrist to the cadaver's clammy skin. "And I doubt she'd go any more now than about, 75 degrees F. So, everything considered, and figuring a heat loss of roughly 3 degrees per hour, I'd have to say about — eight hours."

The lieutenant glanced at her watch. "That would peg the time of death at approximately ten o'clock last night."

Sam Morton shrugged his dumpy shoulders. "Give or take a smidgen."

"How long," Mark wanted to know, "is a smidgen?"

"How high is up?" the M.E. responded gruffly.

The lieutenant ignored her colleagues' idle persiflage. She appeared to be deeply engrossed in her own thoughts. "The girl obviously bled profusely before she died," she surmised aloud, "in an *upright* position. And what do you make of the fact that there's not one drop of blood on the floor beneath her? Weird. But what I'd like to know now, Sam, is precisely what caused her death. The slash to her throat? Or that vicious hook embedded in her back? Either way," she sighed, "it would not have been a happy way to go."

"So, who's entitled 'heppy' lieutenant?" Hymie's muffled voice came from among the folds of the canvas sheet. "These days, *fest* isn't good enough?"

The lieutenant grinned. "You do have a point there, Mr. Lipshitz, but, unfortunately, this lady didn't die 'heppy' or *fest*. What is your opinion, Sam?"

"*My* opinion, lieutenant, will be in the Autopsy Report, which I will duly and eventually complete, and, which you will duly and eventually receive. In the meantime, I'd be much obliged if you'd clear the hell out of here so that I can get on with my job. And lieutenant, how about taking the rest of this rabble with you? Especially this jerk with the camera — " He flinched as another flashbulb exploded. "For Chrissake, Charlie! Enough already. You've done everything now but get her to say 'cheese.'"

LATER THAT SAME MORNING AT METRO'S ELEVENTH Precinct, Chief Henry (Hank) Heller was pacing back and forth behind his desk, looking every bit the gray-headed old rooster he was reputed to be. Every so often, he would stop and peck a peek at his top investigative team, and the stringy wattles at his throat would tense and quiver with exacerbation.

"Do I read you right, lieutenant? Are you telling me that this Lipshitz fiasco is *not* the work of the $1.49-Day killer?"

"Either that, chief, or the grave-yard detail picked up the wrong guy last night."

"What do you mean, the wrong guy? He confessed, didn't he?"

"So they tell me." The lieutenant crossed one gorgeous leg over the other, opened her red-leather shoulder bag, and balanced it delicately on the rounded plateau of her thigh, just above the knee. The chief eyeballed the teetering bag with acute apprehension while the lieutenant, oblivious to the trauma she was inducing, calmly proceeded to trim and polish her beautiful blood-red talons. Mark, meanwhile, was a vision of domestic bliss. He was hunched down in his chair, comfortably catnapping, flaunting an idiotic half-smile on his upturned, dreamy dial.

Hank Heller suddenly stopped his pacing and dumped himself wearily into the chair behind the desk. "Why do I feel like a kid at a circus every time I get together with you two?" he lamented. He shook his craggy head, thrust out his chin, and glowered at the two detectives. "It pains me no end to break up your little high-wire act," he cooed with deadly syrupy malice, "and I hate like hell to disturb that comatose beach-bum you call a partner. *But*, if you don't soon justify that last remark, lieutenant, you may find yourself performing out on the corner of Pan and Handle for the price of a cup of cold coffee."

The lieutenant reacted to his ultimatum with a tolerant sigh and a slow, forgiving smile. She dutifully rescued the bag from its precarious perch, then nudged her burly partner with her elbow. "Mark, did you bring those enlargements with you?"

Mark, with an economy of speed and effort that would have shamed an aging tortoise, reached down beside his chair to retrieve a brown manilla folder. "These are the three shots we had on file," he said with sleepy accord. "The photo-lab will be sending up number four, from the batch they took this morning — soon's it's ready." He yawned and glanced expectantly toward the door. "Should be here directly."

Then, as though by divine decree, the door took that prophetic moment to rumble ominously on its hinges. It opened wide enough to give ingress to a head, a hand, and a brown manilla folder. In that order.

"Here's that pretty snap you wanted, lieutenant," the head said brightly.

Chief Heller buried his face in his hands with a hopeless groan. But curiosity soon compelled him to peek out between his fingers to see what could possibly happen next. He was just in time to see the lieutenant dismiss the courier with a rewarding smile, then march herself magnificently across the office to the notice-board that all but dominated the north wall. The chief followed, moving only his eyes. To look at her, he thought, you'd think she was about to join Charlton Heston at the foot of the mountain with a revised, modern version of the Top Ten.

"BEHOLD!" THE LIEUTENANT SAID WITH A FLOURISH as she finished pegging up the four 12-by-14 enlargements in a horizontal row across the board. She had turned with a defiant toss of her honey-blonde head to face the chief. "These are the actual photographs," she stated, "that were taken at the scenes of the murders. During the last four months, on the second Tuesday of each month, May through August, these bizarre killings have coincided with the $1.49-Day sales events that have long been traditional with department stores in Metro — "

She paused to frown down at the chief until he reluctantly took his face out of hiding. And Mark decided it was as good a time as any to straighten up a little in his chair.

"Accordingly," she continued, in the tritely edifying tones of an eighth-grade schoolmarm, "the murders have now become synonymous with $1.49-Day, and the killer has been aptly labeled, by the Media, as the $1.49-Day Killer."

The chief looked at Mark with Orphan Annie eyes. "Leapin' lizards! He whispered against his palm in exaggerated mock amazement. "Did you know *that*?"

Mark responded with a quick grin and a noncommittal "Arf!"

The lieutenant was not amused and she chose simply to ignore them. She turned back to the board and resumed her graphic dissertation.

"I needn't point out that all four of these photographs (*vis-a-vis* the murders) have the same $1.49-Day theme in common. That is obvious. And there are other similarities, as well. The nudity of the victims, for instance, the fact that they are all women, and prostitutes, the display window locations, to mention only a few. But we have already discussed these factors at length, and I'll not enlarge on them at this time.

"The point I would like to make, however, and the one singular aspect of these murders that most intrigues me now, is not their obvious *similarities*, but rather the subtle way in which this last one seems to *differ* from the others." She turned slowly, almost esoterically to face them. "Gentlemen, do you not agree?"

HANK HELLER AND MARK GLANCED QUIZZICALLY from the lieutenant to each other, then back to the row of photographs on the board. The two men had become suddenly, quietly serious. The four murder scenes, so brutally depicted, blown up into 12-by-14 colored glossies, were not a joking matter. They were nightmare images of mortal horror that had been awesomely frozen in time by the photographer. The two men studied them gravely in this new context, each one in turn:

The first enlargement (labeled: *Tuesday, May 9*) was of a glass-lidded coffin, revealed in all its ornate grandeur in the display window at the Chapel of Chimes. Freshly cut flowers of every variety and color abounded against a backdrop of pastoral splendor. It would have been a somberly restful scene had it not been for the naked young woman imprisoned within the casket; a frail, black-haired beauty, in the rigid throes of her last agony, eyes glassy, wide with panic, mouth agape, fingers bent into claws against the underside of the glass lid. She had been *asphyxiated.* Buried alive, in effect. And strewn over the transparent lid, was a crumpled dollar bill and fort-nine cents in loose change.

The second photograph (labeled: *Tuesday, June 14*) was taken from a similar viewpoint; looking in through the plate-glass window of the Metro School of Hairdressing. Pictured, was a row of upholstered chairs with overhead dryers paralleling a mirrored counter that faded back into the dim interior of the shop. In the chair closest to the window, a woman in her early twenties was slumped in a nude, unladylike sprawl, her hair seemingly still entangled in the overhead dryer. She wore a death-mask that had been grotesquely fashioned by a sudden, surging charge of high voltage from the dryer. She had been *electrocuted.* And on the mirror behind her, $1.49 had been scrawled in foot-high numerals, in a glaring fluorescent shade of red lipstick.

The third photograph (labeled: *Tuesday, July 12*) immortalized Gruber's East Side Confections. It was a 7-11 type catch-all store, with tobacco, pop, magazines and party accoutrements in motley supply. The camera peeked in through the glass entrance, revealing a checkout counter and a floor-to-ceiling rack of magazines in the immediate foreground. And further back, dividing the front check-out area from the shelved interior, was an old-fashioned, "help-yourself" pop cooler. The lid of the cooler was gaped open like a huge metal mouth, and draped over the lower jaw, half in, half out, was the contorted body of a naked woman. Only the buxom twin moons of her bottom and the backs of her long, dangling legs were visible to the camera: her head and torso were buried in the frigid, liquid bowels of the cooler. She had been *drowned.* And on the old-fashioned cash register that sat atop the counter, someone had rung up $1.49.

The fourth and final photograph, taken that same morning at Hymie Lipshitz' East Side shop, had been labeled, *Tuesday, August 9.* It was a cruel replica of the scene met by the two detectives only hours before.

"Well?" The lieutenant stood stolidly before them, feet apart, hands on hips, a look of quiet expectation on her exquisite, inscrutable face.

"Well, what?" The chief pursed his lips and looked up at her through a one-eyed squint. "Each one's about as gruesome as the next (Christ, what a butcher!), except — "

"Except?"

"That last one, lieutenant. The one that came in this morning. Beauty and the Beefs."

The lieutenant rolled her eyes at his rather apt description. "Well," she prompted, "what about it?"

"It's the only one that drew blood."

The lieutenant smiled tightly with grim accord. "Precisely," she said.

"Hey, now! Just a goldarn minute, lieutenant, ma'm. You're not getting off that easy." The chief pushed himself to his feet and came around the end of the desk. "That bit about the blood doesn't prove a damn thing. It could still be the work of the same guy. No M.O. is ever *exactly* the same, lieutenant. And as you've already said yourself, there isn't any lack of similarities."

"That's true, chief, but I just wanted to point out that there is at least one significant inconsistency, even without the time factor."

"The time factor?" The chief and Mark echoed the words in unison.

"Yes gentlemen, the time factor. If Sam Morton was even remotely accurate in his Time Of Death guesstimate, then the man they picked up early this morning couldn't possibly have perpetrated the Lipshitz murder. He was in jail."

THE HEAVY STEEL-BARRED DOOR CLOSED BEHIND them with an ominous, no-nonsense *clank*. The lieutenant and Mark had just entered the detention area on the basement floor of the Eleventh Precinct.

"So the way it looks now," Mark was saying, "is that we've either got a publicity-seeking nut on our hands, who didn't commit *any* of the murders, or there are *two* $1.49-Day killers, and one of them is still out there."

"That about sums its up, Mark." The lieutenant looked trim and nubile in a snug, gray skirt and white tailored shirt blouse. Her three-inch heels clicked out an erogenic rhythm as they traversed the concrete foyer toward the holding cell block. A second barrier glided open as they approached.

"Lieutenant. Mark." Officer McConachie, an elderly, heavy-set Scot, greeted them as they entered. He was seated behind a small desk that was large enough, just, to hold an open body-count book and a cup of coffee. "I'll ha' to *trroble* you to *soign* in," he told them in a pronounced Highland brogue.

The lieutenant signed the book while Mark made an attempt at idle chit-chat. "Hey, McConachie," he joshed, "I hear you're renting out rooms on the side."

"Och, aye, Sarrge." McConachie beamed. "Since the Forrce has went co-ed, I canna keep up wi' the demand." He gave them a sly look of appraisal, and an even slyer wink. Then, in a whispered aside to Mark, he added, "All I got this mornin' though, is a semi-prrivate on Tierr B."

The lieutenant straightened slowly, her eyes flashing like distant lightning. "It is my most fervent hope, Officer McConachie, for your sake, that you are merely jesting."

McConachie's Scottish face turned the color of a Clansman's kilt. "Eh? Oh, aye, Ma'm," he flustered, "now and what else would you be thinkin' — ?"

"McConachie," Mark interjected quickly, "we're here to interrogate the $1.49-Day killer."

"Ah! So that's yourr business, is it?" The old Scot struggled to his feet. "It's that Nazi annihilatorr you'rre wantin'. Adolph Klause, he calls hisself. Bloody butcherr, is what he is. Come along, then. Leave yourr weapons herre, and I'll take you to 'im."

A few moments later, the two detectives were following McConachie down a steel and concrete alley marked Tier C, to the brash accompaniment of wolf whistles and lurid cat calls. Faceless hands and fingers made obscene gestures at the lieutenant from between the bars on either side. By the time they reached the end of the Tier, where an isolated cell stood back, out of sight and sound of the others, the lieutenant was beginning to look thoroughly discomfited.

The old Scot opened the cell door, stood back as they entered, then locked it behind them. "Jus' gimme a shout when you'rre through," he said as he moved away. Under his breath, he muttered, "Damn celibates."

The lieutenant turned quickly and pressed her flushed and lovely face against the bars. "What was that you just said, McConachie?"

"I, uh — I *said*, lieutenant, that I've got to clean up that damn cell a bit." He hurried off before she had a chance to think it over.

ADOLPH KLAUSE WAS A PATHETIC LITTLE MAN IN HIS middle forties, with a thin, disjointed body that appeared to have been haphazardly stuck together from a set of scaled-up tinker toys. A wedge of black hair curled over his forehead in the manner of his given-namesake of WWII fame, but there was no Charlie Chaplin mustache to complete the illusion. He was huddled at the far end of the bottom bunk, hugging his knobby knees to his chest, and looking no more like a mass murderer than a priest at a picnic.

The lieutenant was the first to speak. "Adolph Klause?"

The alleged killer looked up vacantly. His eyes were tar black, small and close together. Bird-like, Mark thought. When the prisoner failed to answer, the lieutenant said again, "Klause? Is that your name? Adolph Klause?"

"Yes," after a dark pause.

"It is my understanding, Mr. Klause, that early this morning you dictated, then signed, a confession. That you did, in fact, admit to the murders of three women. Is that correct?"

"Yes."

"Was it done voluntarily, Mr. Klause? On your part, I mean."

"Yes."

"You were not coerced in any way?"

"No."

"Threatened?"

"No."

The little man had thus far moved only his eyes. His monosyllabic answers had emerged tonelessly from between thin, unbending lips.

"You made a statement, Mr. Klause, at the time of your arrest — "

Klause sat up abruptly. "*I was not arrested!*" he shouted wildly, his body taut with emotion.

"But — "

"You listen to *me*, damn it. I – was – not — arrested. Understand? I turned myself in. *I was not arrested.*" His agitation was acute and volatile, almost maniacal. It was also short lived. After a time, he said "Anyway, who in Hell wants to know?"

The lieutenant moved with deliberation to the center of the cell. "I'm Lieutenant Carruthers," she told him with quiet dignity. She flashed her badge. "This is my partner, Sergeant Swanson."

"I'm supposed to be impressed?" Klause curled his upper lip disdainfully while his eyes scouted up and down her remarkable body as though she were standing there stark naked. "Lady copy, huh? Well as far as I'm concerned, you're no better'n the rest of them sluts." He ogled her with utter contempt. "I know about your kind. Oh, I seen you coming down the Tier just now, bouncin' along, jigglin' and wigglin' your fancy ass, and all them guys locked up in their cells, just ahootin' and ahollerin' to get out at you — "

"*That* is *enough.*" The lieutenant cut him short as Mark moved quickly to her side. After a protracted pause, she said with quiet authority, "Now, suppose you tell me *why* you turned yourself in."

Klause hesitated. He was breathing heavily. "Because I was told to," he said tersely, "that's why."

"You were *told* to?"

"You deaf or something, lady? That's what I said, wasn't it? I was *told* to."

"By whom?"

Klause faced her defiantly, with an I'm-beyond-your-reach-now, born-again smirk on his pallid face. "By *God*," he intoned with righteous finality.

The lieutenant moved closer. "Well, now," she said, her voice gentle, confiding. "And did God also tell you to commit murder?"

"For a fact, yes."

"And pricing your victim's denuded bodies at $1.49 a piece, Mr. Klause, was that God's idea, too?"

Klause's face darkened as though suddenly shadowed by an inner cloud. The whites of his eyes widened in angry circles around their shiny black irises, and his thin lips parted into a moist, ugly red slit, like an open wound. He was visibly trembling.

"That's all they were bloody worth," he spat out, "and a bad bargain at that." The man struggled awkwardly to his feet. His eyes now, like luminous black agates, were rolling in their sockets. "They sold their bodies and their souls into iniquity, and they were paid the going price." He snickered evilly. "Don't you read your Bible, lady? Eh? 'Vengeance is mine, saith the Lord, *I will repay.*"

The lieutenant glanced apathetically at Mark. "This guy's about three bricks short of a full load," she told him quietly. "You might as well call McConachie."

"Aren't you going to ask him if he committed that fourth murder?"

"What's the use? He'd only blame it on God."

"I guess." Mark sighed reflectively. "Sounds like a new twist to that old *the-Devil-made-me-do-it* routine, a la Flip Wilson."

The lieutenant chuckled as she turned her back on the wild-eyed Klause to join Mark at the barred front of the cell. It was an unthinking move, and one that she was to immediately regret.

MARK'S FIRST INKLING OF TROUBLE WAS WHEN his beautiful partner's familiar chuckle suddenly ended in a grim grunt of surprise. He spun around, his big fists clenched instinctively. What he saw brought a startled gasp to his own lips.

The lieutenant was struggling to retain her balance from the unexpected jolt of Adolph Klause's gangly little body that had now, somehow, glued itself to her back. His black head was buried in her long golden hair, and his arms and legs were wound around her bountiful anatomy like the tentacles of a tinker-toy octopus. His skinny fingers raked at the white front of her blouse, and as Mark began to move toward them, the white was being slowly clawed apart to reveal a widening wedge of pink lace and satin, and even pinker flesh.

"Damn it, Mark! Get this loony off me."

The lieutenant was doing her utmost to dislodge him. She shook and shimmied with all the repugnance of a dog getting out of an unwanted bath. But she was in the unhappy dilemma of trying to remove the offending hands, and legs, and feet, while striving, at the same time, to preserve some measure of modesty. It was not to be.

Mark ducked behind them (for which the lieutenant appeared momentarily grateful), and with one hand planted firmly between her shoulder blades, the other circling Klause's scrawny neck, he skinned the man away from her as though he was peeling a banana. Unfortunately (for the lieutenant), Klause's fingers had anchored themselves single-mindedly in the tattered folds of her shirt-blouse, and the garment was inadvertently peeled away with the reluctant loony.

Some minutes later, when Lieutenant Carruthers, Mark and McConachie walked the noisy gauntlet back through the cell block to the entrance foyer, the lieutenant was wearing Mark's tent of a jacket, and a flustered look of steamy discomposure. Mark, in his shirt-sleeves, was close behind her, with his rugged features creased in an idiotic smile of sweet retrospection. McConachie brought up the rear, scratching his hoary old brain-box and debating with himself whether to be governed by appearances, and demand his usual fee, or to try for a little extra on the strength of a *menage a trois.*

IT WAS WELL PAST THE LUNCH HOUR WHEN LIEUTENANT Carruthers stalked self-reliantly into the squad room and headed for her glass-partitioned office. She wore a change of blouse over the same snug gray skirt, and Mark's discarded suit-coat was draped over one arm. As she passed Mark at his desk, she said, "I'd like a word with you," and tossed him his jacket without breaking stride. Mark fought back an involuntary grin as he shrugged into the garment, then followed her into the office.

"I suppose I should say 'thank you' for the loan of that damn jacket," she said as she faced him with an air of cool chagrin.

Mark kicked the door shut and dumped his burly carcass into a convenient chair. "The pleasure was all mine," he told her amiably, "but why do I get the feeling that you're not all that appreciative?"

Cathy Carruthers glared across the desk at him. "And why do *I* get the feeling that you deliberately made a Hollywood bloody production out of getting that damn jacket off of you and on to me?" Her vivid blue eyes sparked angrily. "And, Mark, was it really necessary to help me on with it like that?"

"Lieutenant," Mark said, adopting his well-rehearsed little-boy look of injured innocence, "any true gentleman would have done the same."

"From the *front?*"

Mark smiled wistfully. "I guess I got carried away," he said and then with unexpected warmth and tenderness, he added, "You were beautiful." He met her stormy eyes with his own and held them for some memorable moments. "Besides, it isn't every day I get to see you blush."

As though to prove him wrong (and much to her own annoyance), Cathy Carruthers promptly blushed again. And she was not quite able to repress an embarrassed, reluctant little smile.

"Damn it, Mark," she said with a show of demure temper, "whatever am I going to do with you?"

A SUDDEN RAP ON THE DOOR PRECLUDED THE NEED to do anything with him at all, at least at that particular moment, and the lieutenant seemed to exude an abrupt sense of relief as the door swung in, and an officer of somewhat abbreviated stature appeared in the bottom half of the opening.

"Lieutenant — are you available?"

"Come in corporal."

Corporal Garfield Leprohn (the *Leprechaun*, as he was known to all and sundry in the department), was perhaps the littlest person this side of Fraggle Rock ever to aspire to legitimate cop-hood. And, as Mark was uncommonly fond of pointing out, it had not been easy for the little guy.

"How would you like to go parading through life on a pair of tiddly stilts?" Mark would ask facetiously of anyone willing to listen, "to have to bob and weave among your fellow-men like a truncated flag at half-mast, or to be doomed," he would persist, "to traipse about in a four-foot world fraught with eye-high doorknobs, belt buckles and belly-buttons, of every disgusting size and contour. How would you like that, Bucko? Hmmm?"

The Leprechaun, however, had not been daunted by any such shortcomings (so to speak), real or imagined. He had simply made the most of what little God had given him, and with great dedication and purpose, had managed over the years, to elevate himself (in a manner of speaking) up through the ranks to the lofty position of head of the Records Department, where he was (and is, to this day) duly accorded the reluctant respect and friendly ridicule for which he had so diligently labored.

"Well, if it isn't Gargantua the Great," Mark said with an acute lack of enthusiasm.

"How did you make out?" the lieutenant asked the little man.

"Great." The Leprechaun echoed Mark with a sly smirk. "What else?" To the lieutenant, he said, "I've got the information you asked for, and I must say, your suppositions were uncannily accurate."

"Then the girl in the Lipshitz murder was *not* a prostitute?"

"She was not. And as you surmised, there *are* people in her background. Several, in fact."

"She was married?"

"Well, no. But she was shacked-up."

Mark let loose a noisy sigh of exasperation. "Would someone like to clue *me* in?"

"At your age," the Leprechaun replied smugly, "that would not be an easy task. However, with your permission, lieutenant, I would like to summarize my findings before handing over the file."

The lieutenant made the little man's day with a nod and a bewitching smile. "You have the floor, Garfield."

THE LEPRECHAUN TOOK A COUPLE OF SWIPES WITH his handkerchief at the seat of a vacant chair before elevating his tiny tush into position. He balanced his briefcase on his little lap and began to sort through a horde of file folders. He rejected one file after the other with an exasperated shake of his little head until he apparently found the one he wanted. Then, as he began to rifle through the file's contents, Mark suddenly exploded.

"Oh, for Chrissake!" he blurted out. "Get on with it, you bloody little fidget!"

If looks could have killed, Mark would have been dead and buried, then and there, without the benefit of clergy. In lieu of that unlikely fate, however, he merely groaned and sank a little lower in his chair. The Leprechaun squared his tiny shoulders, cleared his throat importantly, and began his dissertation.

"In the first three deaths," he stated evenly, "the victims were found to be prostitutes. They had no known relatives, and no acquaintances to speak of, other than a disgruntled pimp, a few johns, and a co-hooker or two. Consequently, their deaths were dead-ends. Literally."

"Yes, yes — we're all aware of that, Corporal," the lieutenant said impatiently. "Let's get to the fourth one, shall we?"

The Leprechaun did not enjoy being rushed. "Well — " he drawled, protracting the word out in typical Jack Benny style, "the girl you found in the Lipshitz window this morning, was one Shelley Newcomb, a twenty-three year-old female Caucasian of Anglo descent. At the time of her death, she was living common-law with Max Wineghart, an unemployed high-steel worker. A violent man, Wineghart. Neighbors have reported hearing loud and bitter quarrels on several occasions and from which Miss Newcomb had subsequently emerged with visible scars of battle."

"Hmm. He sounds like a lovely fellow, I must say, and an equally *unlovely* suspect." The lieutenant looked pensive. "But if he was not employed, corporal, how were the two of them able to subsist?"

"*She* worked, lieutenant. As a bar girl in an East End nightclub. *The Playpen*, on South Slater Street. That's the place where the bar girls and waitresses all dress up like little girls, and the waiters and bartenders like little boys. You'd have to see it to believe it. Short, high-waisted dresses for the girls, complete with hair ribbons and knee socks; and short pants and little porkpie caps for the guys. They look like a bunch of erotic children."

"Erotic?"

"With a capital E, lieutenant. When I said the dresses and the pants were short, I *meant* short." The Leprechaun demonstrated by drawing a little hand high across his little lap."

"Sick, sick, sick," Mark muttered. "So why haven't we closed them down?"

"Because," the Leprechaun put in, "the place is legit. And so are the girls. There's no law against dressing up, you know, and a 'no-fraternizing-with-the-customers' rule appears to be strictly adhered to. These are just a bunch of adults acting as if they had never left kindergarten."

"Who runs the place?"

"The club is owned and operated by a forty-one year-old pubescent who calls himself Tommy Flowers. Can you believe it? And he's married to a thirty-nine year-old nymphet named Thelma. She's the club's hostess."

"What was the reaction of these people to Miss Newcomb's rather bizarre demise?"

"Shock and sorrow, lieutenant. At least, that is what they professed. I did the interview, personally, and they seemed genuine enough. They said Shelley Newcomb was supposed to work last night but she didn't show. They hadn't seen her since her last shift Saturday night, which would have extended, of course, into early

Sunday morning."

"What time does she normally go on shift?"

"10 P.M. The club operates from 10 until 4 A.M., every day except Sunday."

"I want the address of that club, corporal, as well as the names of all Shelley Newcomb's known friends and workmates."

"It's all in the file, lieutenant. But I can tell you right now, there's only one other couple who were more than just casual acquaintances. Melissa and Wilson Gibbs. They live in the same apartment block, and Melissa also works at The Playpen. She's a waitress, and just turned nineteen. Her husband (legally, this time), is a longshoreman when he's working, which isn't often."

"Did you get a Medical Report from Sam Morton?"

"No, lieutenant. I checked, but it wasn't ready. I was planning on a trip to the morgue when I left here."

"Don't bother, corporal. We'll check it out." The lieutenant slipped a short caballero jacket over the white blouse as she stood up. "Mark, sign out the Chevy and I'll meet you in the garage in five."

"Where're we going? To The Playpen?"

"No. I doubt there'd be anyone around this time of day. We'll hit The Playpen later tonight, when it's in full swing. In the meantime, I think we'll pay 'just-plain-Sam' a visit. There are a couple of questions I'd like answers to."

"Such as?"

"Such as what caused Miss Newcomb's death, for one."

"And for another?"

"Whether to hit you for the price of a new blouse and bra, to replace those you and your demented accomplice so brutally tore from my body this morning, *or* to settle for a medium-rare with prawns at the local Sizzler?"

Mark chuckled. "I'm game either way," he said. Then, wistfully, he added, "In fact, it will be an *udder* delight."

"I THINK YOU SHOCKED OUR LITTLE IRISH ELF," MARK said as he swung the Chevy into the parking lot of the Metro Central City Morgue. "He's probably still sitting in your office, with his mouth and those ridiculous files hanging open, wondering what really did happen this morning."

The lieutenant grinned. "You didn't help the situation much with the 'udder delight' bit," she reminded him. "In fact, that crack was enough to make a poor girl *cower*."

Mark groaned. "Did you enjoy the steak?"

"Yes, I did. Thank you."

"And the prawns?"

"Mmmm. Those, too."

"I don't suppose you'd care to try for the, uh — 10-ouncer with lobster?"

The lieutenant gave him a dark look of reproach as she got out of the car. "You might as well wait for me here," she said. Then, as though in afterthought, she added, "With luck, nobody will notice you doing it."

"Huh? Doing what?"

"Dreaming the impossible dream," she said, and she blithely walked away.

Mark watched her go with mixed emotions. Coming or going, she was great to watch. "Two down, and two to go," he mused aloud. Where Mark came from, "impossible" just took a little longer.

IT WAS THIRTEEN MINUTES OF MIDNIGHT WHEN THE gray unmarked Chevy ghosted past the front entrance to The Playpen, in Metro's nefarious East End. Mark was behind the wheel, his beautiful partner poised like a jungle predator on the seat beside him. He could see her face in the wan light of the dashboard, intense, alert.

"Want me to park it, lieutenant?"

"No. Not yet," She chewed reflectively on her lower lip. "Why don't we just circle the block. And, Mark, keep it slow."

The car seemed to move of its own will, noiselessly, down the darkened street. As they crept around the second corner, the lieutenant said, "Ah-ha," with a note of grim satisfaction, "just as I thought." She pointed ahead to a storefront that looked somehow familiar, even by the streetlight. But there was no graffiti now to befoul the window, and as they drew abreast of it, Mark could clearly read the gold block-lettering:

HYMIE LIPSHITZ
KOSHER MEATS

"Hey, how about that?" Mark exclaimed. "I knew the Lipshitz store and The Playpen were in the same area, but I had no idea they were this close. They could even be backed up on one another."

"They could at that, Mark. So why don't we take the alley now, and find out."

The soft purr of the idling motor took on a hollow echo as they nosed into the narrow alley. The lieutenant counted aloud as each back entrance drifted slowly by, lining them up with storefronts she had monitored moments before, but it proved to be an unnecessary precaution. The Playpen and the Lipshitz premises were clearly marked for rear deliveries and, as Mark had suspected, they were, in fact, back to back. Only the width of the dark alley separated the bare, low-wattage bulbs that glowed dimly above the deserted doors on either side. Mark braked the car to a halt between them.

"What now?" he said, looking from one bleak and silent portal to the other.

The lieutenant did not answer. Her attention was rivetted on the double back-doors of the Lipshitz store, the same doors that only last night had been forcibly entered by Shelley Newcomb's killer.

"A common length of two-by-four," she said absently to Mark, "jammed into steel brackets on the inside of those doors, has served to ensure the sanctity of Hymie's shop for twenty years. But last night, with relative ease, some knowing miscreant gained access to the premises by simply severing the wooden bar. A sharp saw could have done it in seconds."

"We know it did happen," Mark said impatiently, "but *why?*"

The lieutenant shrugged. "To rid himself of a dead body, I suppose, which was probably the only tangible evidence of his invidious carnage."

"Yes, but why all the dramatics, lieutenant? The hook, and that $1.49-Day hoax?"

"I would guess that was done on the spur of the moment, in an attempt, perhaps, to divert the direction of the investigation that was sure to follow. If you recall, Mark, at the time the hoax was perpetrated, not even we knew the $1.49-Day killer had already given himself up."

"Bad timing," Mark suggested, "And he almost got away with it."

"I hardly think so," the lieutenant replied. "It just seems inevitable, in these last minute cover-ups that they are rarely executed well. This one is no exception."

As she spoke, the lieutenant swung her eyes and her attention across the alley to the rear of The Playpen. There was something strangely forbidding about it. A single, blank door hugged one corner. It had neither hasp, nor knob, which gave it access only from the inside. Then, centered between the door and the other corner, a small barred and bricked-up window (or what once had been a window), added to the atmosphere of a very unfriendly and almost impregnable fortress.

"Okay," the lieutenant said, "I've seen enough. Now, let's see what the joint looks like on the inside."

"Do we flash our badges?" Mark asked routinely as he eased the car ahead, "or do we go incognito?"

"Incognito?" The lieutenant laughed lightly. "Are you kidding? If you went in there wearing nothing but a diaper, Mark, you'd be spotted for a cop before you got one flat foot in the door."

"Not if I took along my rubber ducky."

"Besides," the lieutenant told him, "we have no way of knowing what disguise would be most appropriate until we get in there, and by then it will be too late." She took her .38 Special from her red-leather handbag and spun the cylinder. "You better check your piece, just in case."

Mark looked puzzled. "You expect trouble?"

"Who knows?" The lieutenant was staring at Mark in that vague and obscure way that usually suggested some deep, inner cogitation. "Let's just say that I've got a kind of wild theory about this whole set-up. And if I'm right, we might be in for a bit of a wing-ding."

"You must have picked up some kind of clue at the morgue," Mark speculated.

"No, as a matter of fact, I drew a dismal blank with Sam. The unfortunate Miss Newcomb simply bled to death from a severed jugular, and that is it. We do know, however, that she was impaled on the hook after she was dead, *and*, after she had given up her quota of fourteen precious pints. But *where* she died, *why* she died, and *who killed her*, well — that's still the current conundrum."

MARK AND THE LIEUTENANT WERE GREETED WARMLY at the entrance to The Playpen by what appeared to be, a big boy. A *very* big boy.

"Hi, guys!"

The detectives heard, and saw, but they could only stand there, gaping, rooted in momentary disbelief. Confronting them, was a smiling, boyish face, a thatch of tousled, sun-bleached hair, and a tiny, white, porkpie cap. The face, hair and cap were attached to a body that could only have been spawned on Muscle Beach, but which now bulged obscenely under a dainty white shirt with a frilled bib-front, long sleeves and lacy cuffs. And further down, embarrassingly mature loins had been shamelessly sheathed in tight tom-boy shorts that seemed to end before they began at the height of long, heavily muscled thighs. Finally, at floor level, white ankle socks and matching white sneakers provided a fitting footnote to "big-boy" and his bizarre ensemble.

Mark fought back an incipient smile for fear that it might be misinterpreted. But they were made welcome, regardless, with an animated "Well, come o-o-o-on in," and a knowing, boyish grin that had "I'm-one Are-you-one-too?" written all over it. Cathy Carruthers reached instinctively for Mark's arm as she allowed herself to be herded in over the threshold.

"He looks like the man from bloody Glad, in a bib and a jock strap," Mark said in a loud whisper to his beautiful cohort, as they followed little Lord Fauntleroy's bobbing buns across the entrance foyer and down a short corridor.

The lieutenant chuckled. "Aren't you glad now that we decided not to dress for the occasion?"

"I'll tell you later," Mark demured, "when I see what the girls are wearing."

A door was opened, and they were suddenly assailed by sounds of soft music, the tinkle of ice-cubes on crystal and a murmur of voices. And they were led, like Alice through the looking-glass, into what appeared to be a small, but conventional nightclub, with bar, dance floor (the size of a go-go pedestal) and a stage. A dozen or so tables, half of them already occupied, were scattered about the dimly lit room, and a small group at the rear of the stage were immortalizing the old favorite, *Blue Moon.* Big-boy left them then, but they were not alone for long.

"Hi, kids!"

An extremely well-endowed little girl (or was it a petite young lady?) came skipping up to them with a smile and a happy giggle. "My name is Thelma," she said, "what's yours?"

Thelma looked to be all legs and auburn curls. The little-girl dress she wore, with its high, ruffled waist and flared skirt, though modest enough as far as it went, ended without adequate warning the width of a widow's wish short of propriety. On a child, it would have been cute. On Thelma Flowers, it was blatantly sexual.

Cathy Carruthers flashed her badge and identified herself. "My partner," she added, with a nod toward Mark, "is Sergeant Swanson." The little-girl facade and the smile seemed to melt away as the lieutenant spoke, and Thelma Flowers was suddenly left looking her age. "Well, what do you want with us?" she said impatiently.

"One of your girls was murdered last night, Mrs. Flowers, and we're trying to find out why."

"We've already told the police everything we know," she retorted angrily. "Shelley Newcomb only worked here, lieutenant. Surely you don't intend to hold us responsible for the private lives of all our employees."

"You don't feel then, that her death was related in any way to her job? An irate, or over-zealous customer, perhaps? A fellow worker?"

"No. Of course not. What a wild idea."

"Then you won't mind, I'm sure, if the sergeant and I sort of, look around a bit."

"Look around?" She did not appear to be too pleased with the prospect.

The lieutenant smiled disarmingly. "It's just routine, Mrs. Flowers. After all," she said, softening her voice to a husky, confiding whisper, "we're just doing our job, you know. And, uh —

it isn't every day that Mark and I get to visit a — well, a club like The Playpen." She lowered her eyes and shyly reached for Mark's hand. "By the way," she said coyly, "we think your little dress is just *darling*, don't we, Mark?"

Mark nodded numbly. "Yeah — uh, just darling," he echoed.

Thelma's happy girlish demeanor was slow to reassert itself, and there was a residue of caution in her voice as she struggled to qualify them in this new role. After a thoughtful pause, she said, "Well – " uncertainly, then with a slow smile and a tiny titter of comprehension, she added, "I guess even cops can have their little, uh — preferences." She gave them both another long, lingering look of appraisal. "Grab a table," she said finally, "and I'll tell my husband you're here."

As she flounced away, Mark was quick to notice that the ribbon on her hair matched the pink, frilly hem of her peek-a-boo panties.

THEY CHOSE A TABLE WHERE THEY HAD A GOOD view of the exits and the other patrons, though it was difficult to see much of anything in the subdued light. As they took their seats, the lieutenant's eyes were drawn to a balding, nondescript sort of man, fiftyish, in a dark, expensive-looking suit and (oddly, given the lack of light) a pair of shaded Foster Grants. He had risen from a nearby table and was headed (rather purposefully, she thought) toward the rear of the club. When he disappeared under a small, illuminated sign that said "Gents," she shrugged and turned her attention back to the table.

Mark, meanwhile, was making himself comfortable. The lieutenant watched him patiently, her beautiful golden head resting on one hand, as he hitched up his chair, edging it closer to hers, then closer, until when he turned to look at her, her luminous blue eyes were only inches from his own. "That," she said quietly, "is close enough. And, Mark — "

"Uh-huh?" She was so close, he could feel the soft warmth of her breath.

"Let's try to remember, shall we, that we're here on a serious police matter."

"I'm poised for action."

She sighed tolerantly. "Well, whatever action you're poised for, tiger, I won't be far behind. *You are still holding my hand.*"

"Good grief!" He looked aghast. "And all this time I thought that you were holding mine." He made a move to withdraw his hand, just as another girl came skipping toward them, and he felt his partner's fingers tighten again, firmly over his.

"Saved by the 'belle,'" he chuckled.

The lieutenant groaned.

"My name is Melissa," the girl said brightly. "Can I get you something?"

She was a small person, a possible five feet at most, and she couldn't have weighed more than ninety-seven pounds soaking wet. In her kiddies attire, hair-do, and in the dim light of the club, she looked to be about twelve years old. That is, until she had taken their order, then stooped to clear and wipe off an adjacent table.

Mark coughed self-consciously, then surprised even himself by averting his eyes.

"That 'child,' Mark, must be Melissa Gibbs," the lieutenant asserted, "Shelley's friend. She certainly doesn't look her age."

"How old is she?"

"According to the Leprechaun, nineteen."

"Jeeez-uz!" Mark squirmed in his chair. "This place is beginning to make me feel downright dirty."

"Thank God for that." The lieutenant rewarded him with a tight smile. "But, Mark, have you noticed that almost all the customers are men? There must be thirty people here, and only three of them are women."

"And *we*," Mark noted, "are the only couple."

"So I see." The lieutenant pursed her lips in thought. "Maybe we've been putting on the wrong act."

"There's a first time for everything," Mark reminded her, "but, lieutenant, why the charade at all?"

"I'm just trying to throw them off guard, Mark, give them something else to think about. When we get around to looking this place over, I want it to be on my terms."

The drinks arrived then, in a swirling tease of skimpy skirt and skivvies. "Johnny on the rocks for the gent," the girl tittered, "and creme de menthe for the lady."

"Are you Melissa Gibbs?" the lieutenant asked.

She looked surprised. "Yes, I am."

"I'm Lieutenant Carruthers, Mrs. Gibbs. This is may partner, Sergeant Swanson. We're from Metro Central."

"Oh." She lowered her voice. "You're here about Shelley, aren't you?"

"Yes. Is there anything more you can tell us that you haven't already told the police?"

The girl bit her lip and darted a nervous glance over the lieutenant's shoulder. Her manner quickly changed. "I don't know what you mean," she said.

"The entire staff, lieutenant, has been questioned already, and at great length." It was a male voice, and it came from behind her. The lieutenant turned to see another man-child smiling down at her. "You may go now, Melissa," the man said authoritatively.

The girl hurried away with her saucy little tail wagging provocatively. The man lowered himself into a chair. "I'm Tommy Flowers," he said. "May I join you?"

"It seems you already have," Mark observed dryly.

Tommy Flowers smiled good-naturedly. He was not a big man, but he exuded an air of strength and purpose that even the "little-boy-blue" outfit he was wearing could not dispel. The illusion of youth, however, that radiated from his forty year-old face, had obviously been accomplished with the subtle help of make-up.

"I understand from Thelma," he said with a meaningful glance at their coupled hands, "that you're sort of mixing business with pleasure tonight."

The lieutenant stole a quick look at Mark before lowering her lovely eyes. "I guess we are being a bit obvious, aren't we?" She bit her lip, then shyly withdrew her hand. "It must be the atmosphere of this place."

"The Playpen does have its effect on people," Flowers said proudly. "It seems to bring out ones, uh — hidden proclivities."

The look of bewildered innocence that the lieutenant leveled at Tommy Flowers would have suckered a saint into the life of a born-again sinner. "Mr. Flowers, we really do have to make a guided tour," she told him sweetly. "And that would get the 'business' part of the evening out of our hair, so to speak." She shook her golden head indicatively. "Wouldn't it?"

Flowers smiled. "Sure. Give me a minute with our musicians, and I'll take you around myself."

While the club owner engaged the small group on the stage in conversation, the lieutenant said to Mark, "A guy in a dark suite and tinted shades disappeared under that 'Gents' sign, Mark, when we first arrived."

"So?"

"So he hasn't come out yet. Don't you think it's a bit strange?"

"Did anyone follow him in?"

"Well, yes. Three or four other men have gone in there, but they've all since returned to their seats."

Flowers had left the stage and was threading his way slowly back to them, smiling and nodding at the clientele along the way.

"You stay here, Mark, while I take the tour, alone."

"Do you think that's wise?"

She shrugged out of her jacket without answering, then as the man approached, she rose to meet him. Flowers made no attempt to hide his admiration. "I'll bet you'd be something else in a Shirley Temple outfit," he said as he led her away.

Mark watched them go with a feeling of helpless chagrin. "The bloody pervert must have read my mind," he muttered to himself.

TOMMY FLOWERS WAS DOING HIS BEST TO PLEASE and impress. Perhaps the prospect of adding a new playmate to the fetishistic regulars at The Playpen had temporarily turned his head. Especially one as exquisitely unique as this starry-eyed lieutenant, who drew mewls and drools (not the least, his own) from staff and patrons alike. Nor was he unmindful of what a "sympathetic ear" in the ranks of the police, could do for him and the club, *if*, eventually, she could be persuaded to function in the club's interest; to remain openly sequestered, as it were (in the manner of Poe's purloined letter) while continuing to merge and mingle with the legal lackeys at the Eleventh Precinct. And in her off hours, well —

The "tour" had begun with a slow meander back through the maze of tables, and The Playpen's motley customers had taken advantage of the occasion, fawning, clutching, as they welcomed the six-foot, honey-haired *ingenue* to their collective breasts. Next had come the open ogling and the heavy breathing of the group of spaced-out virtuosos that occupied the stage.

"Way to go, big mama."

"Oh, yeah, foxy — far out."

"He-e-e-e-e-ey!"

They were well into *I'm In the Mood For Love* when the introductions began, and though only half of the band appeared to be playing at any one time, the melody (such as it was) never seemed to falter.

It was off to the bar next, where the lieutenant met a couple of over-aged, under-dressed "kids," one male, one female, who were busy building drinks and bumping bottoms in the narrow confines behind the counter. And then on to the kitchen, where a tall, good-looking black man in a microcosm of steam and stainless steel, greeted them with a broad friendly smile. He wore a chef's hat at a jaunty angle and a long white apron, which, by The Playpen standards, made him look a little over-dressed — until he unexpected turned his back.

"Leroy is strictly gourmet," Flowers said as they turned to leave. "His specialty is *Beef Bourguignon.*"

The lieutenant arched her perfect brows in innocent wonder. "Not buns?"

They went from the kitchen to a small room off a rear center-hall that seemed, almost, to evenly divide the rear half of the premises.

"Let me guess," the lieutenant said as they entered, "this would be your private office."

"Office, yes," Flowers replied with an ambivalent laugh, "but rarely private. We're all one big family here."

I'll bet, she thought, as she surveyed the room's interior. A desk and filing cabinet were crammed against one wall, while the rest of the room was given over to a bar, a sink, a fridge, and a well-worn black leather couch. It was all too typical, the lieutenant decided. The entire place, in fact, was somehow just too blatantly obvious. Too pat. Too — expected.

Even the "change-rooms," where they headed next, fitted into this tiresome malaise of over-done sexuality; a *menage* of mirrors and make-up, in an absurd repertory of puerile, juvenescent clothing, where the staff and an in-group of regulars would come to don their panties and pinafores for an evening of charade.

But it was not until they had reached the tail-end of the tour, and were standing in a kind of receiving area at the rear of the building, that the lieutenant was suddenly rewarded with what she liked to call the "unexpected," and which, as usual, was precisely where (and what) one would least expect it to be.

The room was utilitarian and bare, except for stacked boxes of incoming liquor and food, and the usual pile of refuse and crated empties, destined for the dump. She recognized the blank back door she had seen from the alley, locked and barred on this side, and the bricked-up window, close against the opposite wall. The drab austerity of the place gave it the appearance and the appeal of a sealed crypt.

But there it was. The tell-tale crack in The Playpen's impregnable armor. The very thing she'd been looking for. The *unexpected.* And to the trained eye of the Amazon, it was as obvious and apocalyptic as a pimp on a pulpit.

WHEN THE LIEUTENANT REJOINED MARK AT THE TABLE, a girl in a Shirley Temple wig (and little else), was performing the last rites on *The good Ship Lolly-Pop* from the front of the stage.

"Must be amateur night," the lieutenant said with a grimace as she sat down."

"Yeah. She's kind of cute."

"Are you serious? I've heard axles needing grease sound better than that."

"I'm looking," Mark told her, "not listening. Where's your boyfriend?"

"He'll be back any minute. Did you spot the guy with the shades?"

"Not a sign of him."

"Ah-ha." The lieutenant looked like the mouse with the cheese. "Then he *is* in there."

"What?" Mark stared at her vacantly. "Who's in where?"

"Mark, I'm absolutely convinced that there's a secret room, or something, built into this place. It runs from behind the restrooms, over there, clear back to the alley. And what's more, our mysterious Foster Grant did not *go to the john,* Mark, *he is one.*"

"Prostitution?"

"Of the most abominable kind. You'd better check out that men's room, *pronto.* And Mark, look for hidden or blank doors, or anything else unusual. *Anything* that might suggest an entry into that area. I'll give you exactly one minute to reappear."

"Better make it two, lieutenant. Even *I'm* not that good."

The lieutenant smiled. "Two, then. If you're not out in two, I'll put in a call for back-up and come looking."

"You're really that sure there's something going on back there?"

"I'm really that sure."

Mark levered himself out of his chair and headed directly for the "Gents" sign at the rear of the club. Cathy Carruthers glanced at her watch. She was sipping her creme de menthe, moments later, when Tommy Flowers suddenly appeared at her elbow.

"Are you still working on your first drink?" he asked as he sat down uninvited.

"I'm on duty, remember?"

"You *were* on duty." Flowers caught Melissa's eye from where she was serving drinks at another table. He made a circular sign with his index finger. "Drinks for everyone," he told the lieutenant. "It's time you let your hair down. Thelma tells me she's been looking through our costumes and she's come up with something special, just for you."

"Oh?"

"Wait'll you see it."

"I'll wait."

"Little Bo-Peep," he said excitedly.

Cathy Carruthers looked appropriately sheepish. "Knowing you," she said, "I'll bet there'll be more peep than bo."

"Yeah," he breathed.

Melissa bore down on them then, with another round of drinks, and the lieutenant rose nonchalantly to her feet. "I've got a telephone call to make," she said with a casual glance at her watch.

"I'll only be a minute."

"Reporting in?" he asked with some wariness.

"Not really." She treated him to one of her mind-boggling smiles. "I just don't want anyone waiting up for me."

His answering smile lingered long after she was gone; even, some minutes later, when he saw her leave the phone at the end of the bar and head toward the restrooms. But then, as she went right by the door marked "Ladies," and abruptly disappeared into the men's room, the smile became a puzzling frown.

"That blonde bitch," Thelma Flowers whispered venomously into her husband's ear, "has more on her bloody mind, me thinks, than a tumble with my Tommy."

The club owner shrugged her hand impatiently from his shoulder.

"We'd better see just what in hell she's up to," he said grimly.

"LIEUTENANT? QUICK! HELP ME WITH THIS THING," Cathy Carruthers read the scene in a split second. The guy with the Foster Grant's was out cold in the middle of the men's room floor. His shattered shades hung from one ear and a trickle of blood oozed from a slack, open mouth. Mark was farther back, with one of his size-twelves braced firmly against the end of a row of urinals, and his big fists wrapped around the open edge of a solid blank door. The door, unopened (without hasp or hinges), would have been an unobtrusive part of the wall. Mark was in the midst of what appeared to be a losing struggle to keep it from closing.

The lieutenant moved with lightning speed. She stooped and grabbed the inert man on the floor, then tossed him like a sack of California Whites into the space between the door and the jamb. "That should hold them both for a while," she said to Mark. "What's making it close?"

Mark straightened with a puff of relief. "It must be operated pneumatically," he gasped. "So what do we do now?"

"Find the mechanism, I guess, and blow it away with a .38." But before she could transform the words into action, the door behind them slammed open and Tommy Flowers burst into the room. His ludicrously leggy wife was hard on his heels. "You get the guy," the woman blurted from the doorway, "I'll take care of Bo-Peep."

Mark turned to face the advancing Flowers with a tolerant sigh. "Time for bye-byes," he sang with a lilt, as he lobbed a long, lazy right into the club owner's unprotected face. The man seemed to stop and stiffen in mid-stride, and Mark stood back to watch the "flower" wilt (as he recalled it later) — "like a pansy in a piss-pot."

Thelma Flowers had come charging by her woebegone mate with her feet and fists flailing, right into the waiting, open arms of her smiling opponent. The look on the woman's face, as their bodies collided, was one of angry frustration, then, as the Amazon linked her hands and began slowly to squeeze, the anger turned to mild alarm. Panic promptly followed, and the one-sided encounter soon came to a pitiful end in a wild-eyed, lung-wrenching, desperate struggle for air.

"You'll have to teach me how to do that," Mark said as he took the breathless, gasping woman from the lieutenant's arms, and set her down on one of the toilets to recoup. "We could practice over at my place — "

"Hi, guys!"

They both turned to see Big-boy standing in the open doorway, his round boyish face wreathed in a malicious grin. The huge muscular body seemed to fill the door opening, and one clenched fist held a wine bottle firmly by its neck. Mark had taken a tentative step toward the man when a throaty, dark voice from behind, made him freeze in his tracks.

"Hold it right there."

The lieutenant shot a quick glance over her shoulder. "Well," she said brightly, as though welcoming an unexpected guest to a Sunday outing, "if it isn't our old friend, Buns."

The pneumatic door had somehow released its hold on the wedge of flesh and bone that had prevented it from closing, and now, on the threshold, stood the tall, good-looking black from the kitchen. He was still wearing the chef's hat and apron, and he held a gun in his big right hand.

The lieutenant squinted at him through narrowed eyes. "You're not planning on turning your back on me again, are you, Buns?"

The big black exposed a perfect set of pearly whites. "No way, big mamma, not this time."

"Then I don't suppose you'd object," she said as she tossed her golden mane defiantly and reached for the hem of her gray skirt, "if I turn mine." To Mark, in a guarded whisper, she said, "You take Fauntleroy."

Then, in one aesthetic motion that would have made a ballerina blanche with envy, the Amazon hiked her skirt to a somewhat unseemly height, pivoting as it lifted, until the white's of the chef's eyes were an identical match to the pristine gleam of his teeth. And at that precise moment, she leveled a devastating donkey kick at the hand that held the gun. The weapon went whistling up into a far corner of the room.

And, while there was still more surprise than injury in evidence, the Amazon turned, skirts flying, and lunged with a vicious karate jab to the black man's throat. She struck again, then again, with an eye blurring combination to the left temple. The man dropped to his knees with a rasping gurgle, then toppled forward onto his face.

Mark's view of his partner's somewhat saucy shenanigans, fortunately, was only peripheral. Big-Boy, on the other hand, witnessed the entire spectacle from an eye-to-thigh vantage point that was not a little difficult to ignore. And it was in that split second of heady inadvertence, that Mark hurled himself at his assailant.

The lieutenant was in the process of turning, smoothing her disheveled skirt, when she saw Mark land with both big feet on Big-Boy's bulging thighs. His hands streaked out and clamped themselves around the hulking faggot's neck, and for the briefest moment, the two men were staring into each other's eyes, inches apart. But the big detective's six-foot frame was already answering the call of gravity, falling back, and down, and it was dragging Big-Boy along for the ride. When his shoulders hit the floor, Mark straightened his long legs with a vengeance and sent the other man hurtling high over his head. A long, trailing shriek of rage came to an abrupt end with a squishy *thud*! And when Mark scrambled up to investigate, he found Big-Boy crammed snugly, butt first, into one of the urinals. And he was there to stay.

Oddly, the bottle of wine was still intact, clutched in Big-Boy's big right fist. He was gazing up at the two detectives with a stupid, vacant grin on his face.

"The big jerk's halfway to dreamland," the lieutenant laughed.

"Yeah." Mark relieved the man of the bottle, ruffled the thatch of sun-bleached hair, and said, "Nighty-night," with apparent solicitude. Then he flushed the urinal.

THE SECRET BACK ROOM AT THE PLAYPEN WAS, IN effect, a self-contained apartment. It was long and narrow, with most of the space taken up by four small cubicles that apparently functioned jointly as bedrooms and detention cells. There was also a bed-sitting room and a kitchenette cramped into the far end of the place, complete with T.V., telephone, and a good supply of food and booze. A bathroom, only slightly larger than the facilities it contained, divided one area from the other.

Mark and the lieutenant stood close together in the kitchenette area, watching the specialized teams from H.Q. go over the place with a fine comb. There was barely room to swing a cat, and with all the uniforms milling about, even standing room was at a premium.

"So you figure it was Flowers who killed Shelley Newcomb," Mark said summarily.

"No doubt about it." The lieutenant was filing an asymmetrical fingernail with care. "Now all we've got to do is prove it."

"Which may not be easy."

"Oh, I don't known, Mark. Both Big-Boy and Buns have already begun to sing like a couple of Carolina crickets. And in the process of saving her own skin, you can bet that Thelma Flowers will soon be picking up the chorus."

"Maybe so, lieutenant, but there's still a lot of missing pieces. Damn it, we don't even know where the murder happened, and why."

"My guess is that she was murdered in the change room, Mark, while getting dressed to go on shift, Monday night. That would be consistent with the M.E.'s T.O.D. estimate, plus the fact that she was nude, or near nude, when the killer struck. And with all the blood that flew, it shouldn't be too difficult for the lab-crew to nail down the exact site of the murder."

"And the motive?"

"We may never know for sure, Mark, but I'd be willing to bet that Shelley Newcomb inadvertently (or otherwise) discovered this hidden room, and what it was being used for. In my humble, but considered opinion, she was simply being silenced."

"Salami'd, is more like it," Mark said grimly.

The lieutenant cast a thoughtful eye at the closed door to one of the cubicles. It had remained closed since they had first broken in through the men's room and discovered a young girl huddled in a corner in a state of wild-eyed hysteria.

"There's a policewoman in there with her now," the lieutenant said with a rueful sigh. "Poor kid. Her last visitor must have been that creep with the Foster Grant's. There should be a special kind of justice for an animal like that."

"Lieutenant?"

A uniformed policewoman had just entered the room. She had Melissa Gibbs in tow. "This, uh — person, lieutenant, wants to talk to you. She says it's important." The startling contrast between the child-like Melissa and the policewoman would have been comical under happier circumstances.

The lieutenant acceded with a smile. "Very well," she said, "what is it, Melissa?"

The girl looked uncomfortably around at the people milling about them. "I just wanted you to know," she said haltingly, "that I intend to do everything I can to — to cooperate."

"As a witness, you mean? For the State?"

"Yes, lieutenant."

"Are you saying that you were actually involved with what was going on in here, Melissa?"

The young waitress paled and her lips quivered. She looked to be on the verge of tears. "Yes, but — I mean, it wasn't what you think — "

The lieutenant put her arm around the distraught girl and steered her over to the bed-settee, then sat down with her. "Why don't you tell me about it," she said gently.

Melissa told her story with frequent pauses for tears and self-recriminations, but that did not dilute, in any way, the impact of what she had to say.

Thelma and Tommy Flowers, she informed them, were the principals involved. They were the brains of the operation. Big-Boy and Buns were only muscle. If there were others, she did not know of them.

The Playpen, she explained, was being used as a kind of way station, or pick-up point, for an organized ring of flesh peddlers. Runaways and street-kids, mainly, who seemed to be the most vulnerable and the least likely to be missed.

They were only kept at The Playpen for a few days. Melissa went on, then they were shipped out. To the Middle-East, mostly, Big-Boy had told her once. Some to the Orient. Very few of them were kept State-side. There was big money involved, he had said. Oil money.

When asked where she fitted in, Melissa told them with some embarrassment, that when young girls were in short supply, Flowers would sometimes give her extra money to pose as one of the runaways. "You know, for a customer." The regulars at the club knew her, of course, but many of Flowers' special customers were from out of town. "They never knew the difference," she said with an indifferent shrug of her tiny eyebrows.

The lieutenant sighed audibly through tightly pursed lips. "And Shelley?" She asked ruefully. "What happened to her?"

"I honestly don't know, lieutenant. It happened Monday, when I was off. Maybe they were short of girls that night, and Shelley, well — refused — "

"I get the picture," the lieutenant interjected. "Once she'd been asked, once she knew about that back room, a refusal to play ball could only have meant one thing — "

"Golly." Melissa's eyes widened uncomprehendingly in her childish face. "It seems such a silly thing to — to die for. I mean, it's not like Shelley was even — "

"A virgin?" the lieutenant suggested dryly. "Perhaps not. But then, maybe she wasn't a whore, either."

"WELL, I GUESS THAT PRETTY WELL WRAPS IT UP," Mark said as he and the lieutenant left the entrance to The Playpen and sauntered slowly down the street toward the gray Chevy. It was almost dawn. "It's the Fed's baby now. But who'd of thought The Playpen would turn out to be a front for a gang of lousy flesh peddlers?"

The lieutenant chuckled. "And who'd of thought the real $1.49-Day killer, Adolph Klause, was actually telling the truth all the time?"

"Yeah," Mark said thoughtfully. "It's been some kind of case. But there's still a couple of things I'm not too clear on, lieutenant."

"The graffiti on Hymie Lipshitz's window?"

"Uh, yeah — " Mark gave his beautiful partner a doubtful glance. "After all, that was not part of the $1.49-Day killer's established M.O."

"No, it wasn't. My guess is, it was done by vandals. It had nothing to do with the murder. A simple coincidence, Mark. Nothing more."

"Coincidences aren't supposed to happen in murder cases, lieutenant."

"Nor are beautiful blondes supposed to be anything but dumb." She chuckled coyly. "And certainly not, uh — clairvoyant."

Mark emitted a hopeless groan. "Okay, Swami, so how did you spot it?"

"The secret room?"

"What else?"

"Well, Mark, the 'unexpected' was that bricked-in window at the rear of the club. When we first saw if from the alley, you may recall, it was centered between the door and the opposite wall. But when I saw it again from the inside, either the wall or the window had mysteriously moved. The fact was, or course, that the inside wall was phony, and I might add, about as stupidly obvious as those little one-liners you're so pathetically fond of."

"I'm pathetically fond of a lot of things, lieutenant, not the least of which is to get some practice on that bare-hug thing you were doing tonight."

The lieutenant gave him a sly look. "I can read you like a book," she said. "That's *bear*-hug, Mark, not *bare*-hug."

"As Tommy Flowers would say, lieutenant, everyone to their own, uh — hidden proclivities." He stuck out his tongue and panted. "Anyhow, I bet my way'd be more fun."

MEL D. AMES

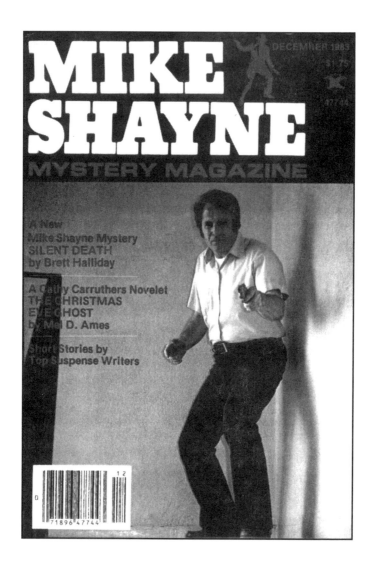

MIKE SHAYNE

DECEMBER 1983
$1.75

47744

MYSTERY MAGAZINE

A New
Mike Shayne Mystery
SILENT DEATH
by Brett Halliday

A Cathy Carruthers Novelet
THE CHRISTMAS
EVE GHOST
by Mel D. Ames

Short Stories by
Top Suspense Writers

0   71896 47744

*Murder never stops — not even for the
holidays! Neither does Cathy Carruthers!*

the christmas eve ghost

DETECTIVE-LIEUTENANT CATHY CARRUTHERS WAS at her desk in her Homicide Division office at Metro Central's Eleventh Precinct. Her burly partner, Detective-Sergeant Mark Swanson, sat across from her. She glanced at the sheet of paper he had just handed her, then looked up curiously.

"What is this, Mark? Some kind of joke?"

"If it is, lieutenant, it's a cruel one."

"It looks like a poem."

"It is," Mark told her. "Read it."

The lieutenant read the typewritten words aloud:

> *"'Tis the night before Christmas*
> *And the thought uppermost*
> *In the minds of the 'children,'*
> *Is the Christmas Eve ghost.*
> *While the Vanderhilles lie snug,*
> *Asleep in their bed,*
> *The clock will strike midnight, and*
> *— one more will be dead."*

A frown creased the lieutenant's beautiful brow. "So? What's it suppose to mean?"

"Well, lieutenant, according to Franklin B. Vanderhille, it simply means that before midnight, tonight, another member of that illustrious family will die, at the hands of the Christmas Eve ghost."

"*Another* member?"

"Yeah. If the ghost carries out its threat, lieutenant, this will be the third year in succession that a Vanderhille has gone to glory on Christmas Eve."

"At the hands of a *ghost?*"

"That's what the man says."

"What man, Mark, and where did you get this?"

"I got it from Franklin B. Vanderhille, himself. *He* got it from the ghost. He's waiting in the outer office."

"The ghost?"

"No, damn it, Franklin B."

The lieutenant narrowed her eyes in sudden recollection. "Wait a second. Not *the* Franklin B. Vanderhille, who lives out in Thornston Heights — "

"You got it."

"Ah, yes. I remember now. There was a bit of trouble out there last Christmas. Didn't a woman fall down a flight of stairs, or something?"

"That's right. But the family denied that she fell — they claim she was pushed."

"Pushed? By whom?"

"By the ghost, I suppose."

"Yes, well — was there something done about it? I mean, was anyone booked?"

Mark shrugged his shaggy eyebrows. "So how do you go about booking a ghost, lieutenant?"

The lieutenant emitted a long, querulous sigh of exasperation. "I guess you'd better just send the guy in and, Mark, I want you to sit in on this, too." As she watched him go out the door, she added, "Scheee. A pushy ghost that writes poetry. What a great way to spend Christmas Eve."

FRANKLIN B. VANDERHILLE WAS A TALL, REGAL-looking man. Impeccably groomed in a grey pin-striped suit, he exuded an unmistakable air of wealth and preferential breeding. His demeanor this morning, however, was obviously out of character. He appeared to be afflicted by a nervous excitement that he was not quite able to repress.

"Mr. Vanderhille, come in. Please sit down."

"You are Lieutenant Cathy Carruthers?"

"Yes."

"I've heard of you, lieutenant." He settled himself stiffly into one of the chairs. "You've really become quite famous," he said with flawless diction. "I did not, however, expect anyone so — attractive."

The lieutenant did her best to accept the compliment graciously, but she had some difficulty ignoring Mark's zany *la-di-da* clowning in the background. "You're very gallant," she said as she fought a half smile, waiting until Mark had dutifully dumped his rugged carcass into the other chair. "Mark said something about a ghost."

The man's already gaunt face paled visibly. The pupils of his restless eyes were pinpoints of fear. He looked to be on the quiet side of panic.

"Where shall I start?" he asked uncertainly.

The lieutenant had placed the tips of her fingers together and cradled her chin in against her thumbs. She looked almost to be praying. "Why not take it from the beginning," she said into her hands.

"Yes," he stammered, "yes, of course. It all began, lieutenant, two years ago today, with the death of my daughter. Her name was Samantha. She was only ten at the time; a twin, actually, to my son, Franklin C."

"You both have the same name?"

"Yes. Except for the initial. My father is Franklin A. If and when Franklin C. has any children, his first born will be called Franklin D. My father's idea, to identify the Vanderhille lineage alphabetically through consecutive generations."

"How did the girl die?" the lieutenant asked.

"She died of fright, lieutenant. She saw the ghost." He looked obliquely at Mark, then quickly back at the lieutenant. His eyes glinted insanely. "The coroner called it asphyxiation, of course, and in a sense, I guess, it was. But fright can do that, you see. It tightens up the respiratory system, constricting the heart and the lungs. The child, that night, would have felt herself to be in a grip of abject fear, an invisible phantom hand, as it were, that squeezed, and squeezed, until the breath and the life had been virtually drive from her little body." He paused to wipe his forehead with an immaculately white handkerchief. "Asphyxiation, perhaps, lieutenant. But *death by fright*, nonetheless."

"Where was the child when it happened?"

"In her bed."

"There was no other possible cause?"

"No. None, whatever. Oh — the police came up with the wild idea that she could have been smothered by someone in the house. You know, a pillow held over her head while she slept, or some such ridiculous scenario. She slept alone, you see. In her own room, I mean. But no member of the family had any better access to her than any other. And, I ask you, what possible motive could any one in the family have to — to kill my little girl — ?"

His voice trailed off disconsolately. The lieutenant, meanwhile, had momentarily closed her eyes, a habit she had when deeply engaged in thought. She gave every appearance of being fast asleep.

"Were there others in the house?" she asked suddenly, without opening her eyes. "Beside the family, I mean? Servants — ?"

"Yes." Franklin B. glanced inquiringly at Mark, then quickly back to the beautifully reposed lieutenant. "Yes, lieutenant. We have three full-time retainers. A cook, a maid, and a footman."

"They all live in?"

"Yes."

"And they had the same access as anyone else, to Samantha's room?"

"Yes, but — "

The lieutenant rose suddenly to her feet. She went to the window behind her desk and stood there looking out at the downtown morning bustle of Central Metro. Last minute Christmas shoppers were darting about the streets like ants in a sugar bowl.

"Tell me about last Christmas," she said without turning to face the two men.

"My mother was taken," Franklin B. said to the lieutenant's engaging back. "She was pushed from the top landing of the front staircase. It broke her dear neck — rest her soul. She — she died instantly."

"At what time of day did this occur?"

"Just prior to midnight, lieutenant. I remember hearing the grandfather clock striking twelve as we came running out in answer to her scream. Oh, the pitiable way she screamed. I can hear it still — "

"And again, everyone in the house (family and servants, alike) had ready access to the scene of death?"

"Yes. And the police, of course, attempted again to obfuscate reality with some inept conclusion that had no basis in fact. They suggested, for instance, that she simply might have tripped on the top stair, or, of all things, that she was sleep-walking, and she had merely lost her footing in the dark — "

"And you find these possibilities unacceptable?"

"Totally." The man was suddenly, seethingly adamant. "My mother had already retired, lieutenant, and she was not in the habit of roaming about the house in the middle of the night. Nor has she ever been known to sleepwalk. Not in her entire life. She was lured from her bed and pushed, lieutenant, you can be assured of that." The lieutenant turned to face him then, as he added in a low, foreboding voice, "*She was shoved to her death, I tell you, by the evil hand of that infernal ghost.*"

THE GRIM PORTENT OF THE MAN'S WORDS ECHOED in the prolonged silence that followed. Finally, the lieutenant gave a Pegasusian toss to her golden mane, and effectively shattered the ominous stillness that had so suddenly engulfed them.

"Mr. Vanderhille," she said with her back to the window, "suppose you tell me about that poem."

"That's the weirdest thing of all," he said softly.

"In what way?"

The eyes that looked up at the lieutenant were those of a frightened little boy. "It was a few minutes after midnight when it happened," he began, "last night, in the first few moments, as it were, of Christmas Eve day. I was just about to ascend the stairs to my bed, when I heard a tapping coming from the hall study. Someone was in there, using the typewriter. My son, Franklin C., was with me, so don't get the idea that I was imagining things — "

"Wasn't that rather late for a twelve-year-old boy to be staying up, Mr. Vanderhille?"

"It *is* the festive season, lieutenant, and this ghost thing has upset the boy terribly, as you might imagine. We had just watched Dickens' *A Christmas Carol* on television, which was rather a poor choice of entertainment under the circumstances, but — "

"I understand. Did the boy hear the tapping?"

"He did, indeed. As a matter of fact, he drew my attention to it. It was very faint, at first, from back of the staircase, but as we approached the study it became appreciably louder. Everyone else in the house was in bed, lieutenant, but, clearly, *someone* was in there using the typewriter. I was about to open the door when Franklin C. caught my arm. I've never seen the boy so frightened."

"What happened then?"

"The typing suddenly stopped. I put the boy behind me and opened the door. My God, it was weird."

"What was weird?"

"My son and I were the only mortal souls in that room, lieutenant. But just before I found the light switch, I felt an icy chill sweep over me, and for one horrifying moment, I had the distinct impression that an invisible and malign presence had brushed past me in the dark. I heard Franklin C. utter a terrified gasp from somewhere behind me. A moment later, with the lights on, we saw the typewriter on the desk, which of course, was precisely where it should have been, but that sheet of paper," he pointed to the poem on the lieutenant's desk, "was jutting out of the machine. Otherwise, the room was empty."

"Is there any other means of egress to the room? Other than the door you entered by?"

"There is not. That study is an interior room. It has no windows, and only the one door. The heat vents and cold air returns are grilled, and much too small to accommodate the body of even a child."

"Could someone have hidden in the room?"

"The only furniture of any size, lieutenant, is the desk. It's of the pedestal type, with one tier of small drawers and the rest open fronted. The walls are paneled and lined with books. And there are no secret passages or tunnels, anywhere in the house. There was just no way a living creature could have hidden in that room, lieutenant."

"Hmm." The lieutenant nudged her pretty nose with an elegantly-flexed knuckle. "You certainly don't give a lowly skeptic much room to maneuver, Mr. Vanderhille."

The distraught man leaned forward in his chair. He was visibly trembling. "Lieutenant Carruthers, I beseech you. Please help us."

"I'm not sure there's very much I *can* do, much as I may wish to. You must remember, sir, that the sergeant and I are attached to Homicide and, as yet, there has been no crime."

"No crime? You don't regard the death of my daughter and my dear mother a crime?" The man was flushed and angry

"Those incidents, as unfortunate as they may be, have already been investigated. It is not for me to re-open the files."

Franklin B. Vanderhille jolted to his feet. "Lieutenant," he blurted, "let me tell you this. I intend to go from here to the office of your Chief of Detectives, Henry Heller. From there, if need be, I will proceed to the Police Commissioner himself. Even the office of the Governor is not beyond me. I am a very influential man in this state, lieutenant, and I usually get what I want."

The lieutenant straightened against the backdrop of the window and she was suddenly silhouetted by the morning sun. Caught in a remarkable halo of sun-glow, scintillating streaks of light seemed to glance off her golden head and ricochet about the room in a dazzling display of daylight pyrotechnics. The affect was so startling the angry man was momentarily shaken. He fell back a pace, then turning abruptly, he headed for the door.

"I'll have you on this case within the hour," he asserted tersely. And with a show of nervous dignity, he was gone.

IT WAS LESS THAN THIRTY MINUTES LATER WHEN Lieutenant Cathy Carruthers lifted the telephone on its first ring and

Chief Hank Heller's gruff bark bounced off her eardrum.

"Lieutenant?"

"Chief."

"What's this about you turning down the Franklin B. Vanderhille case?"

"I didn't know there *was* a case, chief."

"No case?" The chief's voice rose an octave. "You call two corpses and another one threatened, no case?"

"The two deaths have already been investigated, and those cases are closed."

"Then you'd better re-open them."

"Is that an order?"

"It is."

"On Christmas Eve? That's heartless, chief."

Mark, who was sitting on the other side of the desk, groaned. He could not avoid hearing the entire conversation.

"Just think of me as Santa Claus, lieutenant," the chief responded with a mirthless chuckle.

"Or a Christmas turkey," Mark quipped.

"*I heard that*, you overgrown beach bum. I think you'd better go along with her, sergeant."

Cathy Carruthers could not hold back a sudden burst of laughter as Mark did a grotesque mime of a Christmas gobbler losing its head.

"Have your fun kiddies, while you can," the chief retorted grimly, "but just make damn good and sure that Vanderhille threat doesn't materialize."

"Do you happen to know where that 'threat' came from, chief?"

"A note of some kind, I understand."

"It was a poem — "

"So?"

" — delivered by a ghost."

There was a prolonged silence before the chief quietly cleared his throat. "Yes, well —you can fill me in on the whole fiasco, tomorrow. Uh — better make that Monday. Tomorrow's Christmas. And, lieutenant — "

"Yes, chief?"

"Season's greetings."

MARK WATCHED AND REMINISCED AS HIS BEAUTIFUL
partner hung up after the chief's call, then immediately re-dialed, to
ask for the Records Department. It had been well over two years since Cathy Carruthers had
joined the Metro Central Police Force. And in that time, Mark had
literally witnessed the creation of a living legend: this stunning, six-
foot (with heels) honey-haired blonde, possessing all the sex appeal
of a Playboy centerfold, together with a hidden reservoir of such
sheer animal strength and cunning that she had been dubbed *The
Amazon* by her awe-struck colleagues in Homicide. They had
become a credible team, she and Mark, and a deep bond of mutual
respect and affection had grown between them.

"I know it's Christmas Eve," she was saying into the phone, "and
I know those files are closed, but I want them re-opened, as of now.
And, corporal, I want *you* to hustle them up to my office."

Mark laughed as the lieutenant held the loudly complaining
receiver away from her. "When?" she echoed the instrument from
arm's length. "How about yesterday?" she said as she cradled the
phone without waiting for a reply.

"The leprechaun?" Mark asked.

"Who else?" She smiled wanly. "I guess you can't blame the
little guy. This is a busy time for him."

"Damn!" said Mark suddenly, holding his hand to his eye.

The lieutenant looked at him, puzzled. "What's up with you?"

"Something just flew in my eye," he groaned. "Sonofagun!"

The lieutenant grabbed for a Kleenex and came around the desk
quickly. "Let me have a look," she said with apparent concern. But
in the next instant, Mark had pulled her down on his lap and was
jerking a big thumb over his head to indicate a sprig of mistletoe that
was now mysteriously hanging from the ceiling.

Cathy Carruthers sighed compliantly. "The Kissing Bandit,"
she muttered. "I might have known you'd get to it sooner or later."
She faced him with a crooked smile. "Well — get it over with."

Mark did get it over with. And over with. And over with. And
some memorable moments had elapsed before Corporal Leprohn
burst into the office and found the two detectives still as one, so to

speak.

"Oh my," he stammered. "*Lieutenant.* I mean, *really.*"

Cathy Carruthers, flushed and breathless, struggled to her feet. She regarded the little four-foot interloper with a blend of chagrin and embarrassment. "What's *with* you. Leprohn? You want I should get married before I let someone kiss me under the mistletoe?"

"I'm sorry lieutenant, I didn't mean to imply that — "

But the leprechaun never did get to say what he didn't mean to imply. The lieutenant caught him deftly under the arms and hiked him up to her own eye level, and there, with his little feet dangling three feet above the floor, she planted a kiss firmly on his forehead. Then she dumped him with a spiteful jolt onto Mark's lap. "Your turn," she said.

Mark obliged, then set the little guy on his feet, wretching and scrubbing at his forehead, and blinking like a bloody owl. "You'll regret this, Swanson," he sputtered.

Mark wiped the back of his hand across his mouth. "I already do," he said with an uncharitable grimace.

CORPORAL GARFIELD LEPROHN, OR *THE LEPRECHAUN*, as he was widely known, was quite aware of the fact that he was not a big man. As a matter of fact, at four-foot-zilch (on a clear day, with the atmospheric pressure in his favor) he could scarcely lay claim to being even a big boy. Nevertheless, he *was* head of the Records Department and, as such, he was reluctantly tolerated for what he did, in spite of what he was — or rather, in spite of what he wasn't. And at this precise moment, what the leprechaun wasn't, was happy.

He sat perched on the edge of his chair like a pimple on a pickle. His little feet didn't quite reach the rung of the chair.

"Lieutenant," he said with pained solemnity, "before we address ourselves to these two case files, I must register with you my utter dismay at the display of carnal plebeianism I have been forced to endure this morning. And, before we proceed any further, I would like some assurance from you that it will not occur again."

The lieutenant struggled with a rising bubble of laughter. "Speaking for myself, Garfield, rest assured that I shall hold you

MEL D. AMES

inviolate, henceforth, *ad infinitum*."

The leprechaun turned to Mark. "And you, sir?"

"I don't know," Mark said with mock sincerity. "You're such a cute little bugger, it's going to be hard to resist. But in the magnanimity of Christmas, I'll agree to a moratorium — "

"Thank you."

" — until next Christmas."

The lieutenant held up her hands. "Enough already," she said wearily. She reached across her desk to relieve the little man of the file folders, then sat perusing them in rapt silence for several minutes. When finally she raised her head, she said to the leprechaun, "There's not a thing in these damn files that we don't already know."

"You must realize, lieutenant, that in view of the family name, the Vanderhille *eclat*, as it were, these reports were written with a certain reserve."

"That's putting it mildly. The deaths are certainly suspect, but there is absolutely no suggestion of motive. And no one seems to have even been questioned at any great length, except, perhaps, for the servants."

"What motive could there have been, lieutenant, considering who the victims were? A ten-year-old girl and an aging grandmother — "

"Money?" Mark wondered aloud.

The leprechaun shook his little head. "The Vanderhille fortune is 'old' money, buried deep in family trusts and traditions, secure from outsiders. I tell you, there is simply no motive."

"There is always a motive, gentlemen. Even the absence of a motive, constitutes motive of a kind." The lieutenant flipped a couple of pages. "I see the boy is something of a whiz-kid."

"A prodigy in several fields," the leprechaun volunteered, "especially Physics and the Applied Sciences."

"Mmmm. Interesting. And the boy's grandfather, Franklin A., is an invalid?"

"He was bedridden shortly after the death of the little girl. Some type of cancer. Incurable. He apparently never leaves his room."

"That just leaves Franklin B., and his wife, uh — Candice."

"And the three servants," the leprechaun put in.

"Yes," the lieutenant mused absently, "Vanderhilles, A., B. and

283

C., one wife, and three servants."

"And one ghost," Mark added.

The lieutenant gave him a distant look. "And one ghost," she echoed softly.

MARK PILOTED THE GRAY UNMARKED CHEVY BETWEEN the two monstrous stone lions that guarded the entrance to the Vanderhille estate. The high wrought-iron gates stood open for them, and as he nosed the car up the driveway, it was like entering the Holland tunnel in a new nightmare setting through a maze of towering trees. The cold white winter moon was snuffed from view and did not reappear until they emerged some minutes and a good hundred yards later, into a clearing the size of the Rose Bowl. And there, with turrets and spires reaching into the crystalline, moonlit heavens, the Vanderhille mansion stood like the *Vaux-le-Vicomte* itself, right out of the seventeenth century.

"Mother of God!" Mark exclaimed, "would you look at that?"

Cathy Carruthers sat in awe beside him. She had leaned forward to get a better view as they broke out of the trees. "It's easy to see why Franklin B. needed less than half an hour to get us in on his ghost hunt," she said with a snort of frustration.

Mark glanced at his watch. "Almost eight o'clock," he said, "I sure hope they plan to feed us."

"We *were* invited, you know."

"For supper?"

"Mark, these sort of people refer to the evening meal as dinner, not supper."

"Oh, yeah." Mark nodded thoughtfully. "I'd forgotten. Christ had the last one, didn't he?"

The lieutenant wasn't sure whether to laugh or take a poke at him. Instead of doing either, she said, "Mark, do you have a middle initial?"

"Yup. M, same as the first one."

"What's it stand for, Mephistopheles?"

Mark grinned. "I wish the Devil it did." But the big grin quickly turned to a look of bewilderment as he spotted a black-and-white sitting alone in the small black-topped parking lot immediately ahead.

"Did you order in some uniforms?" he asked the lieutenant.

"Not I."

Mark pulled in beside the police car. Officer Fisk was in the passenger seat. She rolled down the window and turned her head lazily toward him. "'Bout time," she said curtly. Beyond her, Mark could see Mayhew slumped behind the wheel.

"What in hell are you two doing here?" Mark wanted to know.

"The chief ordered us out," Fisk said. "He told us to meet you here at seven." She looked at her watch and sighed heavily. "Can't win 'em all, I guess. Bones and Madson were supposed to be on call tonight, *but* (as the chief gleefully pointed out), they're both married, *and,* we're both single (in name, at least), *and* (according to the chief), it *is* Christmas — " She flashed her big brown eyes at him. "Humbug!"

Mark laughed. "I guess we've got company whether we like it or not," he said to the lieutenant. "Where do you want them? Inside or out?"

"We'll decide that later." The lieutenant leaned over the wheel in front of him. "Have you eaten?" she asked Fisk.

"No, and we're starved," Fisk replied.

"Okay. Come in with us and we'll see if we can get you fed." She was about to withdraw her beautiful head when Mark planted a wet kiss on the side of her mouth. She turned angrily toward him and got the full treatment.

"Damn you, Mark!"

But from the corner of her eye, while thus engaged, she could see him jerking his big thumb above his head to where the same, infamous sprig of mistletoe now hung like a twin conspirator from the headliner of the car.

Fisk giggled. "Mayhew brought his along, too," she said.

THEY MOUNTED THE MILE-WIDE STEPS TO THE ACRE-sized porch, four abreast. Huge granite slabs, worn smooth by generations of Vanderhilles, paved the way. Looming before them were massive Cathedral doors, adorned with the heads of the two lions that had greeted them at the gate, replicated here on ponderous brass rings.

"Oh, wow!" Fisk cried excitedly, "twin knockers!"

To Mark, in an aside against the palm of his hand, Mayhew muttered, "Are there any other kind?"

With a flamboyant gesture, the lieutenant gave the young rookie the honor of heralding their arrival. Fisk pounced gleefully ahead, took a door knocker in each hand, lifted, and swung them at the doors. Sadly, she forgot to let go.

"Knocker to knocker, bust to bust," Mayhew canted solemnly as the lieutenant helped Fisk to her feet. Both women turned with blood in their eyes, but the doors took that precise moment to creak lumberingly inward, and a girl in a maid's uniform appeared on the threshold.

She was a petite platinum blonde with a high bountiful bust that made her look off balance, and ever on the point of tipping forward. Her dress was black and short, and she wore a frilly white cap of sorts, like a little tiara, and a matching white apron the size of a dilettante's doily.

To Mark, the girl said, "We've been ex*th*pecting you, Lieutenant Carruther*th*." She curtsied. "My name ith Mi*th*ty. Will you follow me, plea*the*."

Mark gave his beautiful partner a don't-blame-me look, shrugged, and followed after the girl's long, black-stockinged legs. The lieutenant, Fisk and Mayhew joined the little parade and, single file, like a platoon on patrol, they crossed an immense central hall that would have accommodated the Green Berets on war maneuvers.

Misty ushered them into a room that looked like the lobby at the Waldorf. An enormous stone fireplace blazed cheerfully from one distant corner, and a fir Christmas tree that enjoyed enough latent lumber to reconstruct Noah's Ark, stood proudly and hugely in another. The decorations that emblazoned the tree, Fisk was quick to point out, would have cleaned out Woolworth's entire Christmas stock in downtown Metro. The rest of the room was characteristically sumptuous in creature comforts.

"The ma*th*ter will be with you pre*the*ntly," Misty lisped from the doorway. Mayhew, the last to enter, paused there a moment to admire the girl's oscillating rear-end as she flounced away.

"Watch it, Mayhew," Fisk cautioned him. She wet a finger on her tongue and made an imaginary mark in mid-air. "That's twice.

One more slide from grace, and you get the 'Cold Shoulder' award."

Before Mayhew could protest that in fact, all he had been doing *was* watching it, the door he had just closed, swung inward, and Franklin B. Vanderhille entered the room with a stately, silver-headed woman on his arm. The woman held herself uncompromisingly erect, with a stiff dignity that made her look as though she had inadvertently donned her gown without first removing the coathanger.

"Ah, good evening, lieutenant." Franklin B. extended his hand. "I'm so pleased you decided to come after all." The lieutenant acknowledged his little dig with a tight smile. "I'd like you to meet my wife, lieutenant. Candice, this is Lieutenant Cathy Carruthers, the famous detective."

Mrs. Vanderhille looked down her long nose like Morris the cat the night he didn't get his 9-Lives. "A lady detective," she observed tonelessly, "how droll."

The lieutenant's intolerant sigh was both obvious and audible. "This," she said to no one in particular, "is my partner, Sergeant Swanson."

Mark nodded.

"I'm glad to see you've brought reinforcements with you, lieutenant."

"Courtesy of Chief Heller," she informed the man dryly.

"Good." He looked over her mini-entourage with critical approval. "We'll need all the help we can get before the night's over, mark my words."

Misty suddenly appeared in the open doorway. "Dinner *ith* *th*erved, *th*ir, madam."

"Thank you, Misty." Vanderhille turned to lieutenant. "I trust you will be dining with us."

"Thank you, yes. And the officers?"

"Misty will show them to the kitchen, lieutenant. They will dine well, believe me."

"*Thith* way, plea*the*."

When only Fisk and Mayhew followed the sprightly maid out the door, Mrs. Vanderhille pointed her long snotty snoot in Mark's direction. "Oh!" she said with pained hauteur, "will the sergeant be dining with *us*, then?"

AMAZON

"If he doesn't," Cathy Carruthers told the woman bluntly, "you'd better have the cook set another place in the kitchen — for me."

THE TABLE, IT SEEMED TO MARK, WAS THE LENGTH of a football field. Franklin B. sat at one end, Candice Vanderhille at the other, and Mark and the lieutenant sat opposite each other, center field. The starting whistle hadn't blown when a boy entered the room. He was a gaunt little fellow, distressingly thin, with deep-set, hollow eyes and pallid cheeks. He ignored the place that had been hurriedly set for him, next to Mark, and promptly commandeered a chair beside the lieutenant.

"I'm Franklin C.," he said by way of introduction, "You are Cathy Carruthers, of course. I'm a great admirer of yours, lieutenant."

"Oh? Have you added criminology, then, to your many other talents?"

"No. Not really." He committed her to an overtly frank appraisal. "I have only recently entered puberty, you see, and I've made the rather delightful discovery that beautiful blondes really turn me on."

"*Franklin C.!*" Mrs. Vanderhille now aimed her intimidating proboscis at her son. "What a *dreadful* thing to say."

The boy eyed his mother dispassionately. "What could *you* possibly know about it, mother?" Then to a flushed and thoroughly discomfitted Cathy Carruthers, he whispered, "Misty takes it as a compliment." He winked connivingly.

"*Really*, Franklin," Mrs. Vanderhille was livid. "That will be quite enough."

The lieutenant shot a helpless glance at Mark who was having troubles of his own retaining his composure. And Misty took that moment to enter from the kitchen. She was followed by a full-bodied girl with long chestnut hair and a sweet and gentle face. Misty proceeded to uncork a bottle of wine, while her companion, in a somewhat less abbreviated uniform than Misty's, began to serve.

"That's Brenda," Franklin C. confided to the lieutenant in a throaty whisper. "She's the cook. She's not quite the looker Misty

288

is, but she's uh — just as friendly." He winked again. "I honestly don't know *what* I'd do," he confessed with a weary sigh, "if it wasn't for the help."

Cathy Carruthers decided it was time to divert the young Lothario from his recently acquired obsession, temporarily at any rate, and into matters more relevant to the purpose of their being there. "Tell me," she said to the boy, "what are your thoughts on this ghost business?"

At the mention of the word "ghost," Misty upset a glass of wine over Mark's beef Wellington, and Brenda splashed soup on Mrs. Vanderhille's evening gown. The woman was surprisingly calm about it. "Do be more careful, child," she said to an obviously distraught Brenda, and to Misty, she added, "Set the sergeant a clean place, girl, and for pity's sake, do watch what you're up to."

"The ghost," Franklin C. said gravely, in a suddenly serious manner, "is something we do not talk about, lieutenant, and try not to think about."

"But talk and think about it we must," Franklin B. interjected, "at least, tonight. But first, lieutenant, I would like to take this opportunity to apologize for the manner in which I was forced to bring you here. You must understand, however, our desperate plight. We attempt to carry on, you see, to live a normal life, to pretend that what has happened twice before will not happen again. Our staff (and they are loyal souls) as well as ourselves, approach this festive night with fear and trepidation. We are in mortal dread, lieutenant, of a ghostly presence that will shortly walk this earth, on this holy night, for no other purpose than to consign yet another Vanderhille to the grave."

"This ghost," the lieutenant asked, "does it ever manifest itself at any other time?"

"It is the Vanderhille ghost, lieutenant, the ghost of Christmas Eve. It comes but once a year."

"What will you do," the lieutenant queried, "when the hour of midnight approaches?"

"That, Miss Carruthers, is for *you* to decide. It is for that very reason that I brought you here. It is no secret that you possess uncanny insight, that you have an acumen of perceptive and deducive thought far beyond the cognizance of most mortals. We, on the other hand, are as babes in the woods, my dear, *toys*, if you like, playthings of the Devil himself. And I, a Vanderhille, will be in greater peril than my lowliest servant. It is a humbling thing, believe me." He drew a tremulous breath. "Tonight, Cathy Carruthers, we are placing ourselves in your hands. May God go with you."

The silence that followed was electric. The man's portentous words echoed over the table long after he had ceased to speak.

"I shall want to see your father," the lieutenant said, "Franklin A. And your other servant, the footman."

"Yes, of course. And so you shall."

"Are there any others?"

"Only the ghost," Franklin B. replied, almost in a whisper. *"Only the ghost."*

"TALK ABOUT YOUR STAIRWAY TO HEAVEN," MARK observed with appropriate awe. The two detectives were ascending the stairs with their host to the second floor landing, where the room occupied by the bed-ridden Franklin A. was located. "Do you realize that if this staircase could keep on going," Mark fantasized, "down, as well as up, it would probably be wide enough to handle the total daily traffic to the Great Hereafter, from the whole of the U.S. of A."

Vanderhille laughed at the rather bizarre analogy. "But do you really think the traffic would be all that great, sergeant?" he mused. "Going up, I mean."

"You do have a point there," Mark conceded.

"And speaking of Hereafters," Vanderhille added ominously, "that is precisely where I hope to be, come Christmas day."

The lieutenant regarded the man with undisguised amazement. "You hope to be — *dead?*"

"No, lieutenant," he said with a smile, "just *here, after.*"

At the door to the room, Vanderhille hesitated. "The man is quite ill," he cautioned. "And he does babble a bit. I trust you will allow — "

The lieutenant waved him on. "I understand," she said gently.

It was a large room, heavily draped in somber colors. The only light emanated from a pale yellow lamp that sat on the bedside table, bathing the walls and the high ceiling in a sickly, anemic hue. Shadows lurked in every corner.

"Good evening, father."

The old man on the bed turned a tired, drawn face toward them.

"Oh, it's you, Franklin. I thought it might have been that — that hellish spectre again." His voice was a faltering, fragile wheeze. "It's time, you know."

Behind the pallid-looking lamp there was a real-life Christmas tree, about two feet in height, propped up in a small pan of water. It was decorated with a half dozen electric lights that were not illuminated, and the usual garish sweeps of tinsel and hanging ornaments.

"I see that Franklin C. has been in to try to cheer you up," Franklin B. noted with a smile.

"Eh?"

"The miniature tree, father. It's a lovely touch."

"Yes, yes. He's a good boy, that one." He coughed weakly, deep in his throat. "The damned tree's a blessed nuisance, just the same. Felt I should humor him, though. But no lights, I told him. Put my foot down there. Just can't tolerate those confounded lights — "

He broke off into another fit of feeble coughing.

"Rest easy, father. Don't excite yourself. I just came up to introduce you to our guests."

"Guests?" The old man squinted into the obscure shadows behind his son. "Guests, you say? *Tonight?*"

"These are no ordinary guests, father. This is Lieutenant Cathy Carruthers, the celebrated detective, and her assistant, Sergeant Swanson."

"They are going to try to exorcise that accursed spirit?"

"Something like that."

The old man's laugh was a mirthless, gutteral rattling deep in his chest. "You are grasping at straws, my son. You must accept the reality of what is happening, what has now become inevitable. The ghost will come again, tonight, you mark my words." His voice fell to a rasping, portentious whisper. "You, as I, am a Vanderhille. There is no escape."

At that moment, a sudden wintery chill seemed to invade the room, and a ghostly, ethereal mist began to materialize in the gloom beyond the reach of the lamp.

"Do you see what I see?" Mark stood frozen in wide-eyed

disbelief beside the lieutenant.

"Yes, Mark. But what is it?"

"It's the ghost, you poor fools," the old man croaked from his bed. "I can feel its bloodless presence."

Franklin B. had stumbled back toward the door, his face contorted with fear. "Get a cross," he choked. "*Someone get a cross!*"

The sinister mist seemed now to hover and vacillate, as though attempting to take on some kind of shape, then, slowly, it began to sink into the deeper shadows along the floor. Cathy Carruthers suddenly darted toward it, sweeping into it with outflung hands. Mark could see the mist swirl in around her, engulfing her, and he moved quickly. In three giant strides he was at her side, but then, suddenly, strangely, the ghostly presence, or whatever it was, had gone.

"My God, lieutenant!" Mark breathed incredulously, "what unholy horror are we dealing with here?"

The lieutenant chose not to respond. She walked back to the bed. "Do you want someone in here tonight?" she asked the old man, "someone to be with you?"

"No, it would serve no purpose."

"Very well, but if I am going to see this thing through, I must ask that you cooperate to some degree, at least." She turned to Mark. "Check the windows behind those drapes and make sure that they are securely bolted, and otherwise impregnable." To Franklin B., she said, "is there any other access to this room, other than by the windows and this one door?"

"No lieutenant. None whatever."

"Good. I intend to have the room thoroughly checked and searched, then a double guard will be posted outside the door for the entire night. I would like your assistance, Mr. Vanderhille, in seeing that your father submits to these precautions."

"Yes, of course. But how do you hope to protect *them*, lieutenant?"

"Them?"

"The guards," he said with eerie apprehension.

THE FOOTMAN'S NAME WAS ATHOLLE BROWN. HE WAS a short, pasty man, with a dumpy, ill-attired body that looked, even in uniform, to be all ass and pockets. The lieutenant and Mark caught up with him in the scullery, a steamy little hell-hole of dirty pots and pans, off the kitchen.

"Are you Atholle Brown?"

The man looked up, startled. He had been lost to dreamy contemplation of the southern-most parts of a wiggly Misty and a jiggly Brenda, whose northern-most parts happened to be fortuitously poised over the scullery sink.

"I *th*ertainly hope *th*o," Misty retorted with some emphasis, before Brown had a chance to respond. "I'd hate to think there wa*th* more than one of *him* around."

"Ditto!" Brenda concurred with equal feeling.

Brown unfolded a smile that looked like a cob of corn after the birds had been at it. "Heh, heh," he chirped lamely, "couple of great kidders, these two." He levered himself up off a kitchen stool and turned to face the lieutenant.

"You got it right, lady. That's my name."

The lieutenant ignored the man's insolent manner. She consulted her watch. "I want all three of you people in the main lounge in, uh — twenty-seven minutes. That will be precisely ten o'clock. It that clear?"

Both girls turned from the sink long enough to execute a quick curtsy. "Yes, mam," they said in unison.

"Brown?"

"Yeah, yeah — whatever you say, sweetheart."

Mark made a move at the lieutenant's side but she restrained him with a slight pressure on his arm. She had turned to leave then, and was already half way out the door, when Misty's sudden squeal of surprise and indignation made her spin around.

"You do that on*the* more," Misty seethed as she approached the grinning footman, "and I'll cut you where it hur*th* mo*th*t." She brandished a large kitchen knife from one soapy hand.

"What did he do?" the lieutenant asked.

"He goo*th*ed me!" she wailed with righteous wrath.

"Just giving the girls a little treat, lady." Brown twisted his ugly mouth into what was supposed to be a smile. "Nothing to concern you," he added.

"A *treat?*" Misty advanced threateningly, the knife at the ready. "Why you — you — you *Atholle!*"

The man's eyes flared with anger. He grabbed the knife out of the girl's hand and shoved her roughly back against the sink. "Nobody makes fun of my name," he snarled. But the words were scarcely out of his mouth when he felt the hand of the Amazon slip around his wrist and close over it like a velvet handcuff. She exerted a slow, vise-like pressure until the pallor of his face matched the sudden whitening of her knuckles. The knife clattered to the floor.

"I think I've heard about as much from you, Mr. Atholle Brown, as I care to hear." An unsmiling Amazon picked the man up by his pudgy neck with one hand, and perched him on the stool he had just vacated. It put them on more of an eye-to-eye level. "And I'm inclined to agree with Misty," she told him evenly, "that you are, indeed, sir, truly an Atholle."

"Damn you, stop *saying* that!" Tears of frustration had brimmed up in the man's eyes. He struggled violently to free himself, but when he found that impossible, he began to kick out blindly in all directions. A big black boot caught the Amazon squarely in the abdomen, and she jerked forward with a little grunt of pain and surprise.

Atholle Brown realized immediately that he had committed a foolish act. He looked, at that moment, like he would have given anything to relive the last few seconds of his life. But that was not to be. And he simply closed his eyes in a desperate attempt to shut out the visual horror, if not the pain, of the inevitable retribution he knew would shortly be wrought upon him.

In total darkness (as far as Atholle Brown was concerned), he felt himself being levitated across the scullery and, to the sounds of girlish giggles, immersed baptismally, butt first, up to his fifth lumbar vertebrae, into a sink full of pots, pans, and the random residue of Brenda's Beef Wellington.

Atholle Brown suffered in steamy and silent martyrdom until he felt it was safe to open his eyes. When he did, he found himself to be alone. "*That*," he muttered bitterly to the flotsam and jetsam that bobbed about him in the greasy water, "has got to be one Hell of a price to pay for a Christmas goose."

OFFICERS FISK AND MAYHEW WERE COMPELLED TO make the search of Franklin A.'s sick room with the use of flashlights. The only light fixtures that worked were the yellow lamp beside the bed, and the lights on the miniature Christmas tree. All the other bulbs had either burnt out or been purposely screwed out. When Mayhew inadvertently switched on the tree lights, he was subjected to a barrage of verbal abuse from the vicinity of the bed that would have shamed a drunken sailor into signing up for lessons."

But is was the windows that concerned the officers most. They both were fitted with conventional crescent hasps, which did appear to be more than adequate, but on the lieutenant's instructions, a steel wedge was tamped into each window between the sash and the jamb. The heating vents were small and grilled, and obviously no threat to anyone. There was nothing (and certainly no *one*) behind the heavy drapes or in the room's one and only closet. Fisk even checked under the bed.

"Trust you to look under there," Mayhew quipped, "isn't that the old maid's hope chest?"

"That does it, Mayhew." Fisk posted the latest score with a damp finger. "Want to try now for the See-You-Around trophy?"

But it was no more than twenty minutes later (the old grandfather clock had just chimed 10:45) and Fisk and Mayhew were at their post on the second floor landing outside Franklin A.'s door, when Fisk decided quite suddenly (without thought to what it might do to the already struggling Civil Rights movement, or the E.R.A.) to surrender her cold feminine shoulder to the warmth and security of Mayhew's masculine chest.

Mayhew, quite frankly, was glad of the company. For at that moment, some one, or some *thing*, had just dimmed the lights in the main central hall below, and the two officers had groped their way to the head of the stairs to investigate. They saw no one, nothing. Nothing, that is, but the long, empty staircase winding down into the abysmal, cavernous depths of the hall. *Then*, in that eerie, hollow gloom, came the unmistakable sound of footsteps, *thup, thup, thup,* slowly, but inevitably, ascending the wide carpeted staircase toward them. They gaped into the vacant shadows in horror, as apperception slowly dawned. The sound of the approaching footsteps was irrefutably real; but *who*ever, or *what*ever, was coming toward them, was *not*.

Fisk quickly sought the shelter of Mayhew's arms, and together, with their eyes riveted on the empty stairs, they backed up to the door they had been assigned to guard. At this point, at least, it was still locked and secure.

"Who — who's there?" Mayhew called out in a shaky voice.

The footsteps halted immediately, poised, as it were, on the third from top stair. There was a kind of shuffling, as though the ghost was momentarily undecided on what to do next; then, with the same grim stealth they had come toward them, the footsteps began to recede. Slowly, they descended the stairs.

"Wheeeew!" Fisk breathed a long, tremulous sigh of relief. When the sound of the last *thup* had died away, she turned in Mayhew's arms and hung onto him. "I've never been so scared in my life," she said in a choked whisper. "Do you think that was the ghost?"

"It sure as hell wasn't Santa Claus," Mayhew told her with a shudder. "Maybe I ought to go and tell the lieutenant about it."

"And leave me here alone?"

"*You* go, then."

"By myself?"

"We can't *both* go," Mayhew said with exasperation. "This door can't be left unguarded."

"Why don't we, uh — try calling her?"

"Are you nuts — ?"

They were spared any further anguish by a rapid rhythmic thumping that sounded to Fisk like the welcome approach of the cavalry. She half expected to hear the blare of a trumpet, but even without it, she managed to squirt out of Mayhew's arms and into a dignified posture, as a true and stalwart guardian of the law, before the lieutenant and Mark Swanson appeared at the top of the stairs.

"Did you two hear anything up here?" the lieutenant asked them breathlessly.

"Yes," Fisk said quickly, with sudden bravado. "It was the ghost, lieutenant. It came up to the top of the stairs and just stood there, watching us."

"You could *see* it?"

"No, but — it was there."

The lieutenant sighed circuitously. "What happened then?"

"We chased it back down," Fisk replied with a furtive look at Mayhew.

"You chased it back down," the lieutenant said dryly. "Just like that."

"Uh-huh."

Cathy Carruthers reached out an immaculately manicured finger and drew it across a lipstick smear on Mayhew's shirt front. "What do you make of this, Officer Fisk?"

"I, uh — I must have, uh — brushed up against him — in the dark," Fisk stammered through a flush of color. Then, "Damn it, Mayhew!" she added hotly, "why can't you look where you're going?"

Mayhew, Mark and Cathy Carruthers all looked at each other, and grinned.

"*She Oughta Be in Pictures*," Mark crooned softly.

AFTER CHECKING THE SICK ROOM TO SEE THAT Franklin A. was still in fine fettle (relatively speaking), the lieutenant and Mark left the two officers at their post outside the door, and returned to the main lounge. As they were entering the room, they encountered young Franklin C. in the doorway.

"Where have you been?" the lieutenant asked.

"I've been diddling in the dark," the boy replied. "Who snuffed the damn lights?"

"You went to the bathroom?"

"I thought I just said that."

The lieutenant regarded the boy closely. "I think I'd like to see your room, Franklin C., where you pursue all your many interests."

"Great," the young Vanderhille responded. "As a matter of fact, I'm rather involved right now in a somewhat, uh — burgeoning phenomenon."

"Oh? And what might that be?"

The boy grinned. "Girls," he said.

The lieutenant took a deep breath and let it out slowly. "I had to ask," she told Mark in a weary aside. Then, for all to hear, "Make sure everyone stays together in the lounge while we're gone," she said, "and, Mark, take a head count every now and then. I don't want *anyone* wandering around this old house alone."

"You got it, lieutenant."

Mark stood in the doorway and watched his beautiful partner head up the stairs with the boy, past a somewhat humbled Fisk and Mayhew on the second floor landing, and on up and out of sight to the third story. He turned into the room then, to count heads.

Franklin B. and his wife, Candice, were enjoying a bottle of imported cognac by the fire; Misty, Brenda and a sullen Atholle Brown formed a loose grouping around the tree. Mark walked over to the three servants.

"Everyone comfortable?"

"Comfortable," Brenda acknowledged in her gentle way, "but tired, sergeant, and a little anxious."

"That's understandable, under the circumstances," Mark said consolingly, "but it can't last much longer."

"And it won't," Atholle Brown chortled darkly, "at least for one of the Vanderhilles."

"Still feeling a bit surly, Brown?"

"If he wa*th*n't complaining to you, *th*ergeant," Misty put in, "he'd be at the telephone company again for li*th*ting hi*th* full name in the directory, in*th*tead of ju*th*t the initial."

"That's a problem?"

"It i*th* when your name i*th* Atholle Brown, *th*ergeant, and it'*th* *th*pelled out in rever*th*e."

Mark laughed in spite of the evil eye he got from the dumpy footman. The man had changed clothes but he did not look any more presentable. "If your name is a source of such embarrassment to you," Mark told him, "why don't you change it?"

"Hey, that'*th* great!" Misty clapped her hands enthusiastically. "Then he could choo*th*e *th*omething to match that na*th*ty *th*treak up hi*th* back, like, uh — Atholle Yellow."

Mark was about to point out that wasn't quite what he had in mind, when Brenda jumped into the fray, " — or the color of his cold, cold heart," she giggled, "like, Atholle Black."

The two girls seemed determined then, to wade gleefully, color by color, through the entire chromatic spectrum. Mark left them finally at the color Pink, to join the Vanderhilles.

THERE WAS A GRIM LOOK OF *DEJA VU* TO THE TWO second generation Vanderhilles, albeit, one by marriage. Mark approached them with compassion. He wondered how *he* would feel, given the one-to-four odds they had of surviving the next sixty minutes. The threat of the Christmas Eve ghost had taken on a new and eerie credibility since their arrival three hours ago, and there was little doubt in Mark's mind that something sinister was, indeed, afoot in the old house. *Something*, he sensed, *that was diabolically and obscenely evil.*

"One hour to go, sergeant," Franklin B. said with dark foreboding, as the chimes of the grandfather clock began to echo ominously through the rambling old structure. "Whatever is going to happen, will, now, in this final hour." He glanced toward his wife who appeared to be well into her cups. "Are you bearing up, my dear?"

The woman turned slowly, training her great rhinarium conk on the two men. She peered down its imposing length for several tense moments, as though aiming a loaded bazooka, zeroing in. "*Que sera sera*," she said with a note of tearful inevitability, "what will be will be." She then proceeded to quietly sob, in a most refined, subdued, and thoroughly proper manner, as befitting a Vanderhille.

ON THE THIRD FLOOR, WHICH WAS ALMOST ENTIRELY given over to Franklin C. to do with as he chose, the lieutenant marveled at the hoard of paraphernalia the boy had accumulated. Test tubes, beakers and burners; electronic gadgetry of every description; computer systems, feed-ins and read-outs; and wall upon wall of books that appeared to cover every conceivable advance in modern technology.

"This is very impressive," the lieutenant told the boy, "but where do you sleep?"

Franklin C. opened the door to a small room (at least, by comparison) that contained the usual trappings of a bed chamber.

The room was clean and neat, the bed made, and the porcelain in the ensuite bathroom virtually gleaming.

"You're a very tidy person," the lieutenant noted absently.

"Not really," the boy replied. "The girls keep it clean for me."

"*Both* of them? I understood that Brenda did the cooking."

"She does, but they like to help each other with their separate duties. Besides," and he gave the lieutenant a secret smile, "I find them both to be a willing and authentic source of, uh — material, with which to research my current project — "

"Spare me the sordid details," the lieutenant told him curtly. "You are, you know, quite abominable." She hustled him toward the door. "It's time, I think, that we rejoined the others."

As they went over the threshold, and headed for the stairs, Franklin C. said, somewhat magnanimously, "Really, lieutenant, it wouldn't be very sporting of me to play favorites, now would it?"

AT PRECISELY 11:20 WHEN EVERYONE, EXCEPT THE bedridden Franklin A., Fisk and Mayhew, was assembled in the lounge, Misty informed the lieutenant that it was customary at this hour for her to administer medication to the ailing Vanderhille.

"And what," the lieutenant inquired, "is the nature of this 'medication?'"

"I don't know, lieutenant. Either the *thir* or the madam give*th* me the tray to take up to him."

"That is correct, lieutenant." Franklin B. came forward then. "It is simply a pain killer, you see, and a sedative, prescribed by Dr. Quarrels. Quarrels has been our physician for over thirty years. I keep the medication locked in a cabinet in my study."

"This is a usual, nightly procedure then?

"Quite."

"But why, might I ask, do you or Mrs. Vanderhille not administer the medication yourselves?"

Franklin B. sighed heavily. "My father can be somewhat cantankerous, lieutenant, as you have seen, and particularly with myself and my wife. On the other hand, he does like the girls. And they never fail to get him to — to acquiesce without a fuss."

The lieutenant dislodged a fall of golden hair from her forehead with a toss of her beautiful head. "Very well," she said. "Mark will go with you to the study, and from there, he'll accompany Misty, along with the medication, to the sick room."

"As you wish."

The lieutenant remained in the doorway where she could watch Franklin B., Mark and Misty traverse the wide hall to the study, and where, at the same time, she could still keep an eye on the others in the lounge, Candice Vanderhille, Franklin C., Brenda and Atholle Brown. She could even follow Mark and Misty up the stairs, until they disappeared from view on the second floor landing. The entire mission consumed no more than fifteen minutes, with Franklin B. returning first, Mark and Misty shortly after.

"Everything copacetic?" the lieutenant asked Mark on his return.

"Sure." Mark smiled thinly. "The old man is alive, if not too well. And, as you suggested, I told Fisk and Mayhew to stay in sight at the top of the stairs. From there, they can effectively monitor the door to the sick room (which, by the way, I checked out, and left locked), and they can keep us in view at the same time."

"Great." She turned to the six people who were now assembled in the lounge. "I want you all in one group by the fire," she told them. "There are only some twenty-three minutes remaining until the crucial hour of midnight, and until that clock has struck twelve times, I want no one to move from where I can see them. Do I make myself clear?"

They all nodded numbly as they gathered together in a loose group by the fire. Franklin B. and his wife sat aloofly to one side, the two girls flanked their *enfant gate*, Franklin C., on the chesterfield, and Atholle Brown sat glumly alone.

"There is a visual link now," the lieutenant said quietly to Mark, "between all eleven people in the house. All, that is, except Franklin A. And he is secure in a room that is barred and locked, and guarded by two police officers. If that so-called ghost approaches anyone in this house from now until midnight, I intend to know about it."

"What if it goes after the old man?" Mark asked clearly puzzled. "He's all alone up there."

"Fisk and Mayhew will see anyone who tries to enter that room Mark. There is no other access."

"Lieutenant." Mark turned to whisper so that only she could hear. "We're not talking about a flesh-and-blood killer," he said with some frustration, "we're talking about a *ghost.*"

"Yes," the lieutenant said with maddening ambiguity, "and a very enterprising ghost, at that."

"Meaning?"

"Think about it, Mark. The Christmas Eve ghost writes poetry, types threats, has the icy chill of the grave, walks the stairs like an unseen phantom, haunts us as an ethereal apparition, then disappears without a trace — "

"It's damned demonic," Mark breathed. "What will the bloody thing do next?"

"I suspect," the lieutenant said quietly, "*it will attempt to carry out its morbid threat.*"

THE MINUTES DRAGGED ON. THERE WAS A MOUNTING tension in the assembled group that even the brilliant tree or the blazing warmth of the fire could not dispel. What little conversation there had been between them had dissolved into guarded, silent glances of apprehension and fear. The lieutenant and Mark stood apart, near the open door to the hall, each with one eye on Fisk and Mayhew at the top of the stairs, the other on the group by the fire.

"This waiting is murder," Mark muttered to the lieutenant. He looked at his watch. "Fifteen minutes to go."

As he spoke, the clock chimed the quarter hour, and the boy, Franklin C., got casually to his feet. He sauntered slowly over to where the lieutenant and Mark were standing at the door.

"I asked you, Franklin," the lieutenant told him curtly, "to stay with the group."

"Just wanted to stretch my legs," the boy replied. "Besides, what you *said* was not to leave your sight, or words to that effect."

"Whatever." The lieutenant's impatience was evident in her voice. "Now, do as I have requested."

"You're the boss, beautiful." The boy turned, as though to rejoin the group, but he sidled lightly past the two detectives and stepped over the threshold into the hall. He just stood there then, looking up the stairs, smiling, one finger pressed thoughtfully to his lips, the other hand buried in the right pocket of his jacket. "You appear to have things well in hand, lieutenant," he said disarmingly.

The lieutenant suddenly jerked erect with a quick, Amazonian toss of her long golden mane. Her eyes flashed like blue lightning. And she moved with the speed of sound, sweeping the boy up off his feet with one encircling arm, and jerking his right hand free of the pocket. A small plastic box, about three inches by two, by an inch and a half thick, fell from his fingers.

"Mark, hang onto this little monster."

The Amazon put words into action, and Franklin C. went hurtling through the air into Mark's massive arms. She then swung on her heel, hiking up her snug gray skirt as she turned, and she streaked for the stairs. She took them three at a time, a magnificent leggy blur, sky-rocketing upward, her fluorescent yellow hair strung out behind like Haley's Comet. Fisk and Mayhew staggered back as she flew past them, then stood in stunned immobility as she leapt clear of the landing and leveled her fantastic body, feet first, at the door to Franklin A.'s room.

She seemed to just hang there for a moment, as though in suspended levitation, a beautiful battering ram of exquisite proportions, caught and held in mid-flight by the flash of a camera. Then came the violent, wood-rendering *Crash!*, as the door buckled and splintered in all directions — and there, in the midst of mayhem, the Amazon flipped lightly to her feet with the willowy effortlessness of a falling feline.

She hesitated for only an instant, turned, sucked in a lung full of air, and disappeared into the room. Seconds later, she re-emerged, flushed and disheveled, with a struggling, gasping (but very much alive) Franklin A. Vanderhille wrapped in her arms.

"Do *not* go near that room," she cautioned a slackjawed Fisk and a wide-eyed, ogling Mayhew. "And, Fisk," she said with a disparaging look at Mayhew, "pull down my skirt for me, will you please? My arms are full, and I wouldn't want Mayhew's eyes to end up on the carpet."

THE CLOCK STRUCK ONE. IT WAS CHRISTMAS DAY.

Franklin A. was now comfortably ensconced on the chesterfield in front of the fire. All eyes in the room were on him as he complained vociferously to a sleepy-eyed Dr. Quarrels. The good doctor had been summoned from a warm bed (and a warm body) to attend to his elderly patient, and he was now waiting *im*patiently for a well-placed shot in the butt to take effect and "shut the old bugger up," as he so aptly put it.

Franklin B., meanwhile, and his supercilious spouse were off to one side, as was their custom, quietly polishing off the remainder of the brandy, with somewhat mixed emotions. Tears, brought on first by fear, then by shock and contrition, along with the pervasive warmth of the brandy, had reddened the woman's flaming great honker to where it had begun to look like part of the Christmas decor.

Franklin C. had already departed, under escort to Fisk and Mayhew. He had been handcuffed to the comely, brown-eyed policewoman, and, as they went out the door (undaunted to the very end), the lascivious little lech was making a last minute pass at his flushed and embarrassed captor.

The servants were huddled by the tree, Atholle Brown on one side by himself (as was his fate), the two girls whispering secretly between themselves, too excited by the turn of events to think yet of retiring. "Imagine," Misty was saying, "that na*th*ty little Frankie, *th*caring the pant*th* off u*th* like that."

Brenda gave her friend an indignant little nudge. "I wish you wouldn't put it quite that way," she tittered.

"Anyway," Misty sulked, "thi*th* pla*the* i*th* the pit*th*. The entertainment i*th* ju*tht* too young or too old."

"You mean *was*," Brenda sighed, "now it's just *too damn old.*"

The lieutenant and Mark, who had innocently overheard the conversation, grinned at one another as they tactfully moved out of earshot. "Let's take a look at that room now, Mark."

"The sick room?"

"Yes, the air should be clear by this time."

As they climbed the wide staircase, Mark asked, "What suddenly twigged you to the idea that young Franklin C. was up to no good, lieutenant?"

The lieutenant treated him to one of her special smiles. "I could say it was woman's intuition," she said coyly, "and I guess, in a sense, it was. But, still, there had to be some logical explanation for all the weird things that were happening — "

"You don't believe in ghosts?"

"That's not the issue, Mark. If, in fact, it was the work of a ghost, then *whatever* we did would have been totally futile. I simply *had* to proceed on the premise that some*one*, or some*thing*, was the root cause of the mischief. And that, of course, made Franklin C. the most logical suspect."

"Why him? He's only a kid."

"But a bright kid, Mark, with all the expertise. It's been said, you know, that there is a fine line between genius and madness. I was becoming more and more convinced that our young prodigy had already made that awesome transition."

"But, my god, lieutenant, to murder his little twin sister, then his grandmother — and to make a bloody game of it? What motive could he have possibly had?"

"There is no motive in madness, Mark, but madness itself. As you mentioned a moment ago, the boy was simply playing a game."

THEY HAD REACHED THE BROKEN DOORWAY AND the lieutenant entered the room with caution, sniffing audibly as she crossed the threshold. She went directly to an overhead light fixture that hung from the center of the ceiling. It had a large, Tiffany-style shade. With the assistance of a chair, she retrieved a small plastic box that had been secreted in the flanged top of the Tiffany. It was somewhat larger than the box that had fallen from Franklin C.'s hand, when the lieutenant had jumped him in the hall.

"How did know that was up there?"

"I didn't. It just seemed obvious." She held the small box in her hand and pried open the lid with a metal nail file. A swirl of milky ether curled over the lip of the box and began to sink in writhing, ghostly fashion toward the floor.

"There's your ghost," she said, "dry ice. The gas it gives off is heavier than air and will slowly sink to the floor. It will take several seconds to dissipate. And a closer examination of this box, Mark, will show that the lid can be operated electronically, by remote control. Needless to say, it was triggered for a few seconds while we were in here before — hence the illusion."

"I'll be damned."

The lieutenant moved over to the bed, poking at the bed covers, the pillows, the mattress.

"What are you looking for now?"

"I don't know, but I will when I find it."

Mark sighed heavily. "Well, while you're looking, how about filling me in on how that typewriter was being operated without anyone being in the room?"

"But it wasn't, of course. I've been doing some snooping in the past hour, Mark, and the sound of that typewriter had simply been recorded earlier, then played back from a tape hidden in the room. More electronics. Actually, it was behind the grill-work of the heat register. It was the boy, you will recall, who drew his father's attention to the sound to begin with, then, feigning fear, he prevented him from entering until the tape had shut itself off. The boy was no poet, though. That poem was pretty childish."

"What about the icy chill in the room?"

"Dry ice again, hidden in the heat vent with the tapedeck. We felt something of a chill, too, up here. Remember?"

"Do I ever."

The lieutenant had wandered from the bed to the yellow bedside lamp and the miniature Christmas tree.

"Okay," Mark said after some reflection, "what about those footsteps, going up and down the stairs, scaring Fisk and Mayhew witless? That couldn't have been a recording. We heard it, too. All the way downstairs, from where we were standing at the door to the lounge."

"Underneath those stairs, Mark, is an open storage and utility area, fuse panels, etc., and an unfinished washroom for the express use of the servants. Franklin C. was in that washroom at the time the footsteps were heard. He was also the only one to wander away from the group. The way I see it, he simply dimmed the lights at the fuse panel, then with the aid of an ordinary house mop, he created the illusion of footsteps from the *under*-side of the carpeted stairs. As a matter of fact, we met the little ghoul as he was returning to the lounge."

"Yeah. We did, didn't we?"

"*Ouch!*"

The lieutenant gave a sudden cry of pain and stuck one red-tipped finger into her mouth. "That's rather strange," she said.

"What's strange?"

"All the lights on this tree, Mark, are of the cool burning variety, except this one." She pointed to a blue bulb at the base and the back of the tree. "And look at *this*." There was a blob of waxy substance still clinging to the bulb. "Ah," she said softly, "I see now how he did it."

"How who did what?"

"How Franklin C. had planned to kill his grandfather." She sniffed at the liquid in the container in which the tree was standing. "Yes, there's still a faint odor of bitter almonds," she said as though to herself. "That's prussic acid, all right. And I strongly suspect that a small tablet of cyanide-salt crystals was stuck to the back of this bulb, with wax, or gelatin — whatever."

"I don't get it."

"After Franklin A. had been sedated, Mark, his loving grandson must have triggered the switch (electronically) to turn on these lights. The heat from the hot bulb would then have melted the wax, and the lethal tablet had simply dropped into the prussic acid. *Voila!*— *cyanide gas!* Can you believe it?"

"A bloody execution," Mark muttered. "But why would he draw attention to himself, lieutenant, by going out into the hall like that? That's what tipped you off, wasn't it?"

"Yes. And my guess is, that his remote only had a limited range. He had to be in the hall in order to make it work. There's no doubt about it, Mark. That kid was truly ingenius."

"Yeah, I guess." Mark gave it some thought for a moment or two. "But he was too damn smart for his own good, lieutenant. If he'd stuck to holding pillows over little girl's heads, and shoving old ladies down flights of stairs, he might even have gotten away with it. Sometimes," Mark added sagely, "it doesn't pay to get too cute."

"Oh yeah?" Cathy Carruthers smiled slyly. "I happen to think *you're* pretty cute yourself."

Mark always the opportunist, dug frantically into his pocket.

"Damn!" he said. "I must have left it in the car." He fixed her with a pleading little smile. "Any chance for a Christmas smooch without the mistletoe?"

She closed the distance between them. "Well — maybe," she teased, "maybe just the *ghost* of a chance. After all, as Misty would say, it i*th* Chri*th*tma*th*."

"Yeah," Mark murmured against her lips, "and be*th*ide*th*, who believe*th* in gho*th*t*th*?"

308

MAY 1984
$1.75

47744

An Unusual Mike Shayne Adventure
YESTERDAY'S HERO
by Brett Halliday

Exciting Novelets
by Joseph Commings
and Mel D. Ames

Short Stories
and Features by
the Best
Suspense
Writers in the
World

*The sloop drifted in toward shore, with
only one passenger on board — a dead
body hanging from the rigging!*

blood
in the
rigging

THE SAILING SLOOP, *WARM WINDS,* HER SAILS TWISTED
and tattered, emerged like a phantom from the early morning fog and
drifted aimlessly toward the pier. She was two-score and one from
bowsprit to taffrail, thirteen abeam, and fifty dizzy feet to her
masthead. An apparition of majesty and mystery, rocking gently on
the shoreward swell of the tide, her rudderless approach heralded by
the shriek of a lone seagull perched high on her spreaders.

A small group of anglers on Metro's Beachville government
wharf watched in silent fascination as the sleek, shadowy hull
ghosted toward them. When she nudged in against the weathered
pilings at the end of the pier, two men clambered aboard to secure
her mooring lines, then quickly rejoined their companions to stand
and stare, appalled, up into the tangled rigging.

Suspended above them, one trim ankle snarled in the stays'l
halyard, spread-eagled, as though in the throe of a midair cartwheel,
was the body of a young woman, naked as a shucked oyster.
Vertical red tendrils streaked the surface of the mast from a gore of
blood where the raven head dangled, swinging into it with each
rocking yaw of the boat. The man who had secured the bow line

turned suddenly away with a queasy grimace. His eyes focused on a telephone kiosk at the inshore end of the pier. "I'd better call the police," he said.

THE WAIL OF THE SIREN WOUND DOWN TO A MUTED whimper as the gray, unmarked Chevy ground to a halt at the foot of the wharf. The group of anglers turned to watch as two imposing figures advanced over the rough-planked pier toward them.

One, a woman, was a stunning six-foot Amazonian beauty, with long flowing hair the color of ripe wheat. She moved with the inborn power and poise of a jungle cat, a long loping stride that seemed to test the seams of her snug gray skirt with every step. At her side, an equally tall, heavily-muscled male kept pace with her, his rugged, unassuming self-assurance clearly evident even in the distracting presence of his remarkable companion. As they drew near the boat, the fishermen stepped aside to let them pass.

Warm Winds rocked gently as the husky male climbed aboard, but the big blonde hesitated, one foot on deck, one ashore. "Which one of you men telephoned the police?" she asked the group on the pier.

A squat, balding man in dungarees and a red plaid jacket stepped forward. "I did," he said, then with a doubtful tilt of his head, "are you from the police?"

"I *am* the police." The blonde Amazon extracted an ID wallet from her red leather shoulder bag and flipped it open. "Detective-Lieutenant Cathy Carruthers," she intoned with obvious tedium, "Metro Central, Homicide, Eleventh Precinct." She nodded toward her husky companion. "My partner, Detective-Sergeant Mark Swanson. Now — what can you tell me about this?"

The man shuffled gumboots that looked to be about two sizes too large. "*Warm Winds?*" he said with a moot shrug. "She just drifted in outta the fog, n' we snugged her up. Me and Shaklee. Saw the body hanging up there in the riggin' and well — figured I'd best call the cops. That's about it."

The lieutenant looked idly from one bleary-eyed, unshaven face to the other. "Does anyone recognize the boat?"

The anglers shook their collective heads.

"Did anyone go aboard? Touch anything?"

"Just to tie her up, lieutenant." Baldy seemed to be the only one with a tongue. "I was on the bow line. Shaklee, here, he got the stern."

The whole motley group nodded in unison, this time affirmatively.

"Here comes Bones and Madson," the sergeant said from the deck of the derelict. The lieutenant followed his gaze down the length of the pier to where a police car, with cherry flashing, had just pulled up beside the gray Chevy. A towering black emerged from the car like a giant genie out of a bottle, dwarfing his fellow officer by simple comparison .

"Have Madson call in," the lieutenant told her burly partner as she finally stepped aboard. "I want the whole crew out here, with special emphasis on the Forensic team. And get Bones started on this bunch," she indicated the ragged cluster of silent, gaping anglers. "Name, domicile, occupation (if any), whatever — And, Mark," she glanced up at the grisly, swaying body in the rigging, "nobody leaves this pier until I give the okay."

"AYE, AYE, LIEUTENANT." THE VERNACULAR OF THE sea seemed to come easily while standing astride *Warm Winds'* buoyant deck, and as Mark relayed the lieutenant's orders, he could not deny a sudden strange affinity with the Blighs and Ahabs of the past. It was a haunting moment that was as elusive and as fleeting as a leeward echo. When he turned back to his beautiful partner, he found her struggling with the line that had snarled the dead woman's ankle.

"It's no use," she said to Mark. "She's hung up on the stays'l halyard and it's fouled at the masthead. I'm going to have to go aloft."

Mark's eyes followed the mast to its dizzy peak. It was stepped with widely-spaced metal footholds that would take a good arm and leg stretch to maneuver. "You're not dressed for a climb like that," he said with a glance, first to her snugly fitted skirt, then to the group of anglers on the wharf, "though I doubt anyone would mind the show."

"Hmmm." The lieutenant paused thoughtfully. "I see what you mean. It's a man's world after all, isn't it? Well — I guess I'll just have to do it the hard way." She pressed the slack halyard into his big fist. "Keep this line as taut as you can as I climb. And, Mark, watch carefully — "

"I promise, I won't miss a thing."

" — to see that she doesn't come down hard once I've freed the line."

Mark wound the line under one arm and over the opposite shoulder in an alpine hitch. Then, as the lieutenant kicked off her shoes, and stood facing him on tiptoe, reaching for a handhold as high on the rope as she could, Mark found himself confronted by two beautiful blue eyes and a pert little nose that was gently nudging his own.

"Your igloo or mine?" Mark said with a reciprocal nasal nudge of his own.

"At a time like this," the lieutenant told him quietly, "a true gentleman would look the other way."

But Mark was not able, either to qualify as a true gentleman, or to look any way but breathless as she began to climb. She squirmed by him (he could not help but notice) in precise anatomical order, crushing his face against the wriggling ascent of breasts, then stomach, thighs, calves, and finally, ten red-tipped toes; at which point, he looked up to see her rising rapidly heavenward, hand over hand, like an ascending angel. When she reached the top of the mast, he could feel her tugging at the line, freeing it, and a moment later he took the full weight of the dead girl and began to lower her slowly toward the deck.

The lieutenant, skimming down a larboard shroud, with hair and skirt flying, landed lightly back on deck at the same time the dead girl's outstretched hands touched the foredeck. Mark lowered the body gently, almost reverently, over the fo'c'sle hatch-cover, like a beached starfish, he thought, her chalk-white flesh frozen in the rigid grip of rigor mortis. The lieutenant was busy ripping away at the tattered stays'l in order to cover the body, and as she knelt to adjust the fabric over an outflung limb, her eye caught the glint of a silver-colored slave bracelet hanging from one trim ankle.

"*Suzy Q.*," she read aloud. "At least we know her name now, or part of it. I wonder what the Q stands for?"

"There can't be many names beginning with Q," Mark ventured, "but what I want to know is how in hell did she get up there in the first place?"

"Well — she could have been on deck when that stays'l blew out, got her foot caught in the halyard and was yanked up the mast with it. I seem to recall that the weather was pretty squally out in the straits, before this fog set in."

"Or, she could have been hauled up there by some person, or persons unknown. And that, of course, brings up another cogent question — "

"Yes," the lieutenant replied musingly, "like who owns *Warm Winds,* and what has happened to her crew? No true seaman, Mark, would leave a two-hundred thousand dollar boat, unmanned, at the mercy of the elements — except," she seemed to be looking beyond him, out into the clammy depths of the unrevealing fog, "except, perhaps, under the threat of death."

"Or even then," Mark equivocated.

The lieutenant nodded with knowing, sad accord. "*Or even then.*"

MARK EYED HIS SENIOR PARTNER REFLECTIVELY AS she strode the length of the deck to the after-end of the boat with her typical *savoir-faire.* Ever since that memorable day, some thirty months ago, when he had first teamed up with Cathy Carruthers (or *The Amazon,* as she was chauvinistically referred to in Homicide by her staunchly sexist colleagues), they, she and Mark, had shared a secret liaison of mutual respect and affection. It was an intimacy which, over the months, had evolved quite innocently into a covert kind of carry-on that went well beyond the buddy-backup ethic laid down by the Police Academy.

Mark, though somewhat bemused by the relationship, was not unhappy with it. There was, he knew, no place in the legendary mystique of the Amazon for the "conventional" or the "faint of heart." The extraordinary feat she had just performed, the lithesome scaling of the mast to free the dead girl, had simply been one more manifestation of the awesome, *para*-human strength and agility possessed by this angelic-looking creature. She was a paradox of pulchritude and rare physical prowess that was nothing short of mind-messing, *and,* from Mark's vantage point (in more ways than one), a great lady to be around.

He watched her now as she leapt lightly into the cluttered cockpit and stood, one hip against the helm, surveying the havoc and devastation wrought by the wind — or had it been the perverse will of some unknown human hand? Or both? Flotation cushions, life-jackets, and discarded bits of clothing (male and female) littered the well of the cockpit. A pair of shattered binoculars dangled loosely from the gimbaled compass atop the binnacle, and a couple of empty beer cans sloshed idly in the scuppers.

"Looks like panic city," the lieutenant said to Mark as he joined her aft, "a routine day at sea — gone hellishly wrong." A capricious surge of the tide took that moment to lift the hull against her moorings, sluing the rudder. The wheeled helm was quick to respond against the lieutenant's thigh, nudging her gently toward the open companionway, as though by some ghostly resolve of its own. "Let's take a look below," she responded softly, "maybe the boat's log will have something to tell us."

THE SCENE BELOW DECKS WAS NO LESS IN TURMOIL. Charts and tide-tables lay in disarray, books had been thrown from shelves, pots and dishes, and a potpourri of foods and condiments were strewn about the galley. It looked as though a baby tornado had come below and, in the confines of the cabin, copied the sea-whipping wrath of its tempestuous parent.

"Be careful where you step, Mark." The lieutenant stooped to examine a bare footprint, clearly visible in a patch of spilled flour. And then in the lounge area, she extracted a black scuba wet-suit from the rubble on the cabin floor. It looked to be loosely wrapped, or entangled, in a length of yellow nylon rope. "Could be Suzy Q.'s," she said, holding it up, "kind of small for a man."

"What's the rope for, I wonder?"

"Who knows?"

"Oh, oh." Mark hefted an ebony cylinder out of the clutter. "Here's the tank and breathing apparatus." He released a short, hissing spurt of air. "There's still pressure on the gauge."

"Never mind that, look for the log." But a moment later she recovered it herself, pulling it out from under a muddle of charts. She opened the book carefully, to the last entry.

"It's dated yesterday," she said. "A little smudged, but legible." She began to read aloud, *"Hidden Cove. 6 A.M. Woke secure on the hook to clear skies. Skiffed ashore with first mate for oysters before weighing anchor. 7:15 A .M. Set an intermediate course for Tree Island, 285 ° — starboard reach in light to medium airs. 9:37 A.M. Off Tree Island. Altered course to 243 ° — "*

"Well, go on."

"That's it."

"You mean there's no entry after 9:37 yesterday morning?"

"Not a whisper."

"Aw, well — no big deal. It's all gibberish, anyway." Mark scratched his tousled head. "What's it mean by, *woke secure on the hook?*"

"The hook is the anchor, Mark. It was apparently well set and didn't drag during the night."

"Then why in hell'd they have to weigh the bloody thing in the morning?"

The lieutenant regarded her partner with the vexed tolerance of a young mother whose six-year-old had just asked where babies came from. "They didn't weigh it, Mark. They *weighed* it." She let out an exasperated breath. "They pulled the goddamn thing up!" .

Mark still looked a little dubious, as though he'd been fed the line about the stork. "I'm almost afraid to ask," he said tentatively, "what the guy was reaching for, over the side — ?"

"The wind, you dummy. The mother-lovin' wind! And the sails were doing the reaching, not the — say," she narrowed her beautiful eyes at him, "are you putting me on?"

Mark took what he thought to be an opportune moment to try out his injured, little-boy look, but it failed to mask the mischief in his eyes.

"You turkey," the lieutenant told him with a hopeless shake of her head, then, suddenly serious again, "Well, at least now we know he wasn't alone."

"The first mate?"

"Right. And on a boat this size, that's a title usually given to the woman aboard." She flipped to the flyleaf at the front of the log. "Hmmm. Here are the owners: Richard and Debbie Raines."

"So now we've got three people to account for," Mark said soberly.

"Three people, Mark, and a skiff."

"A skiff?"

"The log says they went ashore for oysters in a skiff, yesterday morning. Well, there's no skiff aboard *Warm Winds* now." She tugged open the small fridge beside the galley sink. "There's not even any oysters."

A SUDDEN ROCKING OF THE BOAT SIGNALED THE arrival of the special teams from Homicide. By the time the two detectives had scrambled topside, the decks were swarming with men and equipment.

"Fill the guys in, Mark, while I have a word with just-plain-Sam."

The lieutenant headed toward the bow where a dumpy, disheveled looking man with a symbolic black bag was stooped over the body of the dead-girl. He looked up with seeming indifference.

"What'n hell happened here?"

The lieutenant met his gruff greeting with a tight, forgiving smile. This was a man she had learned to accept at face value. He was Samuel Morton, M.D., Coroner and Chief Medical Examiner for M.C.P.D., *or,* as he was fond of proclaiming at happier moments, "just-plain Sam." His bark, the lieutenant knew, was a damn sight worse than his bite.

"We found her hanging in the rigging, Sam," the lieutenant drew his attention to the violent spatter of blood, high on the mast, "by her left ankle. Her head must have hit the mast repeatedly, probably during a squall."

"How'd you get her down?"

"I went up after her."

The M.E. raised a bushy eyebrow. "Dressed like that?"

"No one seemed to mind."

Sam Morton straightened with a deep, muted, gurgling sound, a poor excuse for a laugh that just couldn't seem to find its way out of his belly. "I'll bet," he muttered. "Just one request, though, before you pull your next *coup de theatre*."

"Well?"

"Wait for me to arrive." He turned to signal the morgue-meds in with a stretcher. "I might want to sell tickets," he added sardonically.

The lieutenant shook her golden head with disapproval. "You see too much of death, Sam. Your sense of humor has deteriorated to the unlively level of your unfortunate clientele."

The shabby little M.E. turned to face her then with a rare show of deep concern. "Listen, lieutenant, if I didn't keep it on the light side, I wouldn't last another damn day in this lousy job." He sighed deeply, sadly. "I thought you and Mark, of all people, would understand that. "

The lieutenant averted her eyes. "Touche," she acknowledged quietly.

"Now," he snorted, with an abrupt return to his customary ill humor, "you're going to ask me how long she's been dead, right?"

"Right. I know you can't be specific, Sam, but an educated guess could be helpful."

"Not this time, lieutenant." The M.E. squinted up into the rigging. "Hanging up there in the wind, in God only knows what temperatures, wrapped in a blanket of pea-soup — Christ! I'm a doctor, not a psychic. The only thing I can say for sure (and, knowing you, you've probably twigged it already), is that she's been dead for a minimum of, say — three to four hours. It would take at least that long for the rigor to set in. But, beyond that —"

He shrugged and turned his palms up in a hopeless gesture.

Cathy Carruthers ruffled the few straggly hairs on his thinning pate. "Your doubtful charm," she told him sweetly, "is exceeded only by the abysmal lack of information you have just given me. I hope you do a little better with the autopsy."

"You'll be the first to know."

"And, Sam, bag that slave bracelet on the girl's ankle and get it over to the lab, will you? It's the only clue we've got to her identity."

"Anything else, *WunderFrau?*"

"Yes, as a matter of fact there is. I'd like to know *precisely* what caused Suzy Q.'s death."

"You don't think the storm killed her?"

"Who's to know? Maybe, as Mark says, she was hauled up the

mast *after* her demise. And what was she doing out on deck anyway, without any clothes on? All we have are questions, and no answers."

"I've got an answer." Mark had appeared suddenly at the lieutenant's elbow. He had a pair of wispy, lavender lace panties in his big fist.

"What's that?"

"Suzy Q.'s missing panties, I guess. I found them inside that wetsuit." He held them up in front of him. "One thing for sure, lieutenant, they aren't mine."

THE FOG HUNG ON THROUGH THE DAY, CROWDING IN over the land from somewhere out in the windless straits. When night fell, it thickened into swirling yellow clouds, stirred and fed by the funereal crawl of traffic along the streets of Metro. Deep-throated foghorns moaned incessantly through the long night and into the early morning hours of a new day.

Cathy Carruthers turned in front of her office window in Metro Central's Eleventh Precinct, causing her statuesque reflection in the fog-silvered glass of the window to turn with her. She stooped to smooth an above-the-knee wrinkle from a shapely nyloned thigh. Mark, sitting opposite, tilting precariously back on the legs of his chair, watched both Cathys with the oblivious, divided zeal of a lovesick schizophrenic. He had just begun to chant, *"Double your pleasure, double your fun,"* when she looked up and caught him sightseeing. He wasn't quite sure then, which of the two Cathys kicked the chair out from under him, but there was no doubt about the end result.

"Whadya do that for?" he groaned from floor level, one seismic second later.

"As if you didn't, know."

Mark struggled to his feet, feigning injury to both body and moral repute, but his winsome, wily partner wasn't buying either one.

"Give it up," she told him flatly. "The only thing bruised is your male ego." She settled into the chair behind her desk and opened a thin, brown file folder. "Is this all that Records could dig up on our two missing sailboaters?"

"That's it."

"There's more information in the log book than there is in here."
She flipped a page disparagingly. "Hmm. Richard Raines, it seems,
is a free-lance journalist, in his middle thirties. Debbie's almost ten
years younger. They've been together for some time, apparently, as
'liveaboards' and joint owners of *Warm Winds* — "

"What's left of it, you mean." Mark had righted his chair and
was tenderly lowering his husky carcass back onto the seat.

"Oh, I think the damage is really quite superficial, Mark. The
tattered sails and rigging will present something of a financial
hardship, of course, but to whom? The real tragedy here, is the
mysterious disappearance of Richard and Debbie Raines, not to
mention the grotesque, and still unexplained death of Suzy Q." The
lieutenant furrowed her perfect brows. "For the life of me, Mark, I
cannot see anyone abandoning a boat like *Warm Winds* voluntarily,
nor can I accept the unlikely premise that they were somehow 'lost
at sea' — washed overboard, drowned, whatever. Not both of them.
Not at the same time, on the same night, in the same storm, without
even a trace —"

"Maybe they were *taken* off, at gunpoint."

"That's a possibility, of course. But *why?*"

Mark shrugged his heavy shoulders. "Drugs, maybe? There's
been a lot of off-shore traffic lately."

The lieutenant pursed her lips thoughtfully. "I thought of that,"
she conceded softly, "but, as yet, there is just no tangible connection.
Still, I think you'd better requisition a couple of uniforms, just in case.
If any bodies have been washed ashore, I want to know about it.
There's a lot of shore-line between Tree Island and the Bay area,
and this damn fog isn't going to help, so the sooner we get someone
on it, the better."

"Gotcha."

"Try for Bones and Madson, if they're on today."

"They are. I met them coming in and I've got them standing by.
Anything new on Suzy Q.?"

"Not a thing." The lieutenant drew a long, frustrated breath.
"Records couldn't even come up with enough to open a file on her.
Which isn't surprising, I guess, when you consider what little we
gave them to start with. Maybe the autopsy —"

Mark was already shoving himself out of his chair. "I'll put a call through to Sam's office to see if he's come up with anything. And for starters, lieutenant, what do you say to Bones and Madson checking with the Coast Guard?"

"Good idea. And you might alert them to the drug theory. And, Mark, while you're at it, sign out the gray Chevy. It says here that *Warm Winds'* home berth is at the Bayside Marina. I think we'd better have a looksee."

"Meet you in the garage in five," Mark said as he went out the door, but a moment later, his head reappeared in the doorway. "Don't forget to bring that girl in the window along with you," he said with mock seriousness, "of the two of you, I think I like her best."

"Oh?" The lieutenant glanced back at her reflection and went right along with the gag. "Why's that?"

"She doesn't play so *goddamn rough,"* he swore ruefully, then ducked out of sight as a pencil went whistling by his ear.

MARK WATCHED CATHY CARRUTHERS MATERIALIZE out of the fog in front of the gray Chevy, an exquisite apparition, gathering mortal form and substance as she narrowed the distance between them. Behind her, the Metro Central City Morgue loomed in the deeper, distant shadows like a giant tombstone. As she drew abreast of the car, Mark flipped the door open and turned the key.

"Where to now?" he asked routinely, "Bayside Marina?"

"Why not?" The lieutenant tossed the file folder containing Suzy Q.'s autopsy report onto the back seat. "We're just marking time here."

"I gather Sam wasn't very helpful."

"Helpful?" She snapped on her seat belt with a disgruntled snort. "He wasn't even *hopeful.* And that goes ditto for the Lab."

Mark was gingerly following the yellow curb out of the parking area. The fog had reduced visibility to about two car lengths. At the exit gate, he turned and eased the Chevy cautiously into the ghostly flow of slow moving traffic.

"Nothing new on how the girl died?"

The lieutenant shook her head negatively. "Her skull was so badly mashed from repeatedly colliding with the mast, there was just no way of determining the precise nature of the blow that actually killed her, or if, in fact, there was a blow at all."

"What?" Mark shot her a quick glance. "How else *could* she have died? "

"Any number of ways, Mark. She could have been rendered unconscious before (or after) being swung from the yardarm, by almost any means, then simply left to bleed to death. There wasn't an ounce of blood left in her body."

"Any sign of drugs, poison?"

"Not a trace."

"No other wounds?"

"There were rope burns on her left ankle, of course, and plenty of bruises and contusions. But they were likely the result of being slammed about in the rigging."

"So we don't know a damn thing more now than when we started?"

"Well, the Lab's still working on a few loose ends, under-nail residue, hair samples, stomach content, you name it — but I'm not holding my breath."

"Then what *are* you holding?"

The lieutenant looked down at her own tightly clenched fist, then slowly unfolded her fingers. The silver slave bracelet lay coiled against her palm.

"All that's left of Suzy Q.," she said tightly.

THE SIGN IN FRONT OF THE BAYSIDE MARINA BOASTED 100 berths and a big NO, signifying no vacancies. On the same sign, a large red arrow with the word OFFICE painted on it, pointed to a weather-beaten, driftwood shack overlooking the fog-shrouded docks. A door with a busted porthole hung half open on one twisted hinge.

"Anyone home?" The lieutenant stepped inside the dimly-lit shack and confronted what looked at first glance to be a smoldering pile of garbage. Then it spoke.

"Wot c'n I do fer yu?"

An unshaven but friendly face had separated itself from what she now recognized to be a cluttered old desk, with an equally cluttered old man sitting behind it. A hand-made cigarette dangled from a pendulous lower lip while two crinkly sea-green eyes squinted up at her through a haze of rising smoke.

"Lieutenant Carruthers," the lieutenant told him, flashing her badge. "This is my partner, Sergeant Swanson. We're here about *Warm Winds.*"

"Yeh, yeh. I hear she come driftin' in on 'er own, down't th' government wharf." The man shuffled to his feet and extended a pudgy, freckled hand. "Name's Skinner. Cecil P. Skinner. I'm th' owner uv this here marina."

As the lieutenant took the proffered hand, she could not help but notice a couple of small flies that appeared to be in perpetual orbit around the old man's grizzled head. Even the smoke from the smoldering cigarette did not deter them, nor did it mask a lingering odor of soured bilge water that seemed to rise off the crusty old salt like steam from a manure pile.

"Tell me, Mr. Skinner, have you seen or heard anything of the *Warm Winds'* owners?" The lieutenant could not restrain a rebellious twitch of her nose.

"Not s'much as a peep, looten'nt, mam. Leastwise, not since day b'fore last." He was giving her a long, honest look of appraisal. "Gotta tell yu, though, that *Po*-lice Academy is purely puttin' out some trim-lookin' hulls, nowaday." He winked a watery eye at Mark from behind a curl of smoke.

Mark grinned in spite of himself. "What can you tell us about them?"

"Rich 'n' Deb? Not much, fer a fact. Quiet pair, those two. He's a writer, yu know. She works in town some're. Flower shop, seems like." He pointed to a solitary, long-stemmed rose sticking out of an empty Coke bottle, on the one clear corner of his desk. "She brung me that. Only fresh thing aboard." He laughed through his nose with a shrill, long, wheezing whistle.

"Do you have any idea what would induce them to abandon their boat, Mr. Skinner?"

"Can't see 'em doin' that atall, mam. Not that pair. Young Rich figured th' sun rose 'n' set on that there boat. Deb, too, fer that matter."

"What do you know about Suzy Q.?" the lieutenant asked suddenly.

The old man blinked. "Suzy who?"

"Q," she said again, "Suzy Q."

Skinner scratched his weedpatch of a head, inciting the flies to widen their orbit slightly. "Nope. Don't figger I know that one. She a parta this cruise?"

The lieutenant ignored his question. She had eased back to the open door where the air was fresher. "Perhaps you can show us where the boat was berthed, Mr. Skinner."

Skinner's ragged and soiled old shirt shrugged its shoulders. "Yep, I c'n do that all right. But ain't nothin' there now, looten'nt, 'cept gullshit 'n' gravity." He detached himself from the desk with apparent reluctance, but in so doing, he effectively diminished the offending mid-room rubble by roughly half. The two detectives were already outside, gulping at the Metro smog with new-found relish.

SKINNER LED THE WAY DOWN A RAILED GANGWAY TO the Bayside's floating dock area. The hinged ramp was steep with the low tide, and the bedraggled little man tumbled down it like a bundle of dirty wash going down a laundry shute. His winged entourage circled in hot pursuit.

The weathered planking rocked lazily under their combined weight as Mark and the lieutenant followed the old man into the unseen maze of moorings. Row on row of boats materialized slowly on either side, then retreated back into the fog as they stumbled along the docks, first in one direction, then another. They halted, finally, before a vacant berth that looked to be strangely ostracized from the others, ominous almost, with the bleak and chilling stillness of an empty grave.

Mark tossed a cigarette butt into the dark well of the berth. The brief *hiss* as it met the water echoed up through the suffocating weight of the fog. "You're right about the gravity, Skinner," he said idly, "and the — "

"Mr. Skinner," the lieutenant cut in, censuring her partner with a grim look, "are all these boats occupied?"

"Hell, no, looten'nt. Mostly fairweather sailors, hereabout. Ain't no more'n half a dozen live-aboards in the whole marina."

"Are there any of these live-aboards (as you call them) in

neighborly proximity to where we're now standing?"

"Uh — yep. Me, fer one." He pointed along the dock with a finger that looked like a pork sausage with freckles.

The lieutenant squinted into the fog. "You mean that empty berth — "

But then she saw it, a low-slung, time-ravaged, plywood ark, cowering like a whipped dog against the near side of the berth. It seemed to be hanging by its own mooring lines in a grim struggle to stay afloat. With eleven inches of freeboard to port (and three to starboard), it defied every visual law of equilibrium known to man. A lush beard of seaweed that would have made the Ayatollah Khomeini look like a hairless youth sprouted from its hull, and the chalky upper surface of its deck and doghouse looked as though it had been the target of every dyspeptic gull from Tijuana to Nome.

"That's a boat?" Mark queried in mild awe.

"That's the *Neverset Horizon,*" Skinner told them proudly. "I renamed it after my wife up'n left me, some thirty year ago." He wheezed out a high-pitched giggle. "I 'member like it was yestiday," he reflected, "seein' the ol' bat go stompin' off the dock, yellin' back at me that she hoped she'd *never set her eyes on* me, or that Godforsaken boat ever ag'in. An' yu know, by golly, she never did."

The lieutenant rolled her beautiful eyes. "Yes, well — I think we can skip that one for the time being. Are there any others, Mr. Skinner, close at hand?''

"Yep. The Duhaneys. Back this way a piece."

The old man turned and trundled wearily back the way they had come, his pungent aura in lingering pursuit. A third fly (a deserter from the deck of the *Neverset Horizon)* had now joined his winged escort.

PETE AND CHARLOTTE DUHANEY PROVED TO BE AN amiable couple. Their boat, the *Confront,* was a spacious forty-two foot yawl, with all the amenities of modern-day seafaring. The two detectives were taken below into a huge, richly-cushioned lounge area that was centered and dominated by a long, communal-type table. The entire, lush interior was made quaint with memorabilia and serene in the warmth of the Duhaney's ingenuous hospitality.

"What a beautiful boat," the lieutenant enthused. She and Mark were settled back on the cushions on one side of the table, while Skinner was being tactfully persuaded to hove-to on the top step of the companionway ladder, where the air could get at him.

"My concrete castle," Pete Duhaney said with an encompassing wave of his hand. Then, as both Mark and the lieutenant raised a questioning eyebrow, he added, "A man's home is his castle, and mine just happens to be made of concrete."

"*Concrete?*"

Pete Duhaney laughed at the look of amazement on both their faces. He was a big, deep-chested man with a big, deep-chested laugh. "It's a relatively new process in small boat construction," he explained. "Ferro-cement, it's called, which is really just another name for reinforced concrete."

"And *it floats?*" Mark wondered aloud.

"Why not? *Warm Winds* is made of steel, and *she floats.* A displacement hull, sergeant, is buoyed by virtue of the relative amount of water it displaces, not the — "

"Pete, come *on* — " Charlotte smiled down from the raised, open galley behind them, where she was in the process of pouring coffee. "You get him talking about boats," she warned them good-naturedly, as she handed Skinner a mug of hot coffee and a fly swatter, " — he'll go on all day about it."

Charlotte Duhaney, in her late twenties or early thirties, was both svelte and disarmingly casual. She was not the hale-fellow extrovert her husband was, but there was a profound and quiet sincerity about her that would readily attract the confidences of others. *A Pied-Piper of troubled souls,* the lieutenant decided. Their eyes met briefly in wary cognizance of that secret intuitiveness that only one woman can recognize in another.

Pete Duhaney sheepishly acquiesced. "Charlotte's right, of course," he said. "We should be doing our utmost to find out what has happened to Richard and Debbie. We *are* concerned, lieutenant."

"You were close friends?"

"Yes. Very close."

"Did they often take off like this?" the lieutenant asked, "without letting anyone know where they were going? Specifically, I mean."

"Frequently." Charlotte placed a mug of steaming coffee before each of them. "They left about a week ago on this particular junket, to cruise the off-shore islands, they said. That's what 'living aboard' is all about, lieutenant. Freedom to do what you want, when you want, without the artificial fetters of time-clocks and time-tables." She snuggled down on the cushions beside her husband. "Specifically? Well, there must be a thousand and one coves and anchorages in the off-shore islands. Precisely where they went and how long they'd stay would depend, I imagine, largely on the whim of the wind."

Mark began softly to croon the first line of the wistful old chestnut: *"Nice work if you can get it — "*

And with a philosophical chuckle, Charlotte followed through, *"— And you can get it, if you try."*

Pete Duhaney took a deep chug of his coffee. "There is one thing, lieutenant, that might or might not be significant. I went over to the government wharf yesterday afternoon, when I heard that *Warm Winds* had drifted in there. There was a police guard on the boat, as you know, and they wouldn't let me board, but even from the dock, I could see that when the stays'l had blown out, and the mains'l boom had broken free, the clew end of both starboard sheets had been cleated in to a close-haul — "

"Give it to us in English," Mark suggested dryly.

Duhaney looked vacantly from Mark to the lieutenant, then back to Mark. Charlotte came to his rescue.

"They're landlubbers," she reminded him gently.

"Oh, yeah." Pete cleared his throat. "What I'm saying, lieutenant, is that when that squall hit, *Warm Winds* was close-hauled on a starboard beat, uh — she was *sailing into the wind."*

"So?"

"So the night before last, as I recall, the prevailing wind was a nor'wester. That could tell us something about where they were heading."

"According to the log book," the lieutenant reflected, "her last course was 243 ° off Tree Island."

Duhaney furrowed his brows. "That just doesn't jibe, lieutenant. A 243 ° heading from Tree Island would bring them home, all right, but a beat into a nor'wester sure as hell *would not.* "

"Then they must have altered course," Charlotte put in, "no mystery there."

"But *why?*" The lieutenant was quick to question the obvious. "According to the log, they had apparently decided to head for home. *Something* must have induced them to change course, *and,* if what Pete says is true, it wasn't the lure of a fair wind."

"I stand corrected," Charlotte deferred graciously. "Now perhaps you'll shed some light on another mystery for me, lieutenant."

"And what might that be?"

"What it is you're clutching so desperately in your left hand."

Cathy Carruthers seemed surprised to discover that she was still tight-fisting the silver slave bracelet. She handed it across to Charlotte without comment.

"Suzy Q.," Charlotte read softly. "Is this from the dead girl?"

"Yes. And we'll require one of you to view the body."

"One of *us?* But why?"

"We haven't yet established, Charlotte, that the girl we freed from the rigging, wearing this Suzy Q. bracelet, was not, in fact, your good friend, Debbie Raines. And, frankly, I'm rather surprised that you haven't already considered that possibility yourself."

"But — but the newspaper account of the story said the dead girl had black hair, lieutenant. Debbie was a blonde."

"*Was?*"

Charlotte shot a quick glance at her husband, as though in search of moral support. Pete straightened defiantly. "Surely, lieutenant, you're not suggesting that Charlotte and I are in any way involved — "

"Relax Mr. Duhaney. When an unnatural death is under investigation, *no one* can be held above or beyond suspicion." She flipped the silver bracelet like a George Raft dollar. "Not even Suzy Q., herself."

OFFICER GEORGE WASHINGTON (TOO-TALL) BONES collared the lieutenant and Mark as they entered the Eleventh Precinct later that same morning. The entrance hall was a hive of activity. Uniforms and civies buzzed around the desk sergeant like a swarm of drones around a queen bee. The big black drew the two detectives aside, into a quiet corner.

"We've just come up with a couple of castaways, lieutenant, but I don't think they're the ones you're looking for."

"Oh? How's that?"

"The Coast Guard picked them up early this morning, a man and a woman, off Desolation Rock."

"Alive?"

"Apparently."

"And — ?"

"They were found huddled together, lieutenant, in a beached Thunderbird — "

"A car?" Mark wide-eyed the big cop with a look of total incredulity. "On *Desolation Rock?*"

"A sea-going Thunderbird," Bones explained condescendingly, "is not a car, Mark, it's a class of sailboat. A twenty-six foot sloop. This particular one is called *The Tired Tush.*" He chuckled ruefully. "It's looking pretty tired now, all right — stove-in and hard aground."

"Did you get the names of the survivors?"

"Not yet, lieutenant. But we're expecting an update any minute. I left Madson glued to the phone."

"Good. Keep us advised."

The lieutenant headed for the elevator, but Mark lingered just long enough to inform Too-Tall Bones that (technically speaking), a Thunderbird was neither a car nor a boat, but a constipated gull with gas. He dodged a playful cuff of the big black's giant paw.

THE TELEPHONE WAS ON ITS THIRD RING WHEN THE lieutenant entered her office. Mark followed her in and closed the door. The voice of the caller came through loud and clear.

"Lieutenant Carruthers?"

"Speaking."

"This is your prime suspect."

"Oh?"

"Charlotte. Charlotte Duhaney."

The lieutenant chuckled. "Did you phone me up to confess, Charlotte?"

"No, lieutenant. I phoned to tell you that I may have found a clue to the identity of your mysterious Suzy Q."

"That so?"

"Take a look in Tuesday's *Metro Examiner*, lieutenant, the day before-yesterday edition. There's an ad in the PERSONALS column, addressed to Suzy Q."

"What does it say?"

"It says, and I quote: SUZY Q., 48-123, 327, BLUE SERGE —"

The lieutenant waited expectantly. "Is that it?" she said finally.

"That's it."

"Blue Serge?"

"That's what it says."

"It doesn't make any sense to me. Do you know what it means?"

"No, but I'm working on it."

"Oh, great. And what makes you think this has anything to do with the girl who came drifting in on *Warm Winds?*"

"Lieutenant, how many Suzy Q.'s do you suppose there are in Metro?"

"You've got a point there, I guess. Well, we'll check it out, but in the meantime —"

There was a sudden spate of activity on the other end of the line, voices raised in surprise and excitement. Then, Charlotte's voice again, "Lieutenant! You'll never guess what just happened."

"Skinner took a bath?"

"It's the Raines's, lieutenant. Richard and Debbie Raines. They just walked in, large as life."

The lieutenant was already on her feet. "Tell those two to sit tight until we get there. Where are you phoning from?"

"The Bayside office."

"We're on our way. And, Charlotte — "

"Yes, lieutenant?"

"Thanks for the tip."

THE OLD CLOCK ON THE METRO CITY HALL BUILDING was striking twelve-noon when Mark steered the gray Chevy into the Bayside Marina for the second time that day. The dilapidated driftwood office was deserted, so they headed directly for the fogged-in dock area. Charlotte was waiting for them.

"Climb aboard," she said in welcome, "you're just in time for lunch."

Confront accepted the combined weight of the two detectives with a tolerant ripple along her waterline. And old man Skinner, again (or still) perched high on his private bleacher, moved aside to let them enter. As they descended the companionway ladder, they were met by Pete Duhaney and two new smiling faces.

Richard and Debbie Raines looked like they had just stepped out of a Marlboro cigarette commercial. Sun-bleached and wind-blown, with that fresh-as-all-outdoors look about them, they seemed to epitomize the best of what "messing about with boats" had to offer. The introductions that followed seemed hardly necessary, but once accomplished, Charlotte posed a friendly ultimatum.

"So what do we do first, lieutenant? Eat, or talk business?" She steered them all toward the main lounge, where it became immediately apparent that lunch aboard *Confront* was going to be more of a banquet than a midday snack. A pot of steaming baby clams now dominated the long communal table, and a half-dozen wooden bowls of hot, liquid butter circled the pot. Side plates of crabmeat (still in its pink armor), fillet of smoked ling cod and coho salmon, and small, pearly-white raw oysters on the open, half shell, provided a tantalizing *embarras de choix* to even the most voracious palate. A covered basket of piping-hot, whole-wheat crispy rolls and a gallon jug of dry red wine added the final, tempting touch to an already sumptuous spread.

"Why don't we talk and eat at the same time?" the lieutenant said in compromise. "I'm anxious to hear what Richard and Debbie have to tell us, but — to ignore this noble repast any longer than necessary would surely be a crime in itself."

Mark set the pace and the mood of the lunch by eulogizing a plump little oyster, held on high in its half shell, with a line from *The Rubaiyat Of Omar Khayyam:* "A jug of wine, a loaf of bread, and *thou,*" he recited solemnly. He popped the oyster into his mouth, swallowed once, and grinned with satisfaction at his amused tablemates.

Debbie tilted her head thoughtfully. "Mark, I know it's customary to eulogize the dead," she told him with mock seriousness, "but that little critter you just swallowed, was still alive."

"*Alive?*" Mark blanched.

"But of course. It wouldn't be very hospitable of Charlotte to serve up a bunch of little corpses, now would it?"

Richard came to Mark's rescue. "Debbie's graphic realism, Mark, is only slightly less obvious than her motive. Given half a chance, she'd tuck away every raw oyster on the table."

"Yeah, well —" Mark's enthusiasm had cooled somewhat. "Maybe I'll try the clams."

"Good choice, Mark." Debbie smiled reassuringly. "You'll just love the clams. The steam may not always 'do them in,' so to speak — but it does render them comatose."

Mark reached for the smoked salmon.

"THE SQUALL HIT US WITH A VENGEANCE," RICHARD told them as he recounted the dark hours that preceded *Warm Winds'* ghostly arrival in Metro. "It came out of nowhere and hit us broadside, in that order."

"But what were you doing on a close haul?" Pete cut in. "You must have been heading almost directly into that nor'wester."

"We were." Debbie picked up the story, along with her third or fourth oyster. "The Coast Guard told us you had confiscated the log book, lieutenant, so you must already know that we had initially set a course for home."

"243 °," the lieutenant confirmed, "off Tree Island."

"That's right. It was mid-morning, sometime, cloudy but smooth sailing. I was at the helm. Rich was below, updating the log. And it was then I first saw the Thunderbird."

"Debbie called me up on deck," Richard said as he took up the tale again, "and we watched the boat for some time. She looked to be in irons. *The Tired Tush,* I mean. Drifting in toward Desolation Rock and certain disaster. We couldn't see anyone aboard."

"In *irons?*" Mark queried.

"Lying up in the wind, Mark, with her sails luffing – uh, just flapping out of control. Anyway, I brought *Warm Winds* as high up on the wind as I could, and headed for the stricken boat."

"We hoped to get a line on her," Debbie explained, "and pull her clear of the rocks. But before we could get close enough, the squall hit."

"What happened after Richard went over the side?"

"I was left alone on board," Debbie responded grimly. "My first thought was to bring *Warm Winds* about, but she was heeled so far over that I couldn't even stand upright. We'd been trailing the skiff from the stern, so I tried to crawl back and get into it. But the moment I freed the line, the wind tore it right out of my hands. All I could think to do then, was to grab a life-ring from the taffrail and go over the side. I just had to get to Rich before he drowned."

"And you apparently did," the lieutenant acknowledged with a glance at a very much alive Richard, "so what happened then?"

"Well, by the time I struggled over to him, and had maneuvered him into the life-ring, *Warm Winds* had veered away, out of reach. I had no choice then but to head for Desolation Rock."

"What about *The Tired Tush?*"

"She was driven hard aground, lieutenant, before we reached the rock. Rich had started to come around (thank God!), or I don't know how I'd have gotten him ashore — if you can call getting up on Desolation Rock, going ashore."

"You still haven't seen anything of the crew or the owners of the Thunderbird?"

"I did see *someone,* or some *thing,*" Debbie recalled disconcertedly, "but I can't say with any certainty *who,* or *what* it was. Just a dark shape popping up out of the churning water, next to *Warm Winds'* listing hull. It seemed to be grabbing for the leeward rail, trying to scramble aboard. It was all black and shiny, lieutenant, like a large seal —"

"Or someone in a black wet-suit?" Mark put in.

Debbie nodded vacantly. "I guess."

"The rest you know, lieutenant." Richard was methodically adding to an already heaping pile of picked-over crab shells that littered the table in front of him. "The squall didn't last long, and when the wind did finally die down, we climbed aboard what was left of *The Tired Tush,* to dry out and wait for rescue."

"Is it common for a wind to come up like that, so unexpectedly," Mark asked, "and subside so quickly?"

"Old salts have a rhyme for weather like that," the almost

forgotten Skinner suddenly proclaimed from his elevated perch. He looked almost Biblical, sitting there, silhouetted against the fog with his winged halo slowly spinning. He recited solemnly: *"Long foretold, long last; short warning, soon past."*

"Old salts have a rhyme for everything," Richard laughed. "And trust Skinner to know them all."

"I wonder if they've got a rhyme," the lieutenant said thoughtfully, "for a naked Suzy Q., or a black mermaid?"

"Or something called *Blue Serge?*" Mark added cryptically.

"I DON'T KNOW NOTHIN' 'BOUT NO SUZY Q.," SKINNER told the six upturned faces beneath him, "an' I ain't never seen no black mermaid nowheres." He hesitated reminiscently. "Jus' white ones," he reflected with a secret smile. *"But, I* do know what *blue serge* means, as any ol' salt worth his vittles should."

"That so?" The lieutenant reached into her red leather handbag. "Then maybe you can interpret this want-ad for us."

Skinner took the folded newspaper and read aloud the advertisement that had been circled in red ink. "Suzy Q., 48-123, 327, BLUE SERGE."

"Well?"

Skinner cogitated silently and was not about to be rushed. He scratched at his patch of weeds, stirring up a small cloud of dust and debris. "Those first two numbers," he said finally, "48-123, sounds to me like coordinates, looten'nt. You know, like 48 ° latitude and 123 ° longitude. An' if I'm not mistook, that partic'lar position'd likely be some'eres right out here in the straits."

Pete had already reached behind him for a chart of the local waters, and he and Richard were soon spreading it out before them on the table.

"Skinner's right," Richard exclaimed grudgingly. "Give or take a few 'minutes,' those two bearings intersect over Tree Island."

"Tree Island? Then the other number, 327, could be a course heading — "

"You got it." Skinner chuckled sagely as they all leaned over the chart to watch Richard draw in the course line. "Which oughta take yu right smack onta Desolation Rock, right?"

"He's right," Richard conceded sourly, "but what in hell has all this got to do with Suzy Q.?"

"And where does *Blue Serge* fit in?" Mark persisted.

Cathy Carruthers eyed the grinning Skinner threateningly. "Come on, you old buzzard, give us the rest of it."

The old man was enjoying the attention he was getting and he seemed determined to make the most of it. "You got t' member back a piece," he told them as he tucked a wad of snoose under his lower lip, "back b' fore th' days uv depth-sounders and sonar, when th' only way a sailor could find a shoalin' bottom was with a 'lead-line.' And as I recall, that line would be 'bout twenty-five fathoms long (for a small yacht the size *o' Warm Winds),* measured off in fathoms by 'marks' or 'deeps.' An' then to make it easier to tally, they 'flagged' the line at the diff'rent marks. Leather strips, fer instance, was used to mark off two, three and ten fathoms; white calico at five; red bunting at seven — *and,* looten'nt, mam, at thirteen fathoms yu got yer *blue serge.*''

"Can you be sure of this, Skinner?"

"Can the tide turn at twilight?"

The lieutenant looked to Richard and Pete for confirmation, and Skinner wheezed out a high-pitched cackle as they both shrugged their shoulders.

"Like it or not, looten'nt," the crusty old mariner continued, "what yu got here is a gen-u-ine type-writ treasure map. That's my figurin'. I don't know jus' what Davy Jones got hidden down there, under them thirteen fathoms, but there ain't but one way t' find out."

"We're all ears," the lieutenant sighed with a skeptical glance around the table.

"First off, mam, yu got t' get a good boat under yu. Then yu do jus' what that want-ad says: yu point out from Tree Island ona headin' uv 327 ° (makin' sure, o' course, yer compass be True swung). And then, mam, bye 'n' bye, when yu start bearin' down on Desolation Rock, yu keep a sharp eye on yer depth-sounder, an' when yu start shoalin' in t' thirteen fathoms, yu jus' hove-to an' drop the hook."

"And?"

Skinner shook his untidy old head. "Do I gotta spell out the whole uv it fer yu?" He grimaced with feigned impatience. "Richard's no stranger t'that new underwater contrivancin', now is he? Well then, jus' git him into his gear an' hustle him over th' side t'have a look."

"For *what*, Skinner?"

"For the same damn thing what Miss Q. was after, mam. Look, th' way I see it, that black mermaid warn't none other than Suzy Q., herself, an' she was right on course with that message in th' want-ad when Rich 'n' Deb showed up unexpected like. Still, the whole finale mighta ended right then 'n' there, plain 'n' simple (cause at that point, who'd a knowd a treasure from a teapot, eh — even at spittin' distance?). No, mam, it took that damn squall t'come blowin' in t'make bouillabaisse outta an ever'day servin' uv clear fish soup."

"Bouillabaisse?"

"Fish soup?"

Skinner wet a finger to mark the wind before propelling a blob of tobacco juice out into the fog. "If yu want t'see this whole thing clear t'the horizon," he told the small gathering below him with a wheezy, almost ominous certainty, "yu jus' got t'go back t'the beginnin', d'yu see, n'do ag'in ever'thin' what Suzy Q. did —"

Debbie gave an involuntary little shudder. "Not quite *everything*," she cautioned.

"Well, not *ever'*thin," Skinner conceded. "Don't see no call t'go naked —" He crinkled his watery green eyes down at a clearly disconcerted Debbie. " 'Less o'course, yu *want to*."

IT WAS THE MORNING OF DAY THREE AFTER *WARM Winds* had come drifting in out of the fog. The time, 6 A.M. Mark steered the gray Chevy into one of the many roadside viewpoints that overlooked Metro's beautiful Beachville harbor. He braked to a gentle stop and turned the key. In the seat beside him, Lieutenant Cathy Carruthers gave him a questioning look.

"We're early," Mark said with a yawn. "I thought you might want to kick this thing around a little before we join the others."

The lieutenant nodded and turned her head thoughtfully toward the ocean. The sun had just begun to take its first peek at the new day, warming the edges of the crisp night air. The fog had lifted and, except for scattered pockets of morning mist that still clung tenaciously to some of the off-shore islands, the view was tranquil and clear. In the middle distance, a small powerboat silently skimmed the water's surface with the dreamy similitude of a beetle in a fish pond. A seagull shrieked.

"I can't believe I'm doing this," the lieutenant muttered querulously. "A treasure hunt, no less. How in hell did I *ever* get conned into it?"

"Everyone loves a parade," Mark chuckled softly, *"and* a treasure hunt. And from what I can see, we're the only ones who haven't yet shown up for it."

The lieutenant followed his gaze down over the viewpoint rail to where, almost directly below them, the government wharf jutted out into the water like an accusing finger. And at its seaward tip, looking from that height and distance like a child's toy, *Warm Winds* sat patiently at her moorings while her crew of would-be pirates made last minute preparations for the day's jaunt.

They were all there; the men on deck, Pete bending on a new stays'l, Richard, fine-tuning the shrouds; the girls, Debbie and Charlotte, their blonde heads visible through the open companionway hatch, bustling about in the galley. Even Skinner was aboard, alone on the after deck. He looked to be running a small black flag or pennant up the backstay.

"They've sure done a beautiful clean-up job on *Warm Winds,* " the lieutenant noted appreciatively, "but what is that man Skinner up to? It looks like — oh, my God, it *is!*"

"The Jolly Roger," Mark laughed. "Can you believe it?"

"I can't believe any of this," the lieutenant replied grimly, "including that want-ad that Skinner keeps insisting is a treasure map."

"Then what are we doing here?"

"As ridiculous as it may sound, Mark, that want-ad *was* placed *before* Suzy Q. was killed. And, as it happens, it's the only lead we have to her identity. We've *got* to follow it up."

"So what do you expect to find," Mark nodded in the direction of the off-shore islands, "out there."

"Well, certainly not fifteen men on a dead man's chest, that's for sure. Still, we have to assume, at this point at least, that Suzy Q. could have been engaged in some kind of nefarious activity. Even that Skinner (God forbid) might be right. Whatever."

"What about the idea of a drug-meet?"

"Hmmm. That again, eh? Could be, I guess. But according to Richard and Debbie Raines, there was only one involved — which reminds me, Mark, did Bones get any kind of a line on that Thunderbird?"

"*The Tired Tush?* It was homemade, lieutenant, as a lot of Thunderbirds are, apparently. It wasn't registered."

"So we don't even know who owns it?"

"Not only that. Unless someone steps forward to claim it, we never bloody will." Mark pursed his lips thoughtfully. "You just said that there was only one boat involved, lieutenant. I counted two."

"*Warm Winds?* You think Richard and Debbie could be in on this. Maybe even — drug connected?"

"We don't have any proof they're not."

"True. In fact, all we have is *their version* of what might, or might not have happened out there."

"And, for that matter, lieutenant, the Duhaneys could be involved as well. Even Skinner."

"Involved in *what,* Mark? Let's not get carried away now. It was Charlotte, remember, who told me about the want-ad."

"Big deal."

The lieutenant eyed her partner closely. "I see what you mean. Big deal, indeed, if all we find out there is a rocky bottom."

"Especially when we're going to have to rely on one of our prime suspects to do the looking for us. What.if there is something down there besides rocks, lieutenant, and what if Richard is part of the scam? Do you think he's likely to fill us in on whatever he's up to?"

The lieutenant shot a quick glance at her watch. "We aren't due to sail until 6:30, Mark, and it's not ten past yet. Do you think you can make it to my place and back in twenty minutes?"

"With time to spare." He turned the key and the Chevy roared to life. "What'd you forget?"

"My scuba gear." She flipped on the siren and reached for the portable cherry. "It could be dangerous at thirteen fathoms, Mark — without a buddy."

"Yeah," Mark acceded warily, "and it could even be a damn sight more dangerous *with* one."

WITH A FRESH TEN-KNOT BREEZE OFF THE STARBOARD
quarter, Skinner was humanely given a healthy dollop of neat rum
and a two-hour watch on the port bow. With a change of course (or
a change of wind), he could just as quickly be watching where he'd
been, instead of where he was going. His immediate fate, it seemed,
was not so dependent on the wind's whim, as on its whiff.

Warm Winds had slipped smoothly away from the docks under
her own power. It was not until they were well out into open water
that the sails had been hoisted and the diesel shut down. The resulting
quiet, the slightly-heeled forward thrust of the boat was met with a
sense of sudden awe and exhilaration by all aboard. Now, running
proudly with the wind, under taut, towering main and jenny, Warm
Winds was quickly dispelling any last lingering memory of the storm-
ravaged derelict that had come ghosting in out of the fog only three
days before.

The lieutenant and Mark found a sheltered spot along the upper
side of the low-profile cabin. From there, they had a good view of the
entire deck area, as well as any activity that might occur in the open
galley. And they could effectively maintain an innocent-appearing
surveillance on all members of the impromptu crew.

"Look for signs of unguarded, obverse intent," the lieutenant
cautioned Mark in a whisper, "or any indication of ulterior
involvement."

Mark curled his lip indulgently. "You said?"

"Keep your eyes peeled for anything suspicious."

"That's what I thought you said."

She eyed him curiously. "Then why do you keep looking at me?"

"Because, mine confrere, I find you infinitely more pleasing to
look upon than Skinner. You smell better, too."

The lieutenant laughed as she turned to look in the old man's
direction. He was slouched in the bow in an untidy, indolent heap,
rocking idly with every dip and yaw of the boat. Above his grizzled
head, she noticed with some amusement, a couple of silver-winged
fishflies had taken over halo duty from their landward cousins.

However, in spite of Skinner's somewhat antisocial effluvial
emanations, he did not appear to fit the lieutenant's definition of
"anything suspicious." Nor, for that matter, did the rest of the crew.
Richard, at the helm, seemed oblivious to anything but the precise

functioning of ship and sail, while Pete, still tidying up loose-lying lines and halyards, looked to be equally abstracted. Even the girls had a guiltless, happy hustle about them.

"Gather 'round, m'hearties. Coffee time." Debbie had popped out of the galley with a tray of steaming mugs. "Name yer p'ison, mates. Sugar, cream or coffee-*royale*."

The early morning dollop of Cap'n Morgan was graciously declined by all but Skinner. And no one noticed (or so it seemed), as that feisty old son of Neptune lay claim to the rest of the bottle and trundled off to the bow with it. "First time I've seen rum used as an anti-pollutant," Mark whispered to a knowing, grinning Debbie.

In the midst of the ensuing coffee-klatsch, Richard quietly handed the wheel over to Pete and drew the lieutenant off to one side. "It's not going to be quite as easy as Skinner makes it sound, lieutenant. Finding the exact spot, I mean."

"You can't hold that accurate a course?"

"Oh, I can hold the course, all right. And the depth-sounder is accurate to within a few inches, given a decent bottom, of course. What bothers me, lieutenant, is the time of day — "

"The *time* of *day?*" But even as she spoke, the lieutenant's troubled blue eyes were slowly brightening, as though a light had come on inside her lovely head. "But of course — " She thumped her brow lightly with the heel of her hand. " — *the tide.*"

"Right. And this time of year, I'd guess the tide to be running about five feet. I'll check the tide-tables for the night and the time of the storm, just to be sure. And, lieutenant, that might not sound like much of a differential, five feet, but whether it is or it isn't, the chance of our finding anything at thirteen fathoms is going to depend largely on the fall-off at that particular point."

"Uh-huh. I see what you mean. If the approach to Desolation Rock is reasonably steep, our pinpointing should be correspondingly accurate, even with that five-foot disparity. On the other hand, if the ocean floor shoals gradually, it could widen our search area to a point where we'll need a lot more than just two divers to be effective."

"*Two* divers?"

"I brought my scuba gear with me. I'm going down with you."

"Oh?"

"That doesn't suit you?"

Warm Winds' tow-headed skipper favored her with a determined little smile. He was a big man, well over six feet, a somewhat less massive, work-hardened version of Mark Swanson. "I guess now's as good a time as any to remind you, lieutenant, there can only be one skipper on a boat. And on *Warm Winds,* that's me. As long as we're afloat, *Miss* Cathy Carruthers, *I* give the orders."

"Hmmm." The lieutenant matched his circuitous little smile with one of her own. "Suppose I put that in the form of a request?"

"Are you qualified?"

"Yes."

"At thirteen fathoms?"

"Would you believe — thirty?"

Raines narrowed his eyes. "Are you serious?"

"Yes. But it's not something that I'd want to do everyday."

"Guess not." The man's wind-weathered face softened perceptibly. He screwed his mouth into an awkward grin. "Tell you the truth, lieutenant, I wasn't looking forward to going down thirteen fathoms alone, without a buddy." His chuckle was a little spurious, the lieutenant thought, as he held out a leathery hand. "Be glad of the company," he said.

THE NEXT FEW HOURS WERE ROUTINE AND RELATIVELY uneventful. They had smooth sailing most of the way, until an unscheduled change of wind forced them to endure two choppy port tacks and one to starboard. Still, by early afternoon, they were standing off Tree Island. All hands appeared eager to begin the final, crucial leg of their mysterious voyage. The new course of 327 ° (courtesy of Suzy Q.), gave them a welcome, steady beam wind and a healthy bow wave.

"How fast are we going?" Mark hollered at a smiling, wind-blown Debbie, now at the helm.

"Seven knots, give or take."

"Seems faster."

"Always does, on a reach."

Mark managed to look vacant and impressed at the same time. "How long before we get there?" he shouted into the wind.

"We should spot the Desolation Rock marker in about an hour."

"And?"

"Add another hour."

Everyone but Skinner and Debbie had gone below to gather around the large booth-type table, off the galley. Mark joined them. He poured himself a cup of coffee and sat down next to Charlotte. Richard and Pete, opposite, had the book of tide-tables open in front of them.

"The tide was on the ebb that night, lieutenant." Raines spoke without raising his head. "Time of the storm, I mean. We're looking at about three and a half feet."

"And now?"

"It's on the rise. But there shouldn't be more than about a foot differential, by the time we get into position. Hardly worth worrying about."

"Any suggestions?"

Raines shoved the tide book to one side. There was a large, detailed chart under the glass top of the table. He pointed with a stubby finger.

"Well, it looks from the chart like a steepish bottom. And rocky. That could be either good, or bad. Bottoms can be tricky. Might be wise to switch the depth-sounder from FATHOMS to FEET, about a hundred yards off. We'll hove-to, then, right on seventy-eight."

The lieutenant smiled. "You're the skipper. Now, how about an E.T.A.?"

Everyone watched Mark then, as he leaned thoughtfully over the chart, his thick beefy finger tracing a course that was about fifty nautical miles off the mark. "Uuuh — I'd say, 'bout two hours, lieutenant." He looked around the table with feigned sagacity. "Give or take."

And as though on cue, the cabin was rocked by shrieks of uninhibited laughter. Richard, finally, with tears streaming down his face, found his voice. And when he did, it all began again.

"The funny thing is," he choked, *"he's right!"*

DESOLATION ROCK WAS A LOW PROFILE OF SOLID granite, barely visible above the surface of the water. It was the size of a city block. In a heavy sea, it would be next to invisible. But on its bleak and shallow crest, a huge white beacon stood like a silent sentinel. And every five seconds, in a 360 degree arc, it flashed out a solemn warning.

"It looks like a candle on a cake," Mark mused aloud.

Raines squinted up at him. "Huh?"

"The marker light."

"Oh. Yeah." But neither the light nor the threatening rocks were what held the skipper's attention. His eyes were glued to the depth-sounder, mounted on the after-side of the cabin bulkhead. He had switched it on at about 100 fathoms, then monitored the slow progress of the red electronic signal, as it inched around the edge of the dial. When it got to 25, he leaned over the wheel and flipped the calibrations to FEET. The bleep jumped instantly to 150.

"We're getting close."

Mark shot a concerned look ahead where Desolation Rock loomed up off the bow like a watery tomb. "A little too close, maybe?"

Raines did not appear to hear the warning. "I'm going to bring her up into the wind," he sang out with casual authority. "Let's get her undressed, Pete. Smartly now. You take the jenny. Skinner?"

"Aye, skipper."

"You drop the hook."

Skinner belched affirmatively.

"We're shoaling fast, now —100 — 90 — all hands! — 80 — 75! Mark, mind your head!"

The heavy boom whistled over Mark's head as the boat suddenly veered to starboard, and there was a great frenzy and milling about as the rigging shuddered, chains rattled, sails flapped and fell. It was a time of clamor and orderly confusion that peaked and ended as quickly as it had begun. Then, in the subdued after-effort of furling canvas, hauling taut on the anchor, cinching in, stowing lines — a sense of ominous expectancy seemed to settle quietly over the boat.

It was into that uneasy calm that Cathy Carruthers emerged from the companionway hatch like a second sunrise. Her remarkable six-foot physique was sheathed in a bright yellow wet-suit that appeared to be in perpetual conflict to reveal and conceal at one and the same time. The reveal side was currently winning, hands down.

"*Ma-ma mia!*" Richard Raines drew black looks from Mark and Debbie as he sauntered aft with wide-eyed approval. "How *about* that — a buddy with a body!"

"Down, boy," Debbie cautioned, then added in a back-to-business voice, "come on, I'll help you get your gear on." She shoved him toward the companionway hatch, then followed him down into the bowels of the boat. When she reemerged five minutes later, she beckoned to Pete. "He wants you," she said simply, then nonchalantly ambled forward to maneuver Charlotte into a quiet huddle.

Mark shot a curious look at his senior partner and got a knowing wink in reply. He moved close to her on the pretext of straightening a twisted tank strap. "I've got this feeling," he said in a surreptitious whisper. "Watch yourself down there."

"I'll do that," she replied softly. "You, too. Keep your eyes open."

He tapped her tank as Richard, then Pete, began to ascend the companionway ladder. She turned toward them.

"Ready to go, skipper?"

Raines answered with a ready smile. He was fully geared in black; wet-suit, fins, tank, et al. "Whenever you say, body — uh, buddy."

He parted the lifeline just aft of the port shrouds, then turned with a grin to extend an open hand. The lieutenant duck-walked to his side and took his big fist in one of her own. She gave him a quick nod and they slipped over the side. There was a single, unified splash.

Mark watched as the yellow and black suited bodies jack-knifed under water like a coup of performing dolphins preparing for a leap. But instead of shooting up toward the surface, they headed straight down into the murky depths beneath the boat. They were almost out of sight when Mark felt the world around him suddenly explode in a flash of blinding light and pain.

THEY DESCENDED SLOWLY, THEIR HEADLAMPS TURNED on. The only sounds were the gurgle of escaping bubbles and the rhythmic, hollow rush of air through the demand-valves on their aqualungs. They had first located the anchor line off the bow, then Raines had taken the lead and followed it down into depths that were cold and heavy with plankton. But even at thirteen fathoms, the sun still managed to penetrate the murky water. It cast an eerie glow over a tilting ocean floor that was strewn with sedimental rock and almost hidden under an undulating carpet of sea moss and rockweed.

Raines hovered weightlessly above the snared anchor as he unclipped a portable lantern from his weighted belt. He lashed it to the chain-lead on the anchor line and flicked it on. He swung to face the lieutenant, pointing to his wrist watch, holding up five fingers. He flashed his compass and swept his other arm in a 90degree arc. She lieutenant nodded and repeated the signals, confirming her designated search area and a rendezvous time of five minutes. The lieutenant turned away from him then, and with one engaging wag of her yellow derriere, she was gone.

Raines waited until she had dissolved into a watery blur, then he turned and headed off in the opposite direction. The lieutenant, with a stealthy glance over one shoulder, saw him go. And in the dwindling illumination of the rendezvous light, she watched him suddenly veer and angle up an incline of rocks and lichen, into an area not covered by the proposed search. She let him get ahead of her, extinguishing her own light as she paralleled his course. When she could no longer see him or the lantern on the anchor line, she made an abrupt right angle turn in an effort to intercept him. Thirty seconds later, in the cloudy distance, she saw his light.

He was not aware of her approach. He was bent intently over a florescent orange bag that was tethered to an upright metal shaft, imbedded in the ocean floor. But when she reached out and touched his shoulder, he whirled, his eyes wide with alarm.

Raines gave a bubbly snort of displeasure when he recognized her. He moved in close and pressed his face-mask tight against hers with an angry *clack!* His voice came through to her in a burst of bubbles, distorted but intelligible.

"Whatta yu trying to do? Scare the bejesus outta me?"

"You want I should phone ahead?"

Raines sputtered irately into his mouthpiece but Cathy Carruthers was no longer listening.

"What's in the bag?" she burbled.

"How'n hell should I know?"

"You went right to it," she insisted. "You *knew* where to look."

The frustration and smoldering hostility in the man's eyes suddenly flared like twin lasers. Before she could shove away from him, he had reached out, grabbed one of her breathing tubes, and yanked it free. She tasted seawater as a torrent of air and bubbles shot toward the surface. And through the wavering, watery turmoil that abruptly engulfed her, she caught the unmistakable glint of naked steel.

ON BOARD *WARM WINDS*, PETE DUHANEY HAD SWUNG hard with the weighted sap, then stood back, anxious, as the big detective seemed to take forever to react to the vicious blow. But the heavy shoulders finally, slowly drooped, and Mark toppled forward over the rail. Duhaney waited for the splash before turning to the two women.

"One of you get the shotgun out of the cabin," he said tersely, "and we'll need the boarding-ladder." He stuffed the sap into his back pocket and reached for a gaff-pole that was slotted in against the shrouds. "I'll keep him occupied, but *hurry*, damn it."

Debbie headed for the cabin while Charlotte began rummaging in the cockpit's under-seat stowage for the ladder. "Where is it?" she flustered. There was a hint of panic in her voice.

"It's there, some bloody place. Jesus, woman, just *look*, will you?"

Mark's head took that moment to pop to the surface. The shock of the cold water had cleared his brain but he was having trouble focusing his eyes. A large, looming shadow, *Warm Winds*, filled his vision, and he could see a smaller blur of movement, slightly higher, that seemed to be lunging at him. Threatening. Before he could move away, something hard and pointed stabbed painfully into the hollow of his neck, forcing him back, and down. He tried to suck in a lungful of air before going under, but seawater was already swirling in around him, backing up into his nose and throat, making him retch and gag.

He groped blindly at the source of pain and his fingers closed over the iron tang of the gaff. He tried to ease it away from against his neck, but as he struggled, he was inadvertently forcing himself deeper down into the water, standing himself on end, his feet buoyed up toward the surface. His left foot, thrashing out, came into jarring contact with the side of *Warm Winds'* rounded steel hull and he felt, rather than heard, the hollow ringing echo.

To Mark, it was the bell for the last round.

With his lungs in the grip of a giant, squeezing fist, he maneuvered his body so that his feet were planted firmly against the hull. Then, in one final, desperate bid for survival, he pistoned back with his heavily muscled thighs, with every ounce of strength remaining. There was a momentary tightening on the gaff-pole, then a quick release — and he was suddenly shooting through the water, off and away from the boat. Seconds later, he surfaced, gasping for air.

He had hardly filled his lungs, when Pete Duhaney's frantic face bobbed out of the water, directly in front of him. The man's eyes and mouth were wide with panic.

"Help!" he choked. "I — I can't swim."

Mark looked on dispassionately as Duhaney splashed and struggled to keep his head above the water. "You tried to drown me," he snarled. "You sniveling bastard."

"No, no! I was trying (choke) to reach you — to (cough) pull you out —"

Mark's big right fist skimmed the water and caught the man squarely on the point of his jaw. " — and I'm just trying to shake hands," he snorted. Duhaney's eyes glazed and closed, and he sank peacefully out of sight.

"He's going to drown!" It was Charlotte. She had just hooked the boarding-ladder into position, over the port rail, and was kneeling behind it, livid with fear and shock. "*You can't just let him drown!*"

Mark had already reached into the water and had Duhaney firmly by the hair. He was not in the business of killing people. Not even someone who had just tried to kill him. He swam with the man to the ladder, and there, with Charlotte pulling, and him shoving, they managed to get the water-logged Duhaney up onto the deck.

But then, as Mark tried to follow, with one hand and a foot on the ladder, he found himself squinting up into the barrel of a 12-gauge shotgun. Debbie Raines was on the other end of it, looking more scared than murderous. Especially, Mark decided ruefully, when she closed her eyes and pulled the trigger.

ON THOSE OCCASIONS WHEN CATHY CARRUTHERS felt the need to awaken the specter of the Amazon that slept within her, the resulting metamorphosis was often swift and spectacular. She had not expected the sudden assault on her air supply. It had left her momentarily disoriented. And it had given Raines that thin edge of surprise, allowing him to move in on her, knife drawn, held low in both hands.

And it was in that split second, before myth became reality, that Cathy Carruthers was only able to thwart, and not totally evade, the first deadly thrust. She spun in the water on her own axis, as the knife advanced, offering to her assailant a somewhat less lethal, if no less vulnerable a target. And in the instant that followed, as naked steel sliced into the fleshy hill of her right buttock, it was not Cathy Carruthers who felt the pain. It was the Amazon.

And it was the Amazon, with the inherent speed born of a jungle kill, that reached behind her and took a knife-wielding wrist in each hand. Fingers, instantaneously paralyzed, deserted their hold on the knife's grip as she brought her arms up over her head with torpedo-like force, slicing the man through the water in a giant arc that terminated abruptly on the rocky ocean floor.

Blood leaked from around the deeply imbedded blade in her hip, but the flow, she noticed, was minimal, held in check by the knife itself and the chilling pressure of the deep salt water. She decided to leave it there, in its fleshy scabbard, until she could reach the surface and, hopefully, medical assistance.

Air was her most desperate need at the moment, and she filled her aching lungs from the tank on Raines' back. Then, with the florescent orange bag in tow, and Raines in an encircling, crippling grip of steel, she floated slowly toward the surface, sharing the one remaining air supply with her captive. The carefully monitored ascent was necessarily slow, and when finally she, and the bag, and a still groggy Richard Raines, all popped to the surface together, it was just in time to witness the culmination of Mark's and Debbie's desperate, deadly drama.

INSTEAD OF A DEAFENING ROAR, AS THOSE WHO watched the horrifying scene expected, there was a hollow, metallic *click!* And instead of ten pounds of raw meat where his head should have been, Mark's still unscathed countenance reflected the awesome relief of one who had just been plucked from the brink of certain death.

An unkempt, clown-like apparition suddenly materialized behind the now drooping, trembling figure of Debbie Raines. Skinner, in all his abhorrence, with cigarette dangling, smoke and fumes rising, flies cavorting, stood grinning out at the world like a one-man circus. He held three red shotgun shells in one triumphantly raised hand, while with the other, he commandeered the gun from the girl's unresisting fingers.

"I took pr'cautions," he chuckled, as though enjoying a private joke, "on one o' my freq'nt li'l jaunts to th' head. Th' way I see'it, yu can't never trust a femin-ine gal with a loaded gun."

"Thank God for strong urges and weak kidneys."

At the sound of the voice, Mark turned to see his partner's golden head moving over the water toward him. She had shoved back the diving hood and face mask but, still, she was almost upon him before he noticed the grim look of pain and pleading in her haunting, liquid blue eyes.

"I'm hurting," she told him softly.

Mark reacted with compassion and dispatch. In quick succession, the orange bag, then the bleary-eyed Raines were tossed unceremoniously up onto the deck. And with his arm around her waist, supporting her, he and his sailing partner came up the boarding-ladder together. They were just stepping onto the cluttered deck when he noticed the knife protruding from the yellow wet-suit.

"Skinner," he ordered sharply, "reload that gun and herd those four misfits up on the bow. And do whatever you have to, to keep them there."

"Aye, matey."

"And hang onto this." He kicked the orange bag in Skinner's direction, then tenderly scooped up his own golden treasure in his massive arms and headed for the cabin. But before disappearing with her down the companionway ladder, he hesitated just long enough to give the motley group on the bow a look of dark intimidation.

"You bunch better start praying like bloody crazy," he told them grimly, "that this lady is going to be A-okay."

CATHY CARRUTHERS WAS STRETCHED OUT ON HER stomach on the settee in *Warm Winds'* spacious lounge area. The tank suit she had worn under her diving gear was tugged up, exposing her right buttock. Her face was buried in her hands and pressed tight against the cushions.

She moaned aloud with indignation and pain. "This has got to be just downright *embarrassing!*"

Mark chuckled. The danger had passed. "I could always send for Skinner," he told her, "though I think he'd infect the wound just by looking at it."

"Damn it, Mark. Just get it *over* with."

The blade had come out easily, if painfully, and he had already cleansed the open gash with antiseptic. There was surprisingly little blood. He had found a first-aid kit in the ship's head, and was now applying a clean bandage, taping it in place.

"How much longer?" she groaned.

Mark straightened and gave the good side of her engaging rump a friendly pat. "Done," he said. She lost no time in squirming over onto her side.

"You'll need a tetanus shot, I imagine, soon's we get you in," Mark said brightly, "but I think you'll live."

"Thank you, Doctor Swanson. That is nice to know."

Mark covered her with a blanket. "How about a shot of rum to ease the trauma?"

"Whose? Mine or yours?" She gave him a knowing look. "And speaking of rum, Mark, where's Skinner?"

"He's holding our *fierce*some and not-so-friendly foursome at bay with the shotgun. I've taken it for granted he's one of the good guys." He handed her a tumbler half full of straight rum. "Have fun, pardner, while I go topside and see about getting us under way." He turned to leave.

"Mark." She looked up at him with a constrained but woeful little smile. "Thanks for the R and R."

Mark shrugged. "No big deal." He mirrored her smile. "I was just bumming around, anyway."

She looked for something to throw at him but the only thing handy was the knife, and that, she decided, had done enough damage already.

WARM WINDS GLIDED QUIETLY THROUGH THE VELVET night. In the distance, a full-round moon hovered like a watchful eye, just above the horizon. The moon and the boat seemed to be umbilically linked by a streak of light that glittered across the placid water between them. The only sounds were of the boat's own gentle impetus, the comforting, resonant chug of the diesel, the soft creak and tug of the idle rigging, and the unending, bubbly ripple of the bow wave.

"It's a night made for dreams," Cathy Carruthers mused poetically. She was stretched out in the cockpit, on the long, fore-and-aft seat that Mark had padded with extra cushions and blankets. And himself. She had her head in the crook of his big arm, lazing against his chest.

"Don't you mean — nightmares?" Mark muttered, recalling his own recent brush with death.

Skinner chuckled in his high-pitched, wheezy way. He was perched up on the pilot seat behind the helm, seeming somehow secure (if not particularly refreshed) in his own debilitating aura that even the cool night air was unable to render totally innocuous. He had a new, near-full bottle of rum in his pudgy fist and the flies had settled down on his hoary old scalp for a well-earned rest.

"That bunch back there jus' might have somethin' t'add t'that," he said with a bleak laugh that seemed to bubble up from his own bellybound bilge of old rum and snoose scuz.

Mark glanced back over his shoulder to where their four prisoners sat shackled together in an inflatable dinghy, skimming along behind the boat on the end of a thirty-foot tow-line. He could just make out their faces in the faint glow of the running lights. They did not look to be enjoying the ride.

"What will happen to all that Horse we salvaged out of the orange bag?" Mark asked idly. "There must be a street value there of three to four million dollars."

"At least." The lieutenant nestled her flaxen head deeper into the hollow of Mark's receptive shoulder. "We'll just turn it all over to the Narcs, along with those four would-be drug-pushers."

"So it'll be their baby from here on out?"

"Correct. But we're not off the hook, Mark. What we — uh, *you* will have to worry about now (seeing that I'm incapacitated), is a lengthy and detailed report —"

"You're too kind."

" — on how we managed to get ourselves into this mess in the first place."

"Talk about a 'bum' rap," Mark lamented. "Besides, we don't even *know* what really happened —"

"Speak f'r y'rself, sarg'nt." Skinner took a fresh pinch of snoose and lit up a cigarette. Counting the liquor, he now had pollution going for him on three fronts. "Whilst you was down there in th' cabin, mam, gettin' yer purdy fantail tended to, I was up here havin' a reg'lar ol' chin-wag with them bunch o' live-boards."

"So?"

"So yu want to hear about it, or doncha?"

"I want to hear about it."

"Hmmmph!" Skinner put another match to his flagging cigarette and belched. A tongue of blue flame leapt out into the night, and he had to wait for the dragon-fumes to abate before beginning his narrative. "It all started," he said finally, "with Charlotte seein' that Suzy Q. advert in th' noospapers. She figgered, right off, it was directions to a drug cache an' told Pete about it. They didn't do nothin', though, Pete 'n' Charlotte, not until Rich 'n' Deb showed up, 'bout 2 A.M. —"

"Richard and Debbie? But — "

"Yeah, I know. They was s'pposed to be over t'Hidden Cove that night. But I was aboard th' *Neverset Horizon,* looten't, 'n' I seen 'em. They musta doctored up that log book, later on, figurin' t'throw you off some. Anyhow, they got themselves t'gether in a conflab, aboard *Warm Winds.* Charlotte had th' thing all ciphered out, she told 'em, 'cept fer the BLUE SERGE bit — but Debbie'd been readin' some ol' sea yarns (young fella name of Melville, I think) an' she twigged right on to it. Well, wasn't nothin' fer them t'do then, but t'go after the 'big money,' as they seen it. Pete 'n' Charlotte was t'stay an' keep an eye on home port, while Deb 'n' Rich (Rich havin' th' divin' rig 'n' all) was t'head right out t'try t'beat lil' ol' Suzy Q. to th' loot."

"Just *who was Suzy* Q., Skinner?"

"Didn't know then; don't know now. But fer a fact, looten'nt, she was in t'this drug scam up to her purdy neck. Anyhow, Rich 'n' Deb spotted her aboard *The Tired Tush* 'bout mid-mornin' th' next day, then followed her right over to Desolation Rock. When they saw her drop th' hook and go over the side in her scuba outfit, Rich moved right in. He got his own gear on while Deb hove-to, then he went over after th' girl. Twern't long for he had 'er back up on *Warm Winds* an' all tied up in 'er wet-suit. They left 'er down there in th' cabin then, figurin' on Rich goin' over th' side ag'in to get th' drug cache — but that was when th' storm hit. And, as you know, all hell busted loose."

AS SKINNER TALKED, CATHY CARRUTHERS WAS wistfully weighing the pleasure of having her left temple caressed, against the obvious denial of her professional dignity. After some deliberation, however, she decided that she'd continue to consider the matter just a little longer.

"It musta been like wrigglin' outta a straightjacket," Skinner was saying. "Without touchin' a single knot, that girl left her wet-suit in a bundle on th' cabin floor, includin' th' ropes that stayed right in place, *and* a pair of lavender panties that didn't."

"At least we know now where she lost her clothes," Mark put in.

"Yeah, well — she went hustlin' topside then, in her altogether, and caught both Deb 'n' Rich lookin' th' other way, too busy tryin' to control th' boat t'notice her. She jus' shoved them over th' side, then went scramblin' fer the anchor line. She made it, too, an' even managed t'haul the anchor up, but b'fore she could get offa th' bow, that stays'l blew itself out an' th' halyard whipped her clear up inta th' riggin'. And, well, I reckon yu know th' rest uv it."

"Hmmm. *Warm Winds* was blown away in the storm and *The Tired Tush* was beached. Then, I guess, Richard and Debbie had little choice but to head for Desolation Rock, hoping to pick up the drug cache at a later date, I suppose. That it?"

"That's it, looten'nt."

"Skinner, I'm impressed. But I can't help but feel that you put the skeleton of that little story together from garnered information. First from the four miscreants back there, and from Mark and me. But all that meat you've been padding on the bare bones of fact, sounds to me like it came from your own imagination."

Skinner grinned, and his watery sea-green eyes shimmered in the moonlight. "Sounds a little that way t'me, too, looten'nt."

"You old fake. You knew those four were up to something almost from the beginning, didn't you? Why didn't you tell us about it?"

"I did tell yu, looten'nt, when yu first come in t'the Bayside office. I told yu I'd seen 'em day b'fore last, but I guess you was just too taken up by my, uh — personality to notice."

The lieutenant drew in a slow, patient breath. "So how do you explain away the fact that it was Charlotte who told me about the ad in the first place? And *why?*"

"To throw yu off course, looten'nt. She knew you'd never figger out that sea-goin' jargon in a million years. An' fer a fact, yu never did. It wasn't until I spilled th' beans that things started goin' wrong for those would-be *pi-rates*. It was *me* what suggested th' treasure hunt, if yu 'member, an' they just didn't have no choice but t'go along with it."

"But why try to kill us? That seems a little drastic, doesn't' it?"

"Not with a few million green-ones in yer net, it don't. Th' way I see't, looten'nt, once them fellas an' their gals got as far's Desolation Rock, with yu an' th' sarg'nt in tow, an' yu bein' so dead set on goin' over th' side with young Rich — well, there jus' wasn't any turnin' back then. If they was ever goin' t'get that money, yu two jus' had t'be 'liminated, no mistake 'bout that."

"So where do you fit in, Skinner? You were just as much a threat to them as we were."

"Maybe so. But I'm not yer ever'day kind of mess-about,

looten'nt. Most people like t'pretend I'm not there, even when I am. They tend t'want t'ease me off t'one side, outta spittin' distance, yu might say, and that gives me plentya elbow room t'mess with. Oh, they'd uv got around t'me soon enough, I 'imagine, but I'd a been ready fer 'em."

Cathy Carruthers chuckled softly. "You are without doubt, Skinner, an inveterate old reprobate of the first water. But you did save our lives and for that, we thank you."

"Amen," Mark assented with feeling.

"Just one last question, Skinner."

"Aye, looten'nt."

"Whatever happened to that missing skiff?"

"And the oysters?" Mark added.

"The skiff was took away by th' storm, looten'nt, no myst'ry there, and there never was any oysters."

"Then let's see if we can't add the same kind fate to that Jolly Roger up there in the rigging, *before* we get to Metro." Cathy Carruthers groaned in grim anticipation. "I'd sure hate to have to explain *that* to the chief."

MEL D. AMES

COLD BLOOD II

Edited by Peter Sellers

Peter Robinson

Jack Barnao

Peter Sellers

John North

Eric Wright

Charlotte MacLeod

Mel D. Ames

Sara Plews

Ted Wood

Elaine Mitchell Matlow

Jas. R. Petrin

William Bankier

Tony Aspler

MOSAIC FICTION SERIES

"He's dead, Charlie. Christ Almight,
he's dead!"
"What? Who's dead?"
"The Messiah, hisself, that's who. He's
been iced, Charlie, in more ways than
one."

the devil
made me do it

NIGHT WATCHMAN OTIS SCROGGS, PADDED HIS WAY
stolidly down the short hallway behind the concession stand in Metro
Central's Memorial Arena. A glance at his watch told him it was
forty-seven minutes after three a.m. He was on schedule, in spite
of the ugly hue and cry that had arisen in the wake of the *Messiah's*
resounding victory over his arch foe, *Satan*, in the pro-wrestling
main event. Fans and wrestlers alike, of both good and evil bias, had
been seemingly bent on one last glorious moment of mayhem before
reluctantly vacating the Arena. But now, amid the shambles, and in
the deserted building's eerie hush, Otis felt grimly alone as he
approached his tenth and final check point. There was meager
comfort in the knowledge that each rendezvous point on his round of
the huge sports facility, including this one, was under constant
surveillance by closed-circuit television.

The security phone was midway along the hall, in full view of the
camera and directly across from a small walk-in freezer. The
freezer was used communally by the concession stand (for the
preservation of food), and by a never-ending flux of professional
wrestlers, all with an undying passion for the recuperative power of

frozen water, in both their ice packs and beer buckets.

Tonight, however, as Otis suddenly saw to his horror, there was more in the freezer than ice cubes and frozen franks. He did a gut-wrenching double-take at the small frosted window in the freezer door, and the hair on his scalp stiffened in a prickly sweat. A human hand, with an ugly red scar in the center of its palm, had wiped a streak of inner frost from the glass and *a benign, beared face that could belong to no one but Christ himself,* was pressed in lifeless rigor against the pane. The glazed, icy-brown eyes seemed to be locked pleadingly on Otis's own as he made a grab for the security interphone.

"Otis?" The sound of his name echoed thinly in the empty hallway. "You okay?"

Otis swallowed hard. "He's dead, Charlie. Christ Almighty, he's *dead!*"

"What? Who's dead?"

"The Messiah, hisself," Otis blurted into the mouthpiece, "that's who. He's been iced, Charlie, in more ways than one."

DETECTIVE-LIEUTENANT CATHY CARRUTHERS PICKED up her telephone on the second ring, with obvious chagrin. Her bedside digital said 5:30 A.M.

"Give me your number," she told the instrument tersely, "and I'll call you back at an earthly hour."

"This is Heller," the telephone responded, "and this is as earthy as it's going to get."

"I said *earthly*, chief, not earthy."

"Whatever — now listen up, lieutenant, I need you down here on the double. It's PR problem time again, and it's going to take a great deal of finesse and expertise on your part to — "

"On *my* part?"

"Believe you me, lieutenant, you're the only one for the job. This baby's right up your bailiwick."

"But, chief — *bailiwick?*"

"Glad to see you're with it, lieutenant, so early in the A.M." Captain Henry (Hank) Heller's voice had the cacophony of half-inch gravel rattling down an empty drainpipe. "The media is on the case already," he rasped, "like a pack of bloody jackals. They're calling it the most heinous crime since Cain slew Abel."

"But, chief — "

"And what was *the* most heinous crime, you ask?"

The lieutenant stifled a yawn. "Okay, so I'm asking. What was *the* — ?"

"That, lieutenant, is what it's all about. *That*, don't you see, is the PR problem, precisely. As a matter of fact, the morning papers have already hit the streets with it, and you wouldn't believe the screamers."

"Try me."

"In three-inch type, no less. I kid you not, lieutenant — listen, MESSIAH DIES MARTYR'S DEATH — "

"Jesus Christ!"

"Those are your words, lieutenant, not mine. And get this one, DIVINE MESSIAH SELF DESTRUCTS — and again, MESSIAH CONTRIVES OWN DEMISE —"

"Hold it, chief, *hold* it. Wait up a minute. You're obviously referring to that professional wrestler, are you not? The one who's been fighting Satan on a nightly basis?"

"Too true, but — "

"Well, then. Don't you think — uh, in view of the notoriety of the *defunctee*, so to speak, that we could discuss the sordid details of the case just a little later — ?"

"Later?" A crescendo of fresh gravel hit the drainpipe. "What's with later?"

"Because, *Mein Kapitan*, at this moment, I am somewhat indisposed."

"You're still in bed?"

"No, I am not in bed, but I *was* in the shower."

"Was?" The gravel made a chuckling sound. "My, my — when *will* they perfect those new tele-view phones?"

"And when *will you* hang up and let me — "

"Okay, okay. Just get hold of that beach bum you call a partner and meet me down at Lil' Oly's in half an hour. They open at six. I'll fill you in over breakfast, and lieutenant — "

"What now?"

"If you're there on time, I'll spring."

The decisive click of the receiver precluded any further discussion, pro or con. With an indolent shrug of her dripping shoulders, the lieutenant punched out Mark's home number. The phone rang four times before a querulous voice grunted, "Yeah?"

"The chief wants us at Lil' Oly's in half an hour. He's picking up the breakfast tab."

"Half an hour?" Detective-Sergeant Mark Swanson growled his displeasure. "Can't make it. I'm still in the shower."

Cathy Carruthers chuckled. "So was I when the chief called me." Then, after a brief but thoughtful pause, "You've got a telephone in the shower?"

"No, damn it, but I'm shedding water even as I speak, and it's going all over the bloody floor."

The chuckle swelled to a hearty laugh. "We're in parallel plights," she confided, "let's hang up."

"You mean — well, well, well. This has all the happy aspects of an obscene phone call." Mark did some heavy breathing. "Want to go first?"

"Yes. Cool down. Dry off. And get dressed. In that order. And that *is* an order."

"Spoil sport."

"I'll pick you up in twenty minutes."

MARK STALKED BACK TO THE SHOWER WITH ALL THE alacrity of a wounded bear. Dressed, Mark Swanson was a big man; naked, he was herculean. His shoulders were mountainous, his abdomen flat and ribbed with muscle. The girth of his compact loins seemed scarcely larger than any one of his massive limbs. As he began again to soap his body, the thought of his comely partner doing the same brought a wistful smile to his handsome, boyish face. He drifted happily away into an X-rated daydream.

Meanwhile, towel in hand, Cathy Carruthers faced her full-length bedroom mirror. She was clearly unaware that a conceptual clone of her naked self (*in the figment of one over-active imagination*) was, at that very moment, cavorting with girlish glee in Mark's steamy shower stall. But no mere mortal, however biased, could hope to justly personify the superb creature that now looked into, and out of, the polished glass.

Her long, lion-like mane seemed to reflect the vibrant colour of ripe wheat, her eyes, the limpid ethereal blue of a summer sky. When she chose to smile, the effect was tantamount to a flash of friendly lightning. Her body was rife in the pulchritude of a Playboy bunny, yet, inexplicably, rippling with the awesome strength and stealth of a jungle cat. She carried her full, firm breasts proudly high, and, when in motion, the musculature in her slender haunches undulated beneath the tawny velvet of her skin with a sensuous mix of womanly grace and raw, predacious power.

She was *The Amazon*, aptly styled by her friends and colleagues in the Homicide Division of Metro Central's Eleventh Precinct. And she was held in deferential awe, as much for her legendary manifestations of almost para-human intelligence, as for the more obvious attributes of her physical presence. No one, other than Mark Swanson, her one true friend and cohort, had ever enjoyed the close personal intimacy vital to even a glimpse of the woman beyond the Amazonian mystique, and then only on regrettably rare occasions. But it was Cathy Carruthers, the woman, undeniably, who toweled dry on this morning of the Divine Messiah's death, and reached for her clothing.

LIL' OLY'S WAS THE OFFICIAL *UN*OFFICIAL SCOFF-trough of the Eleventh Precinct. In little more than two years, it had burgeoned under the all but exclusive patronage of the local constabulary; from a sandwich-cum-coffee bar, to cafeteria, to full-fledged restaurant, replete with a *chef de cuisine* (Frenchy to the boys in blue) and mini-skirted waitresses. It was one of the latter, Mavis, who now approached Captain Hank Heller.

"May I help you, captain, sir?"

Heller's grey eyes flicked impatiently from the waitress's friendly smile to the restaurant's busy entrance, then narrowed keenly as he spotted Cathy Carruthers and Mark Swanson entering through the glass double doors.

"Three coffees, posthaste," Heller told the waitress, "and four breakfast menus. And, Mavis, if you can hold Swanson down to one normal serving of ham'n'eggs, you'll earn yourself an extra tip."

The girl giggled, then flounced away. By the time she had reappeared with coffee carafe and menus, the two detectives were already seated at the captain's table.

"So," Cathy Carruthers said brightly as she surveyed the restaurant's first thin crop of omnivores, "what's up, chief, apart from your early morning ire?"

Heller scowled at his watch. "I've asked the leprechaun to join us," he said, matching the lieutenant's good cheer with his customary brashness. "He's been putting a file together for the past couple of hours, so we'll wait to hear from him first. In the meantime, we may as well give Mavis our order."

"Great." Mark smiled warmly up at the girl as she waited, pad and pencil in hand. "How're the breakfast steaks this morning, love?"

"Well — uh — " Mavis looked unduly flustered, torn (Heller speculated) between the promise of monetary gain and a 'maid'-to-order opportunity to gladden the eye, and the stomach, of the precinct's most eligible hunk. "Aaah — not so good, really," she hedged with a sheepish glance at Heller, then, straightening, she bravely added, "but I'm sure I can find a nice one for you, sergeant."

Mark rewarded her with a wink (more than she had hoped for) and Heller let his displeasure be known with a surly grunt and a compensatory order of toast and marmalade.

"Make mine the usual," Cathy Carruthers told the girl, "egg-nog, if you please, three raw with a touch of nutmeg and — well, speak of the devil — "

The "devil" who had caught the lieutenant's eye was an elfin little man who was advancing with comic haste toward their table. He carried a huge bundle of files under one little arm while his abbreviated legs seemed to propel him forward in a frenzied kind of whirl, just above floor level.

"He's doing his Jesus walk," Mark noted dryly.

It was, of course, the *Leprechaun*, nee Garfield Leprohn, Corporal, the littlest blue-coat this side of Smurfsville (according to Mark) and the incontrovertible *major-domo* of the Records Department. The little man braked to a breathless halt beside the one remaining empty chair, and while his three colleagues looked on in thinly veiled amusement, he proceeded to elevate himself to table-top level with the aid of all but one of the bulky files he had so laboriously carried in. And only then, squinting out from between the ketchup and the cream jug, did he acknowledge the presence of the other three at the table.

The leprechaun wasted no time in formalities. "We've got ourselves a real puzzler this time," he began in a tiny voice befitting his stature. "Murder? Suicide? Accident? Who knows? The only thing I could ascertain for certain, chief, is that a man is dead."

"Yeah, well, Leppy — ," Mark took unholy pride in being the little corporal's most devout irritant, "Just give us the facts, eh? We'll do the ascertaining."

The leprechaun bristled. As much as he hated that ignominious epithet, Mark's truncated version of it was even more offensive, aggrandizing one indignity, it seemed, with yet another.

"But the media is calling it suicide," Heller cut in, ignoring Mark's nugacious needling.

"Don't you mean *sacrifice*, chief?" The leprechaun leafed through a well-filled file he had balanced on his little lap. "They (the media) are actually suggesting a comparison, of sorts, between the wrestler's death last night and the historical crucifixion of Christ on the cross. Not in so many words, mind, but most assuredly by implication."

"That's journalism at its yellowest," Cathy Carruthers stated emphatically, "and obviously without the slightest basis in fact. Knowingly, or not, the media are simply aiding and abetting a bunch of money hungry promoters in the perpetuation of what has recently become the most farcical show on earth." She loosed a tremulous sigh. "*The Messiah*" versus "*Satan*" — yee gods! What next?"

"What is next," the leprechaun asserted, "is that the Messiah (myth or mystic) is undeniably dead. And to the many thousands of rabid devotees of professional wrestling, this means that the second coming, in prophecy and in fact, has come and bloody gone."

"That, Garfield, is somewhat less than funny." The lieutenant's mild rebuke was mollified by her use of his given name, a courtesy he cherished dearly. "You surprise me, really."

The leprechaun dutifully hung his little head.

"I suggest we start by putting this whole mess into some kind of perspective," the lieutenant said to the table at large, then, to the chastened leprechaun in particular, she added, "now suppose you tell us precisely how the man died."

"That's easy, lieutenant, he froze to death in the sports arena's walk-in freezer."

"Did he go into the freezer of his own accord?"

"Apparently so."

"Was he bound, or in any way constrained?"

"No."

"Was he drugged?"

"That, I can't tell you."

"Was the door to the freezer locked?"

"No."

"Then what in heaven's name would deny the man the option of simply walking out?"

"That lieutenant, if it were on Lil' Oly's menu this morning, would be the *delimme de jour*."

MAVIS HAD HARDLY BEGUN TO SERVE BREAKFAST when the leprechaun plunked his one working file on the table and began to expound. Dishes were pushed aside to accommodate the rude intrusion.

"As I see it, thus far," the little man said importantly, "there are four principals in the case, including the dead man. Two males and two females, all of whom are wrestlers. A fifth person, the one who discovered the body, is a night watchman called Otis Scroggs. He is not otherwise involved." He paused to take a sip of coffee. "I have a brief history on each of the other four," he added.

"Start with the stiff," Heller told him bluntly.

The leprechaun cleared his tiny throat. "The Messiah, aka The Almighty, or The Prince of Peace, among other tasteless aliases, was born in Oporto, Portugal, in 1945, and has been wrestling for most of his adult life, primarily in Europe. But the name given him at birth was Jesus Podera."

"Jesus Christ!" Mark blurted around a mouthful of medium rare.

"No," the leprechaun countered calmly, "Jesus Podera. Podera, by the way, roughly translated from Portuguese, means power."

"Jesus Power?" Heller gave a rare grunt of amusement. "With

a name like that, who needs, Messiah?"

"In Portugal," the lieutenant said in an edifyingly patient voice, "the name, Jesus, is as common as Tom, Dick or Harry on this side of the Atlantic. Still, its religious connotation may have given a certain impetus to the man's somewhat bizarre bent for professional nomenclature."

"Yes, well." The leprehaun coughed softly into a little fist, then went calmly on. "About two years ago, Jesus Podera took up with a lady wrestler and married her. They've been together ever since, working the circuits. According to the marriage license, her maiden name was, uh — Mary Mandomski. The name she is currently using in the wrestling ring, however, is Mary Magdalene."

Mark choked into his coffee cup and Heller let out a guttural whoop that vaguely resembled a burst of laughter. The lieutenant lifted her beautiful eyes heavenward. "That sounds like more of Jesus Podera's obvious proclivity to sacrilege, don't you think?"

The leprechaun was clearly miffed, "It's not my job to moralize, lieutenant, I simply relate the facts as I see them. Now, if you'll permit me to continue – "

"Please do."

The leprechaun please did. "The other male wrestler," he said quietly, "Satan, has also appeared under a multitude of misnomers. The Prince Of Darkness, or Of Devils, or Of Demons — you name it. But the appellation given him at birth, was — " and here, the little man looked around uneasily " — Mephisto Schmidt."

"Mephisto!" Mark echoed the name with a howl.

Heller wiped his eyes on his napkin. "Are you sure you've opened the right file, corporal?"

"May I remind you, captain, it's not my job to — "

"Yes, yes, we know. Just the facts, Ma'am. Right? So why don't you give us the name of the other female, corporal? We may as well get this over with."

"Viki Viper," the leprechaun stated flatly, then settled back to weather the predictable outburst. When an element of calm had returned, he carried on.

"Needless to say, Viki Viper is teamed up with Schmidt, and rumour has it that there's been some sort of emotional intrigue brewing between all four of these people."

"One question, corporal." Heller was back to his usual ill-humoured norm. "What makes these three in particular our only suspects in the Messiah's death?"

"Circumstance, captain, nothing more. They were seen with the victim just prior to his death."

"Seen? By whom?"

"By closed-circuit television. The security camera picked up all three wrestlers as they entered the freezer with the Messiah."

"Then it must have also picked them up as they all came out without him."

"It did."

"Then the camera would also show if anyone had deliberately locked him in there."

"It would, but it didn't."

"So, to all appearances, Jesus Podera remained inside the freezer entirely of his own accord."

"Yes."

"And you find that premise to be untenable?"

The leprechaun could not suppress a little shiver. "Don't you?"

"Hmmmm. I presume they have all this on tape, corporal."

"They do, sir."

"Then get it."

Heller singled out the lieutenant with a steely stare. "One dead Jesus, a Devil's cauldron of Judases, and a videotape of a perfectly normal ice box. What more could you ask for?" He gulped the rest of his coffee and got to his feet. "Like I said, lieutenant, it's right up your bailiwick."

For the lieutenant's ears only, Mark muttered, "Up yours, too, chief."

Heller scrawled his John Henry on Mavis's order pad. "There's a tip in there," he told the girl, "somewhere between the steak and the eggs. You might try hitting the hunk for the balance."

THE METRO CENTRAL CITY MORGUE WAS A LOW STONE structure with long empty echoing halls and quiet tenants. Mark swung the grey unmarked Chevy into a parking slot and killed the motor. He turned to his beautiful partner who graced the seat beside him.

"Don't you think we're a mite early, C.C.?"

"For what?"

"For the autopsy, what else? I doubt if Sam — "

"We haven't come to see Sam, Mark. We've come, you might say, to meet our maker. I want to examine this so-called Messiah before Sam gets at him."

"To what end?"

"To the end of the controversy, I hope. In spite of the chief's colourful prose, Mark, what we have here is one of three distinct scenarios: murder, suicide, or just plain misadventure."

The lieutenant left the car abruptly and Mark followed. He drew abreast of her as they crossed the acre of concrete that prefaced the ornate, heavily-doored entrance. A group of news-people were gathered just inside, clearly visible through the glassed-in front.

"Let's duck that mob, Mark. Sam's got a side entrance just around the corner."

She promptly converted words to action, with Mark hard on her heels. They sped toward a door midway along the side of the building, on which a modest sign was affixed:

SAMUEL MORTON, M.D.
CORONER & CHIEF MEDICAL EXAMINER
M.C.P.D.

The lieutenant tried the door. It was locked. Mark leaned heavily on the bell. A few gesticulating forms appeared around the corner, heading toward them. The door finally inched inward, and the two detectives pushed past a short, dumpy man in a once-white, well-laundered smock that still bore the indelible marks of past mortal migrations under the knife.

"To what," the man snuffed heatedly, "do I owe this outrageous intrusion?"

The lieutenant jerked her golden head toward the open door. "Take a look."

One glimpse of the wildly advancing media types was enough to shift Sam Morton into a Keystone-cop reverse. He slammed, locked, and bolted the heavy door, then stood with his back to it, surveying the two interlopers with mild exacerbation.

"We've got to stop meeting this way," he said with no apparent attempt at humour, "and it's not as though I don't know why you're here."

The lieutenant gave him one of her melting smiles. "Then you'll let us have a look at him?"

"For you, *Wunder Frau*, anything." He met her smile with an endearing leer, then led the way out of his office and down a narrow inner corridor. "I assume you're referring to the Divine One, lieutenant, the guy who came in last night dressed in priestly robes and looking like an iced-lolly."

"The same." She laughed aloud. "Do you treat all your guests so dispassionately, Sam?"

"Only until I get them on the table, my dear." Sam Morton suddenly became Peter Lorre incarnate. "My fondest caress is with my scalpel," he mimed.

The ensuing laughter abruptly fell away as they entered a large tiled room where the cryptic chill of death seemed to burden the very air they breathed. The room's one occupant reclined somberly beneath a sheet that had been noticeably subjected to as many fruitless ablutions as the M.E.'s smock.

"You haven't begun the autopsy then," Mark noted hopefully.

"Are you kidding, Mark? Remember how long it took to thaw out your last Christmas turkey?"

Mark and the lieutenant exchanged ashen glances.

"Well, add to that the complicacies of rigor mortis and you'll get some idea of what we're up against. That's why he's in here, to hurry up the process."

"Why the rush?"

"What Heller wants, Heller gets," the M.E. stated flatly, "come Hell-er high water." He chuckled at his own quip, then added, "Sometimes."

"Have you examined him, Sam?"

"Only perfunctorily, lieutenant."

"Did you happen to notice any epidermal signs of possible drugging?"

"No."

"What about external marks of restraint?"

The dumpy coroner shrugged his shoulders. "He was not bound when he arrived here, but, let's take a look." He drew aside the soiled shroud.

The two detective's were visibly startled at the indisputable likeness of the dead man's countenance to the graphic depictions of Christ as portrayed by the Renaissance masters. The facial hair, the high cheek bones, the sensuous mouth; every detail appeared to be meticulously replicated from a fourteenth century canvas. Even the long white flowing robes he wore were indicative of that period in time when the Gallilean walked the earth.

"Look at his hands," Mark said with a note of awe.

Both palms bore the scars of what might have been the running through of spikes. The feet, too, just below each ankle, had similar wounds. There were no detectable signs of rope burns.

"Plastic surgery," Sam Morton said without hesitation, "the nail scars, I mean. Quite obvious, in fact, to a medically trained eye."

"And spurious," the lieutenant added. "Those who were unfortunate enough to be crucified by nailing (some were tied), the nails, of necessity, had to be driven through above the wrists, in order to support the weight of the body. Let's look at his side."

The M.E. bared the man's right torso. A long ugly red scar marred the otherwise unblemished flesh.

"The man was an unconscionable charlatan. He has obviously gone to preposterous lengths to fabricate a macabre and tasteless hoax." The lieutenant turned and headed for the door. "I've seen enough."

THEIR EYES MET OVER THEIR COFFEE CUPS AS THEY sat across from each other at a small table outside Luigi's, a sidewalk cafe half a block from Metro Central's Memorial Arena. It was lunch time.

"So what's on the agenda, beautiful?"

Cathy Carruthers treated her favorite tellurian to a flash of friendly lightning. "What do you say to some *t'ai chi chu'an*?"

Mark beamed. "Chinese food? Great. Your place or mine?"

"*T'ai chi chu'an*, Mark, is a form of Chinese wrestling."

"Better still. Your place or mine?"

The lieutenant laughed. "Why don't we settle for the Arena? It's less than a block away. I'd like to get better acquainted with those two lady grapplers, Viki Viper and Mary Magdalene — not to mention the notorious Herr Mephisto Schmidt."

"Well, each to his own proclivity," Mark muttered ruefully. "After our last encounter with a wrestler, I just hope these three weirdos are still alive."

"And talkative."

THERE WERE HALF A DOZEN MEN LAZING ABOUT THE ring, large men, in a motley array of casual attire, save one, and he stood out from the others like a leper at a love-in. He was dressed in black; black hood, black cape, black leotards, black body-shirt, black boots and gloves. Even his face was a congenital black. The only relief from that ominous hue was a pair of red horns jutting from his hood and a red pitchfork emblazoned across his enormous chest. He was, without question, Herr Satan.

The ring was lit, and two women in abbreviated tights and tops, were listlessly rehearsing a variety of wrestling moves. One was heavy-thighed, thick-waisted and busty; the other, lithe and shapely, almost pretty, with an obviously concocted air of chasteness about her that made her look more vulnerable than she deserved beside her beefy opponent. It was not difficult to distinguish between Mary Magdalene and her arch foe, Viki Viper.

The approach of Cathy Carruthers and Mark Swanson went unnoticed, until they came in under the canopy of light that illuminated the ring. The Satanic one was the first to spot them.

"Vell, vell," he intoned gutturally, "vas dis?"

"Are you Mephisto Schmidt?" the lieutenant asked quietly.

"And who vants to know?"

"Just answer the question, clown," Mark told the man with steely evenness.

The big German black was not accustomed to being told to do anything by anyone, much less be called a clown. He locked his dark eyes firmly onto Mark's, looking for an edge, a sign of weakness. The huge arena had become as silent as a tomb.

"Answer the question," Mark said again.

"I am Mephisto Schmidt," the big black snarled, "who the hell are you?"

The lieutenant flashed her badge and went through the routine of introduction.

Schmidt ignored her. "No one calls Schmidt a clown," he said to Mark.

"I just did," Mark asserted softly.

For a big man, Schmidt moved swiftly. He lunged at Mark with a squawk of anger, his big paws clutching wildly at thin air as Mark stepped adroitly to one side. Then, before the enraged wrestler could regain his balance, a fist the size of a leg-o'-mutton slammed squarely against the point of the big black's jaw. Satan dropped to his knees like a repentant sinner.

Mary Magdalene let out a squeal from the centre of the ring. With practiced opportunism, she spied an unsuspecting Cathy Carruthers standing a scant two feet from the ring's edge. She leapt like a rabbit, grabbing two handfuls of golden hair and with the aid of the ropes, she hoisted the startled detective up into a loping jackknife. A cheer went up from the ringside wrestlers as the lieutenant landed in a tangle of limbs and disheveled clothing in the middle of the canvas, her head nodding dizzily.

"Go get her, Mary."

"She's a doozer."

"Yeah, get some of them clothes off her."

"If you don't." someone bellowed, "Viki bloody will."

There was a chorus of laughter as Viki Viper took the bait, moving in to join the fray.

Mark jumped to the apron. He was about to duck under the ropes when strong hands grabbed at his legs. He looked back to see five large men holding his feet firmly to the canvas. Satan was still well out of it.

Then a sudden spate of activity drew his eyes back to the ring. And Mark knew, as he saw the veil of vertigo leave her eyes, that it was no longer Cathy Carruthers in there, skirt and blouse, half on, half off, flipping suddenly to her feet as though propelled by a steel spring, tossing her would-be assailants aside like a couple of rag dolls.

It was *The Amazon*, tall and proud, front and centre. One in each hand, by the scruff of their necks, she lifted the two stunned lady wrestlers three feet off the canvas floor and brought their heads together with a resounding *thwack*! that could be heard in the most distant reaches of the arena. They fell senseless, in a convoluted heap at her feet. Then, with lightning speed and precision, the Amazon leveled her superb body in a blistering dropkick, squarely at the heads of two of the wrestlers still clinging to her chosen cohort. The hapless pair sagged back and down to join Satan on the concrete floor.

Mark then diminished the odds further still by pistoning the heel of one freed foot into the already cauliflowered visage of one more witless grappler. All that remained now was a little mopping up, which the Amazon left in Mark's capable hands (and fists) while she went about retrieving her dissimulated ensemble. With a nip here and a tuck there, plus a few minor adjustments, she resurfaced, moments later, as a slightly soiled but highly presentable, Cathy Carruthers.

"YOU WERE GREAT," MARK TOLD HER AS HE NURSED the knuckles of his right hand.

"I can handle myself when I have to," she replied indifferently.

"Yeah," Mark grinned, "that too."

Uniformed police arrived soon after the scuffle had ended, at the behest of Arena Security (who had seen the entire incident on closed-circuit television). They were gathering up the addled behemoths to cart them off to the pokey when the lieutenant addressed one of the uniforms.

"Hold the two women for questioning, officer, and that guy in the devil's outfit. As for the rest, just hang onto them until they've seen the light."

"Yes, ma'am." The officer's eyes were saucers of wonderment. "But by the look of them, lieutenant, that might be a while."

"And he ain't just whistling Dixie," a deep, throaty voice said behind her. She turned to face a large, rumpled-looking man whom she guessed to be in his late sixties. He was bald and noticeably bereft of all facial hair. He reminded her of Telly Savalas, without eyebrows.

"I'm Garth Gibson," he said, proffering a large hairless hand, "also known as the Albino Assassin." He laughed good-naturedly. "But that was back in my misspent youth. Today, I run this joint. I'm the current promoter of Central City Wrestling."

The lieutenant took his hand. "What can I do for you?"

"It's not what you can do for me, lieutenant, it's what I can do for you."

"Oh?"

"I saw the whole donnybrook on Security TV," he said with unbridled enthusiasm, "and, well — I was impressed."

"Were you, now?"

"No, no. Don't get me wrong, lieutenant. I'm not talking cheap thrills here." His pinky-looking eyes were painfully apologetic. "I'm willing to offer *you*, and that guy you're with, one million dollars, lieutenant, for twelve months work. God's truth. Of course," he said apprehensively, "he'd have to quit using those bloody great fists of his. We all want to survive, you know."

The lieutenant heard Mark's playful chuckle at her elbow. "Did you hear that?" she asked him.

"Faith, and I did at that," he responded in his best Irish accent, "But I'd be warnin' yu, sir. I'll not be settlin' fur nuthin' less than top billin'."

The already bemused promoter looked suddenly stunned. "You mean — "

"The *man*, himself, begorra." Mark was doing what he could to look godly and serious at one and the same time. "Now, I ask yu," he spoofed, "how else yu goin' t'be teachin' the likes of that black divil to toe the line?"

WHEN THE SHENANIGANS WERE OVER, AND THE pallid promoter had given up all hope of recruiting new talent from the M.C.P.D., he proved to be a veritable well-spring of information.

"Oh, yeah, the Messiah was good," he told Mark and the lieutenant over a cup of coffee in his office, "that guy's probably drawing crowds right now, in heaven — or wherever the hell he went to." He laughed at his own inept humour. "He had this hold, see?

AMAZON

He called it the 'laying on of hands'. Can you believe it? He'd grab
a guy by his traps (that's the *trapezius* muscle, between the neck
and the shoulder), and he would squeeze on some nerve, or
something. And, well — that'd be all she wrote, lieutenant.
Manana."

"Come o-o-on." Mark was unimpressed. "A so-called
submission hold? I've seen them all. And they are all as phoney as
a tit in a tantrum."

"Mark!" the lieutenant gave him an elbow.

"Not this one," Gibson insisted. "In fact, that's where the trouble
all began. The other guys were willing to fake it. For self
preservation, if nothing else. But Jesus came on with this bolt-of-
lightning bit like he was God Almighty, himself."

"So he wasn't particularly liked."

"Lieutenant, he was hated. Any one of dozens of men would
have gladly pulled his plug."

"What about the girls?"

"Well, it don't take much savvy to see that Viki Viper is on an
AC/DC circuit. Both she and Mephisto have the same diddly itch
for little Mary."

"But Jesus was in the way?"

"You got it right, lieutenant, *was* in the way."

"Mmmm." The lieutenant grew quietly pensive. "We seem to
have ample motive, as well as ample opportunity. And while we still
can't prove the Messiah's death to be anything other than
misadventure, the circumstances surrounding his demise are so
bizarre, we simply must assume he was in some way coerced into
remaining inside that freezer after the other three had left."

"How long was it before they discovered the body?" Mark
asked.

"Just shy of four A.M.," Gibson stated firmly. "I happened to
know because they got me out of bloody bed when they found him."

"Yeah, but how long was he in there?"

"A good three hours."

"And he was frozen solid?" The lieutenant looked perplexed.
"That hardly seems long enough to — "

"Aaah," Gibson broke in, "a good point, lieutenant. Under
normal functioning, the inside freezer temperature would be about –

– 10 Celsius, which is pretty damn cold and may well have done the job in any case. However, when the Messiah's body was found early this morning, the temperature in the freezer had dropped to almost -25. Someone had tampered with the thermostat."

"But if the temperature in the freezer is controllable, why couldn't the Messiah have simply turned it down? Or off, for that matter?"

"The thermostat, lieutenant, is mounted on the *outer* wall."

"Outside the door?"

"Yes."

"In view of the security camera?"

"Yes."

"Well, now we're getting somewhere. Anyone tampering with the thermostat would have been seen by the camera, right?"

"I would think so."

"Then it's time we took a look at that videotape." The lieutenant got to her feet, then hesitated. "Mr. Gibson," she said, "Before we leave the Arena, do you think you could join us in a brief visit to the scene of the deed, as it were?"

"Don't you mean the scene of the *dead*, as it *is*?" the promoter replied with a crusty chuckle. "Either way, lieutenant, it'd be a pleasure."

THE HALL WAS FOUR FEET WIDE AND APPROXIMATELY fifty feet long. They came into it as Otis Scroggs had done, from behind the concession stand. Midway down the hall, on their right, the security interphone rested in a small niche, directly across from the walk-in freezer.

"This, then, is the thermostat," the lieutenant observed, as she pointed to a plastic wall-mounted dial, about two feet from the heavy casing of the freezer door. She looked up to locate the camera, which hung suspended from the ceiling at the far end of the hall. "Anyone touching that thermostat," she mused aloud, "could not possibly escape the eye of the camera."

"But why," Mark queried, "would anyone deliberately incriminate themselves in front of a camera? They must have known it was there."

The lieutenant shrugged her impeccable eyebrows. "Why indeed?"

"But it *was* tampered with," the promoter insisted, "the camera must have picked up *something*."

"We'll soon see," the lieutenant said idly, her attention now drawn to the handle on the freezer door. It was a one-sided pull-type lever, hinged inside a sturdy metal housing. She tugged the door slightly ajar, then closed it again. When in the closed position, she noticed, a small oblong gap was exposed at the butt end of the handle, large enough to accommodate two of her well-manicured fingers. She tried opening the door with her fingers still in the gap and found she could not. But most surprising, was the lack of any meaningful pressure on her fingers as she tugged on the handle.

"The mechanism in this thing is certainly well engineered," she said as she opened the door again and went inside. The icy chill of the freezer enveloped her at once and her breath came out in misty puffs. The room was about twenty feet by ten, the walls lined with shelves of frozen foods. A huge ice-cube unit dominated the far wall. As she turned to leave, the lieutenant saw that simple egress was ensured by pushing on a round, dish-like handle which responded to the slightest pressure.

"Mark," she called around the door's edge, "when I close the door, put your finger in that gap at the butt end of the handle." she re-entered the freezer, and with Mark's big finger in place, she tried again to open the door. This time, it remained closed, and no amount of pushing on the handle would budge it. She signalled him through the small glass window to let her out.

"It seems clear enough," she said as she joined the men in the hall, "that any object, about an inch and a quarter long, by maybe three-quarters wide, and deep, if placed in that gap, would prevent the door from being opened, from either side."

"There was nothing in there when they found the body," Gibson reminded her. "The guys from security just walked right in and pulled him out."

"Of course, it could have been removed."

Gibson gave a raspy laugh. "You're back to the camera again, lieutenant."

"Right." The lieutenant dropped to one knee and sighted along an imaginary line from the door to the camera. "If some foreign object was inserted in the door handle, and subsequently removed, the camera would, indeed, have seen it. Come on, Mark, let's go to the movies."

THE LEPRECHAUN WAS READY AND WAITING AS THE lieutenant and Mark entered the Eleventh Precinct's dimly-lit projection room. A lone police woman sat in one of the leather seats with her eyes glued to the television screen.

"Thank God you're finally here," she said wearily, "Nothing has moved up there for almost three hours."

The TV screen showed the camera's-eye-view of the empty hall in the Arena where the two detectives had parted company with promoter Garth Gibson less than an hour before.

"I had to have someone monitor the screen," the leprechaun explained from the shadows behind them, "from the time the wrestlers left the freezer until the watchman, Otis Scroggs, finally found the body. Scroggs, by the way, is due to appear any minute now."

"Fisk," the lieutenant said, addressing the pretty brunette rookie, "are you saying that no one has entered that hall since the wrestlers left?"

"Not a soul, lieutenant. Four wrestlers went into the freezer, three came out. That's it."

"And nothing since?"

"Nothing."

"Here's Scroggs," the leprechaun said suddenly.

They all looked on as the night watchman acted out his traumatic discovery of the Messiah through the window in the freezer door, along with his subsequent call to Security. Then, in a matter of minutes, another guard appeared, and together they opened the freezer door and dragged out the dead Messiah. At that point, Scroggs left, only to reappear seconds later with a blanket to cover the body.

"They sure as hell didn't have any trouble opening the door," Mark noted.

"Tell me about it," the lieutenant said with a heavy sigh, "so there goes the convenient foreign-object-in-the-handle theory." She turned to the leprechaun. "Run it back, Garfield, to where the wrestlers first appear. Maybe this time we'll get lucky."

The videotape took some time to rewind and the lieutenant used the interlude to further solicit from Officer Fisk her absolute assurance that nothing had moved in the empty hall during her long vigil. The young woman was unshakable.

"My eyes never left the screen," she stated emphatically. "I'd have seen a fly move, had there been one."

"I'm more interested," the lieutenant told her, "in insights, than insects."

"Ready when you are," the leprechaun announced with as much felicitous flair as he could muster.

The lieutenant waited patiently while Mark fired up a coffin nail. "One dead; one dying," she said with a sigh of mild reproof, then, "Okay, Garfield, roll it."

The screen lit up with the same view of the empty hall.

"There's a lead time here of about two minutes," the little man told them. "Prior to this shot, there was traffic in and out of the freezer from both wrestlers and staff, but nothing out of the ordinary."

There was another minute of empty silence before the screen came alive. The four wrestlers could then be seen approaching the freezer in a tight group, their backs to the camera. The Messiah was first, then Mary Magdalene, with Viki Viper close behind. Herr Satan brought up the rear, carrying an empty ice bucket, while his broad back was managing to eclipse a clear view of the other three. But even then, as they passed the thermostat, there was an almost imperceptible flicker of movement between Satan's back and the wall.

"Hold it," the lieutenant said quickly, "run that back a bit."

The leprechaun deftly followed instructions. Then, with the tape rolling again, and on the lieutenant's sudden cry of "*There!*" the wrestlers all froze in mid-stride. The blurred image of a white hand had made contact with the dial of the thermostat. It was impossible to tell to whom the hand belonged.

"That," the lieutenant asserted quietly, "is the hand of the murderer. But whose hand is it?"

"It sure as hell isn't Satan's," Mark said with certainty, "wrong colour."

"And one would hardly expect the Messiah to assist in his own demise," the lieutenant added.

"Which," the brown-eyed Fisk chimed in brightly, "only leaves the two women."

"Good thinking," the lieutenant said with an amused chuckle. "Can this scene be blown up, corporal?"

"Yes, there is a process. But it will take some time."

"Do it. And see that tiny glint of light on one of the fingers? That's what I'm after. Okay, let's see the rest of it."

The wrestlers sprang to life again, only to disappear one at a time, into the freezer. After about a minute, the door opened and Satan re-emerged, his bucket, now filled to overflowing with ice cubes, in one hammy fist. He was out of the picture in seconds. Viki Viper came out next, closely followed by Mary Magdalene. Both women moved off slowly toward the camera.

"Hold it, corporal."

The tape stopped on the lieutenant's command. "Roll that back a little, to just before the door closes. That's it. Now let it come – slowly — "

There was no sound in the projection room as all eyes focussed on Mary Magdalene, the last one to leave the freezer. They saw her purposefully, gently, ease the door shut, then, as she walked away from it, her hand trailed lightly, almost casually, along the lever-like handle, until it finally dropped away.

"Nothing there," Mark said as the two women moved out of camera range.

"Agreed," Fisk piped up, happy this time to have an ally.

"To be frank, lieutenant," the leprechaun said tentatively, "I, too, saw nothing."

"Get a blow-up of Mary Magdalene's hand on the door handle, corporal." The lieutenant rose lightly to her feet. "No rush. But it would be nice to wrap this case up, sometime tomorrow."

"Wrap it up?"

"There are always loose ends at the conclusion of every case. You know that, Garfield." She turned to Mark. "How about some *sushi*, and a bottle of dry wine?"

"Does this mean what I think it does?" Mark asked cautiously. "You now know who done what to who?"

"To *whom*, Mark, and I'll ignore the rest of the sentence. But, yes, I do know. Now all we have to do it prove it. So, what about that *sushi*?"

Mark wondered if he would ever be able to take his partner's sudden augeries in stride. He decided to capitulate. "Your place or mine?" he sighed.

"Mine." Cathy Carruthers flashed one of her iridescent smiles. "I feel safer on familiar territory."

LIEUTENANT CATHY CARRUTHERS SAT SIDE-SADDLE on one of the many desks in the Eleventh Precinct's spacious squad room. Mark Swanson, as could be expected, was close at her elbow. The three disgruntled wrestlers, Schmidt, Magdalene and Viper, had been given chairs on the low, room-wide dais in front of the desks.

"So vat's dis about?" the Satanic menace wanted to know.

"Yeah," Viki Viper muttered, looking dumpy and mannish in a loose-fitting sweater and slacks.

"Yeah," echoed a mini-skirted Mary Magdalene, her ring-wise aura of innocent vulnerability having seemingly evaporated overnight.

"All in due time — " the lieutenant began, then turned abruptly as chief Hank Heller came bursting into the room like an early morning sand storm.

"Don't have much time, lieutenant," he rasped, "let's get this over with."

"We're waiting for the leprechaun," she told him calmly.

"Again?"

"Again." The lieutenant glanced impatiently toward the door. "And here he is."

The leprechaun did not exactly burst into the room as his chief had done; he sort of popped in, like a pea out of a pea-shooter, with his usual bulky bundle of files tucked securely under one little arm. He dumped himself into a chair behind one of the desks and promptly disappeared from view, an embarrassment he was quick to rectify, with the help of a goodly portion of his documental burden.

The little corporal's colleagues politely refrained from any outward display of amusement, but the somewhat less-than-saintly Mary Magdalene was not so gracious. "A midget wrestler," she giggled. "Oh, I love the little darlings — "

"Did you bring the blow-ups, corporal?" the lieutenant cut in quickly, hoping to defuse a visibly irate leprechaun, who, at that moment, looked to be on the verge of blowing up, himself. The little man rummaged in his reams of data to produce not two, but several large photographs. He then basked openly in the lieutenant's commendatory smile as she took them from him.

"I see you've second guessed me, Garfield," she said as she scanned the enlargements. "Good work. Good work, indeed."

The lieutenant then ascended the dais to stand before the three wrestlers. "May I see a show of hands, please?"

The three grapplers looked confused, then, one by one, with some reluctance, they held their hands out in front of them. The lieutenant singled out Mary Magdalene, on whose left hand, alone, a thin platinum ring reposed.

"Would you agree, Mary," the lieutenant asked as she thrust one of the enlargements under the woman's nose, "that this is your hand?"

Mary Magdalene glanced sidelong at the photograph and shrugged her shoulders. "How would I know?"

"It has your ring on it."

"So what?"

"Only this, dear lady. That hand belongs not only to you; it is also the hand of the person who murdered Jesus Podera."

There was an audible hush in the room. The accused wrestler looked open-eyed from Viki Viper to Mephisto Schmidt, then back to the lieutenant. She was overtly distraught.

Schmidt spoke first. "Don't let her scare you, Mary. Jesus' death was an accident. That picture don't prove nothin'."

"No, it doesn't," the lieutenant agreed, "not in itself, but rest assured, we have more to go on than that. Nor am I suggesting, Mr. Schmidt, that you and Viki Viper are in any way blameless in the Messiah's murder. But first, Mary, let me pose a scenario, a sequence of events, if you like, of what really happened last night, prior to the discovery of Jesus Podera's frozen body."

THE LIEUTENANT SEEMED TO GROW IN STATURE AS SHE paced, slowly, back and forth behind the three detainees. Their eyes followed her warily as she moved into, and out of, their peripheral vision. Mary Magdalene, in particular, was visibly shaken.

"As I see it," the lieutenant began, "it had already been decided among you, for whatever reason, that Mary Magdalene would be the one to reach out and trip the thermostat on your collective way to the freezer, amply concealed (so you thought) from the camera's view, not just by huddling together, as you did, but by the broad back of Mephisto Schmidt. However, as this enlargement testifies, that part of your nefarious scheme has clearly failed."

The lieutenant paused to draw an errant tress of flaxen hair from her forehead with an elegantly arched middle finger. The silence in the room was profound.

"How you persuaded an unsuspecting Jesus Podera to lead the way into the freezer," she continued, "and then linger there, while the rest of you made a hasty exit, we may never know. Still, I seriously doubt that a simple deceit of this nature would present much of a problem. But then, and again according to plan, once the Messiah was left alone in the freezer, it fell to Mary Magdalene, with those same cunningly manipulative hands of hers, to keep him there." She confronted the lady wrestler directly. "And that, Mary, is precisely what you did. We have it all on tape."

Mary Magdalene was on the quiet side of panic. "What've you got on tape?" Her voice was a susurrus hiss. "What've you got on tape, lieutenant?"

"Take a look." The lieutenant spread the enlargements and held them up in front of her. "They show you doing it."

"Doing what, for chrissake?" She struck the prints from the lieutenant's hands. They fluttered to the floor where Mark and Heller promptly retrieved them. The leprechaun was smiling smugly.

"Some small object," the lieutenant told the room at large, "had to be inserted into that gap at the butt end of the outer handle, to prevent the man inside the freezer from opening the door and escaping. There was no other way to keep him in there. But that 'object' had to be something that would not later have to be retrieved in full view of the camera."

Mary Magdalene was on her feet. "Bullshit!" she screamed. "You ain't pinning this rap on me."

"Shut up," Schmidt snarled. He tried to tug her back down into the chair. "Just *shut up!*"

"*You* shut up, you Nazi bastard. I ain't taking no fall for you. And I ain't taking no fall for that quirky queen of yours, neither. You were the ones who set this all up in the first place."

Schmidt and Viper rolled their eyes in unison as they sagged back in their chairs. The lieutenant moved in quickly.

"Are you prepared to make a statement to that effect, Mary?"

"Yeah, sure. Why not?" She gave a grotesque little giggle of defeat. "I know when I'm licked, even if they don't." She shook her head ruefully. "But you've got to give the devil his due, lieutenant, Mephisto had it figured out pretty good."

"But not good enough," was the lieutenant's grim response.

MARY MAGDALENE SAT AT ONE OF THE DESKS IN THE squad room, laboriously reading through a statement that had been drawn up in preparation for her signature. On the other side of the room, the lieutenant, Mark and Heller were gathered around the leprechaun who was still propped up on his pile of data like a toddler waiting for his first haircut.

Mark was shuffling through the enlargements. "You know, C.C., these things don't really show anything substantial at all." He kept his voice low, out of reach of the lady wrestler. "Some of them are just a bloody blur. I doubt a magistrate would even accept — "

"Not the point, Mark," the lieutenant told him softly. "Mary Magdalene accepted them, and that's what counts."

"But she hardly glanced at them."

The lieutenant chuckled. "Maybe that's why. But let's not forget, Mark, that she *is* guilty, by her own admission, and is willing to confess to it. How she arrived at that decision is immaterial."

"What *I* want to know," Heller barked under his breath, "is how they got the guy to stay inside that freezer while all the rest of them were getting the hell out, lickety-split?"

"The way Magdalene tells it," the lieutenant reflected, "was that she had intentionally 'forgotten' to bring along their ice bucket, hers and Jesus', and on the pretext of going back to get it, she obligingly left him there to wait for her return. He had no reason, then, to think that she would not return. The videotape bears her out, if you recall, which shows only Mephisto Schmidt carrying an empty bucket into the freezer."

"No, I don't recall it, lieutenant, but I'll take your word for it. Now what about the 'foreign object' bit? How was it done? Locking him in there, I mean."

"Ingenious, but simple, as all ingenious things are," the lieutenant recounted, "a common ice cube, chief, in the dexterous hand of Mary Magdalene was surreptitiously dropped into the gap at the butt end of the handle as she left the freezer. By the time the body was found, the ice cube had melted, restoring unobstructed access to the freezer. The small residual melt from the ice cube had either dried up by then, or gone unnoticed."

"So all this BS about blow-ups," Mark said in a disparaging undertone, "was just so much hogwash." He grinned at the little man on his stack of papers. "You might even say that the whole effort fell a little short."

The leprechaun blinked and blushed as only he could. But he kept his cool. The knowing smirk he had donned when the lieutenant had first taken the prints from him, was still implacably in place.

"Not entirely, Mark." The lieutenant treated the leprechaun to a reassuring smile. "As blurred and as indistinct as some of the prints were, they did serve to corroborate a rather tenuous theory. The first print, to be precise, exposed the ring on Magdalene's finger as it touched the thermostat. So far, so good. The second and third prints revealed what might reasonably be construed as the ice cube being skillfully dropped into place in the handle. A bit thin, but credible. But the last three or four, which were taken from the tape some time after the wrestlers had left — "

"One hour later, lieutenant," the leprechaun proudly interjected, "precisely."

"Yes, well, what they showed (and clearly this time) was a minute flow of water, trickling from the handle as the ice cube melted. That clinched it."

"Well, as the promoter, Garth Gibson emphatically informed us earlier, Mark, Jesus Podera was hated by all and sundry. The needless cruelty he apparently inflicted on the other wrestlers in the ring, he carried over into his private life. He must have put his wife (if you'll pardon a bad pun) through Hell. And although it was actually Mephisto Schmidt who planned the murder, he found in Mary Magdalene, a willing, if not eager, accomplice."

"Lieutenant?" Mary Magdalene was timidly approaching the small group still gathered around the leprechaun.

"Yes?"

The woman looked painfully dispirited. "It says here," she said, tracing her finger along a line in the prepared statement, "that Mephisto and Viki were, uh – 'accessories, *after* the fact,' and that it was me, lieutenant, who really killed Jesus."

"Well?"

"But it was *him*, lieutenant, Mephisto. I wouldn't have done nothing if it hadn't been for him. He *made* me do it, lieutenant, him and Viki." She was on the verge of tears. "I think that should be in here, lieutenant."

"Fair enough, Mary. We'll type in an addendum to that effect." The lieutenant took the statement from the woman and handed it directly to the leprechaun. "Did you get that, corporal?"

The leprechaun looked momentarily at a loss. "What should I say?"

"What else?" Cathy Carruthers could not suppress a wide mischievous grin. "Just say, *'The devil made me do it'.*"

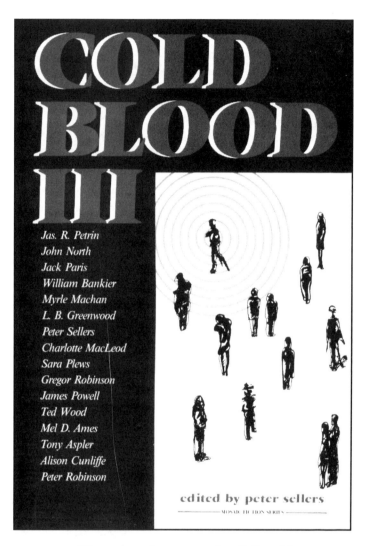

COLD BLOOD III

Jas. R. Petrin
John North
Jack Paris
William Bankier
Myrle Machan
L. B. Greenwood
Peter Sellers
Charlotte MacLeod
Sara Plews
Gregor Robinson
James Powell
Ted Wood
Mel D. Ames
Tony Aspler
Alison Cunliffe
Peter Robinson

edited by peter sellers

MOSAIC FICTION SERIES

"You cannot have a murder, C.C., with-
out a murderer, and the only mortal soul
in that house last night was the victim."
"So it would seem."

the murder that couldn't happen

"MURDER," SHE SAID.

"How can you say that, lieutenant? There just isn't any way it could have happened." Detective-Sergeant Mark Swanson sat teetering on the hind legs of his chair with his size twelves (and her desk top) holding everything in tender balance.

"But happen, it *did.*" Detective-Lieutenant Cathy Carruthers regarded her junior partner with an exasperating mix of angst and chagrin. "It happened, Mark," she reavowed with ominous calm, "just as surely as your jarring descent to the floor level is about to happen, *if you don't get you goddam feet off my desk.*"

"Temper, temper," Mark chided, but he hauled in his brouges and rocked the chair back onto all four legs, thereby defusing a moment he knew from experience to have reached the brink of imprudence. Still, he persisted. "But you cannot have a murder, C.C., with out a murderer, and the only mortal soul in that house last night, was the victim."

"So it would seem."

Mark heaved an intolerant sigh as he watched his favorite

sleuth-person take a small blood-red bottle from her desk and begin calmly to lacquer her flawless nails.

"What you fail to realize, Mark, is that suicide, by your own criterion, was also 'impossible.' Suppose you tell me how a man could shoot himself in the back of the head, without leaving powder burns on or near the wound, nor the slightest trace of powder residue on the hand that purportedly held the gun?"

Mark grinned. "Lieutenant, I do believe you've got yourself another puzzler." Cathy Carruthers, he knew, was in her element. There was nothing that piqued her inherent acuity more than a genuine 'honest-to-God' *puzzler.*

THE TWO DETECTIVES WERE SEATED IN THE lieutenant's office at Metro Central's Eleventh Precinct. Through the wide picture window behind her desk, Mark could see the late afternoon sky fast becoming a murky solid gray (a harbinger of more snow, perhaps) and lights were already winking on like a gathering swarm of fireflies in the deepening shadows of the city's concrete jungle. Mark glanced at his watch. It was just shy of five o'clock.

"My stomach and my watch are out of sync," he complained. His words were punctuated by a low growl from the vicinity of his abdomen.

Cathy Carruthers laughed. "Was that a fluke?" she asked, "or can you perform that little trick at will?

"That 'little trick,'" Mark told her with feigned gravity, "was an alarm going off on one of my biological clocks. It is not something I usually care to ignore."

"Do tell." The lieutenant hung her freshly painted nails up to dry, elbows on the desk, wrists limp. "Dare I ask what other clocks you've got ticking in that Herculean carcass of yours?"

"You wouldn't want to know," Mark assured her with a playful leer, "hunger is not priority one, you know."

Mark watched her get to her feet and stand before the window. Her reflection had begun to materialize in the polished glass, against the darkening sky. Mark coupled her reflection with her engaging silhouette and smiled wistfully.

It was hard to believe that almost three years had elapsed since he had begun working second i.c. to the *Amazon*, an epithet that had been bestowed upon her (with admiration and affection) by her burly colleagues in Homicide. She was six shapely feet of honey-haired womanhood, with the physical prowess of a jungle hellcat and the deductive acumen of a walking think-tank. The Amazon's remarkable and totally unpredictable exploits had become legendary at the Eleventh Precinct, together with the unspoken respect and intimacy that they, she and Mark, had obviously come to share. The good-natured derision that initially had been targeted at Mark by his male cohorts, working side-kick to a (cough) woman, had long since been usurped by a rabid pandemia of green-eyed envy.

Cathy Carruthers turned from the window and flashed a smile that could have halted rush-hour traffic on the Metro freeway. Mark groaned inwardly. He knew he was about to be conned out of a quick trip to the local food emporium, but a sudden jangle of the telephone put his culinary unrest on hold.

"Carruthers, here."

"I've got the Lep – uh, Corporal Leprohn, up here in my office, lieutenant, and I'm finding this Briscombe caper a little hard to swallow." It was Captain Henry (Hank) Heller. His voice had the cacophonic appeal of an amplified death rattle. "I understand that you, and that beach bum partner of yours, were first on the scene."

"You understand correctly, chief, but — "

"Then get on up here for chrissake, and fill me in. Did the guy commit suicide? Was he murdered? Or was it some kind of bizarre accident? We're not talking a bad night on skid row, lieutenant. Briscombe has just been named to the bloody Senate. Or didn't you know?" There was a deadly pause. "Lieutenant, mam, I need some answers."

"Be reasonable, chief. I wasn't there when it happened, but I do have a — theory."

"A theory." The death rattle seemed to be edging ever closer to the Great Divide.

"Now why didn't I think of that?" His voice took on the smarmy tones of mock servility. "No, commissioner, I really don't have a clue what happened to Briscombe last night, but – guess what, commissioner? — I got this terrific *theory*!"

"Be right there, chief."

THE DAY HAD BEGUN INNOCENTLY ENOUGH, WITH
Mark meeting his comely partner in the restaurant of her apartment-
hotel in the fashionable west end of Metro. They had enjoyed a brief
but pleasant breakfast and were on their way in to the Precinct when
the call came through.

"Possible homicide at the Briscombe residence out in Thornston
Heights." The dispatcher's voice was crisp and efficient, and
decidedly feminine. "Can you respond?"

The lieutenant took the mike. "10:4," she said, "give me the
address."

Mark watched her write it down, then hung a hard right at the
next intersection. The roads were slushy from a fresh fall of snow
during the night and the gray, unmarked Chevy was having a little
trouble holding the road.

"Briscombe," Mark mused. "Didn't they just name a John A.
Briscombe to the Senate?"

"They did, indeed," the lieutenant concurred, "and judging by
the address, there could be some connection." After a few
moments of silent contemplation, she added, "I hope the news media
hasn't got a hold of this."

They were met in front of the house by a telephone maintenance
truck and a linesman who had just descended a power pole. There
was no one else at the scene.

"Were you the one who phoned for the police?" the lieutenant
asked.

"Yeah. Name's Carl Bogner. You can't see nothing from here,
cause of the house being on a kind of a hill, but from the top of the
pole —"

"What did you see?"

"In that glassed-in middle section — " Carl Bogner began,
pointing up toward the house.

"The atrium?" the lieutenant prompted.

"Yeah, well, there's a guy lying on the floor in there, toes up, and
he hasn't moved since I got here half and hour ago. I dunno. Maybe
he's just drunk. You know, passed out or something. But he sure
don't look very comfortable."

"Where did you phone from?"

The linesman unhooked a compact telephone unit from his belt. "I just hooked into the line. That's my job."

"And what brought you out here this morning?"

"Service call," the man replied. "Some interference on the line. Nothing serious. Just a loose connection."

"Right. Well, we'll take it from here, Mr., uh — "

"Bogner. Carl Bogner."

"Thank you, Mr. Bogner."

As the man withdrew to his truck, Cathy Carruthers and Mark faced an unbroken expanse of snow between the road and the house, and as far as they could see on either side. The entire intricate roof of the huge dwelling, including the glass roof of the atrium itself, was hidden under a white blanket. Even the top of the power pole wore a snowy cap and the electrical wiring swept down from the house to the pole in two parallel white lines. Only the telephone wire on which the linesman had been working, it seemed, was bereft of snow.

"I love the snow," Cathy Carruthers confided as they crunched up the front walk. "It makes everything seem so serenely hushed and pristine."

They had closed to within a few yards of the house and the interior of the atrium was now clearly visible. And there, amid the abundant and decorative greenery, a man lay stretched out on the tile floor with his head resting in a matted pool of blood.

"Serenely hushed, I'll buy," Mark muttered, "but pristine?"

THEY ENTERED THE HOUSE THROUGH THE FRONT door which was not only unlocked, but slightly ajar, then went directly to the atrium.

"It's Briscombe all right," Mark noted, "I've seen his picture on the front page many times. And he looks to be as dead as Senate reform."

The lieutenant stooped and pressed a red-tipped finger to the man's carotid artery, which, in view of the cold gray-white fettle of his flesh, seemed a needless precaution. "Don't you find it a little surprising, though," she said thoughtfully, "at the amount of blood, especially from a head wound?" Rigor mortis had already set in and she had to lift the head to see the bullet hole just above the nape of the neck.

Mark, meanwhile, had moved to the rear of the atrium and was looking out at the open area behind the house, then to either side. The white blanket of snow was virginally unmarred in all directions.

"Well, one thing's for sure, C.C.," he stated emphatically, "unless the murderer is still on the premises, Briscombe was shot well before one A.M. this morning. That's when it quit snowing and, apart from our own tracks up the front walk, there is no sign of anyone having come or gone since."

The lieutenant straightened, wearing a deep frown. "Mark, put a call through to H.Q.," she said, "we'll need the forensic team, a photog, the coroner, the works — and, uh, get them to send over a couple of uniforms to do a thorough search of the house. And, oh yes, I want the Leprechaun to do a number on Briscombe, and tell him to keep it quiet, out of the news media. There's a phone in the hall; I noticed it when we came in."

"No sooner said." Mark responded.

The atrium, the lieutenant noticed when Mark had left, was connected to either side of the house by two large double-glazed doors; one giving access to the living quarters, from which they had entered, the other to an elaborately paneled hallway that provided entry to a number of bedrooms. Both doors were of the sliding type, that closed automatically, ensuring a controlled environment for the profusion of flora in the atrium. It would also provide, the lieutenant speculated, a consistent room temperature by which the coroner could determine the cooling rate of the body and thereby establish a reasonably accurate time of death.

She sauntered over to the rear window and looked out at the unbroken sheet of snow that surrounded the house. It gave her a moment of bemusement. She had already made an educated guess at the time of death, given all known factors, and she had pegged it at a minimal six hours prior to eight A.M. That would mean that Bricombe had been shot at approximately two A.M., at least one hour after the snow had ceased to fall.

A BLACK-AND-WHITE WAS FIRST TO ARRIVE, CHERRY flashing, snow flailing in all directions as it slewed up the driveway to the front of the house. A tall black uniformed officer rose out of the car like a genie from a bottle; a giant, about to grant the wish of some lucky mortal. It was, in fact, George Washington Bones, better known at the Eleventh Precinct as Too-Tall Bones. The big black would have looked more at home with the Harlem Globe Trotters than the Metro P.D. His partner, Dave Madson, a Caucasian of moderate stature, was dwarfed by his imposing cohort.

They were met at the door by Mark Swanson, "You guys into drag-racing, or what?"

"A back-up call is a Code 3, Sarge. Just doing our job." Too-Tall gave him a wide gleaming smile. "We were in the neighborhood."

Mark admonished them with a grunt that said "Who's kidding who?" then led them into the house. Bones ducked through the door with practiced aplomb.

"We want a thorough search of every room, "Mark told the two officers, "except the atrium. That's the greenhouse that separates the sleeping quarters from the rest of the house. Start with the garage. And work together."

"Where's the stiff?" Bones asked.

"In the atrium."

"What're we looking for?" Madson wanted to know.

"Anyone living or dead, or anything at all that looks out of place or unusual. There's a possibility that someone could still be hiding on the premises, and if they are, they could be armed. Now go to it."

Bones and Madson headed for the kitchen where they hoped to find a door that opened into the attached garage. They were scarcely out of sight when Mark heard the approach of more vehicles. It was the 'special' teams and they came trooping in with their equipment, leaving a trail of melting snow between the front door and the atrium where Mark had directed them. The last one to arrive was the coroner.

"Hello, just-plain-Sam," Cathy Carruthers said in greeting to a dumpy, grumpy little man whose official appellation happened to be Samuel Morton, M.D., Coroner and Chief Medical Examiner,

M.C.P.D., or, as he was fond of proclaiming at lighter moments, "just-plain-Sam."

"I'm in no mood for levity," Sam Morton muttered, but he gave his favorite investigator a lascivious wink. "How's your love life, beautiful?"

"It's currently on hold," the lieutenant quipped back. "I've been waiting for you to grow up."

"Be kind," Sam cautioned, "if you want to know how this guy was snuffed."

"I already know *how*," the lieutenant told him, "what I want to know now is *when*."

"Everybody want a T.O.D. at the scene," the M.E. grumbled. "Can't it wait?"

"Not this time," the lieutenant asserted evenly, "the man is attired conventionally in shirt and trousers and this room has been at a constant temperature of 20 degrees Celsius since he died. Now give."

"Feisty this morning, aren't we," Sam grinned (in his own particular way), then, as he fumbled beneath the body, he reached for a pen and hooked out a gun by the trigger guard. "Did you know he was laying on a gun?"

"I do now." The lieutenant transferred the gun to a pen of her own, then handed both to Mark. "A pearl-handled thirty-two — well, well."

The M.E. stood up. "They can do their chalk lines and snapshots now," he said, "then I'd like some muscle to get this guy into a body bag and into my wagon."

"What about the T.O.D.?" the lieutenant persisted.

Sam Morton was doing some calculations on a small note pad. After a time he looked up. "Six hours," he said finally, "give or take."

"Give or take what?"

"A smidgen."

"What in hell's a smidgen?" Mark wanted to know.

"Let's say, an half hour, either way."

"*Damn*," the lieutenant muttered, "Sam, are you sure?"

"Under these conditions, sure as shootin'. Why?"

"Because," Cathy Carruthers said with deadly calm, "unless Bones and Madson find a stowaway aboard, we've got ourselves a murder that simply couldn't happen."

CATHY CARRUTHERS WAS IN NO MOOD FOR ANY OF Chief Hank Heller's habitual ill humor. She hammered on his office door with a vengeance.

"Come," a raspy voice commanded, then, as she and Mark entered the office, the chief added, "You can shut the door behind you, lieutenant, if there's anything left of the bloody thing."

The lieutenant blatantly ignored Heller and addressed herself to an obviously frightened little man perched precariously on the edge of a wooden chair. "I thought I told you to report to *me*, corporal." she said with an audible restraint of anger.

"He's here on my orders, Lieutenant Carruthers," the chief snarled, "or am I now obliged to get your permission before consulting with my own Records Department?"

"You assigned me to a case, chief," the lieutenant responded tersely, " and for your information, it's a bitch. I have my own methods of operating, as you know, and I will not stand still for your needless meddling."

Mark stood numb with awe. Corporal Leprohn quaked with apprehension. And Chief Hank Heller turned scarlet in a mix of wrath and outright disbelief. "Lieutenant," he said between clenched teeth, "I suggest you find yourself a chair, sit down, and permit us to discuss this matter in a civilized manner."

The lieutenant seated herself disdainfully in an over-stuffed leather chair, then crossed one magnificent leg over the other, thereby obfuscating all rational thought on the issue at hand.

Mark sighed wistfully. Heller exhaled noisily in a helpless wilt of surrender. The little corporal demurely averted his eyes.

"Well?" Cathy Carruthers folded her arms across her bountiful chest in an attitude of abject defiance.

"Briscombe." The chief said simply.

"Chief," the lieutenant began condescendingly, "we have here a two-plus-two-equals-three murder case. It just doesn't add up. I need more time, more information, and *less interference*. If I can leave this office with the Lep — uh, Corporal Leprohn, and have privy to the data he has perched on his little lap, I see no reason why

I will not eventually arrive at a logical solution to the murder." She drew a tremulous breath. "Chief, why don't you tell the commissioner we're working round the clock on a hot lead and that you'll have him off the hook no later than this time – tomorrow."

Heller consulted his watch. "5:30 P.M." He was not ignorant of the Amazon's legendary exploits. She had got him out of many a tight spot in the past. "Can I count on that?" he asked curtly.

"Indubitably."

Mark gave his comely partner a gentle elbow. "Are you nuts?" he asked in a hoarse whisper.

"Indubitably," she said again.

CORPORAL GARFIELD LEPROHN WAS NOT A BIG MAN, in fact, at four-foot diddly-squat, the little corporal had never gained the physical stature of even a big boy. Still, he did have a remarkable talent for gathering data, and it was this expertise that had given him rise (so to speak) to achieve his current post as the indisputable head of the Records Department.

He was perched now, on a high stool, at his own desk, comfortable in his own environment where everything was made specifically to accommodate him, rather than the gargantuan creatures who shared his day-to-day world. Seated around his desk, on conventional furniture, were Cathy Carruthers, Mark Swanson, Too-Tall Bones and Dave Madson.

"Gentlemen," Cathy Carruthers began, "I regret keeping you all working late, but we've just got to get a handle on this bizarre murder. I'd like to start by doing a quick recap on the day before hearing from Garfield."

The little corporal swelled with secret gratification. The lieutenant was the only one who called him by his given name, Garfield, instead of that demeaning epithet, 'Leprechaun.' Mark, the little man's most devout irritant, had even brutally shortened the scurrilous affront to 'Leppy.'

Too-Tall Bones shifted his huge frame in the suspiciously low chair he had been given to sit on. "Lieutenant," he said tentatively, "you know we drew a blank on finding anyone in the house, but Mark also told us to look for anything unusual, or out of place. Well, I've been thinking about it since, and there *was* a couple of things."

"Yes?"

"You know that loft off the living room, like a mezzanine floor above the larger room? It looked to be used as a den or office, and there was this typewriter on the desk, papers all around."

"So?"

"The typewriter didn't have no ribbon in it."

"Maybe it was in the process of being changed," Mark offered.

"Weren't no used ribbon in the waste basket, nor any where else. My wife types, lieutenant, and she never takes an old ribbon out without she's got a new one right there, ready to put back in. Anyway, I thought you ought to know."

"I'm glad you told me, Bones. Anything else?"

"Yeah, well," the big black stirred the tight crinkly curls on his head. "I don't want you thinking I'm trying to solve this thing on my own, but, there being no one in the house and no way to get out without leaving a trail in the snow, I noticed that the telephone wire ran right up to within reach of the window in that same loft. And it was the only wire that wasn't coated with snow."

"You think someone could have done a hand-over-hand all the way down to the pole?"

"Don't know about that. It's a hell of a long way, two-hundred feet at least. *I* wouldn't want to try it. But if they had something like a pulley to skitter along on — "

"Like the reels from the typewriter ribbon? Could be, I guess. Good thinking, Bones. And here's something you might tie into it. That same wire had a loose connection fixed first thing this morning. Might do to call up, uh, what's his name — ?"

"Bogner," Mark recalled, "Carl Bogner."

"That's it" the lieutenant concurred. "It'd be interesting to know if there was snow on that wire *before* he started working on it. You can follow up on that, Bones. Bogner's with Metro Telephone."

"Right on, lieutenant."

"Then there's the blood," Mark put in, "I never saw a guy bleed like that from a head wound before. Want me to check with Sam?"

"Do that, Mark. I meant to bring it up myself, at the scene. And you might want to confirm my cursory conclusions of there being no powder burns near the wound and no residue on the hands. That would rule out suicide, definitely. Madson?"

"I remember seeing a half empty jar of Vaseline on the bathroom countertop. The lid was off, sitting to one side. Didn't think too much of it at the time, but — "

"Something to grease the reels with? Better check out the telephone wire for traces of Vaseline. Good work, Madson. You two better work together on that angle."

The lieutenant looked at each man in turn. "Anything else?" she asked.

The Leprechaun coughed softly into a little fist.

CATHY CARRUTHERS KNEW THAT THE LITTLE CORPORAL had been eager to take the floor ever since they had begun to talk. The obviously abbreviated legs of the chair on which she sat made it necessary for her to look up at him, a new page in the three year history of their relationship. Mark, Bones and Madson sitting on either side of her, seemed also to have subtlely settled into a floor of quicksand. She could not suppress a chuckle. They had unwittingly, but very effectively been reduced to size in the magical kingdom of the Leprechaun.

"Garfield," the lieutenant said with a magnanimous smile, "you now have the floor."

The little data gatherer was well prepared. He was also determined to make the most out of his kick at the cat. He opened a file on his desk, shuffled a few pages, then donned a pair of wire-rimmed half glasses that would enable him to peer over the top, to assess the impact of his newly acquired revelations.

"At the risk of restating the obvious," he finally began in an appropriately timid little voice, "I will start at the beginning. You asked me to 'do a number' on Briscombe, lieutenant, so that is precisely with whom I began."

Mark gave an impatient huff. "Oh for chrissake, Leppy, get on with it."

The Leprechaun bristled. "I thought I had the floor, lieutenant."

"You do," she assured him, struggling with her own composure. "Mark, let him say his piece."

"Briscombe," the Leprechaun began again, "is (was) a

womanizer. It was a public secret. Everyone knew of his on-going infidelities. What they did *not* know, however, was that his erstwhile devoted wife, Julia Briscombe, had recently decided to join him in a sordid game of tit for tat. She chose as her lover, a close friend of her husband, one Ryan Westwold, a well-known local realtor. As a matter of fact, Westwold, together with another mutual business acquaintance, Edward (Eddy) Marshall, branch manager of the Metro Central & District Credit Union, were both at the Briscombe residence last evening. The three men were rumored to be flipping properties to the financial advantage of each, and their meeting last night was not an unusual occurrence."

"When did the meeting break up?" the lieutenant asked.

"Both Westwold and Marshall left when it began to snow, about eleven o'clock, not wanting to get caught in a traffic snarl. Mind you, either one could have returned without the other knowing."

"Alibis?"

"Wifely assurances that obviously have to be taken with a grain of salt. They claim to have gone directly home."

"Where was Mrs. Briscombe during the meeting? And where was she all last night? In fact, where in hell is she at this moment?"

"Julia has an aging mother —"

"How strange," Bones chuckled in his deep subterranean voice.

"— who is struggling to maintain her independence," the Leprechaun went on, ignoring the interruption, "in a condominium out in the Beachville area, overlooking the yacht club. Westwold, coincidentally, has a forty-foot motor launch moored within sight of the condo. A home away from home. Julia has always spent a lot of time with her mother, often staying the night to keep her company. Too, she has lately been seen spending prolonged periods of time aboard the yacht, both in and out of harbor."

"Briscombe wasn't suspicious?"

"The man was too wrapped up in his own affairs to notice. Besides, the time that Julia allegedly spent with her mother, gave Briscombe free rein to carry on with his own libidinal pursuits. The recent Senate appointment must have given him a boost in ego that left no room in his life for family restraints of any kind, however fragile they already must have been."

"So where was Mrs. Briscombe during the meeting?"

"At her mother's condo, or so she claims."

"And she spent the night there?"

"Yes. She said the roads would have been too treacherous to attempt to drive home in the snow. Her mother concurred."

"And where is she now?"

"Mrs. Briscombe? The desk sergeant has her cooling her heels in the reception room. We picked her up at the condo this afternoon. Her mother (who is not too articulate, mind) claims she had been there since her arrival early last evening."

"Westwold? Marshall?"

"We have had to release them after questioning. Nothing to hold them on. But I did have them routinely tested for powder residue, as well as the grieving widow."

"And?"

"Negative."

"What about the pearl-handled thirty-two?"

"It's registered in the name of Julia Briscombe, given to her by her husband early in their marriage. For protection, she says. She apparently spent many nights alone, even then."

"Prints?"

"Only Briscombe's."

"Mmmm." Cathy Carruthers extricated herself from her kindergarten chair with great difficulty and a rewarding show of Amazonian leg. Mark, Bones and Madson also struggled to their feet, and the fun-house mystique of the Leprechaunean illusion was at once dispelled.

"Mark." The lieutenant turned to her favorite side-kick. "I noticed Lenny Brewster still working in the Forensic Chemistry lab on my way in here. See if he's still there, and if so, whether he has the results of the paraffin tests on Briscombe. I'll meet you in the reception room. Bones, Madson, you might as well call it a day. We'll meet you out at the Briscombe place first thing tomorrow morning. Garfield, thank you. You've done a highly professional job, as usual."

The Leprechaun sat perched on his elevated stool for several minutes after the others had left, beaming with pride and pleasure, while the lieutenant's complimentary parting words still chimed in his little ears.

MRS. JULIA BRISCOMBE WAS A PETITE BRUNETTE. She was seated on a leather settee when the lieutenant entered the room, her shapely legs revealingly crossed well above the knee. She looked like anything but a grieving widow. Her impatience at being detained was visibly apparent.

"Mrs. Briscombe. I'm Lieutenant Carruthers."

"I insist on speaking to someone of authority," the woman said with cultured venom, "otherwise, I shall simply walk out of here. It's absurd, inhibiting me in this manner."

"I'll be very brief," the lieutenant told her calmly, "then you'll be free to go."

"Indeed," she sniffed indignantly.

"May I see your purse, please?"

"My purse?" Julia Briscombe stiffened. "Whatever for?"

"You may refuse, of course," the lieutenant said evenly, " but that would then require me to obtain a warrant, a sometimes lengthy procedure — "

"It's simply an embarrassing imposition," the woman said bitterly as she handed over her small black bag. "I'll have something to say about this through my solicitor."

"You do that."

The lieutenant took the bag to the table that centered the room. She sat down and opened the clasp. The musky lingering scents of perfume and face powder rose from the open bag, together with another familiar odor she recognized but could not immediately identify. She turned the bag over and emptied its contents onto the table. Cigarette pack, lighter, compact, lipstick, car keys — all the usual accouterments of the modern woman, including a pair of black gloves.

Mark took that moment to enter. "Negative," he said simply, "on both counts."

The lieutenant was methodically putting everything back into the bag. She noticed a small gold key on the same ring as the car keys, looking a little out of place. When she came to the gloves, she hesitated. She had suddenly recognized the illusive odor. Cordite.

"Mark, has Brewster left yet?"

"Not for another half hour, at least."

The lieutenant handed the gloves to Mark and the otherwise replenished bag to Julia Briscombe. "The sergeant will give you a receipt for the gloves, Mrs. Briscombe. I'll see that you get them back tomorrow morning."

"Well, of all the goddam nerve." Julia Briscombe snatched at the bag and stood up. "Just forget the receipt, sergeant. You can have the bloody things." She stalked stiffly out of the room.

"Let her go," the lieutenant said as Mark made a move to follow, "just get those gloves down to Brewster before he leaves. I'm sure I caught the smell of cordite on them."

MARK PULLED THE GRAY CHEVY OVER TO THE CURB in front of the Briscombe residence. It was just ahead of eight A.M. There had been a fresh fall of snow overnight and all signs of activity around the house was once again obliterated. The rooftops, the power pole, the electrical wires, all carried their share of new snow, including, this time, the telephone wire.

"What now?" Mark asked.

Cathy Carruthers treated him to one of those esoteric little smiles that meant she had something cooking of which he was not yet aware. "We know now that Julia Briscombe fired the shot that killed her husband," she said reflectively, "but I don't think we've got a strong enough case to stand up in court. We can prove she fired the gun all right, wearing those gloves, but we can't prove *when*."

"Yeah," Mark agreed, "she could claim that she fired the gun, for whatever reason, well prior to the established time of death. And yet, if she did do it, C.C., how in hell did she get out of that house without leaving a trace?"

"A good question." The lieutenant had her hand on the door handle. "You wait here for Bones and Madson, Mark, there's a little something I've got to check out."

He watched her go up the walk with that long loping stride she had, her snugly skirted hips see-sawing sensually as though pivoting on some unique inner fulcrum. He permitted himself a wistful sigh of approbation as the front door finally closed behind her.

Moments later, Mark's rear view mirror came alive as the

black-and-white bearing Bones and Madson pulled in behind him, and then Carl Bogner's yellow telephone maintenance truck followed them in. All four men got out of their vehicles and gathered on the sidewalk.

"I got your call," Bogner said, "What's up?"

"We'll know soon enough," Mark told him. "The lieutenant has just gone into the house. She'll be out directly."

"Tell me," Bones said to Bogner, his voice sounding like a quiet peal of thunder, "how did that telephone wire look when you went up the pole to fix it, yesterday?"

"You mean was there snow on it?"

"Yeah, before you might have shook it off trying to tighten it up."

"Hmmm." Bogner thought back. "Can't rightly say for sure, officer. Might've been, might not."

"Great." Bones delivered a disquietingly deep groan of disaffection. "You think about it now, eh?"

It was then that Cathy Carruthers appeared at the front window, the one that looked out from the loft above the living room. She opened the window wide, then began to attach something to the telephone wire, instantly dislodging its cover of snow.

"Oh, no," Mark lamented. "She's going to try that typewriter reel gimmick that you thought up, Bones."

"Well, it *should* work," Bones said weakly, "at least in theory."

"That, in case you haven't noticed, Bones, is not a theory up there."

"I've seen her pull a lot riskier stunts than this," Bones persisted. "That lady's got nine lives."

"Yeah? Well, if she takes a tumble, Bones, you better have at lease two of your own." No one but Mark would have dared to address the big black in those terms.

"That line won't hold her weight," Bogner broke in, "if that's what she's — "

He never finished the sentence. The Amazon hurled herself from the open window in a Haley's Comet of golden hair, her hands above her head, clutching the device she had rigged up from the reels and the ribbon of a typewriter. Her body seemed to swing unsteadily below the wire — sliding forward — then stopping with a jerk — forward again — stopping — She'd gone about twenty feet when the line parted from the power pole.

It was the Amazon, Mark prayed, not Cathy Carruthers up there at that moment. He saw her body twist in an arcing circle of descent as she still clung to the wire, drawing her in toward the house. She hit the wall with out-stretched legs, easily absorbing the shock before the end of the wire that was connected to the house, also parted.

She landed in a puff of snow like a contorted Barbie Doll, all limbs and blond tresses, and a titillating flash of pink panties. Mark was at her side before she could adequately repair her shattered modesty.

"Are you nuts, or what?" Mark scolded as he helped her to her feet. "You could have been killed."

"Tell Bones his theory stinks," she laughed.

"It was only a theory," Bones pleaded humbly.

"Anyway," the lieutenant stated unequivocally, "we now have only one other possible solution to the murder, and I do believe I know what it is."

Mark sighed in defeat. Why fight it?

"Hey," Bogner whined, "what about that wire you just pulled down?"

"I guess you'll just have to put it back up." The lieutenant told him sweetly, "and while you're up there, don't forget to close the window. I hear there's more snow on the way."

MARK MANEUVERED THE GRAY CHEVY ALONG THE Seaview Esplanade that fronted onto the Metro Yacht Club, then, with his blonde Amazonian idol at his side, he swung the car into the underground parking lot of a large condominium. He eased into a slot reserved for guests and the two detectives rode the elevator to the fifteenth floor.

"It's number seven," the lieutenant said as they followed the numbered doors down a wide plush hallway. "I hope she's still here."

Julia Briscombe answered the door, her face immediately registering acute annoyance.

"What now?" she said thickly.

"May we come in?" the lieutenant asked.

"Do I have a choice?"

The lieutenant took a folded document from her inside jacket pocket and held it up. "No," she said, smiling.

The petite brunette stepped back to allow them to enter. "I hope this won't take long," she muttered, "I was just on my way out."

In the living room, the lieutenant chose a chair facing the chesterfield on which an old lady sat knitting.

"This is my mother," Julia Briscombe said, sitting beside her. The old woman's vacant gaze rose to acknowledge the lieutenant's presence, then wordlessly returned to her knitting. "She's not well," the younger woman said simply.

Mark was drawn to the huge picture window that looked out over the harbor. The view was spectacular. Row on row of sailboats with towering masts rocked idly in their berths, while motor launches with shallower draft levels nosed neatly into open-ended boathouses that hugged the shoreline. He wondered absently which one belonged to Westwold.

"Mrs. Briscombe," the lieutenant was saying, "when did you last see your pearl-handled gun?"

"Oh, heavens, I don't know. Months ago. It was kept in a drawer of the desk, up in the loft."

"Was the drawer kept locked?"

"Yes. Always."

"Would that small gold key on your ring of car keys be the key to that drawer?"

"Uh — yes. I guess so."

"You *guess* so?"

"Yes, damn it. That *is* the key."

"The *only* key?"

"Uh — yes," the woman said hesitantly, as though fearing she was being led into saying things she didn't really want to. "But John knew where it was," she added hurriedly, "he could have taken it at any time."

"But he didn't take it the night he was killed."

"How can you be so sure?"

"Mrs. Briscombe, if the key was on your ring when I questioned you at the Precinct, late yesterday afternoon (and it was), and you had not been home since early the previous evening, how could *anyone*, but you, have had access to that gun?"

"How the hell should I know?" Julia Briscombe was looking more uncomfortable by the moment. "Maybe somebody jimmied the lock."

"I checked that desk myself this morning, Mrs. Briscombe. There is only one drawer with a lock on it and it had not been tampered with in any way."

"That doesn't prove a thing."

"It proves that you did return to the house that night and, because you were not seen by either Westwold or Marshall, it must have been shortly after they had left. Then, wearing these same black gloves," the lieutenant went on, drawing the gloves out of a side pocket, "you took the gun from the drawer and shot your husband from behind as he was passing through the atrium. You probably dropped the gun in panic and when your husband fell on it, you were undoubtedly too frightened to try to retrieve it. Now isn't that about the way it happened?"

"No, and you can't damn well prove a thing."

"You're wrong there, Mrs. Briscombe. These gloves were on the hands of the person who killed your husband. The lab found residues of gun powder on both of them, and like the key to the desk, no one had access to them but you. I'm afraid I'm going to have to ask you to accompany us to the Precinct. You are now under arrest. Sergeant, please read the lady her rights."

CHIEF HANK HELLER GLANCED AT HIS WATCH. "IT'S precisely 5:30 P.M.," he said.

Cathy Carruthers, Mark Swanson and the Leprechaun were seated randomly around his desk.

"So it is," Cathy Carruthers said cheerily, "and you have the murderer of John A. Briscombe safely in custody with a solid case against her, just as promised."

"Not so fast, lieutenant. While I agree with you that you do have a reasonably strong case, thus far, Julia Briscombe has not yet confessed or pleaded guilty, nor is she yet aware of the time frame discrepancies that make it virtually impossible for her to have been at the scene of the crime when her husband was shot. And while she doesn't know about the conundrums of the untrodden snow, it won't take those high priced lawyers of hers very long to put it all together. Read my lips, lieutenant, *reasonable doubt*, remember? And that's all she's going to need to go scot-free."

"Oh," the lieutenant said off-handedly, "didn't I explain all that?"

"Not to me," Heller grunted.

"Nor me," Mark assured her.

"Nor me," the Leprechaun squeaked.

"I've got a call in to Sam Morton, chief, and I'd like his corroboration before spelling it out. He should be calling any minute. Meanwhile, why don't we hear from the Lep — uh, Garfield, about motive."

"No shortage of that," the Leprechaun piped up, delighted to have the floor, "apart from their marriage being an absolute mockery, Mrs. Briscombe had plenty to gain financially. Not only did she stand to inherit all of Briscombe's holdings, but also there were a couple of substantial insurance policies that would have double indemnified on the man's violent death. Julia Briscombe had become well acquainted with the good life, and I guess she was willing to stop at nothing to preserve it."

The telephone rang.

"Heller. Yes, Sam, she's right here."

The lieutenant took the phone. "Yes, Sam — uh-huh — uh-huh — I see — uh-huh — thank you, Sam. Bye."

"Well?" Heller rasped impatiently. "Does uh-huh, uh-huh, uh-huh, mean you had the wrong time of death?"

"No," Cathy Carruthers stated clearly, "we both had agreed separately on the time of death and we were both right. Briscombe did die at approximately 2 A.M., about one hour after the snow had stopped falling — "

"Then how — ?"

That was when the man *died*, chief, but it was not when he was *shot*. The bullet from Julia's gun penetrated Briscombe's skull in such a manner as to render him comatose, but it did not kill him instantly. He apparently lay there, unconscious, for a good two hours before he finally gave up the ghost. Julia, by that time, was long gone, long before her hasty exit would have been recorded in the snow."

"Sonofagun," Mark murmured.

"It was the excessive amount of blood at the scene that first tipped me off," she continued, "as long as his heart continued to pump, the wound (up to a point) would continue to bleed. Had he died the instant he was shot, there would have been very little blood. Once Sam knew what to look for, he was able to acquire the medical evidence we will eventually need in court. He's preparing a new report."

"Well, I'll be damned," the Chief grated out.

"How long have you known, lieutenant?" the Leprechaun asked in a little voice laden with awe and adoration.

"Not before this morning," Mark ventured, "or you wouldn't have tried that stupid stunt with the typewriter ribbon."

"Typewriter ribbon?" the chief growled. "Would that have anything to do with the one in my secretary's typewriter having disappeared overnight?"

"Oh, yes," Cathy Carruthers said, getting to her feet. She withdrew a snarl of black-and-red ribbon from her pocket and, together with two bent and twisted reels, placed it all on Heller's desk blotter. "As you can see, chief, the damn thing didn't work any better for me than it did for that antiquated dinosaur that graces your secretary's desk. I think it's time you got a computer, don't you?"

Heller's face was a study in wordless aporia. When Cathy Carruthers quietly closed the door behind the Leprechaun, Mark and herself, moments later, he had not moved, nor had he taken his eyes from the small tangled pile on his desk.

MEL D. AMES

AFTERWORD

by Peter Sellers
Editor, Cold Blood anthologies, Mosaïc Press

And that, ladies and gentlemen, is Cathy Carruthers.

Chances are, you will not see her likes again. Not this week, anyway. Are her stories politically correct? Probably not. But when it comes to crime and mystery fiction there are higher laws that must be obeyed. Laws that say you play fair with the reader at all times. Laws that say you have to present every clue for due consideration. Laws that call for imagination and dramatic effect and a satisfying conclusion. And Mel does that as well as anyone writing these days.

There's something old fashioned about Mel's writing. Not old fashioned in theme or attitude, but in how Mel uses words. He is not a minimalist. He uses a lot of words. A lot of big words. His stories are not pared down. They're lush, ample, ripe with image and metaphor.

You've seen how dramatically they open. Crucified bodies. Bodies dangling from the rigging of abandoned sailboats. Department store Santas murdered in front of dozens of witnesses.

Everything about the stories, like everything about Cathy, is larger than life. But then, Mel himself has lived larger than life. For the past twenty years, he's been an orchardist in the Okanagan Valley. He's used that setting to excellent effect in his stories about B.C. based private detectives Stu Blaze and Connie Wells. Check out *The Ogopogo Affair*, published by Mosaic Press, and "The Disappearance of Sarah-Sue," a Blaze/Wells story published in *Cold Blood IV*.

Before settling down to raise apples, Mel worked as a guard at B.C.'s Oakalla Prison. As a teenager he worked on a CPR Steel Gang, replacing light rails with heavy steel. He sold lingerie in the Yukon. He was a railroad policeman for Canadian Pacific. He drove taxis, built houses, even worked in the advertising business in Toronto.

The winter when he was twelve, Mel almost froze to death riding the rails from Winnipeg to Toronto. He stayed alive by hugging the steam pipes on the coal tender. In summers in his youth, he lived in a remote cabin on the Whiteshell Reserve where he learned to shoot and fish, live on his own and fend for himself.

Mel has built sailboats with his own hands. In 1939, he joined the Canadian army. Later in that same war, he flew planes with the RCAF.

I've never known anyone else quite like Mel Ames. When I started editing the *Cold Blood* anthologies, he was one of the authors I went out of my way to track down. And I was happy to be able to include the two most recent Cathy Carruthers stories in the anthologies *Cold Blood II* and *III*.

Have we seen the last of Cathy? Only Mel knows for sure. But with any luck, there'll be another bizarre impossible murder committed sometime soon and it will take an Amazon of towering intellect and ability to solve it.

Peter Sellers
Toronto, 1998

MEL D. AMES

Québec, Canada
1999